TOO MANY BONES

BLOOD FROM A STONE

RUTH SAWTELL WALLIS

INTRODUCTION BY CURTIS EVANS

Stark House Press • Eureka California

TOO MANY BONES / BLOOD FROM A STONE

Published by Stark House Press
1315 H Street
Eureka, CA 95501, USA
griffinskye3@sbcglobal.net
www.starkhousepress.com

TOO MANY BONES
Originally copyright © 1943 by Ruth Sawtell Wallis and
published by Dodd, Mead & Company, New York. Reprinted by
Dell Publishing Company, New York, 1946. Copyright © renewed
July 30, 1971 by Ruth Sawtell Wallis.

BLOOD FROM A STONE
Originally copyright © 1945 by Ruth Sawtell Wallis and
published by Dodd, Mead & Company, New York. Reprinted by
Bantam Books, New York, 1947. Copyright © renewed April 13,
1973 by Ruth Sawtell Wallis.

"Ruth Sawtell Wallis" copyright © 2020 by Curtis Evans.
"Foreword" copyright © 2020 by Nancy Wallis Ingling

ISBN-13: 978-1-951473-09-9

Book design by Mark Shepard, shepgraphics.com
Proofreading by Bill Kelly

First Stark House Press Edition: October 2020

RUTH SAWTELL WALLIS

By Curtis Evans

American crime writer Ruth Sawtell Wallis is an outstanding example of the sort of person whom detective fiction boosters used to employ in the 1930s and 40s to bolster the intellectual respectability of the craft, which though popular was not necessarily prestigious. (Actually, we are still doing the same issue today, for crime fiction still has its scoffing naysayers, just as it had in the past.) If someone as brainy as Ruth Sawtell Wallis not only liked reading mysteries but enjoyed writing them as well, so the thinking went, surely no one should be ashamed of their own private mystery fiction addiction, no matter how much scolds like Edmund Wilson (who in 1945 notoriously asked with utmost scorn in the pages of the *New Yorker*, "Who Cares Who Killed Roger Ackroyd?") tried to shame mystery fans into dutifully "elevating" their reading.

Barring the sexism rampant at the time (something with which we are still dealing today) Ruth Sawtell Wallis might not have written any mysteries at all, however. The future crime writer was born in Springfield, Massachusetts on March 15, 1895, the only daughter of Grace Quimby and Joseph Sawtell, owner of a haberdashery and a proud member of the Sons of the American Revolution, being a descendant of Thomas Cogswell, a figure of note in the American Revolution. Cogswell had served as an officer at the battles of Lexington and Concord and Bunker Hill as well as being the Continental Army's Chief Wagonmaster, in which capacity his logistical expertise aided the American revolutionaries in pulling off, along with their French allies, their game-changing victory over the British at the Battle of Yorktown.

Over a century later, young Ruth Sawtell demonstrated that she possessed more than a modicum of her distinguished ancestor's fighting spirit as she battled her way through the treacherous groves of academe, which in those days could be markedly hostile terrain for women. Ruth attended Vassar and Radcliffe colleges, graduating with a BA in English from the latter institution in 1919. She thereupon decided to do advanced work in anthropology at Radcliffe, where she obtained her MA four years later. Awarded a Radcliffe Travelling Fellowship in Science in 1923, Ruth embarked for Europe, where she did research work in France, Germany and England. With her colleague Ida Treat she spent a summer excavating Azilian culture graves at the village of Montardit in the French Pyrenees. After returning to the United States in 1929, Ruth and Ida Treat published both a scholarly account of their findings and an entertaining popular one, *Primitive Hearths in the Pyrenees* (1927); and nearly two decades later Ruth would draw on her experiences in the Pyrenees for her similarly entertaining crime novel *Blood from a Stone* (1945).

Back in the United States, Sawtell transferred from Radcliffe to Columbia University, where she worked as research assistant for the Chairman of the Anthropology Department, Franz Boas, known today as the "Father of American Anthropology." One of her jobs with Boas was to take measurements of Sicilian heritage families in New York—which partly explained her hiring, it seemed, since, as she told friends, "Sicilian men in 1926 would never have allowed a male researcher to measure their wives." Between 1926 and 1930 Ruth also worked in New York City as a physical anthropologist for the Bureau of Education Experiments (now the Bank Street College of Education), a progressive institution founded by a trio of women who operated a demonstration nursery school. Her work there served as the basis for her doctoral dissertation, which she successfully submitted in 1929 at Harvard University.

With her PhD in hand, Ruth in 1930 became a charter member—one of only two women to do so—of the American Association of Physical Anthropologists and the University of Iowa hired her as an assistant professor of anthropology. The next year, she published an academic monograph, *How Children Grow* (1931), and she wed the distinguished Oxford educated cultural anthropologist Wilson Dallam Wallis, a widower nine years her senior with two teenaged children, who, rather shockingly, were not informed of their father's marriage until he arrived home with his new bride to Minneapolis, where he was a professor of anthropology at the University of Minnesota.

Ruth accepted a position as an assistant professor of sociology at Hamline University in neighboring St. Paul. However, she was terminated in 1935, in her belief because of "envy over the dual incomes" which she and her husband enjoyed "in the midst of the Depression." (Even my own mother, some three decades later, recalled hearing the same thing from people about her employment prospects after her marriage to my father, who taught at the University of Wisconsin.) So, over the rest of the decade, with university employment seemingly barred to her on account of her dual strikes of marriage and gender, Ruth like many of the other able unemployed at the time found positions with the U. S. federal government, first with the Works Progress Administration and then with the Department of Agriculture's Bureau of Home Economics. During World War Two she served as a Labor Department analyst for the War Manpower Commission and, most significantly for our purposes here, she began writing detective novels, ultimately publishing five of them in all. Like other talented women of her generation who had promising career paths closed to them on account of then prevalent cultural bias, Ruth Sawtell Wallis sought fame and fortune in the field of crime fiction. Happily she proved a natural crime writer.

□ □ □

Ruth Sawtell Wallis wrote her debut mystery novel, *Too May Bones*, the first of two Wallis mystery novels included in this volume (the other being *Blood from a Stone*), in 1942 while she was summering with her husband in a cabin on the Gunflint Trail on Minnesota's North Shore. When it was published the next year (with a smashing dust jacket by artist Henry Koerner, a talented émigré Austrian Jew who lost his family in the Holocaust), the novel made a decided splash in detective fiction's bloody pond, winning the annual $1000 Red Badge Mystery Prize from publisher Dodd, Mead for best first novel by a novice mystery writer.[1] (Previous winners included Marco Page, Hugh Pentecost and Christianna Brand.) This was actually Ruth's second literary prize, as she enjoyed relating in later years. Way back in 1903, when Ruth was but eight years old, she had won five dollars from Johnson's bookstore in Springfield, Massachusetts for her essay about Mr. Johnson's newly-established toy department. Asked whether she wanted her money in goods or in cash, little Miss Sawtell—"plain, proud and puny"—stoutly piped "cash," dismaying her mother, who conveyed to her daughter "the clear implication that once again I had done something not quite lady-like."

Decorum and ladylike deportment not being necessary (far from it) in a crime novel, Dodd, Mead eagerly boosted the gripping and occasionally grisly *Too Many Bones* as "one of the most sensational—and most carefully developed in its plot and characters—that the Red Badge Editors have read in many years"; and book reviewers contributed their own encomia to the cause. In the *San Francisco Chronicle*, for example, noted mystery reviewer Anthony Boucher lauded *Too Many Bones* for a "[w]ell-prepared climax, literate writing and some authentic shivers" and its author as "a notably competent newcomer," while in the *New York Times Book Review*—where *Too Many Bones* received a three-col-

---

[1] The next year Henry Koerner also splendidly illustrated the jacket for Wallis' second mystery novel, *No Bones about It.*

umn assessment of some six hundred words, separate from the other mysteries—mainstream fiction reviewer Beatrice Sherman pronounced that Wallis in her novel "has assembled a group of very interesting, well-drawn characters, and has done a fascinating job with her anthropological background." More recently internet reviewer John Norris of the *Pretty Sinister* blog after assessing Ruth's debut detective novel concluded: "It's no wonder that…Wallis received the Red Badge Detective Award" for *Too Many Bones*. I share the enthusiasm expressed in these assessments. In my judgment, *Too Many Bones* remains, thirteen years after I first discovered it, one of the best "firsts" by a mystery writer that I have read and a stand-out achievement in vintage American crime fiction, sustaining interest up to the very last page not only in its startling tale of thwarted passions and murder but for its superbly dramatic situations, atmospheric setting and compellingly crafted characters.

Too Many Bones hugely benefits from the wealth of fascinating personal and work detail upon which Ruth Sawtell Wallis drew in writing it. The protagonist of the novel, earnest twenty-one-year-old anthropology student Kay Ellis, in many ways resembles the author herself. When the novel opens (in 1940), she is on her way by rail to Hinchdale, an obscure Great Lakes village in the Middle West that unexpectedly is home to the famous Holtzermann Collection of six hundred European skeletons, which were dubiously smuggled out of Germany in the late 1920s and later purchased by Hinchdale's William Henry Proutman Museum for the impressive sum of $50,000. Once she arrives in the little community, Kay is to assist in cataloging the collection, a formidable task given its scope. (There are, one might say, too many bones.)

The William Henry Proutman Museum was named for Hinchdale's leading citizen, a wealthy corset manufacturer who went to his final reward fifteen years ago but left behind a fetching and much younger (if rather coarse and common) widow, Zaydee, who herself now is nearing the dangerous age of fifty, like the author when she wrote the novel. ("I think [Zaydee] has been feeling her age a good deal lately," comments another character. "She does not like to feel her age.") Zaydee maintains control over the museum, but her main interest is not the bones and relics gathered inside (including her husband's creepy collection of corseted dummies), but rather the flesh and blood and disarmingly handsome young anthropologist John Gordon, whom the man-eating widow has hired "at a Hollywood salary to study the collection in any way he likes." Also employed at the museum, Kay finds, are Alpheus Harvey, its vaguely off-putting director; Alice Barton, librarian and proud founding member of the local chapter of the Daughters of the American Revolution (D. A. R.); Mr. Jensen, the booming-voiced Swedish-American engineer; and Esquire Williams, the Bible-quoting black caretaker, who takes more than a passing interest in Isabelle, Zaydee's dignified black maid. It seems that each of them, along with Kay, has reason to want Zaydee Proutman gone from this earth, and, when Zaydee finally disappears, Kay finds the convenient solution that she was murdered by one of her discarded lovers, who then himself accidentally expired, a little too convenient to believe. Will Kay learn too much about the distressing and deadly affair for a murderer to allow her to live?

The mystery of Zaydee's disappearance and presumed murder should keep readers riveted to the last the page, but along the way there are additional enticements. First, there is the sharply etched drab small-town Midwest setting, like something out of the pages of a novel by the great satirical Minnesota writer Sinclair Lewis. To Kay, Hinchdale, where the greatest excitement for women is found in attending church socials and monthly D. A. R meetings, proves every bit as soul-crushing as Lewis' Gopher Prairie did to Carol Kennicott in *Main Street* (1920). Ruth Wallis Sawtell based Hinchdale on an actual place she had visited: Three Oaks, Michigan, a town then of under 1500 people that is located in the extreme southwestern corner of the state, about five miles from Lake Michigan. Three Oaks owed what small measure of fame it possessed to being the home of the Warren Featherbone Company, founded by local capitalist Edward K. Warren, maker of stays and corsets constructed from turkey feathers rather than whalebone. Edward Warren founded the town's Chamberlain Memorial Museum, which is the model for *Too Many Bones*' memorable and remarkably sinister Proutman Museum.

Another source of the appeal of *Too Many Bones* is simply that it is a well told and exceptionally gripping story, with some of the dramatic urgency we associate with noir crime fiction and films. Indeed, one could visualize Joan Crawford, bedecked in gold tissue blouse and Mexican silver costume jewelry, righteously slagging every poor soul in sight as does man-crazy, wrong side of the tracks Zaydee, assuming the actress ever would have consented to take a second-tier part. Ruth once stated that her favorite mystery writer was a sister Minnesotan, Mabel Seeley, who during the period from 1938 to 1943 was doing much to enliven and invigorate the subgenre of women's suspense fiction, then associated with the old-fashioned and often stodgy "Had-I-But-Known" school of Mary Roberts Rinehart. Seeley's novels were roundly praised for their greater sense of realism and more up-to-date, relatable characters, and they sold in great numbers. With *Too Many Bones*, Ruth established herself as a worthy successor to Seeley, who departed from the mystery field for seven years after 1943 to write mainstream fiction (coincidentally the period when Ruth published her own mysteries).

Too Many Bones is packed with credible and convincing characters and authentic frissons of fear. (In its sometimes grisly clinical detail the novel might be said to have prefigured Patricia Cornwell's Edgar Award winning landmark 1990 crime novel, *Postmortem*.) Take, for instance, the love triangle—if such this personal geometric arrangement actually is—among Zaydee, Kay and John. Zaydee is a palpably hateful presence in the tale, to be sure, but Kay and John are far from the banal love interest so typical of mystery fiction of that era. Is John really a good guy, or not? Even Kay, who like all suspense novel heroines inevitably is drawn to the magnetic Byronic figure in the story, finds herself thinking, when she gazes at John, of the deadly antiheroes of the Thirties films *Night Must Fall* and *Love from a Stranger*. Kay herself can be hard-bitten at times, just like her creator (a most formidable woman of severe manner and dress, in her step-granddaughter's recollection, who with her toothy smile begged comparison with a stage witch), being ever so weary, at the age of twenty-one, of the baneful institutional sexism with which she has had so frequently to deal. Significantly Ruth in a show of professional female solidarity dedicated the novel to Constance Ashenden, the longtime Assistant Librarian at Yale University's Peabody Museum of Natural History.

Many of the secondary characters are memorable as well, including the museum's Mr. Harvey and Miss Barton, but I want to spare a few words here for Ruth's portrayal of the two black characters in the novels, Esquire Williams and Isabelle. So often in Golden Age mystery, whether in its hard-boiled or more traditional forms, the portrayal of black characters simply is, in a word, shameful. Even in the occasional book, like Q. Patrick's *Murder at the Women's City Club* (1932), where such depictions are more sympathetic and nuanced, treating the black characters as real human beings rather than comic simpletons, there is apt to be a patronizing tone. Like Ruth Fenisong, another American mystery writer who appeared on the crime scene in the 1940s and has recently been reissued by Stark House, Wallis manages to portray her black characters without any quantity of condescension, and her already impressive novel is all more impressive for it.

□ □ □

"[The authors] discovered, owing to the experience of the husband of one of the ladies, M. Paul Vaillant-Coutourier, who contributes to the book over a hundred pen-and-ink drawings, a cave containing relics of prehistoric man. This was situated at Montardit, on a limestone ridge of the Plantaurel, five miles from the famous caves of Les Trois Freres. They lived close by in a peasant's cottage, and worked all of the sum-

mer. Their discoveries read like a romance."
                    —*Spectator* review of *Primitive Hearths in the Pyrenees* (1927), by
                                                                    Ruth Sawtell and Ida Treat

"Ah, Mademoiselle," a gleam rose to the blue eyes bright in the old face. "You also? You already love this country of mine? And what do you love? Ruined towers, ghosts, caves?"
                              —*Blood from a Stone* (1945), by Ruth Sawtell Wallis

Readers of *Too Many Bones* likely were left wanting to hear more about Kay Ellis after the novel's powerful denouement, but, if so, Ruth Sawtell Wallis left them disappointed in that regard. However, in 1945, Ruth published a third mystery novel, *Blood from a Stone*, which pleasingly featured another winning anthropologist heroine. As well it should have, since when Ruth wrote *Blood from a Stone*, she drew heavily on *Primitive Hearths in the Pyrenees*, the popular anthropological study which she had published eighteen years earlier with her work colleague, paleontologist (and future journalist and Vassar professor) Ida Treat. Ruth's deep knowledge of the French Pyrenees (the southernmost region of France, separated from Spain by a rugged mountain chain) is one of the great strengths of *Blood from a Stone*, but happily the novel's mystery plot and its cosmopolitan characters—American, British, Russian, French and German, if one counts a fierce dachshund named Seppel—are strong assets as well, as contemporary reviewers recognized. On the novel's publication at the end of the World War Two, Anthony Boucher in the *San Francisco Chronicle* lavishly praised it as "a honey" of a book on account of its "[f]ine emotional tensions, well-conceived characters and locale, fascinating scientific dividend and superlative economy of narration," while the *Saturday Review* avowed that it was an "expertly mixed" mystery story with "some exceptionally shivery scenes."

Blood from a Stone, which Ruth wryly dedicated to her three very young step-granddaughters ("none of them can read," she noted) is set back in time to the summer of 1935, in the valley of St. Fiacre, not far from the commune of Foix, located between the city of Toulouse and the Spanish border. In it Ruth paints a fascinating portrait of culture clash, as the red-haired, young, single and modern anthropological researcher Susan Kent shocks traditionalist natives by residing with another young, single woman in a dwelling, locally dubbed La Catine ("The House of a Woman of Bad Habits"), and intrepidly venturing forth, with only a male assistant in tow, into ancient mountain caves to dig in hard stone and earth for bones, flints and shards.

Steeped as it is in history and romantic legend, the novel reminds me of the tale of the impossible murder that takes place atop a ruined medieval French tower in John Dickson Carr's splendid—and splendidly eerie, with its intimations of vampirism—mystery *He Who Whispers*, which appeared a year after *Blood from a Stone*. At the beginning of the latter novel Susan Kent is even mistaken by a night crawling group of young boys for an ominous supernatural dame blanche/dama blanca (white lady), presaging the miasma of animus and suspicion that later envelops her, as dead bodies—recently slain ones—start to turn up in the most unexpected corners of Saint Fiacre. Susan knows that she is not the source of the menace—but just who is, and what could be his/her motive for perpetrating such wicked mayhem?

Suspicious characters abound, including even Susan's sumptuous friend and housemate, the Latvian (of white Russian heritage) Neva Borodin, who is exceedingly free in her behavior and outspoken on all matters, including sexual ones. (This is one of the few crime novels of the day where I have seen the dread word *abortion* actually uttered, especially without any explicit condemnation.) Then we have:

- Moise, Susan's lovely house servant
- Father Bigorre, the local priest
- Monsieur and Madame Dumas, the local
  schoolteacher and his wife
- the elderly Comte de l'Arize and his aloof son,
  Marc, the local gentry
- earthy Madame 'Ri and her offspring, Jean-Marie,
  who moonlights as Susan's assistant
- Sir Cyril Brooks-Brooks, dilettante scholar and
  suspiciously textbook correct Englishman

In this bewildering nail-biter of a mystery only Susan's feisty and loyal pet dachshund, Seppel, seems unquestionably above suspicion—and even he has taken to behaving oddly, as when he simply will not let go of that primitive ochre-painted stone Susan brings back with her from the cave to La Catine. Contrary to popular wisdom, can you get blood from a stone? If anyone can find out, it should be that intrepid scholar and investigator Susan Kent.

□　□　□

Ruth Sawtell Wallis published two more mysteries after *Blood from a Stone*, both of which featured her series sleuth, FBI man Eric Lund, who debuted in Ruth's highly praised second crime novel, *No Bones about It* (1944); yet disappointingly neither book received the high level of praise of her first three and she published no further mysteries after 1950 (though in 1949 she conducted a three week summer seminar on mystery writing at the University of Colorado at Boulder).[2] After Wilson Wallis' retirement from the University of Minnesota in 1954, where he had been appointed chairman of the Anthropology Department, Ruth published anthropological work with her husband and taught at Annhurst College in South Woodstock, Connecticut from 1956 to 1975. Finally retiring herself at the age of eighty, Ruth passed away shortly thereafter on January 21, 1978, seven years after the death of her husband. Perhaps in her later years she was better known for being the stepmother of Wilson Allen Wallis, a noted American economist and statistician who served as President of the University of Rochester and an advisor to four Republican presidents, from Dwight D. Eisenhower to Ronald Reagan. All of Ruth's novels had remained out of print for nearly three decades before her death (though in the Forties her first three books had been lucratively reprinted in paperback editions), and this neglectful state of affairs regrettably remained so until 2020, when now, thanks to the diligent archaeological efforts of Stark House, fans of vintage crime fiction—or simply good crime fiction of any era—can dig into a couple of superlative recovered Golden Age mysteries.

—Germantown, TN
June 2020

[2] Ruth's successor at the UCB seminar the next year was, appropriately, Mabel Seeley.

Curtis Evans received a PhD in American history in 1998. He is the author of *Masters of the "Humdrum" Mystery: Cecil John Charles Street, Freeman Wills Crofts, Alfred Walter Stewart and British Detective Fiction, 1920-1961* (2012) and most recently the editor of the Edgar nominated *Murder in the Closet: Essays on Queer Clues in Crime Fiction Before Stonewall* (2017) and, with Douglas G. Greene, the Richard Webb and Hugh Wheeler short crime fiction collection, *The Cases of Lieutenant Timothy Trant* (2019). He blogs on vintage crime fiction at The Passing Tramp.

FOREWORD
by Nancy Wallis Ingling

When my father Allen Wallis and his younger sister Virginia were in their teens, their mother Grace Allen Wallis died of tuberculosis, the dreaded contagious disease that took so many lives at that time. Not long after her death their father, anthropologist Wilson Dallam Wallis, surprised them by arriving home from an anthropology conference with a new and much younger wife, Ruth Sawtell Wallis.

Not an easy introduction for Ruth, only 17 years older than Allen, and with no parenting experience. However, she had a Harvard doctorate and was known for her excavations in France and other professional work, so she certainly had the potential to be a quick study.

Joining the Wallis household must have been as awkward for Ruth as it was shocking for Allen and Virginia. Everyone, especially Ruth, agreed that she never would be called "Mother" or anything similar, so everyone in the family just called her Ruth, and that continued even for those of us two generations younger than she.

When my parents, younger sister Ginny and I traveled to Minnesota's Twin Cities we would occasionally visit Ruth and Grandfather Wallis in their Minneapolis house, but we always stayed overnight with my Mother's family in their more spacious Saint Paul house. This house featured an exciting third floor that contained books, toys, trunks of old evening dresses, capes, top hats, and other items well suited for dress-up games. I had been thrilled by gifts from Ruth of well chosen dolls and books and she would eventually add a few of her own "ball gowns" to the collection we inherited.

After graduating from high school in Chicago, I left home to enroll at Wellesley College near Boston, and Ruth encouraged me to visit them, since it was an easy bus ride to their house in South Woodstock, Connecticut, where they had moved after retiring from the University of Minnesota faculty. They made the move partly because Ruth had grown up in New England, and partly because the weather was somewhat milder than Minnesota. They were pleased when nearby Annhurst College, a Catholic college for women, invited each of them to teach part time. Most of the faculty members were nuns, and my grandparents especially admired a Sister who had a doctoral degree from Harvard. Ruth also had family nearby, so she and Grandfather purchased a former carriage house on an old estate, remodeled it into a pleasant house for themselves, and encouraged me to visit on weekends or holidays.

I quickly found that those visits offered pleasant relief from Wellesley's restrictions on its all-girl students, among which were those requiring us to wear a skirt to dinner, keep dorm rooms tidy and clean for room inspections, sign in when arriving back at the dorm later than nine or so at night, and to refrain from bringing cars on campus until a student's last few weeks before graduating. Never had I or many of the other students lived with such restrictions, except those of us who had attended a boarding school.

In addition to these somewhat insulting inconveniences, I found teaching methods far different from those I was familiar with at the University of Chicago Laboratory School, relying more on memorizing and less on questioning or evaluating. So it was refreshing to stay with my grandparents where disagreeing was not considered rude, and almost always led to interesting discussions and even laughter.

Ruth and I now had a chance to become better acquainted, and I discovered that her experiences as an undergraduate at Vassar College, then a college for girls only, had led her to transfer and graduate from Radcliffe College at Harvard University. Knowing this helped build my courage to leave Wellesley and transfer to the University of Pennsylvania.

After earning our undergraduate degrees, each of us proceeded to earn a doctorate, Ruth's in anthropology at Harvard and mine in experimental psychology at the University of Rochester. Discovering these similarities was a revelation that brought us much closer together.

For the rest of Ruth's life I visited whenever an opportunity arose, even after I lived in Ohio and had young children. For a few years after my grandfather died, my father flew with me and one or another of my children to visit Ruth during the Christmas holidays, probably the best possible Christmas gift for her. He also helped my grandparents financially to the extent that they were willing to accept it.

My own weekend and vacation visits from Wellesley marked the start of a long close friendship. Ruth and I spent hours chatting, often sounding more like two girlfriends than granddaughter and grandmother, especially when we discussed why we had left women's colleges for Ivy League universities, or when talking about anthropology, family, and many other topics.

Ruth talked about some of her best and worst experiences, from publishing a short story in a Springfield, Massachusetts newspaper while still a child, to losing her faculty job at the University of Minnesota during the Depression, when it was considered unfair to pay two members from the same household. My grandfather was chairman of the Anthropology Department there and a full tenured professor, so he earned a higher salary, yet one still inadequate for the needs of two people. I barely knew them then, for I lived with my parents and sister in California, New York, or Chicago, also spending long summers in Michigan, where Ruth and Grandfather visited at least once.

Ruth needed to find another way to make money after losing her position, and jobs were scarce. She had been a fan of murder mysteries for years, and often felt that she could write them herself, even making use of some of her experiences in anthropology. Her very first attempt, *Too Many Bones*, was published by Dodd, Mead & Company in 1943, winning her a $1,000 prize and additional royalties in the semi-annual Red Badge new mystery story contest. That was followed by *No Bones About It* in 1944, *Blood from a Stone* in1945, *Cold Bed in the Clay* in 1947, and *Forget My Fate* in 1950. Altogether the royalties derived from the sales of these works more than replaced her former salary.

When Ruth and I chatted in her Connecticut living room, my grandfather would occasionally emerge from his office, perhaps with his pipe, and exchange a few comments while tending to a fire in the fireplace. We would sit on a comfortable gray sofa beneath a rather gloomy framed picture of Stonehenge, the prehistoric monument in Wiltshire, England. I understood why Stonehenge intrigued the two anthropologists, but I secretly thought the picture too gloomy for an otherwise cozy living room.

Ruth and I never ran out of things to talk about, but before we became so much better acquainted, she had seemed serious and even severe. She was not warm, playful, and plump like my Armstrong grandmother, who had had four children and always wore loose dresses, often with a long loose cardigan sweater over them, and lace-up black granny shoes with thick heels, her grey hair inevitably straying from its bun.

Ruth, in contrast, was slim and dressed neatly in dark colors, sometimes in slacks. She wore her auburn hair in a neat bun at the back of her head, and she had spent much of her time talking with adults about things I couldn't comprehend.

Ruth sometimes pointed out that she was not my real grandmother, but to me she was my real Wallis grandmother, the only one I'd ever known. At last it occurred to me to point that out to her, and she seemed relieved, even pleased, to realize it was true.

Becoming a stepmother to Allen and Virginia almost immediately after their mother's death must have been a challenge to the two children, especially since they had had no warning. Surely they still were griev-

ing for their mother. They had suffered through her dying of tuberculosis before there was a vaccine for it. Tuberculosis was contagious and
greatly feared, so families often tried to keep the disease a secret.

Allen and Virginia may have initially resented Ruth's arrival, though
gradually they must have been impressed that she was a successful professional, a talented writer, and eventually a friend. For many years my
father went out of his way to visit Ruth when he was near the East
Coast on business, and for the last years of her life, during the Christmas holidays he would fly with me and one or the other of my older children to visit Ruth for a day.

But the last time we saw her, we did not take a child, for Ruth was in
a local hospital with a heart problem, and all three of us knew she was
on her deathbed. She was unable to speak, yet her face expressed joy
and gratitude that we had come. Soon after we arrived a young nurse
came into her room and tried to get Ruth to eat a sandwich, treating her
rather severely, as one might treat a recalcitrant child. Ruth no longer
could talk, but I knew from her expression that she was insulted, so I
explained to the nurse that Ruth had a Ph.D. from Harvard, was a well-
known anthropologist and also a successful author of murder mysteries. The nurse looked startled, and immediately began to treat Ruth
with some of the respect she deserved.

After Ruth died my father asked her doctor, an old New Englander,
about the official cause of death. He paused thoughtfully, then replied,
"Well, it was like *The One Hoss Shay*," referring to the Oliver Wendell
Holmes poem about the sturdy 100-year-old cart that all of a sudden
falls completely apart. I think Ruth would have been amused by that.

—Gambier, Ohio
June 2020

TOO MANY BONES

RUTH SAWTELL WALLIS

To
Constance Ashenden

CHAPTER 1

Whenever I think of Hinchdale I think of death. Death brought me there—the death of six hundred men, women, and children—and I thought it was fun. Death sent me away—one death—and I may never laugh freely again.

On that long gray afternoon on the dirty little train jerking between stubby cornfields, I thought no girl of twenty-one could be heading toward a brighter year. With college commencement only four months behind me, I was going to assist in the study of the great Holtzerman Collection of human skeletons. To me those thousands of bones laid down long ago in normal death did not mean lost human life; they were scientific adventure and my first job. But murder was to mean the sudden horrible death of someone I knew and hated, committed only too probably by someone I knew and loved.

A week before I took that train I had never heard of Hinchdale.

"I don't know much more about it than you do, Kay," Professor Alden had told me. "It's a village in the Middle West, with twelve hundred inhabitants, and it owns the Holtzerman Collection, as unlikely a combination as you could imagine. The Holtzerman Collection was smuggled out of Germany in the late twenties, and they were asking $50,000 for it. That's a devil of a lot of money to get the trustees of even the richest museum to pay for stuff that has no appeal to the public. So no sale. Now it belongs to the William Henry Proutman Museum of Hinchdale, where the public must be practically nil. Why they ever bought it is a mystery. Find out the answer, Kay, and let me know. I'm just plain curious."

I never did tell Professor Alden why the William Henry Proutman Museum bought the Holtzerman skeletons.

"Those people," Professor Alden went on, "seem in a way to realize the value of what they've got. First they hire John Gordon at a Hollywood salary to study the collection in any way he likes. He's absolutely first rate, the best of the recent Ph.D.s. Now I have this request from Alpheus Harvey, the museum director, for an assistant for Gordon, someone with training in anthropology and statistics. It's a small salary but a big chance to work on the most important material for the study of inbreeding ever gathered together. How about it?"

I said it was just all right with me and watched Professor Alden write the telegram to Alpheus Harvey: "Kay Ellis will arrive Tuesday tenth to assist Dr. Gordon." All this telegraphing and rushing off in a week seemed strange and unacademic. You would think that, after waiting in a graveyard for three hundred years, those bones could lie quiet for a few weeks longer.

Tuesday, the tenth, the gray day, the endless flat brown fields so alien to my eyes that they seemed a barrier more impenetrable than mountains or sea between me and the land I had always known. It was four in the afternoon, and I was very hungry and a little afraid.

"Hinchdale!" bawled the brakeman.

Already? A moment before there had been only the fields. No suburbs, no outskirts, not a single house. The mean town had "snuk up" on me. I pulled my hat harder over my eye, flung on my coat, grabbed my bag, and landed on the platform hard. There was another bang, and from the baggage car ahead my trunk landed harder.

"Kinda got off on the wrong foot, didn't yer?"

The little man had a blue agent's cap pushed back of his gray forelock, and his mustache matched the smutty yellow station. His eyes were dark and sharp. I turned my back on him. All I saw were fields, miles of brown stubble from roadbed to horizon. I turned back.

"You couldn't live on the wrong side of the railroad tracks in this town," I said pleasantly.

"You ain't planning to live anywheres in Hinchdale, 's my guess." The little dark eyes were curious—not, I thought, unkind.

"Oh, but I am," I said. "So if you'll tell me where I can find a taxi ..."

He slowly pulled a twist of paper from the pocket of his old gray sweater, opened it, and shook out a little snuff. "Ain't none." He swallowed the snuff. "Where you goin' in town?"

Suddenly I realized I didn't know and said so.

"You sure you got off at the right place, young lady?"

"Of course. I've got a job here," I said proudly.

The impression on the stationmaster was real, but not quite the one I intended. His eyes, appraising the silver fox jacket and the violet homespun, were shrewd; he couldn't know they were the only things rich Aunt Jane ever had given or ever would give me. One knobby hand waved toward my pigskin bag while the other did double duty in wiping snuff and a grin from his mouth.

"Just where you expectin' to be employed in Hinchdale, lady?"

I had asked for it, and I answered, "At the Proutman Museum."

I was glad to see him astounded. He found speech, hesitating ...

"Does ... ah ... Museum folks know you're comin'?"

"Oh, yes. I just meant I don't know where I'll be living. About the trunk ..."

"Ain't much place to stay in town. Maybe Alph Harvey or Miss Barton's got somethin' fixed up for you. 'Twon't really matter much. You won't be stayin' here long."

I was mad. "Oh yes, I will," I declared. "For years and years." Then suddenly I was frightened. I wasn't awfully good at statistics, and jobs were hard to hold as well as get. "I mean," I added, "if they like my work."

"It wasn't your work I had in mind. I was just thinkin' I'd like to be there when ..." The grin broke out again, not one I felt like joining.

Then he became brisk and helpful, put my trunk and bag in his old car behind the station, and offered to drive them for me anywhere in town if I would call his house after the 5:33 freight east. Name was Epp Marks. The street, 'bout the only one in town, began back of the station, and if I just kept goin' I couldn't miss the Museum opposite the bank because they wuz both just alike. And that gray one-story building with the stucco front was where his wife run a restaurant. The boys called it the Greasy Spoon but 'twasn't; 'twas real nice and clean.

The street was called Broadway with perfect propriety. It was the widest thoroughfare I have ever seen and the thoroughest. It seemed to go on forever across the world; probably it bisected the whole of the United States. I hoped I was on the Museum side of it, because, tired as I now began to feel, I'd probably have to lie down and rest during the crossing, preferably between holes. There were, I noticed, a good many of these and a lot of dust. Altogether not a cheerful street, at least at the station end of town. Brown and gray paint and weather stain or dull yellow brick covered the straggle of shanties, shops, and stores that gradually closed ranks. Not a lively street, either. In fact, the place was as still as death. At that moment two girls came giggling out of the chain grocery. They saw me and stopped. For a moment they stood still, mouths open; then they turned and scampered ahead. Every yard or two their heads bobbed back at me, and there floated toward me words in a sixteen-year-old gasp, "Just like in the movies!"

So my hat was as pert, the silvery fur and violet wool as soft and smart as I hoped they were. It was thrilling to be here in an utterly new kind of town and wonderful to be starting work on the world-famous Holtzerman Collection under the direction of Dr. John Gordon, "the best of the recent Ph.D.s," perhaps the youngest!

And then I saw those twin mausoleums, the Proutman Savings and Trust Company and the William Henry Proutman Museum. Towered and arched, bedizened and labeled in gritty red sandstone, they faced each other squarely across Broadway—not large buildings, but clearly the expression of somebody's big ideas in a little puddle.

I crossed Broadway, Hinchdale, and climbed the five stone steps to the Museum entrance. A large glass case stood on the porch at the left of the door. It seemed an answer to the prayer of a serious young scientist who did not wish to be caught prinking in the public street. The case contained one of those sections of a giant California redwood that live for hundreds and thousands of years, their unjust reward to be defaced with little tagged landmarks of human history: this ring was laid down when Columbus discovered America (wisp of red, white, and blue); this tree was so big when we signed the Declaration of Independence (marked by miniature quill pen); and so on for a long time.

Columbus and the Declaration were on this one, along with the high-jacking of Hinchdale from the Kickapoo Indians; but all this was mere background for the career of Mr. W. H. Proutman. He seemed to have been born (circa 1860), got his first job, built a factory, a bank, and a museum, and died. His outstanding achievement must have occurred in 1915, for the marker at that tree ring was easily twice the height and ten times the splendor of any other. It was one of those figures from wedding cakes, a bride in white, complete with veil, bouquet, and simper; but instead of the blond locks usually brushed modestly over the china ears, hers were flaming orange. So William Henry Proutman, having lived a successful life for fifty-five years, finally fell for a redhead.

I entered the Proutman Museum for the first tune laughing.

CHAPTER II

The hall of the Museum was dark and cold. To the left and right of the entrance were closed doors; a slip of white paper was attached to the one at the right. Beyond these doors the hall widened; and at the right, gray light from above showed a broad stairway. The hall ended in a dim doorway evidently leading to the exhibits. I had a vague impression of a human form in its twilit distance, a feeling of being watched, but there was no sound or motion.

I walked over to the right-hand door and read the slip which said, in genteel script, that the library was closed for the day. A near view of the left-hand door revealed the faded information, "Office of the Director." It looked like an uncommonly thick door, and I knocked hard. I hadn't noticed that it wasn't quite latched, and for that reason I was somewhat unexpectedly launched into the presence of Mr. Alpheus Harvey.

For me it was a bad beginning, but Mr. Harvey did not know it. The gray curls, looking almost like an Uncle Tom wig above his yellow face, continued to bend over the papers before him. I moved timidly nearer the large old desk, covered but not littered with pamphlets, rock fragments, ink, paper clips, and a stuffed weasel. There were no ash trays, no stubs. A neat gold chain held the pince-nez to Mr. Harvey's large saffron ear. I was standing over him now, but still he did not raise his head, and his purple-veined, freckled old hand continued to move slowly across the paper with a silent pen. At the bottom of the paper Mr. Harvey looked across his desk for a blotter, and saw me. Then his eyes were on my face, suspicious, annoyed. They did not leave it while his hands sought the desk drawer, pulled out a small black disk, screwed it into his ear.

"What do you want?" It was a low voice, but it was sharp.

And I stammered. "You're ... I'm ... Professor Alden said ..."

"What do you want?"

I took a deep breath and said, "I've come to work for Dr. Gordon. I am Kay Ellis."

Mr. Harvey's eyes narrowed, and if he had looked suspicious before, he now looked as if all had been confirmed. "Repeat that."

I raised my voice far too much and did it.

Mr. Harvey glowered. "I heard you perfectly," he said. "No one needs to shout at me. I merely wondered if you would say exactly the same thing."

Deep down in my tired and hungry insides tears began to form, but before they reached my eyes I managed to murmur, "There isn't anything else I could say. It's the truth."

Mr. Harvey reached for the weasel, set it in the exact center of the window sill behind him, and slowly drew toward him the marbled pasteboard file that had served as its perch. Fanning it open, he fished into its depths and brought forth two papers, one yellow, one white. The white paper, a thin onion skin, he scrutinized long. He scrutinized me longer. Then he began to read:

"'The Proutman Museum wishes to secure at the earliest moment the services of a former student of Professor H. J. Alden of Oldwick University. Training in anthropology and statistics is essential; knowledge of typewriting is highly desirable. The salary is $150.00 per month. A reply by telegraph collect is requested.'" He paused. "You are not a former student of Professor H. J. Alden."

"But I am," I gasped. "I majored under him in anthropology, and I minored in statistics, and for the last two summers I've been Professor Alden's secretary."

"His secretary, doubtless"—a yellow tooth appeared between blue lips—"but the Proutman Museum did not send for a stenographer. The rest of your story is hard to believe. Even in the Middle West we are fully aware that Oldwick University is not coeducational."

"But there's Edgewood College for Women," I explained anxiously, "just across the river. We have an all-Oldwick faculty, and the same courses and degrees. I ... I think I have all the requirements."

"All but one," said Mr. Harvey. "The telegram gave the distinct impression that a man was coming."

He handed it to me. It was the same message I had read in Dr. Alden's office. No, not quite. Two letters were missing. It now read: "K.

Ellis will arrive Tuesday tenth to assist Dr. Gordon."

I took out my pen and added the *a* and the *y*. "This is what Dr. Alden wrote. I saw it."

"Why did he use a nickname in a business document?"

"Because it isn't a nickname. It's all I have. Just Kay."

Mr. Harvey grunted. "We had every reason to expect a man."

His face waved before me. Was this the end? No chance to study the Holtzerman Collection, no work, no money, and all that train fare gone?

I tried to smile. "Professor Alden couldn't really know that, could he?" I suggested timidly. "I think the letter doesn't say anything about a man. He didn't know you hadn't heard of Edgewood College. It wasn't his fault that I have such a name."

"Why did Professor Alden send you?" he asked. He seemed a little mollified.

"It was late in the year," I explained with a little more courage, "and all the really good men were placed. He thought I was ... better than any man he had left. And the salary is awfully good for a girl, but not quite as high as a man can usually get. And you ... the Museum seemed to want someone at once."

A complete change came over Alpheus Harvey's face. The eyes almost disappeared, the tight channels of yellow skin broadened, lips rolled back from sharp canine teeth. Mr. Harvey shook silently. And so did I. I did not then know that this was Mr. Harvey's way of laughing.

Suddenly he stopped shaking and rose. "So *you* came at once," he said. "Well, Miss Ellis, I'll take you to Dr. Gordon's laboratory."

"I can stay?" It was hard to believe that I had won while his sparse yellow teeth still showed in that ghastly smile.

"So far as I am concerned," he said. "You probably have the training Gordon needs, or Professor Alden wouldn't have sent you. He wrote very highly of Gordon. Yes, you'll suit *Gordon* all right."

Harvey would accept me, Gordon would be satisfied; but was there still something wrong? Was there someone else whom it would be harder to please, someone who wanted only a man? Who? As I followed the director's stooped shoulders to the door, the strangeness Professor Alden had mentioned so casually became dark and tangible. The fifty-thousand-dollar Holtzerman Collection in Hinchdale. The size of Dr. Gordon's salary. The haste to find an assistant. Then I was once again in the grim hallway of the Museum. Our footsteps sounded loud on the tiles.

"Through here," said Mr. Harvey. It was the doorway of the shadowy exhibition hall whence, I had imagined, vague human forms had watched me arrive. I crossed the threshold and stopped dead. It was not imagination; they were there all about me, women, dozens, with great staring faces, trailing, ghostly skirts, masses of hair. They did not move, and neither did I. But Mr. Harvey, with a dry little cackle, stepped to a window and raised the shade.

My breath came then in a gasping laugh. They were wax dummies of another day, pink and white and simpering, with piled and waved coiffures, and tucks and pleats and flounces. Their clothes ranged from dull street costumes to rainbow *décolletage*, from the modes of 1880 to the styles of 1914, but each bore the same incongruity. Between breast and knee they wore over their other garments tight cases of whalebone and satin and lace.

"Upstairs," said Mr. Harvey, "we have a very fine department of Indian Relics and Early Pioneer Life. This is the original museum. Mr. William Henry Proutman made his fortune as a manufacturer of ladies' corsets."

There seemed to be nothing I could say.

"The Holtzerman Collection," he added, "is in the basement," and led the way.

At the foot of narrow stairs, Mr. Harvey opened a door and flung his bomb. "This is *Miss* Kay Ellis." The big young man in the mussed laboratory coat who sprang up from his desk, pushed back a lock of black hair with one hand, and grasped mine with the other was the kind of boy I had known in Professor Alden's seminar; only this man was a little older and more poised and, perhaps, exciting.

"What a surprise you turned out to be," he said, and not at all angrily. "You're an Edgewood girl, I suppose?"

Mr. Harvey's jaw relaxed. Check. My story was true.

"Dr. Gordon," he said, "I will leave it to you to break—er, to make the announcement of *Miss* Ellis's arrival to—er ... the proper sources," and with a ghost of that horrible smile he departed. It seemed to me that the hesitating, the feeling for words, was as contrived as the grin, but Dr. Gordon did not appear to notice it. He was already in the midst of the work we were going to do together.

This was his office, he said ruefully, indicating the dazzling modern desk and leather chair; but this, flinging open a door, was the workroom. It was our kind of room. You find them in museums large and small all over the world. Yellow varnished wood counters and tables and wall shelves stacked with scientific litter—trays and boxes, calipers, accession registers, a bottle of India ink without a stopper on top of Grey's *Anatomy*, record blanks in neat piles and in utter confusion, and dust everywhere. All the trays were full of human bones.

Dr. Gordon drew the nearest toward me on a counter and said, "What do you make of it, Miss Ellis?"

His smile was encouraging, and I plunged in. The thigh bones arching above the tray were long and heavily marked for muscular attachment, and the skull I took in my hands had heavy ridges above the eye sockets and strong square cheeks.

"A hard-working gentleman who departed this life aged forty," I guessed. "But I'd have to see the pelvis to be sure he wasn't she." Then, turning over the skull and looking at the jaw, I added, "He either died of toothache or often wished he could."

"O.K., anthropologist," he laughed. "I think you'll do."

"Oh, I hope so." It was my kind of room and he was my kind of person. "I'd love to work with—with such a lot of bones."

"Do you realize there are six hundred skeletons in the Holtzerman Collection, all in perfect condition?" he teased. "Two hundred per skeleton times six hundred makes 120,000. That might be too many bones even for you."

"There couldn't," I declared, "be too many bones."

"Miss Ellis," he said, "I'm a lot more worried about how you're going to stand life in Hinchdale."

We were sitting on opposite ends of the counter, the tray of bones between us. His hands were clasped round his knees, his head thrown back. I had pulled off my tight hat and dropped it on a chair with the silver fox jacket. I had forgotten Mr. Epp Marks and Broadway and the threat of the Greasy Spoon.

"I can stand it if you can," I said smartly.

There was no response in his voice. "Sometimes I can't," he said.

"But that could happen anywhere."

"Yes." But it was not an affirmative. Then, with a return to his former tone, he said, "What I meant was this is a hell of a place for decent eating and sleeping and even washing. I've chased all around town hunting for a room for this Keith or Kirk or Kaspar Ellis we thought was coming. I found a fairly decent hole for that guy, but it isn't so good for you."

"I can make it," I said, suddenly feeling awfully tired and probably looking it, because he said quickly, "It's really very clean. Mrs. Hawks is a kind old soul but a little too interested. We'll go over and see her now."

"Can't I find it alone?"

"You could. You could probably do anything." There was sudden teasing intimacy in his tone. "But I'm coming," he went on firmly. "I have to explain about your turning up in the wrong size and color, so to speak. Be with you in a minute." And, pulling off his lab coat, he strode into his office. "Tomorrow," he called out companionably as he gathered up his street clothes, "Miss Barton may be able to find a better place for you to live."

"Miss Barton?"

"The Museum librarian. She's a nice little lady of the first family of Hinchdale and related to the second, third, and fourth, which include the doctor, the undertaker, and the sheriff. She's away this afternoon."

"Leaving a most ladylike note on the library door."

"Observant young scientist, aren't you? She's gone to the monthly meeting of the D.A.R. Don't be shocked, you little provincial snob. It does exist west of Massachusetts."

He came out, laughing at my flush of acknowledgment.

"You know what we might do," he said, and, to my complete surprise, my heart quickened a bit. "Something to break Hinchdale to you gently. We could meet Mrs. Hawks and settle your baggage, then drive over to a town on the lake where we could have a steak in front of an open fire." He held out my silver fox. "That is, if you think that coat could bear to ride fifty miles in my so-called car. It's not quite a jalopy."

"Your car?" I thought of the salary as large as Professor Alden's and was incredulous.

"My one and only car." His tone was harsh. "Your coat?"

I put my arms in it, probably not hurrying very much. "My one and only coat. Given me by my rich and only relative because I got a job. She never gave me so much as a sweater, you understand, when I was workin' my way through collitch."

He patted my collar into place. "This job means a lot to you, then," he said.

"It means everything."

Our eyes met for a long moment. "I feel the same way," he said slowly and soberly. His face was a little flushed, and my cheeks felt hot. It seemed as if a fine life was about to begin. "It's a date?" he asked, certain of the answer, and I laughed.

"I'd love it. Does a nice girl go out with her boss in Hinchdale? You are my boss? Or is it Mr. Harvey?"

The telephone stopped his answer. With a gesture of mock irritation he picked it up. "Gordon speaking," he called gaily, and then stiffened and turned his back on me. "Yes," he said. "Yes." I had not heard that guarded tone. "Yes, a short time ago. —Well, not quite as we had planned, but perfectly satisfactory. —No, no, you'll approve of the choice, I'm sure. —I shall report to you fully in the morning." There was a sudden metallic rasp. Only women can make that sound on a telephone. It went on for a long time. "Yes," said John Gordon when it stopped. "I had forgotten. Yes, it was unpardonable. —Yes, at seven. Thanks very much."

He replaced the receiver quietly on the hook and turned to me, still stiff, still guarded. "Miss Ellis," he said, "I'm sorry that I can't take you to dinner tonight. *That* was the boss. Harvey's, yours—and mine."

CHAPTER III

Mrs. Sarah Hawks was kneeling on her parlor sofa with her nose against the windowpane. Viewed from the rear—grayed red hair, plump hunched shoulders, and hips wrinkled over by a brownish housedress from the hem of which tapered shoe soles and runover heels—she looked like a rutabaga that has spent the winter in the root cellar. A little faded and wrinkled, but still round and good at the core.

It was seven o'clock of an October morning when I came out of my bedroom and found her thus, with the peculiar shock that you feel when you see anyone older than yourself in a comfortably undignified posture. She may have heard the creak of my door, she may merely have been talking to herself. What she said sounded like, "There goes that jig again! What's he doin' back in this town, I'd like to know. And they say this Dr. John Gordon's a real hardworkin' feller."

She turned and plumped herself straight, saying, "I don't know why I do this every mornin'. But I always have. My husband used to be foreman there across the street, and there was always somethin' to see out of this window when the shop was runnin'. It's been closed, though, for 'most twenty-five years. William Henry Proutman was a real smart man, but 'twas hard on the town when the corset shop shut down for good."

"It closed because the styles changed?" I asked listlessly. There had been no blankets on my bed, and I had spent a heavy night under two cotton-stuffed quilts.

"Before they changed," Mrs. Hawks said. "William Henry Proutman was smart." She pulled at something evidently pricking between her ribs. "Not that corsets have ever gone out for *me*."

"Well, they're in again now for all of us more or less," I responded politely, smoothing the two-way stretch across my 34-inch hips.

Mrs. Hawks chuckled. "I hear Zaydee wears quite a contraption now. Pink silk and velvet where it shows, but plenty of bones where it hurts."

Again she did not explain, and thus at so early a moment I subconsciously linked Zaydee, "the jig," and Dr. John Gordon.

Dr. John Gordon was not a happy thought with which to begin my day. The humiliation of the broken date, the altered attitude, had lain more heavily on me all night than Mrs. Hawks's quilts. With it mingled fear— fear of the loss of work because I was not a man, fear of the unknown hostility suggested by Mr. Harvey and by the station agent's, "You won't be stayin' here long." And "here" was this dark old room with the towering walnut bed and the glowering family "enlargements."

"You have a pretty good night?" inquired Mrs. Hawks, moving toward the dining room.

"Yes, thanks. Which way do I turn to go to the restaurant?"

Mrs. Hawks stopped in the doorway. "Oh, you don't want to go eatin' there on an empty stomach," she declared. "Addie Marks's chicken-fried steak's real good, but her scrambled eggs always soak grease. You better have your breakfasts with me. You can pay me twenty-five cents, and I guess you'll get enough. It's my one good meal of the day."

It was a good meal and enormous—oatmeal porridge with heavy cream, bacon and sausage and muffins, and griddle cakes with honey, maple syrup, and raspberry jam were the main items. And the talk of Mrs. Hawks was as plentiful as her food.

"I was real sorry I couldn't give you a good hot supper last night," she said, "even though you said you had too bad a headache from the train to eat more'n toast and tea. But I always plan to eat so much at the D.A.R. teas that I never have a thing in the house those nights."

"It was awfully kind of you to give me anything at all," I said.

"Oh, I was glad to. That Dr. Gordon was real solicitous about you. He told me two or three times at the door to look after you, and how tired you probably was."

"I'm afraid I was a nuisance to both of you."

"You were a big surprise to *me*," said Mrs. Hawks. "I'd always said I'd never have a roomer in my house, let alone a girl. But Mrs. Jim Watson, where this Dr. Gordon lives, thinks he's somethin' wonderful and a real honor to Hinchdale, so she worked on me to take in the young feller that was comin' to town to help him out. And in you walk."

"I seem to have been a mistake all around," I said dolefully.

"No, no, now you're here I begin to think maybe a girl would kind of be company." She buttered her fifth hot cake and looked me over thoroughly. "You're a pleasure for me to look at," she said, "but I'm wonderin' about how you'll strike Zaydee."

I was about to say that I had no idea how I would please a lady who wore pink velvet corsets, but I had no chance.

"Yes," Mrs. Hawks went on, "you'll be a shock to her all right," and there was sudden malice in her hitherto good-natured face.

"Who," I asked, "is Zaydee?" I wasn't at all sure that I wanted to know.

"Who is Zaydee?" repeated Mrs. Hawks. "Do you mean to tell me you don't know?"

"No. Should I? I arrived only yesterday."

"Yes, indeed, you should know Zaydee." Mrs. Hawks was vehement. "But I guess maybe you'll know her soon enough. Zaydee is Zaydee Proutman, Mrs. William Henry Proutman, and she pretty nearly owns the whole Museum."

Suddenly I realized that I already knew several things about Mrs. Zaydee Proutman. She had red hair, she had a metallic voice, and she wouldn't want me to work in her museum. Everyone—Epp Marks, Alpheus Harvey, John Gordon, Mrs. Hawks—had told me so. And I knew one more thing about her—John Gordon had broken his first date with me to go to her.

"Is she," I asked Mrs. Hawks, "is Mrs. Proutman ... young?"

I would have given much to have withdrawn this revelation, but to Mrs. Hawks it was merely an invitation to continue. "Well, you wouldn't think so," she said, "though she still seems kind of young to me and to some of the old fools in this town. Yes, and to some of the younger ones here and maybe elsewhere if half we hear's the truth."

I rose hastily. "Thanks for the wonderful breakfast. It ought to fortify me against anything." John Gordon might be one of the younger fools, but I felt I couldn't stay to hear it.

As I came down Mrs. Hawks's front walk, wind whipped my face from the great open space across the street. Along the sidewalk ran a neat fence of the same red stone as the Trust Company and the Museum, and a stone archway was cut with the name "William Henry Proutman Park." I crossed Broadway and looked through the entrance. On the flat field under a few leafless trees were disconsolate picnic tables, a tennis court covered with dead weeds, empty sand boxes, swing frames. At this season of the year they did not give a very festive air to what was obviously the site of the late corset shop. I wondered how much the unemployed of Hinchdale had enjoyed their leisure here in the last twenty-five years.

Well, for the moment I was employed in the William Henry Proutman Museum, which was "pretty nearly owned" by the menacing Zaydee. As I struggled with the quarter-mile wind to its portals, I ardently hoped she wouldn't shut that down until the last bone of the Holtzerman Collection had been measured and I had found another job.

The street door of the Museum was hooked back beside the encased tree section, and before entering I stopped for a glance at the red-haired bridal doll. Again I smiled at its ridiculous swank. No woman could be completely formidable who had that rather endearing kind of bad taste, I thought, and it was the kindest thought I ever had about Zaydee.

The Museum hall was still shadowy. Mr. Harvey's door and that of the library were shut, and the shades were still drawn in the exhibition hall, but the grotesque ladies held no terror for me today. Their dimly perceived smirks seemed to call for some politeness, and so I offered it aloud. "Good morning."

"Good mornin', Miss Ellis."

It was a gentle southern voice, and I responded with a small shriek.

"I certainly am sorry I frightened you. I thought when you spoke like that, you must have seen me." A dignified colored man, a long brush in hand, appeared round the nearest group of dummies.

"Oh, don't be sorry," I said. "I was just being silly and talking to these."

"I understand, Miss. I often do it myself. There're some right nice ladies among 'em, when you get to know 'em, but they certainly hit me funny at first."

"They frightened the life out of me yesterday," I admitted, "but they never will again."

"You turn to the right for the basement stairs, Miss Ellis. My name is Esquire. Esquire Williams. I'm comin' down to do the floor there now. Rest your coat behind the door."

Slipping on my smock, I moved over to the shelves and examined the Holtzerman Collection. Empty wooden boxes about thirty inches long were stacked along the entire north wall, each labeled "Proutman Museum, Holtzerman Collection."

Along the south wall the shelves were crowded with the six hundred paper cartons containing the skeletons to be labeled, catalogued, and finally packed in the strong boxes across the room.

I took one down and carried it to the counter. The most conspicuous objects within were the two long thigh bones lying on top of limbs, ribs, vertebrae, and at the end the skull on its side, together with the lower jaw. It is hard to explain why I like so much to work with human bones. To me they have always seemed fine things, clean-cut, graceful, enduring, smooth and firm to handle, adaptable to sure measurement, each one telling something of the external facts of a way of life, but completely impersonal—I almost said inhuman. Anyway, I never thought of them as having been parts of people.

I was holding up a skull in profile and murmuring, "Supra-orbital ridges medium, alveolar prognathism slight," when Esquire Williams entered with his brush.

"Ezekiel's Daughter!" he exclaimed.

"Ezekiel's which?"

"I ask your pardon, Miss Ellis"—he leaned on his brush and surveyed the layout before me—"but you surely do remind me of Ezekiel's vision."

"A wheel or something, wasn't it?"

"Not the time I have in my mind. Ezekiel had a vision of a land of dry bones. 'Behold there were very many in the open valley, and lo, they were very dry.'"

"I hope so for his sake," I said. "Bones with moist meat on them smell."

"You certainly do seem at home with 'em," Esquire commented. "But sometime you take down your Bible and read the rest about Ezekiel's vision. Maybe you'll laugh, but maybe you won't. Very many and very dry. There's too many bones around here."

"Not for me," I said, taking down a second carton.

"You're at work pretty early in the morning."

"I'm not working," I admitted. "Just playing with the bones because I like them. I can't really do anything until Dr. Gordon gets here."

"He's likely to be a little late this mornin'," said Esquire, "'count of socializin' last night."

I put down the box. That sore little wound in my vanity had jumped at the thought that even the janitor knew that Dr. Gordon had had a date with his boss.

"Big doin's," Esquire continued. "Crabs from See-attle and oysters from Maryland, and eight courses in all. Sheriff Brown, he choked on the artichokes. He! He! A young lady I know told me."

It didn't sound like an intimate party.

"But it wasn't what you'd call a real jollification," Esquire mourned. "No alcohol was served. No cocktails, no wine, no brandy, no highballs in the evenin'. Undertaker Phelps, he's a real nice man in many ways, but he don't touch a drop of liquor."

The sheriff, the undertaker, and nothing to drink. John Gordon must have had a merry evening.

"And Mr. Harvey and Miss Barton, they're a little fussy, too, maybe. Too bad. Mrs. Proutman certainly has a proud cellar."

"Was this an official party?" I inquired out of curiosity thinly masked to myself as polite interest.

"No. What you might call the Four Hundred of Hinchdale. Mrs. Proutman was right pleased to get them all to come to her house, so the young lady told me. They never've come before. But"—and his eyes twinkled—"she's had some right lively parties."

He went out, and I was left with the question why the richest woman in town should be so delighted to entertain a lot of elderly teetotallers. And one dark handsome young man? The answer was easy to that one.

At this moment the young man walked in.

"Hello," he said casually. "You look as if you'd been working here for years."

"Give me something to do, and I'll be glad to live up to appearances," I said.

He found plenty during the next hour to keep me busy for weeks ahead, and then was off to his office, leaving me with outline directions for filing, cataloguing, and numbering bones, and the pleasant assumption that I was capable of finding out the details myself.

Two hours or more passed while I moved from shelf to file drawer to counter. Behind his closed door Dr. Gordon's typewriter clacked away, and I hummed as I worked. The sun came out and fell warmly on the yellow varnish and brought out reddish tones in the bone I was labeling.

The typewriter stopped, a chair scraped, and I heard a voice. It was a woman's voice, not high and metallic but deep and full. I think mellifluous would about describe it as it came to me through the wall. Occasionally Dr. Gordon's tones punctuated the flow. This seemed to go on for a long time. I pretended to be much busier and accomplished much less, and waited for the door to open. The volume of the voices changed. The man and the woman had evidently risen. The doorknob turned.

"Oh, I might as well look at the girl," the woman said, and beneath the honey was a little clink of brass. I intended to keep my eyes glued to my work, but when the door opened I looked up and saw Zaydee Proutman walk into the laboratory.

CHAPTER IV

Nothing I had heard about her had prepared me for the overwhelming fact that Zaydee Proutman was beautiful. It was color that I felt first, deep rich color, deep rich curves moving toward me in lovely lines. Bronze hair in sculptured masses, smooth breasts and thighs molded in sheer marigold wool, long, tapering legs in copper-hued hose, copper itself in barbaric plenty around neck and wrists, and great red-brown eyes fixed insolently on my face. I got to my feet in sheer admiration and moved a step toward her. She stopped, and her eyes traveled up and down my slight smock-clad self, rested on my blond hair, which naturally grows in a mop. She lowered her lids as if she did not like what she had seen.

"Mrs. Proutman"—from her shadow issued Dr. Gordon; over his arm hung a sable coat—"this is Miss Ellis, the new anthropologist Professor Alden recommended for the Museum."

Zaydee Proutman raised her heavy white lids and looked at him. "I know," and there was no honey in her voice. "You've just shown me her teacher's letter. We don't need to go over all that again. She can probably use her hands on the Collection, so that you'll be free for the brain work. That is, if she's a good worker." She flipped a wrist toward me as if to say: If she doesn't stand around gaping like this all day.

I was back on my laboratory stool, my hot face bent over a shin bone, trying to steady the marking pen in my angry fingers.

"She was at the laboratory an hour before I got here this morning," said Dr. Gordon quietly.

I knew what she would reply. "New brooms. Perhaps she might use one on this floor. Esquire does nothing these days but hang around Isabelle. But wasn't last night really too grisly, John?"

The last word did not come out quite so smoothly as the rest. I raised my head a little. Zaydee stood in profile to me. It was not her best angle, for beneath a chin probably never so firm and finished as the rest of her, soft turkey-gobbler folds were beginning to sag.

Dr. Gordon's face looked almost as red as mine felt. "I had a good time, Mrs. Proutman."

She laughed and laid a long, lovely hand on his sleeve. Her nails matched her hair, and I wondered meanly if the same person dyed them both. "John, you really are sweet. Those old crows. You should have gone in for diplomacy instead of science."

"I liked those people."

"Oh, John, don't make me laugh. You couldn't. Sometimes, you know, you remind me of the dearest boy in the Swedish diplomatic service. He's tall and dark. I thought all Swedes were pure blond. Or do anthropologists know better?"

"Some of us do."

"But he was awfully serious, too, when you'd least expect it. If I asked him why, he answered me in Swedish. Cute of him. I've got a letter from him here." She sat down at one end of my work table and opened an enormous bag of orange suede monogrammed in jet. "I've been carrying it around for days, meaning to ask someone to translate some Swedish in it. It might be anything from him. Miss Ellis."

"Yes, Mrs. Proutman." I was working too hard to look up.

"Can you read Swedish?"

"No, Mrs. Proutman."

"I suppose your education was narrow. I had none myself." She made it sound like all the advantages. "Well, go and get Jensen. He'll have to do it for me."

"I don't know who Mr. Jensen is, but I'll be glad to go."

"You don't know Jensen?" We were looking full at each other again. "What have you been doing since you arrived?"

"I have been working in this room."

"Jensen is the engineer," Dr. Gordon said hastily. "I'll get him, Miss Ellis."

"Please, no," I said and was out of the room. In the dark passage a soft voice whispered, "You come this way, Miss," and I followed the lurking Esquire to an iron door labeled "Furnace Room."

"Mr. Jensen?"

The big blunt-faced man shut the furnace door and smiled at me.

"Good mornin'. You the new bone girl?"

"That's right."

"You want a little more heat in your graveyard already?"

"No. Mrs. Proutman is there." I hadn't intended the juxtaposition.

"Then you got plenty."

"She wants to see you right away."

"I bet." Jensen pushed his cap back on his head. "What for now?"

I shook my head. It seemed better not to know.

"Oh, well, I come. If I don't, you get in bad." He was in no hurry.

When I returned to the laboratory, Zaydee was holding her open letter.

"Oh, here you are, Jensen," she said.

"Yah." He didn't remove his cap. "What you want?"

"Look at this letter where I've folded it back, and tell me what it says in English."

Jensen regarded her with a piscine eye, looked at the narrowly creased letter in his paw, and dropped it on the table.

"Bah! Svenske!" he said.

"All right, Jensen. What does it say?"

"What does it say?" Jensen's pale face was a shade whiter between the specks of coal dust. "How should I know? You know damned well my old man come from Denmark. That stuff ain't my language."

"There's no difference," said Zaydee. "You could read it if you really tried. Or can you read?"

"I can read," said Jensen and picked up the letter and smoothed out the crease. "Dear Lady: Remembering our so well-enyoyed days together when you were pursuing your Car-i-been cruise I would with all my heart await your early return. But most unfortunately at the warious dates you suggest I am to be occupied with special work for my government, the most humanitarian in the world toward all but its poor civil servants.' The rest is all Swedish talk. There ain't much of it, though."

The bronze nails of Zaydee's left hand cut into the table and the huge diamond quivered on her finger. "O.K., Jensen," she said, and smiled. "Go on back to your job." Before the door closed on him, she went on, "Quaint local characters. You've just got to overlook them. I think I'd make a first-rate anthropologist."

John Gordon looked at me, and we were two against one, but it was only my response she saw. "All right, Miss Ellis. Go up to the library and look up this stuff in the Swedish or Danish or what not dictionary, and do a good thorough job of it. I'll stop there for it before I leave."

The moment I crossed the threshold of the Museum library at the end of my bruised and beaten retreat, I knew that I had found a refuge. The open shelves invited use; pots of small pink chrysanthemums and African violets stood on the magazine table, and Miss Alice Barton was glad to meet me. As Dr. Gordon had said, she was little and a lady, gray-haired, stiff-backed, smiling with a reserve which did not resemble suspicion. She came forward to meet me and said, "You are Miss Ellis. I am Miss Barton. I was coming downstairs to see you as soon as my early-morning duties were finished. I like to do things in order." Her voice, like her person, was small, dry, and very neat.

"I've come to bother you about one of my early duties," I said. "Can you tell me where to find a Swedish dictionary?"

"I can tell you," said Miss Barton. "I will get it for you in a moment. Mr. William Henry Proutman was a—lavish buyer. We have dictionaries in twenty languages, but in twenty years not a single person has asked to consult a single one. Would you mind telling me why you wish to consult the Swedish dictionary on your first morning here? Is there important anthropological work published in that language?"

"Yes, there is, a lot of it," I said, "but I can't read it. I've got to struggle to make out a few Swedish words in a letter. For—Mrs. Proutman."

"You've met Mrs. Proutman." It was a statement without color.

"Yes." I tried to make my own as pale. "She's waiting for me to do it. Mr. Jensen couldn't read it for her."

"And I can well imagine the result. I'll get the dictionary right away."

She brought it at once, together with paper and a sharp pencil. "Oh, thanks so much. It was dreadfully careless of me to come off without my tools."

"I don't think you would have done it under ordinary circumstances," she said primly, and left me with the little fat Swedish-English dictionary and the elegant sheet of paper over which the dearest boy had spread his writing exceedingly thin.

Laboring over the strange diacritics, I was glad that he had been even charier of his native language than of the English so engagingly enunciated by Jensen. There were in fact but ten Swedish words, and after a half-hour of checking and rechecking I could make of them nothing more intimate than, "I hope this will find you in health and happiness." Which would not perhaps satisfy Mrs. Zaydee Proutman. Since there was no typewriter in sight, I printed the translation in my neatest laboratory script and attached it to the letter, all the time painfully aware that Zaydee was still with Dr. Gordon and that I had been told to wait here.

Miss Barton, stiffly reading, did not look conversational, so I walked over to the modest card catalogue and opened the A drawer. It was a simple file without guide rods. There were very few cards under *Anthropology*, all written in the well-bred hand I had noticed the day before. A few titles in brighter ink suggested their acquisition since Dr. Gordon's arrival, including a pamphlet, "Did Sinanthropus Practice Cannibalism?" which I decided to read at an early date. I hoped that Zaydee had not seen it; it might give her ideas. And still she did not come. I thumbed through the index cards, *Antiques,* "Old Spinning Wheels from Hinchdale, Barton County," by Alice Barton, published by Amanda Adams Barton Chapter, D.A.R., 1920, ten pages; *Archaeology*, with a dozen articles on stone implements and pioneer plows by Alpheus G. Harvey, one of them a reprint from the *American Anthropologist*; *Architecture*, of the Holy Land and of the Proutman Museum (builder's plans); *Astrology* ...

"Star-gazing, Miss Ellis?" It was the honey voice just above my ear. She was standing close to me, her eyes shining with malice. "When you'd finished, you were going to begin my work, perhaps?"

"I have finished everything, Mrs. Proutman," I said and took the letter from the pocket of my smock. "I've been waiting for you."

Color mounted in her cheeks, and as she took the paper a jagged fingernail, roughened by her jab at the laboratory table, scratched across my wrist. Her perfume was stupefying. She glanced at my translation and then at me, eyes narrow with suspicion, and opened her mouth as if to question the honesty of my work, glanced at it again, and, deciding that all too probably it was correct, snapped it into her purse.

"What are you playing with now?" The long fingers swept deep into the index drawer, and the loose cards flew in all directions and flopped to the floor. Zaydee Proutman laughed.

I stooped to retrieve them. Miss Barton had risen from her desk and was looking steadily at us.

Mrs. Proutman laughed again. "Pick them up, Alice," she ordered. "And you"—she tapped my bent shoulder—"get up and go back to your own work."

In my flight through the library door I brushed against Mr. Alpheus Harvey and saw his horrible yellow smile.

Dr. Gordon was standing at my laboratory table, a shin bone in his hand. "Neat labeling," he said. "I hope you don't mind a pipe. This place smelled more like Evening in the Harem than Morning in the Laboratory."

CHAPTER V

"Will you come in and visit with me for a bit?" Miss Alice Barton stood at the library door as I was returning from my drugstore milkshake. "I am sure you haven't been absent for an hour. You should rest at noon."

"Thank you," I said, slipping off my camel's-hair coat and perking flattened curls. "I simply couldn't eat a thing more after Mrs. Hawks's breakfast."

"We all know Sarah Hawks's breakfasts. She is the finest cook in the Amanda Adams Barton Chapter. She is a direct descendant of two generals and a veterinary surgeon of George Washington's army. It is very fine old stock." Miss Barton paused and then added, "Mrs. Proutman is not eligible for the D.A.R."

And nothing, I felt, looking at the drawing together of her faded lips, could be more pleasing to Miss Alice Barton. There was a brief silence. "Are you a Daughter, Miss Ellis?"

I missed the capitalization and said stupidly, "My father and mother are dead."

"Oh, my dear"—her voice was shocked and gentle—"I did not mean ... I regret ... I did not know ... Then you are alone in the world?"

"I have a great-aunt," I said. "I have seen her only two or three times. She—" but this was not the place to be bitter or brutal about Aunt Jane. "She was once State Regent of the D.A.R."

Miss Barton looked for a moment at the hands folded on her desk. "I do not wish to intrude," she said finally. "This work means a great deal to you?" They were almost John Gordon's words.

"Oh, yes, everything." The remembrance of the last hours of the morning was strong within me. "It's a wonderful chance to work with Dr. Gordon. And with the Holtzerman Collection. And, of course, I have to eat. The salary is good for a girl."

"That is the difficulty, isn't it," said Miss Barton. "You are a girl."

"I know. That's why it was probably silly to go into anthropology, but I like it so much. Mr. Harvey seems to think it's all right, though, and I don't think Dr. Gordon minds."

"I am sure Dr. Gordon doesn't mind." There came another of Miss Barton's uncomfortable pauses. "Mrs. Proutman minds."

How could I have forgotten for a moment? Back it all came, the color, the scent, the words, "that girl—she can probably use her *hands*." —"She might use the brush on the floor." —"Your education was narrow." —"What are you playing with now?" I saw the little red scratch on my wrist. Against the rise of angry tears I blurted out, "I know. Everyone has been telling me about it, from the station agent to you. Why does she hate me so? Why did they all know she would?"

Miss Barton's dry tone steadied me. "Look at yourself."

"Look at myself? Mrs. Proutman is beautiful."

"Yes, Zaydee is a handsome woman; but Zaydee, however she may act at times, is a smart woman. When she looks at you, she thinks of how often her hair has to be tinted and how many pounds she weighs and how many years have gone by since she was twenty-one. Are you twenty-one, Miss Ellis?"

I nodded.

"When Zaydee was twenty-one she married Mr. Proutman. That was twenty-five years ago. I think she has felt her age a good deal lately. She does not like to feel her age." Another long pause. "Do you know why you are here, Miss Ellis?"

"To save Dr. Gordon's time?"

"Yes," said Miss Barton.

So that he would have more time for Zaydee. It lay unspoken between us.

"Miss Barton—" I had to know. "Can she do anything she likes about me?"

"Yes. Was there anything in the letter to your professor about the length of time for which you were offered a place at the Proutman Museum?"

"No."

"No, there would not be."

"Aren't there any trustees? Doesn't Mr. Harvey have anything to say about things? Or Dr. Gordon?"

This time the silence was so long that I rose to go. "Sit down," she said. "I think that you should know about Mr. Proutman's will. It affects you as deeply as it does the rest of us."

She sat even straighter in her stiff chair. A faint color came into her crumpled skin. "Mr. William Henry Proutman," she said, "was a remarkable man. He was a poor boy who left here to work in a corset factory in Connecticut. Later he returned and founded one here. It was the first industry in the town. Mr. Proutman was a pioneer type.

"In 1914, it seemed to him that the business might be less profitable in the immediate future, so he decided, very wisely, to close it down. He owned 95 per cent of the stock, and the rest of his money was most carefully invested. Mr. Proutman wanted to do something handsome for the town. He decided to found a museum to preserve the traditions of Hinchdale."

For the town which had no hospital, no adequate school building, no community center nor home for the aged, and which, thanks to rugged Mr. Proutman, was to lack, henceforth, an industry.

"He was, quite naturally, most concerned personally with the exhibits on the first floor. The preservation of Indian relics and the remains of pioneer days are the work of Alpheus Harvey. I was proud to lend my advice. I am a college graduate. Mr. Proutman felt he did not need to seek help apart from his fellow citizens."

"Then Mr. Harvey," I asked, "was living in Hinchdale?"

"He was a bookkeeper in the Proutman Savings and Trust Company. But he had spent most of his leisure time collecting arrowheads and wampum."

"It must have taken a long time to get an entire museum going." I added to myself: Even a museum like this.

"Oh, no." Miss Barton's dry little voice softened. "Just a year. Mr. Proutman was a—very vigorous man. It was a very wonderful year."

"And then"—the softness went, the color in her cheeks grew red—"he married Zaydee Riggins."

I thought she would not go on, but she did, very firmly. "Zaydee worked in the One-Arm Lunch. She understood Mr. Proutman."

Understood him better than a college graduate did, and that was the end of Miss Alice Barton's one wonderful year.

"Mr. Proutman lived until 1925. They spent most of their time in Los Angeles, Atlantic City, and Miami Beach. I do not think they were very restful places. Mr. Proutman was only sixty-five when he died."

But not, I thought, until he had had a pretty good time.

"He left a million dollars to Zaydee and another million to the Proutman Museum. Alpheus Harvey is to be director for life. I am life-librarian. But there is a proviso: if we are judged incompetent at any time because of illness or other cause, we will be retired on pensions equal to our salaries. The judge of our competence will be Zaydee. She controls all Museum funds throughout her lifetime. All salaries are paid by her. She approves the purchase of all collections. She hires employees and dismisses them. There are no other trustees. At her death Alpheus Harvey, if living, becomes immediately in full control of the Museum until his death. Beyond that, no provision is made."

"But why did a smart business man like Mr. Proutman give her all that power?" I demanded.

"Because Zaydee was smart, too. She had been, so everyone believes, a faithful wife to Mr. Proutman and she had a good feeling for business affairs. And she did everything he liked. When they came to Hinchdale every year, she was always dressed very quietly in black and white or gray, and she hardly ever said anything before others. It was only after Mr. Proutman's death that she began to enjoy herself in her own way."

"Like Willa Cather's *Lost Lady*."

Miss Barton's lips narrowed. "Zaydee Proutman was never a lady," she said. "I suppose," she went on, "she wanted to own the Museum so that she could wield power in this town that had scorned her. In the last few years she has spent longer periods here with her—friends. She has been entirely honest about the money, and she is a keen investor. We have an income, I understand, of nearly fifty thousand dollars a year, more than we ever have spent. We could afford to buy the Holtzerman Collection—that is, we could afford the money."

"But why did she want to buy it? I wouldn't think it would have appealed to her in the least. It isn't beautiful or exciting, or famous even, except among a small group of anthropologists."

"It meant a great deal to those few, didn't it?" inquired Miss Barton, her eyes holding mine steadily. "It meant something to you. It means a considerable reputation to Dr. Gordon. Dr. Gordon is a young man."

In the silence that fell I faced an ugly possibility. John Gordon was young in the field of anthropology, with his career to make; he was a man younger by eighteen years than Zaydee Proutman.

"She knew him?"

"Miss Ellis, we shouldn't judge. He does not seem to know her well even now, and I think he is a frank person. And you can tell nothing from Mrs. Proutman's manner. I have seen her that way before with several young men. One was a nice young missionary who is now in West Africa. Another one is not so well off."

"She—she rather has us all, hasn't she?"

"Yes, she has. Neither Mr. Harvey nor I wish to retire and live on our pensions. This Museum is his life, and I should be lonely without my days here. She has done our work no harm thus far, but"—she stiffened in every line—"many little things are hard."

"But she can drop the rest of us at any time. Dr. Gordon and Esquire and Jensen and me?"

"Yes, but I do not think she will do so immediately. Certainly not Jensen. He is the engineer at the bank and the school and doesn't particularly care whether he keeps the Museum position. But he likes to annoy Zaydee. His wife worked with her in the lunchroom, and Jensen used to go to the same barbecues and shivarees that she did as a girl. He is very friendly with"—her lips tightened—"a connection of hers."

"I like Esquire. I don't want anything to happen to him."

"At present she has a special reason for wanting to dismiss him, but Williams is well-liked in this town, especially in the Methodist Church. Zaydee is just beginning to be received by some of our better people. I think she will hesitate to tell him to go.

"You are a stranger here. My dear, if you will assure us of your eligibility to the D.A.R., we shall welcome you in the Amanda Adams Barton Chapter."

CHAPTER VI

During that long October, life in the Proutman Museum was not gay. Suspicion, gleaming through Alpheus Harvey's pince-nez, was steadily directed at potential fingermarks a young female who had unfairly sneaked an education from Oldwick University might leave on his sacred glass cases. If he momentarily missed anything, from a thumb tack to a totem pole, he asked me where I had last seen it. Miss Barton, after her invitation and her warning, withdrew to her habitual reserve.

Dr. John Gordon was no more than the anthropologist I assisted in his study of the Holtzerman Collection.

As we worked in the laboratory he was always the serious young scientist. For days, while he deciphered the Holtzerman documents in his office and I labeled and catalogued skeleton after skeleton, I knew little of him except for the clack of his typewriter or the smell of his pipe.

But there were other days when we would work side by side at the laboratory table, he with calipers and steel tape in his long brown fingers, I with record blanks and pen, reading back and recording his finely made measurements.

"Not much like newspaper anthropology," he commented, leaning back and stretching stiff muscles. "Not 'a moment's thrilling revelation of secret ceremonies never before witnessed by white men.'"

"Nor the 'quick, keen glance of the scientist probing the mystery of human origins.'"

"No," he grinned, "just the seat of the pants to the seat of the laboratory stool."

I looked at the shelves crowded with bones. "I hope," I said, "that you are upholstered in the best quality of tweed. We could be sitting here together for the next three years."

"I can take it," he said. "I can take a lot, so long as I am the only person who has a chance at this material."

He did not smile. He meant literally what he said. Back of the ambition of the selfless scientist seeking knowledge for its own sake, there was something hard, driving, personal. He, John Gordon, and he alone, would study the Holtzerman Collection. Even at a price set by Zaydee Proutman.

In our little scientific world the Holtzerman Collection was unique. In the late seventeenth century, in a remote pocket of the Carpathians, four families of grimly religious dissenters had taken up their home. The bare country and their stark outlook on life had discouraged invaders. During the next three hundred years they had intermarried, given birth, and finally died out, among the rocky pastures and dark forests.

About 1900 the abandoned graveyard had been excavated by a Herr Professor Doktor Holtzerman, not with complete permission of the authorities. Nor did he turn over the loot to the anatomical department of his Central European university. He seems always to have regarded it as his private treasure trove; and as such it was smuggled across the border in the last year A. H. (ante Hitler), then across the ocean under proper invoice, offered in the United States for a large sum by Holtzerman's widow, and finally purchased by Zaydee Proutman for a reason by no means so mysterious to me as it had been to Dr. Alden.

What made these bones so interesting was that we knew so much about the people. Over the centuries a good many visitors, lumber and cattle buyers, hunters, and a few intrepid missionaries, had stayed briefly with the strange little colony, and in a dozen or more obscure newspapers and magazines accounts of it were left in Hungarian, Czech, and German. Fragmentary and prejudiced as the descriptions were (one literary missionary had been sent down the mountain with his face to his donkey's tail), they nevertheless told us what these people ate, something about their illnesses, and how they looked. One article was illustrated with rather fanciful sketches, and the latest with three dark photographs.

More valuable were the moldy records from the old church relating in almost illegible script the dates of all births, marriages, deaths—everything the austere sect had found worthy of note. Only four surnames appeared on this register, evidence that the original stock had received no reinforcement. It was this fact that made it so valuable a source for the study of human heredity.

Not all the skeletons delivered to the Proutman Museum were from the Dissenters' graveyard. Frau Holtzerman had evidently bundled up a lot of odds and ends and added them, either as a bonus to the buyer or to clean out the attic. There were two or three specimens of the skull and right limbs sold to anatomy students, all of fresh green bone, which is actually very white and in marked contrast to the reddish-brown patina which the old bones had taken on from long years in the ground. There was also the skeleton of what Dr. Gordon thought was a collie dog, perhaps the late Professor Holtzerman's pet; and among a litter of old novels, official reports, and rusty nails I unearthed a large black umbrella with a heavy head of solid ivory carved in the form of an anthropoid ape. John Gordon laughed and laughed.

"It's probably a presentation on the twenty-fifth anniversary of his doctorate," he said. "Can't you see the old boy going out on the brightest days with his derby and his frock coat and this?"

"Absolutely," I giggled. "But what will we do with it?"

"Give it to Mrs. Proutman," he said. "It will be something to show for her fifty thousand dollars."

This was the gayest interlude of our month's work. It was his only reference to Zaydee.

I was smiling over Aunt Jane's reply to my inquiry about my Revolutionary pedigree one morning when he came in with his calipers.

"What's the good news?" he asked, as I hastened to get out my record sheets.

"Just a letter from a rich aunt," I said shortly. "I'm ready to begin, Dr. Gordon."

But he was not. "Did she send you a million?" he asked, "or isn't she that rich?"

"She's twice as rich," I said, "and she sent me what she always does. Nothing. Unless you count a family tree. Miss Barton wanted to know whether I was eligible to join the D.A.R., and I find that I am to the extent of three generals and a lieutenant colonel."

"Doubtless a blow to an admirer of Grant Wood, but go ahead and join. I belong to Kiwanis; Harvey proposed my name. He belongs as Museum director, I as scientist (*sic!*). It's a damned good thing for academic people to get out of their little world and see what real values are to the common man. Besides, I've got a weakness for old Alpheus." I evidently looked my surprise, for he went on: "I know you don't like him. And he isn't very engaging at first sight. He's quite different when you get to know him, and he would fight to the death for what he believes is right. Not many people would do that, Kay."

At this use of my name, the feeling of my first day came back suddenly. He went on, "I go over to his house once a week and play anagrams with him and Mrs. Harvey."

"He's got a wife?"

"Of course. You haven't been thinking of him as human, have you? Almost every man has a wife. Except," he laughed a little, "a few really serious anthropologists."

So I joined the D.A.R. Miss Barton flushed with pleasure when she saw Aunt Jane's meticulous and glorious genealogies, which had come to me with no other word; and Mrs. Hawks was voluble in her unselfish admiration of my extra general and the colonel who outranked her Vet.

"There's another blow for Zaydee Proutman," she triumphed.

A cold spot formed in the pit of my stomach. "Why?" I asked. "I shouldn't think she would be much interested in the D.A.R."

"She was interested enough to pay to have some fake genealogies made up for her back East, but Alice Barton was too well educated to swallow 'em. She hasn't loved Alice much since then." She turned to the window where she was again kneeling at her daily ritual. "I declare, there goes her jig again. That's twice I've seen him in the last month."

"Her jig?" I asked. Anything about Zaydee Proutman, I felt, might be useful for me to know.

"Uh-huh, you know that song that used to be on the radio all the time a few years ago." She raised a quaver, "'Just a jig-a-something, tum-tum, turn-tum-turn!'"

"A gigolo?"

"Well, maybe not. I ought not to talk that way. He used to stay in the cottage out on her place, and he didn't work at anything here. He played the piano. He left town more'n a year ago, and folks that worked for her said Zaydee kicked him out. I don't know about that, but I do know this is no time Zaydee would want him back. He's still got that open red and gray car she gave him. Don't look so bright now. I'm real glad you're joinin' the D.A.R. You'll get a note from our secretary, Mrs. Jim Watson. Where Dr. Gordon lives, you know."

I knew not only where he lived, but how he spent his time, for Mrs. Watson was an intimate friend of Mrs. Hawks. He read "till you think he'd hurt his sight"; he had his weekly evening with Alpheus; he dined with the better families and attended Kiwanis committees; and not infrequently his shabby old car headed for the big Proutman house two miles out of town on tiny Lake Laurel. No one, according to Mrs. Hawks, thought John Gordon was Zaydee's jig, but a lot thought she was trying to marry him, and a few said she would succeed.

The day when Zaydee descended upon us while we were measuring a pelvis I was grateful for the impersonality of our relationship. The bones of a human pelvis are three. To measure the total width of the pelvis, all three must be held in place; and I did the holding with both hands while Dr. Gordon bent over me with the big sliding calipers extended. It was routine for us, but viewed from the rear it had an unjustified effect on Zaydee.

"I am intruding," she said, "and I shall continue to do so."

"Two hundred and seventy-two point three," read Dr. Gordon, and straightened up slowly, sliding back the big brass bar.

"Two hundred ..." I repeated, releasing my grasp on the joints. The three bones flopped down gently on the table blotter as I picked up my pen, "... and seventy-two point three. Good morning, Mrs. Proutman."

John Gordon was shaking hands with her, and our lack of confusion seemed almost as enraging to her as had our supposed intimacy. Zaydee did not like to be put in the wrong. She was looking extremely handsome in purple homespun and red fox, and both my eyes and his frankly told her so. She smiled.

"John, you work too hard," she said. "It's stunning of you, but it really goes too far. I've come to take you off to lunch at Emily Garrett's in Warrenton. It's a beautiful day for a drive."

"Lord, I'd like to," said Gordon and looked the part (or was it a part?), "but I can't. I've got to finish a paper for the State Academy meeting. That's only three days off, you know."

She frowned. "Oh, you can dash anything off in five minutes for those people," she said.

"No, I can't. A lot of them are smarter than I am."

"Blah! I don't get it. You're so inconsistent." She was trying to hide her annoyance in a teasing tone. "You tell me again and again that you won't have any results to show from your work for years, and then you have to stay home and write a paper about them a few days later. Explain that one."

John laughed, but not as he did with me. "This is just a very short general note about the condition of the group's teeth. The entire result could be put in one word: they're bad."

"Oh," said Zaydee, "that's rather disgusting, isn't it? You know, my teeth are absolutely perfect. I've never lost one. I've never even had a filling." Dr. Gordon's back was now toward me. "You look as if you didn't believe me."

"Well, it's rather remarkable, you know."

She smiled widely, showing a lot of white, even dentition between warmly reddened lips. "Would you like to examine them one by one?"

"I'd like to see a complete mouth X-ray," he said. "You know what anthropologists are. I've got a little souvenir for you from the late Herr Professor Doktor Holtzerman, no less. Where is it, Miss Ellis?"

I found the umbrella and he gave it to her.

"I think it's terribly cute," she said. "And you know, I think the silk is still perfectly good. If it is, I shall use it."

"Let's see," said Gordon, stretching out his hand.

She drew back sharply, "God, no. Never raise an umbrella in the house. It means a death. You anthropologists can laugh, but I know. It's happened again and again in my own family."

"Well, we didn't open it," said Gordon, "so no harm is done."

Zaydee Proutman's fingers curled beneath the ape's solid ivory neck. "He really is sweet," she said, no longer frightened. "I think I shall call him Johnnie. And we'll drive to the State meeting on Wednesday and start early enough to lunch in the Westerman cocktail lounge."

"That would be fine," said John, "if you think Mr. Harvey and Miss Barton would enjoy it. They're going with us, you know. To give us social standing. They're charter members."

He stood close to her when he said it and smiled, and she took it, and liked it.

On the day of the State Academy meeting, to which no one had suggested my going, I found it hard to settle down to work. The Museum was empty and too still. Jensen had given the furnace door its last echoing slam until evening. Esquire, dourly murmuring that Mr. Harvey had laid out enough work for him polishing showcases in the attic to last a week, gave my floor a last soft brush and left me alone. I lighted a cigarette as a gesture of rebellion against unwritten law. Miss Barton, I knew, was offended by women's smoking; and Alpheus Harvey, while quite unconcerned by John Gordon's perpetual pipe, would be certain that I would burn the Museum to the ground. At that moment I almost wanted to, particularly that ridiculous old corset room. Cigarette in hand, I strolled up the basement stairs, defying no one but myself.

In William Henry Proutman Hall the usual shrouded gloom prevailed. As I entered I could dimly see the three seated ladies in evening dress who were Esquire's favorites. They were very fluffy wherever the corsets permitted, with great diaphanous sleeves floating loose from their bare shoulders and falling over their ruffled skirts. They were very sweet, and in spite of all Esquire's careful brushing, more than a little dusty.

And then in the gray quiet there came a sob. It came from one of the seated ladies. As I listened in straining fear, it was repeated. Even in my fright I realized that it came from lower than the ladies' waxen heads. It was, then, probably human. With more courage than I wish I had had to summon, I walked toward the sound, which at once ceased. The nearest figure was seated with her back to the door by which I had entered the hall. I walked around her and saw a woman kneeling at her feet. She had a tiny electric lamp beside her on the floor, and by its beam she was mending the dummy's pink chiffon flounce.

"Hello," I said weakly. "I thought you were a ghost."

She looked up at me. Her face was a lovely rounded oval in the eerie light, and the whites of her dark eyes shone. She put her finger on her lips and rose. She was a tall girl, wide-hipped.

"I'm certainly acting like a haunt," she whispered, laughing.

I laughed and whispered my reply. "Come on down to my laboratory and tell me what you're doing."

She followed me, and as we entered the light of the window over the basement stairs I saw that she was a mulatto and that she had been crying.

"I'm Isabelle," she said. "Isabelle Jones. I'm Mrs. Proutman's personal maid."

"I work for her, too," I said. "Please sit down."

She hesitated. "Should I?"

"If you have time. I'm all alone."

"You know what I was doing, Miss Ellis?" she said. "It was a little surprise for Esquire. He was terribly upset because he had brushed that old dress just a little speck too hard and tore it. The material is just about ashes, but I've put in a lot of little cobwebby stitches and it don't show a bit."

"You must be awfully skillful," I said. "I wouldn't dare touch it."

"You could do it with a little practice," said Isabelle, "Esquire says you're clever with those fine little pens. You have kind of spooky work, haven't you? I don't know as I'd like it."

"I like it. And anyway I have to eat."

The friendly glow died a little in Isabelle's face. "Ain't we all?" she sighed. Then she laughed and resumed her former manner. "How do you enjoy yourself in Hinchdale, Miss Ellis?"

I had lied about this often to Miss Barton and Mrs. Hawks, but to Isabelle I said frankly and without fear, "I hate it."

"I'm sorry," she said. "I've hated lots of places, but I'd love to stay here for the rest of my whole life."

She was beautifully groomed, dressed in pale tan wool, her only ornaments swinging gold earrings. "Why do you like it here?" I asked. "Isn't your work the same anywhere?"

"My work is," she said, and her eyes grew shadowed. "I've lived all over the world with Miss Zaydee, Paris and everywhere, but I guess all your life that counts anywhere is your—is the person you love best. Isn't it that way to you, Miss Ellis?"

I looked at her, feeling suddenly empty before her completion. I forgot the shadows of tears under her eyes.

"I shouldn't be talking to you in this way," she said.

"Oh, please do. It would be that way with me if—if I loved anybody. I ... just don't."

"Oh, I'm sorry," said Isabelle softly. "I guess Esquire misunderstood."

What had I shown to Esquire? Something I had not quite shown myself. "I like Esquire," I said.

Isabelle's face glowed softly. "He's the finest man I've ever found. In Paris or anywhere else. He's my fleecy lamb." She giggled. "What a way to talk to you—I must go home fast and finish up all the sewing Miss Zaydee will expect to see done when she gets back." She rose. "Thank you for your hospitality, Miss Ellis. I hope you'll get to like Hinchdale. It's a real nice town. The people here are nice to us. They aren't, everywhere. Yes, I'd like to stay here all my life. If I could live here the way I want to." There were tears in her eyes as she left.

I thought often about Isabelle, but the remainder of October passed without my seeing her, though I wondered about her tears.

On the last night of October I set out for supper with a high heart. There was nothing in the black village street swept by a fierce wind from the Great Lakes to cause a cardiac upheaval, and not much in the prospect of eating at the Greasy Spoon.

Mrs. Marks's little restaurant, which owed its traditional name less to the condition of the silver than to the constant smell of the griddle where her perpetual steaks and pancakes were produced, was warm and neat enough. The Markses were kindly souls, their customers mainly truck drivers and store clerks, and the food acceptable if you avoided something called "chicken-fried steak," an unlikely combination of bread crumbs, fat, and old leather belts. Tonight I could have eaten even that with relish. Tomorrow was pay day, and I would get one hundred and fifty dollars; and tonight, unbelievably, I was going to the show with John Gordon.

An hour ago he had stretched out stiff muscles and risen from his desk. "Pay day tomorrow"—he yawned and laughed—"and I'm pot broke. Lord, it seems a miracle every month. To prove it's true that I've still got a dime in my pocket, I ought to take a girl out tonight. How about the second show? I'll meet you at the Greasy Spoon."

I lingered over my apple pie and coffee so that it would last until he came. There was only one other customer in the restaurant, a thin man at the table next the door. He looked young and sick, the skin tight over his cheeks and his eyes red-rimmed and sunken. His skin and eyes were pale, his hair red.

He sat with a cup of coffee which, most of the time, he regarded steadily. He did not drink any of it. Twice he raised his head and looked at me with a glazed stare, as if he were a little drunk, but when he rose his movements were steady and rather graceful, and he pulled on his old felt hat with an air.

Just as he reached the door it opened and John Gordon, broad-shouldered, alive, eyes looking for me with a smile, came into the room. For a moment the thin stranger blocked his path. I saw Gordon's face question his action, and then the other stood aside and Gordon came toward me, looking glad. Behind him I saw the thin boy turn and give him a long stare, and there was hate in the laugh with which he shut the door.

"That Randy Bill," Mrs. Marks yelled to her husband above the crackling grease, "someone ought to run him out of town."

CHAPTER VII

"'There was a noise, and behold a shaking, and the bones came together, bone to his bone. And when I beheld, lo the sinews and flesh came up upon them, and the skin covered them above but there was no breath in them!'" Esquire's soft intone came to an end. "When you're all alone down here, Miss Ezekiel, don't you ever have that vision of the land of dry bones?"

"Do you, Kay?" John Gordon came out of his office with two long envelopes in his hand. "This would be an appropriate time. The ghost walked here last night."

"Don't say that!" Esquire was ashy. "Don't say that, Dr. Gordon!"

"That?" He pulled a long pink slip from one of the envelopes. "Haven't you ever heard that expression, Esquire? It means the paymaster has been around. Here's yours, Miss Ezekiel."

The slip in my envelope was short and white. It said:

Miss Ellis: Please come to my office at your early convenience.

A. HARVEY

I sat by his crowded old desk and looked at the stuffed weasel. I waited certain dismissal, cold hands clasped. The hackneyed words passed through my numb mind, "as in death." Death to hopes, death to— Why can't he tell me quickly and get this over forever?

Alpheus Harvey hooked the gold eyeglass chain slowly into the gray wool behind his left ear, adjusted the black hearing disk, and edged open the drawer of his desk. His fingers crept in, found a paper, and held it out to me. It was a long pink slip.

"I want it made very clear, Miss Ellis"—Mr. Harvey's voice was a low rasp—"there was never any salary agreement between you and the Proutman Museum. In the letter to Professor Alden requesting the recommendation of an assistant there was the suggestion of a stipend of $150.00 per month, but no assistant was specifically named. It is quite clear that you have no claim upon this institution?"

I looked at the check in my hand. "Kay Ellis, October salary, one hundred dollars only."

Mr. Harvey went on, "I want you also to know that your work is satisfactory. I have no fault to find with you. But it has been suggested that the higher figure is somewhat out of proportion to your needs in this town. A young woman, I believe, does not have expenses commensurate with those of a man."

Relief had displaced fear so quickly in me that I did not realize anger had followed. "You mean," I said, "that women can do their own washing? And cut their own hair?"

A jagged tooth appeared between his lips. "That is the idea," he said. "Do you accept this salary, Miss Ellis?"

"I'll have to." I was at the door when he called me.

"Miss Ellis, I should like to say that this—monthly figure—is not my decision. However, that is of little consequence. The decision is final."

I fled to the laboratory, filled with some ill-conceived plan of sobbing on the broad shoulder that, last night, had rested against mine at the movies; but there I met only emptiness and the second disastrous note of the morning. It read:

K. E.: Gone to Warrenton to buy a new bus, compliments of the October ghost.

J. G.

In the first moment of blind rage I was sure that he had known the meaning of my summons to the director's office, and that this triumphant crow satisfied some subconscious inferiority. I was about to give way to a soliloquy on the basic unfairness of life, particularly to women, which might well have run on all day, but there was never time for that. For at that moment there was a straining, bumping bang, and a packing case landed flat on the threshold with Esquire moaning on top.

"If it's bust, I'm bust, good Lord," he sang, rising not without dignity.

I looked at the letters painted a foot high. "If it's come that far, it's probably had worse whangs than this," I said, pointing to "From the Rev. Albert Steinhardt, Gombo Christian Mission, via Freetown, Sierra Leone, West Africa."

"You right, you right. But look, Miss Ellis, this here box is a special present for Mrs. Proutman."

"Who you killin' off in here, Villiams?" Jensen lumbered in. "By golly, a whompin' big box for Zaydee. From Reverend Steinhardt. Yah, Reverend Steinhardt, by golly." He slapped Esquire on the back and guffawed. "Excuse me for laffin' so, Miss Ellis. You don't know who was Reverend Steinhardt?"

"No." What had Miss Barton said about a nice young man who had gone to Africa?

"Yah, well, he was a preacher at Methodist Church four, five year ago. Blond, tall, but not a heavy feller. Zaydee was havin' a lot of trouble with her soul all that winter. And in the spring, preacher's wife tells him he has a call to foreign field. Yah, foreign field." He pointed to the box. "You call up Zaydee right away, Miss Ellis. She was a girl that always liked a present."

"Esquire can call her," I said.

"Thank *you*, Miss." And a moment later I heard murmured into John's phone, "Honey? This is me. You all right? Uh-huh. You tell Miss Zaydee there's a great big present here for her come all the way from Africa."

Five minutes later I answered the buzz of the phone. "Miss Ellis, I want Dr. Gordon."

Indeed you do, I thought; and said, "He isn't here, Mrs. Proutman."

"Where is he?"

"He has gone to Warrenton."

"What for?"

I hesitated.

"What for?"

Well, after all, any news went over Hinchdale in half a day. "About a new car."

"In time for tonight." She was pleased. "Look here, what's this about a little package for me from Africa?"

"It's a case about six feet square."

"From Bertie Steinhardt, I'll bet. I'll be right down."

She burst in upon me, as I had not seen her before. Her hair was flying about her face, and her sable coat blew back from a plaid blouse frayed at the ruffles. Comfortable beige pumps slipped about her heels. She greeted me with a gay wave of a hand only half manicured. She wasn't jealous or malicious or triumphant: she was a child about to receive a new toy and eager to show it off to another little girl who hadn't one of her own. She tapped the box, and her eyes glowed as she urged on Esquire's hammer and screw driver with lusty shouts.

"West Africa is full of kings and slaves, isn't it? This should be something pretty fancy. Barbaric."

When the cover was half off, her fingers were probing straw. "It's ivory," she cried. "It's hard and white. See? Come here, Miss Ellis. Don't hang back. It's too small around for an elephant tusk. It must be something carved. Feel here."

I felt of something smooth, very hard, slender and flat at about the middle of the case. It was dead white. I was almost certain of what it was, and I wished to heaven that John Gordon were there to break the blow to Zaydee that this would not look well over her fireplace.

At last, in spite of her interference, Esquire got all the boards off the top of the box and lifted the last layer of straw. It was just as I had thought.

"My God," shrieked Zaydee, "it's a man! The little bastard has sent me one of his dead niggers!"

Looking at Esquire's rolling eyes, at Zaydee's quivering mouth and chin, I stifled laughter and went over to the box. "No, it isn't, Mrs. Proutman." I lifted out the white thing with the stiff outstretched arms and brutal jaw, which was almost as tall as I. "It's the skeleton of a chimpanzee."

And then, with the idea that Zaydee Proutman must be kept in good humor at all costs, I proceeded to sell her renewed pride in her present. He was interesting, and we didn't have one in the Museum. I couldn't honestly say he was rare, but he was an awfully good specimen of a young male.

"He is rather cute," said Zaydee.

I discovered a somewhat hypothetical anomaly of the pelvis and made it into something of importance, and for that sin against science I was to pay a heavy toll. Zaydee asked if a paper could be written about it. Just one of those notes of John's. Perhaps it could, I said.

"I'd like to read it at the November meeting of the Academy of Science," she said. "Have it ready for me by then."

I was to write, she was to read. "Mrs. Proutman," I explained, "it would take a lot longer than that to get it ready."

"Just a note?" she scorned.

"No, I meant the ape. The bones would have to be taken apart and cleaned before I could find out exactly what we need to know."

Zaydee looked at the bleached skeleton on the table. "He looks marvelously clean to me."

I explained that the skeleton was only partly preserved, that some parts, muscles, tissues, were now holding the bones together, and until these were removed, the ape could not be measured and studied in detail.

"Remove them tomorrow," she said, "if you know how."

At Oldwick, I said, we didn't do maceration. When Dr. Alden had been sent a gorilla in a state similar to this, he had put it on the museum roof in the summer and let the tissues dissolve in the sun.

"I'm not going to wait till summer." Her eyes fixed on the laboratory stove. "If it's heat you need, I should think you could cook it. Well, couldn't you? What's wrong with that?"

"Perhaps I could," I said, "but I'm not sure boiling would be awfully good for the bone. Dr. Gordon might not want me to do it. It would be rather ... messy."

And at once she was the Zaydee of our previous meetings. "You don't work for Dr. Gordon," she said, and the old gleam was in her eye and she was remembering everything. "You work for me, and whether that work is what you call messy, you will do it. I suppose you mean it will smell."

"It will indeed," I retorted. "And fill the whole Museum. But if you don't care, I don't. What do you suggest I use for a kettle?"

"I've got an old clothes boiler that will do perfectly," returned Zaydee in triumph. "Cut off the legs and arms if they don't fit; you're going to take it to pieces anyway. And if it's too delicate to stand boiling, simmer it." She gathered up her sables and smiled. "And, Miss Ellis, don't cut it up until morning. Tell John Gordon to sit it up in the front seat of his new car when he drives out to the house tonight. I'm going to get a kick out of that."

It was late afternoon when John Gordon burst into the room, his cheeks bright with cold, his eyes with his new possession. "Kay, come out and see my bus," he almost shouted, the black lock I sometimes found engaging flopping between his eyes. He was the second person who had wanted to show me a new toy that day, and if I did not quite feel that I could have killed him, I must have looked it, for, slightly blighted, he said, "What's the matter? Are you— Well, I'm damned! Where did you get the boy friend?"

He marched over to the chimpanzee and stood him on the counter.

"He is Zaydee's, not mine," I said in ill-chosen words, "and you are to put him in the front seat of your new car and drive him out to her house for dinner tonight. She thinks he's cute. And tomorrow I'm going to cook him in a wash boiler. And I guess you'll quit laughing like that when you smell it." At which perfect moment I burst into tears.

"What the hell! Kay, where's your sense of humor?"

"Where would yours be," I roared, "if you'd had fifty dollars cut off your salary because you're the kind of girl who loves to do her own laundry? Boo-hoo!"

"She did that?"

"Didn't you know?"

"You know I didn't."

"I don't know anything except that I'm a fool. I haven't cried for twenty years. Please go away until I stop, and—and take your damned ape with you."

He went into his office and shut the door, and a moment later, as I powdered my pulpy nose, I heard him say shortly into the phone, "Isabelle?" I blew my nose and the rest of his speech was lost. I was re-powdering the nose when he opened the door.

"Get on your things," he said. "I'll take you home to get dolled up. We're going places tonight."

I looked at him. "You have a date tonight for dinner with your boss. Haven't you forgotten again?"

His face was expressionless as he repeated, "Get on your things."

I began to obey meekly, but I stopped before I slipped my arms into the coat he held out. "If we go out together for two nights in succession, Mrs. Hawks will spread it all over town, and it might end both our jobs."

"I can manage Mrs. Hawks," he said. I did not move toward my coat. "If it's necessary, there are ways of managing—our boss. I haven't used them to date."

"And there are ways of managing me?"

He took my defiant chin in his hand. "I don't want to manage you, Kay. I just want you to go out with me tonight. If you want to go. I'm telling you it can be done without any of the mountainous consequences you're raising. Do you want to, Kay?"

Well, that was good management, and so was his work on Mrs. Hawks. She clumped into my room while I was assembling the violet tweeds and the silver fox jacket, thankful that I had set my wave the night before.

"Kay, I want you should know I think it's all right for you to go over to Spirit Falls with Dr. Gordon tonight," she said, sagging onto the edge of my bed. "He told me you wouldn't go out there with him unless I agreed. It'll do you a lot of good to wear your best rig and go off with a fine-looking feller, and have a fine dinner. The Lawsons that run Spirit Falls Inn are my husband's second cousins, and they've always kept a decent place. And you can count on me to see that this never gets to Zaydee. You're a nice girl, Kay. I don't know many girls nowadays would care what an old woman like me thinks about anything."

I surprised her further by a guilty farewell kiss. How, I wondered bitterly, would he manage the other one? There now seemed little doubt that he could.

He had chosen a demonstration car of a handsome make, and it ate up the flat black miles smoothly. For the first time, leaning back in the deep seat, letting my shoulder slip a little toward his, I felt the beauty of that wide, almost empty land, where no lights and no hills kept you from the sky. The road narrowed, scattered bare branches changed to thick pines, and the air, mild for a northern November night, felt colder; and then we came out on the Lake shore.

"You can see it by moonlight before we leave," Gordon said. "We turn up the trail here to Spirit Falls."

The inn was full of pleasant things—a log fire, cocktails, steak and french frieds, hot rolls, and ice cream with chocolate sauce. It was an evening such as I had spent before but better because it was so long since anything like it had happened and because John Gordon seemed the most attractive man I'd ever known. He wasn't the ambitious scientist, the wary staff member of the William Henry Proutman Museum. He was a man taking out a girl and liking it. We had coffee on a settee in front of the fire, and his arm lay across the back and he sometimes touched my hair.

"Kay"—his voice was low and kind—"I hate to blight this, even for a minute, but there's something I need to know. How badly off does this salary cut leave you? I don't want to intrude, but I've been through the mill the hard way. I've stoked furnaces and been night orderly in a hospital; and even so, ended up my doctorate in debt. I can't go to—anyone, about your salary because it would only make it worse, but will you let me do anything else you need?"

"I would," I answered his troubled look, "but right now I can manage perfectly well. I'm not in debt. It really is awfully cheap to live in Hinchdale, and I can save a good deal of the hundred dollars. You see, I've got a little of my father's insurance left, and I wanted to add to it as fast as I could to go back to Edgewood for my Ph.D."

"And leave me alone with all those bones?"

"They'll all be measured before I have the money. I'm not in a hurry."

He put my cup on a table and took my hand, turning the fingers slowly, looking at them. "It must have been bad for you when your father died."

It would have been easy to say so, easier than the truth. For it really hadn't mattered very much. Mother had died when I was born, and after some years of a vaguely remembered grandmother, there had been schools and camps which I had usually liked, and rather awkward intervals with a cheerful, generous man who didn't like responsibility, nor my company for very long at a time. During my sophomore year at Edgewood he had been drowned in a speedboat accident at Rio. I hadn't seen him for two years. His insurance was a thousand dollars, and with most of it and scholarships and small jobs I had finished college easily and with no emotional scar. I said so briefly.

"You don't bay at the moon, do you, Kay?" He dropped my hand and clasped his brown fingers around his knees. "My life has been a lot different from yours. I've got a father and a mother and six brothers and sisters. My father is a druggist in a town about like Hinchdale, only in the mountains. None of my brothers or sisters went to college or give a damn because they didn't. I was bright in school, and the principal was a one-lunger from the East. He got a regional scholarship for me at Oldwick, and I waited on table and shoveled coal, and Dad wore shiny pants for four years. You can take it on from there."

"A Ph.D. and a Packard." I smiled. "Success story."

His eyes darkened. "Not quite yet," he said slowly.

"But when the Holtzerman study comes out, you can go to any university you like," I said confidently.

"And nothing will keep me from finishing it." His mouth was straight and hard. He laughed to soften it, not successfully. "I told you we were different, Kay. Do you know who you're really like? You won't appreciate this. You're like old Alpheus Harvey. I'd do a lot of things neither of you would do to finish my work. You two might go out with flaming swords and commit murder to right a wrong, but you wouldn't compromise."

"How do you know?"

"I know. Because compromise is just one word for lying and cheating and theft. I'd do them all to finish the Holtzerman study."

"Don't boast," I laughed at him. "I'll remember these brave words and throw them back at you when I catch you doing a shamefully honest deed."

He drew me to my feet. "The next deed is to show you the moon on the lake."

A moon on a lake is how you feel about it, and almost everyone has felt as we did that night. We drove out a long narrow point of rocks and stopped under a giant pine. The limitless water seemed all there was of the world. Before the second kiss he said, "I've wanted this ever since you first walked into the laboratory. You knew it, didn't you, Kay?"

"At first. Never after that."

He raised his head for a moment and stared out at the water. I stirred a little away from him, and his arms tightened round me. "Let's be happy tonight," he said.

CHAPTER VIII

It was the first Friday in November, and the effluvium of anthropoid ape permeated the Proutman Museum. It filtered through the chiffon and lace of the corseted wax ladies, crept into the pores of the polished stone axes, clung to the fur of the weasel on the director's desk, and insulted the nostrils of every visitor and staff member. It was not a stink. A stink has tang and savor and character, but the waves of smell that rolled through the registers and heaved up the stairs were dull, heavy, and tasteless like old boiled mutton.

For two days the chimpanzee had been simmering in the wash boiler, and my prognosis of the operation was proving true. A few of the bone shafts had cracked from the heat, and the lumps and gray shreds of gristle and strips of muscle, the yellow disks of cartilage floating in thin brown broth, could be justly termed a mess. Also according to prediction, John Gordon disliked my occupation intensely.

"God, I hate to see you cleaning out that fellow's filthy nose," he would say as I held the skull between my knees and scraped out the long, flat, narrow nostrils. "That's no job for a woman."

"It's not unlike a mother's happy days," I said. "Should you prefer to do it yourself?"

"Hand me a scalpel, and I'll dig out the holes in the sacrum. I hate to see you do this alone."

"All meaning that you want me back on your own work."

"Kay, you're a hard gal to woo."

"I am—during office hours."

But Zaydee Proutman had guessed right, too. A pile of clean bones of legs and arms and hands and feet, so nearly human, now almost filled a plain wooden box. Her method had been quick, if unpleasant, and the bone damage had really been slight. In another day everything would be ready for measurement, and the aromatic clothes boiler returned to the sender. Zaydee had not been to the laboratory to inspect work in progress.

On the morning following her demand, her chauffeur had delivered the boiler in the station wagon. Zaydee's servants, with the exception of the faithful Isabelle, were almost unknown characters in Hinchdale because they came and went so rapidly. It was no surprise, then, when this latest too-smart youth in the Proutman plum-colored uniform announced, as he banged down the lid, that this was his last job for that dame and that he and the cook and the waitress were leaving on the afternoon train. Zaydee, according to him, who was always hell had been twice hell last night "when your boss stood her up for dinner in front of her girl friend, Mrs. Emily Garrett, and *her* boy friend. So I'm off, Blondie. Somebody else'll be seein' you."

Although Zaydee did not come to the Museum, she had telephoned each day, and from the even flow of tones and the lack of metallic rasps I felt that John had made his peace with her. How and where he had done it I did not want to know.

If John disliked the anthropoid cookery, Mr. Harvey loathed it as an insult to his person, his position, and his institution; and as he watched me reaching elbow deep into the vat and coming out dripping with a lot of soup and a very small toe bone, there was real human pity in his usually ambiguous face. It was not the sort of thing that Alpheus Harvey could ever have considered funny. Nor could Miss Alice Barton. Driven out of her reserve and also out of her library, which was immediately above the laboratory stove, she had descended with dignified sorrow to commiserate with "you poor dear child" and murmur refined imprecations against Zaydee as she sniffed the bubbling pot. Jensen's comments were not refined and were confined to brief words whose origin is common to all Teutonic languages, including Swedish, Danish, and Anglo-Saxon. It was Esquire from whom I had expected an amusement akin to my own. But apart from a half-hearted, "Not much dry about *these* bones," he made no response. He looked gray and his steps dragged; but, contrary to Zaydee's insinuations, his work continued to be quietly thorough.

At five-thirty I turned out the gas under the wash boiler, leaving the left leg, the last of the stiffly articulated extremities, to soak overnight. John came in from his office, saying, "Poor Kay, off to the Greasy Spoon while I feast on Mrs. Jim Watson's orange shortcake."

"This isn't the night to make me mad with that kind of talk," I said. "After I've been hanging over that stew all day, everything from soup to sliced cold cuts looks like chimpanzee to me. In a month or two I may have an appetite."

He crossed to me and kissed me hard. "You're a sport, Kay," he said.

"So far," I replied, a little shaken as I straightened my hat. "Good digestion!"

Later, as I was picking at a tomato-salad sandwich, which at least did not have anthropoid resemblances, and waiting for my coffee to cool, someone spoke to me.

"May I sit here?" he said. The words came slowly and slightly slurred. It was the thin boy, Randy Bill. "I … I'd rather not be alone."

He looked so forlorn that, though I certainly didn't want him near me, I assented. He sat down. "I've been drinking," he said, "but I'm not drunk. You know I'm not drunk, don't you?"

"Of course you're not," I said, by no means certain.

"And if I were drunk," he rambled on, "you wouldn't have any reason to be embarrassed. I never make passes at women when I've been drinking. I never do, anyway, at girls like you. I don't know any nice girls now. You're a nice girl. I had to talk to you."

It all seemed pointless and unpleasant, but he found his focus and went on. "You work for Zaydee Proutman. Fellow told me that. Fellow named Epp Marks. You look out for her. Zaydee's hell."

I tried to keep all expression out of my face.

"I used to work for her, too," he said, "in a way. I was going to be a great musician two years ago, greater than—he articulated the name carefully and correctly—"Vlad-i-mir Hor-o-witz. Do you know how you get to be a great musician? There's just one way." He coughed, reached for my glass of water, drank, and went on, "You practice. Every day. All day. There wasn't any time to practice. Clipper to Paris, Caribbean cruise, playing Gershwin for her friends. No Bach, no Debussy, no Schoenberg. So I wasn't a great musician. And so"—he dug a fork deep into the table cloth—"Zaydee kicked me out. Eighteen months ago. And I'm not a great musician today either." In the silence I hoped was final I tried to sip my tepid coffee.

"This fellow she's after now," he went on, "he'll come out better than

I did. She's crazy about him. A man can get a lot out of Zaydee if she's that way about him. I—" he looked straight at me, and his eyes with their reddened rims and long, childlike lashes were sober—"I'm the one who loved her."

I reached for my coat, and he stood up. "I've got one thing left from the wreck," he said. "She gave me a car. Someday soon I'll sell it for a few meals and a suit of clothes. In the meantime it's good for picking up dames. Not girls like you. Not nice girls. I had to talk to a nice girl. Nice of you to let me."

"I was glad to," I said in a choked voice.

"I'll walk along with you," he said. "My car's parked on the edge of town. I've been drinking. I'm not drunk, but I don't like to drive a car until I'm perfectly fit. I've had my supper, and the walk back'll fix me up O.K."

I hoped it would.

"Two things to remember," he said. "Never drive a car when you're drunk. Never go near Zaydee Proutman. Both are death."

We were at Mrs. Hawks's door.

"Good night," I said.

"Will you shake hands with me?" he asked. "Thanks and good night. You're a nice girl."

It was while I had hold of his limp hand that a car passed and the lights flashed full on his sick face. He drew back with a blurred exclamation. I had not seen the driver, but I am sure that Randy Bill knew who it was.

CHAPTER IX

When I look back on the day that was our ruin, I wonder how much was due to the real tragedy of hate and fear and how much to the old device of the *deus ex machina*. Whether it was god or devil who brought us death and apparent deliverance, there can be no doubt about the machine.

It stood before the sepulchral front of the Proutman Museum, that dark Saturday morning, an irrelevant affair of light sporting lines and open seat of red leather. Not, Mrs. Hawks had said, so bright now; but still a car for adventure and good for picking up dames.

A shiver of distaste went through me as I approached it, a fear of some sordid mixture of drunkenness and mutilation rising out of Randy Bill's condition on the previous evening. I had little faith in his remembering to refrain from driving. But on nearer view the car showed no trace of accident, and a look inside, for which I summoned a certain valor to carry through, showed nothing more significant than three or four bronze bobby pins on the crimson seat.

Relieved, I turned away to mount the Museum steps and halted, astonished. Through the glass upper half of the storm door someone was looking down at me, a face distorted by reflection. It was not until my hand was on the knob that it retreated.

Once inside I recognized the bald head, drooping red mustache, and heavy eyes of a familiar figure at Hinchdale gatherings, Sheriff Barton Brown, Miss Alice's cousin, who had choked on Zaydee's esoteric vegetables. Alpheus Harvey was standing by his side, a bunch of car keys in his extended hand. Around them the hall was full of the stale smell of chimpanzee.

The Sheriff stopped his contemplation of my advance. "Well, hang onto those keys till she gets here, Alpheus," he said. "Kind of a dirty job, but duty's duty. Your own ain't all so sweet either, I guess. Phew!" He sniffed and lumbered out.

John, with an expression not much more cordial than the Sheriff's, walked out of his office while I was hanging up my coat.

"Can you have that ape cleaned up by afternoon?" he asked.

"By the middle of the morning," I replied. "Has Mrs. Proutman phoned about it?"

"She'll be in to inspect it this afternoon." I walked over to the boiler, rolled up my sleeve, and thrust my arm into the clammy depths.

"What were you doing last night?"

I dropped the meaty shin back into the juice and looked at him. "What," I asked, "were you?"

"I was not asking out of curiosity. Have you done anything to stir her up against you?"

"Not since Wednesday. But you were going to take care of that, you know."

"I did."

"Oh, well, then there's nothing for me to worry about, is there?" I smiled unpleasantly and returned to my fishing.

He went back to his office and closed the door. I took the bones to my table and sat down and scraped. Esquire came in with a cloth and began to dust the shelves. On his face was a dark expression, which was just the way I felt.

"Kay"—John came out of his office and over to me—"let's not have a row."

"It might interfere with your work, mightn't it?" I didn't look up, and so I did not see the approach of the storm that was to stop all anthropology for days to come. John's hand was laid heavily on my shoulder, whether to shake me or caress me I do not know. His fingers relaxed, withdrew, and I looked up and saw Randy Bill.

He was leaning on the door frame, his hat pushed back on his head. His necktie was loosened and slipped to one side, and on his drawn face the hairs of his beard stood out as they do on the faces of the very ill. Deep circles lay under his pale eyes, but his mouth was firm and his words clear-cut.

"You dirty double-crosser," he said.

The Sheriff's stare, John's probing, this insult—all unwarranted blows had fallen on me that morning, and I sat numb.

"You took my girl," Randy went on, and then I realized that the taunt was not to me. "I suppose I can't blame you for that. She asked to be taken. But this is different."

He straightened and came toward us, his eyes blazing. "I want my car."

John stepped forward between me and Bill's advance. "I haven't got your car." His tone was quiet and even.

"Oh, no," jeered Randy. "Oh, no you haven't! You don't know anything about it, do you?"

"No, I don't."

"You don't know that the Sheriff picked it up this morning in front of—well, skip where. He took the keys away from me. You don't know why, do you? You know, all right, but I'm going to tell you in front of the blonde you're two-timing Zaydee with. Zaydee! She never changed the registration to my name like she told me she had. She sent Brown to pick it up so she could hand it over to you. First herself and then the car. You can keep her and welcome, but I—want—my—car."

"I haven't got anything of yours." John blocked my view of Randy's face. "Come outside and talk this over."

"Yes," snarled Randy, "let's go outside and sit in our car. You've parked it in a handy place right in front of the Museum."

"I haven't seen it." John, moving to the wall to take down his topcoat, revealed Randy, white and quivering. "It wasn't there when I got here—walking."

Randy turned on me. "Was it there when you came to work?" he demanded. "You're a nice girl, in spite of the guy you run with. You wouldn't lie to me, would you?"

"Your car was there," I said; "but Mr. Gordon didn't have anything to do with it. He was already in the basement at work when the Sheriff brought it."

"Yeah, but he's got my keys." He launched himself at John, and out of the corner Esquire, whom I had forgotten, moved silently behind him. "Hand them over, God damn you. The law may be on your side, but the right's on mine."

"Mr. Bill"—I spoke so sharply that he turned back to me—"no one here has your keys."

"I'm not so sure," he said. "Last night I thought you were my friend, but I don't trust you now. Has he handed them over to you, sweetheart?"

Both John and Esquire were behind him. I cried out as they closed in. "The Sheriff gave the car keys to Mr. Harvey. I saw him. He told him to keep them until Mrs. Proutman comes for them. She is the only person after your car. Dr. Gordon has a new car of his own. He bought it only a few days ago."

Randy Bill smiled. "He bought a new car of his own? With whose money?" No one answered him, and he went on, "Well, it's in his own name. He's got all the luck." He looked at the black hand on his left shoulder, the white on his right. "Let me loose. You don't have to give me the bum's rush. I'm through with the bunch of you stooges, but I've got just one job to do."

He shrugged free, and John and Esquire ushered him toward the stairs. In the doorway stood Alpheus Harvey. Randy paused, straightened his lean height, and looked down on the stooped figure. "Well, well, Little Alphie," he said. "I'll bet you've got my keys all locked away in your pretty little safe. You're the boy who always does his duty. But you don't like the old bitch any better than I do. If I get my hands on her, yeah, if I get my hands on Zaydee Proutman, wish me luck. You'll have no good wishes for her, the lot of you. Out of my way."

Silence fell in the basement laboratory and lay heavily over that curtain speech.

Esquire and John, who had shadowed Randy to the Museum entrance, came back to their work; and I incised muscles from the chimpanzee's toe bones so fast that my fingers were a mass of tiny cuts. No one spoke. An hour passed, and then Miss Barton came gently in.

"May I talk with you a moment, Miss Ellis, while you go on with your work?"

Esquire bowed low and passed behind her out of the room as she came to me. I was grateful for the break in the tension.

"It is about tonight," she explained, seating herself with her back to as many bones as possible. I had almost forgotten that the D.A.R. was having a pageant committee supper at Mrs. Jim Watson's house to discuss the Washington's Birthday celebration, from six to half-past eight. "Something very serious has happened."

This, it seemed to me, was just the day for it.

"Mrs. Watson, our secretary," she continued precisely, "has received a letter from Mrs. Proutman. She has made the Chapter an offer. If we will hold the pageant in her house, she will supply us with costumes and music from Chicago and a turkey dinner. I do not believe that such things alone would sway our members to hold an important commemoration in the home of one who was not eligible to be a Daughter. But she has brought forward an argument that may seem important to some earnest people. She says—and I believe with some authority—that her house is built on the site where the husband of Amanda Adams Barton made the first payment to the Kickapoos."

I gouged out a tiny foramen in the left great toe and said in shocked tones, "Really?"

"Precisely. Zaydee is a smart woman. But so are you, my dear. You can see through this move as well as I. I can count on you to vote for our original plan to hold the pageant in the Community Church?"

I would have liked nothing less than to stage-manage that ladylike affair under Zaydee's lifted eyebrows, and I said fervently, "You can count on me."

I did not go out to lunch. Randy's visit had cut down my working time, and I had no desire to incite another scene by presenting an unfinished task for Zaydee's inspection. John came back from his dinner, bearing a large paper sack containing Mrs. Watson's idea of a simple picnic lunch which he was to consume in the laboratory, lest he break in upon the Revolutionary conspiracy.

"I suppose she'll be here any minute now," I said nervously, hastily running my hand and arm through the liquid in the boiler. "There, I guess, those bones are all out."

And now there was nothing to do but wait for Zaydee. I set the stage carefully for a quiet scene. I pulled back my hair and pushed it flat behind my ears, and put on the reading glasses I really didn't need. Then I pulled down the big accessions register and slowly and neatly began to copy the record cards that we had filled out before the chimpanzee detour. I was sure I looked like a clerk whose job no one could think was interesting, and like a girl no man could ever love. Behind his closed door John seemed to be carrying out a similarly impersonal program with thoroughness. The typewriter banged and rang so continuously that he evidently hadn't even time to fill his pipe. At four o'clock the rain began, heavy and cold, beaten against the frozen ground and pounded on the basement windows. At five John stopped typing and came out of his room, looking relaxed and entirely natural.

"How about an hour's measuring, Kay?" he asked.

"Fine." I arose and exchanged the register for a Holtzerman skeleton and his calipers and tape. It now seemed certain that Zaydee would not come.

We sat down in our usual places and picked up our tools. My pen was poised to record the first diameter, but he put down the skull.

"Kay, what have you done to yourself?" His voice was apologizing for the morning; so were the fingers turning my meek coiffure into turbulent curls. And Zaydee Proutman came into the room.

She stood very still looking at me, and I knew that in the battle to come I was lost; for in this skirmish, unlike our former ones, there was some truth in her charges. Her lips moved slowly into the position of a smile, her eyes opened very wide, and the weak chin quivered. Then she spoke.

"Such a busy little girl," she said, "and such a promiscuous little girl."

Struck dumb by the adjective, I stared back almost without seeing her.

"You look dazed," she said, "and no wonder. You must be tired after so much—night work."

John was on his feet. "Mrs. Proutman, what do you mean?"

"You," she said, and she was enjoying herself, "don't know the half of it."

"Do you," he asked, "know just what you are saying?"

"I do. On Wednesday night you and she drove out to the Spirit Falls Inn and did some drinking. No one else was there. You got back to Hinchdale at one in the morning. Am I right?"

She was right and she was wrong. We had one cocktail each. It takes an hour to drive back to town, and there were a half-dozen employees in evidence throughout our stay at the Inn. "Am I right, John?"

"You're a wonderful detective," he said.

"Not so wonderful. Evelyn Garrett had dinner at the Inn on Thursday. The Lawsons loved telling her about having people for two successive evenings in the off season. And when you got back to the edge of town you filled up your car at the only all-night station."

"Perfect."

"The rest is better. I saw it myself. I can't account for the way the girl spent Thursday night, but on Friday she was standing in front of her house, necking with Randy Bill."

"I don't believe you." John's face was remote from us both.

"Don't you? Miss Ellis, can you deny there's truth in what I've said?"

And stupidly, angrily, I replied, "You're picking your words carefully, aren't you?" and felt John turn to stare at me.

Her smile was full on John. "Don't think I care what you do," she tried to say gaily, but anger was there. "You're free to take all the fun you want. But I'd rather not have the girl working in the Museum. It makes unpleasant talk in town."

There was a moment of silence, and then John laughed. It may have been in frustration, in rage, in post-adolescent nervousness, anything. It was harsh and crude, and to Zaydee Proutman it was a goad. She turned on me, and all the restraint she had summoned to make her effect broke. Her voice was shrill, and she raised her arm. I noticed for the first time every detail about her: the Mexican tourist jewelry, little silver sombreros swinging in her ears, bulging on the breast of her gold metallic blouse, and lumped on the hand that clutched the umbrella of the late Herr Professor Doktor Holtzerman. Her words were just what I had expected: "Dirty little bitch."

Clang! The end of the clumsy umbrella, much longer than she was used to carrying, caught the side of a three-foot glass measuring tube, crashing it to the floor, along with its iron stand.

I am not altogether clear about the sequence of the next events. I got up and retreated to the stove by the rain-soaked window. Jensen and Esquire were in the room almost at once. John took the umbrella from Zaydee. And in a minute or two Alpheus Harvey was there. Miss Barton, like a censorious ghost, came to the door for an instant and vanished.

Jensen looked at the flushed Zaydee and at the floor. "Bin throwin' dishes, Zaydee," he roared with joy. "Good old days come back, huh?"

"If you want the good old days, you can have them," blazed Zaydee. "Get out, you big Swede."

Jensen stood before her, hands in pockets, teetering on his heels. "I'm goin', Zaydee, and I ain't comin' back. I couldn't work for a lady that didn't act refined." He started for the door and stopped by Alpheus's side. "You don't have to worry none about the heat, Mr. Harvey. The Doctor can take my place just swell. He's got second-class engineer's certificate along with his college education. Trust Zaydee to pick a useful feller."

"Mrs. Proutman." Alpheus stepped into the center of the room. Under the bare white laboratory light he looked little and old. "What," he asked, "is this all about?"

At his feet Esquire, kneeling with dustpan and brush, looked up, his eyes large and white in his dark face. John stood in shadow by the counter where he had laid the umbrella with the heavy ivory ape.

Zaydee, quiet now, stood patting her vivid hair. "About very little. I happened to knock over some glass stuff with that quaint old relic. And before that, I was giving notice to Miss—er ... you know ... that girl."

"You said you were giving her notice? Of what?"

"To leave. To quit. To get out." There was spite in her laughing voice.

"Mrs. Proutman"—Alpheus Harvey's words fell like a judgment—"you have no just cause."

But it was she, not he, who had the power to pronounce sentence. "I don't have to have one," she said, "but I've a case. The girl is—lazy and insulting."

"I have never found her so."

"Alpheus"—the insulting purr came into her tones—"you're an innocent old lamb."

"I am not altogether an ignorant old man. I know why you are doing this, and the whole town will know why, without one word from me. Do you still wish to dismiss Miss Ellis?"

She was quiet a moment, but she had gone a long way.

"Yes," she said. "I'll give her a check for a month's wages. I want her out of town by Monday night."

"If she doesn't choose to go, Mrs. Proutman, I don't believe you can make her leave Hinchdale." Alpheus's voice had a sneer. "There's a limit to the dirty work Barton Brown will do for you." He straightened his old back. "And there's a limit to what I will do, too. If Miss Ellis leaves this staff, I leave it, too."

Zaydee's breath came hard. She half-turned her head toward the corner where John Gordon stood, and turned back again. From where I stood his face was a blank shadow. He seemed, like myself, a spectator at a play in which we had no part. Alpheus stood stiff. Zaydee leaned back against the table. The rain swished against the window. She spoke, "You leave, too."

He was not so erect now, but he did not waver. "I'll give you my keys at once," he said. "You will regret this."

"Oh, no, I shan't," she told him. "The Proutman Museum can get along without you just as well as it can get along without Jensen."

At the name of his beloved institution a look of pain came into Mr. Harvey's wrinkled face, but in a flash another look replaced it. "Possibly. And for much the same reason." His face was now a yellow leer. "I repeat, you will regret it."

Did I expect John Gordon to take up this challenge, to resign like Alpheus, to refuse to take his place, to tell Zaydee she had lied about me? He did not leave his corner, and after a moment I left mine and got my hat and coat and purse and, without looking back, went up the stairs.

I walked slowly, partly to avoid catching up with Mr. Harvey, who, followed by Zaydee, was making his last trip to the office he had ruled for twenty-five years. Partly I hoped that John would call me back, would tell me he had a plan to save us all and was just remaining cool while everyone else was in a rage, would tell me how much my trouble was his trouble, too. There was a step below me on the stairs, and I turned, my heart beating with hope. It was Esquire.

"I'm distressed, Miss Ellis," he whispered. "It's evil. Some judgment will visit that devil woman."

I held out my hand. "Good-by," I said. "Remember me to Isabelle."

"Yes, Miss. Thank you. She"—there were tears in his eyes—"she is a very lovely person. I think you are, too, Miss Ellis. If I may say so."

The light from the director's office was a glare against the dark hall.

"To safe, to basement, to the exhibition cases," Zaydee was enumerating. "Leave the books on your desk. I'd better go over your accounts tonight."

From the dimmer library came the faint sound of a desk being closed and locked. To avoid explaining anything to Miss Barton, I sped across the checkered tiles and shut myself out in the black wind and rain. Outside the Museum stood the car that had once been Randy Bill's.

Numb in mind and body I moved down the street toward Mrs. Hawks's house. It was dark, with no glimmer of light. Forgetting that she, like Miss Barton, had probably just left for the D.A.R. supper, I stood there for a moment in bewilderment, and then automatically turned and dragged off to the Greasy Spoon. Thoroughly wet and shivering with cold and nervous shock, I opened the door into the steaming brightness just as Randy Bill was about to leave. There was no doubt of the degree of his drunkenness tonight. He could walk steadily enough, but his voice was blurred and his hands shook. I turned away from him as fast as possible, but he caught my arm.

"Sorry," he said. "Sorry about today. Make it all up to you soon. Something I want to tell you. Tell you tonight maybe. Tell you later."

"Yes, later," I said, smiling to get rid of him and fearing that our words were audible to Mrs. Marks.

He went. In a few minutes, unable to eat, I was moving back along wet empty Broadway. Completely empty. As I passed the Museum I saw that the car was now gone from the front of the Museum, and Alpheus's office window was dark. Zaydee had evidently driven home. Altogether, she had gotten a good deal today.

I forced myself to go into the dark old house, into the dark old room with the black walnut bed, the marble-topped table, and the enlargements of the late Mr. Hawks in life and in death. Suddenly I realized that it was my home, the place to which I had returned from good days at the Museum and from bad, where my books were, my clothes, my feelings. I had come back here from that night on the Lake and lain awake, recalling each moment. Never think of that again, never think of John.

I couldn't bear it. I had to do something, something hard and heavy and dull. There was no train out of Hinchdale until Monday, and in any case I would need to wait for the bank's opening before I could buy my ticket for the long way east. But I could pack. I hauled up my trunk from the basement, dragged down my suitcase from the closet shelf, and went to work.

At eight-thirty Mrs. Hawks came home and though I prayed she wouldn't hear me, she did and came in. She saw my stripped room, the door open into my empty closet, the hollow drawers pulled out of my chest and dresser.

"My land!" was her first exclamation. "How'd you ever get all that done in one evening?"

CHAPTER X

Monday morning came after another dreadful day of rain, during which I had nothing to do. Mrs. Hawks was enormously kind. She fed me and asked me few questions. She had always said—and she said so again and again—that Zaydee Proutman wouldn't keep a young girl very long at her Museum. I didn't tell her about Alpheus Harvey. It hurt every time I thought of him and of what he had lost through me.

Other feelings were less acute. Mainly, I suppose, I just waited for John to telephone. He did not do it, and to save myself from reality I built up a fantasy in which he spent the time pleading with Zaydee to keep both me and Alpheus. However, when I considered the most probable means of accomplishing this, the anesthetic value was completely gone, and it seemed wiser just to turn on the radio. Not too loud, however, because, after all, the telephone might ring.

Once it did, for me. It was Miss Alice Barton. She had talked to Mr. Harvey, and her distress was real for me as well as for him.

"My dear child," she tried to reassure me, "I still think something can be done," but her tone was not cheerful. She would be over to say good-by to me the first thing in the morning.

So when the doorbell rang at eight o'clock I was expecting her. Mrs. Hawks came back from the door, breathing hard, her eyes round with excitement.

"It's for you," she wheezed. "In the parlor. Sheriff Brown."

The red mustache seemed to droop lower than usual, and his face sagged with fatigue. His big boots were covered with mud. His voice, however, was loud and strong.

"You are a friend," he stated, "of Randolph Bill."

So, in spite of Harvey's warning, the Sheriff was going about Zaydee's dirty work at an early hour.

"No," I said.

"You had a talk with him last Saturday night at 5:51 o'clock. You made a date to see him later."

"No, I didn't. He was leaving Mrs. Marks's restaurant. He spoke to me. I hardly know him."

He took a paper from his pocket and read to me, "'Tell you something tonight. Tell you later.' That's what he said, and you said, 'Yes, later.' Sworn statement of Mr. and Mrs. Epp Marks. Do you deny it?"

"No," I said, "but he didn't have anything to tell me. He didn't make a date to meet me. I said anything to get rid of him. He was awfully drunk."

"Where were you on Saturday night?"

"Here. In this house. Why do you want to know?"

"I'll answer that later. If you still think it's necessary. Where were you?"

"Here," I repeated wildly. "Ask Mrs. Hawks. She'll tell you."

The Sheriff hauled himself up and plodded to the door. "Sarah!" he yelled.

She came, obviously from a very short distance, and, with much circumstantial detail, told all she knew. What it, of course, came to was that I had been at home from 8:30 onward, and that I had not attended the D.A.R. supper.

"O.K., Sarah. Now, Miss Ellis, where were you between six-twenty, when the Markses swear you left their place, and eight-thirty, when Sarah says she found you here at home?"

I told him.

"Any proof you were here for those two hours? Any callers? Any phone calls?"

"None."

"Operator said you didn't have any calls." Why had he already been checking on me?

"I have proof," I said, hoping it was that. "I did a job here in the house that couldn't be done in less than two hours." I turned to Mrs. Hawks. "It's true, isn't it?"

The Sheriff stemmed the resulting flow by telling her to leave the room.

"Miss Ellis, what was this job you did?"

"Packing."

A gleam of success came in his eye. "To leave town?"

"Yes."

"I thought," he said, "you would be." And suddenly I knew that this was not the end of his business, that he was not present to see that I carried out Zaydee Proutman's desire.

"Skipping town," he said. "Now tell me all about your last meeting with Randy Bill."

The word "last" was ominous. I repeated my former statement, and the things we had said in the doorway of the Greasy Spoon sounded worse at the second hearing.

"So after that," said the Sheriff, "you left the restaurant. You were too excited to eat, and you met him in his car and drove—maybe to Lovers' Point?"

"Lovers' Point?"

"You know where I mean." He was watching me carefully for his effect. "Out on the lake. Long narrow point runs out in the water. Big pine tree. Great place for parked cars in the summer time. Know it, don't you?"

I said nothing, as a wave of memory swept over me, and he thought he had all the answers, until from the depth of misery and bewilderment I dragged out words, "I never went anywhere in my life with that poor drunken creature. I don't know why you care if I did. Ask him. He must be sober enough to tell you the truth."

The Sheriff leaned heavily back in the protesting morris chair. "I've got plenty of reasons," he said, "to care whether or not you were out with Randy Bill on Saturday night. I'll have to find out everything from you. He can't tell me anything, and I guess you know it. Randy's dead."

I felt cold. "Dead?"

"Don't you remember? Hitting the tree? The fire in that car? Out at Lovers' Point? Funny you weren't hurt at all. How did you get back to town?"

I choked out the words. "I don't know anything. How can I? I wasn't there."

"Someone picked you up on the road."

I said nothing.

"Suppose someone's come forward and told us."

Of course no one had, and I gained a little confidence. "Can't you believe I saw him only three times in my life, and for every time I have witnesses of our conversation? He was nothing to me but a pathetic and rather repulsive wreck of a boy. I'm sorry he's dead, but if he was driving a car on a night like Saturday and was as drunk as I saw him at six o'clock, I should think a fatal accident was pretty likely to happen."

The Sheriff was silent for a moment. "All right. You had no part in Bill's death, we'll say, and you weren't a witness to the accident. Then why were you packing up to leave town in such a hurry?"

"Because I lost my job."

He had a grim, satisfied smile. "Lost your job? At the Proutman Museum?"

"Yes."

"Like your job?"

"Yes."

"Needed your job?"

"Yes."

"Who told you to go? Harvey?"

"No."

"Young Gordon?"

"No."

"Was it Mrs. Proutman who fired you?"

"Yes."

"So you had a reason for not liking her very well, didn't you? Didn't you?"

"Obviously."

"Obviously," he mocked me. "And Randy Bill had another. The lover she cast off for another fellow. And maybe you like this other fellow pretty well, too. Do you?"

"Like? What is this all about?" I cried.

"I think you know," said Sheriff Brown slowly. "I'm afraid it's about murder."

"Randy Bill was murdered?"

"No, I don't think Bill was murdered. I think it was an accident like what you said, or suicide maybe."

The silence was dreadful. I had to break it. "Who was murdered?"

"Do you really want me to tell you?"

Through my mind ran just one possibility. The other fellow whom I liked pretty well. John! "Tell me."

Sheriff Brown got to his feet and stood over me. "Mrs. Zaydee Proutman hasn't been seen since Saturday night at six o'clock. We have evidence that she is dead. We think she was killed by Randy Bill, and that you can tell us all we need to know about it."

CHAPTER XI

How should a person behave who is innocent of a crime? I sat perfectly still, and from the frozen feeling of my face I doubt that it had any expression at all. That, I soon discovered, was the way not to behave.

"A poker face ain't going to help you," the Sheriff explained to me. "What did Bill mean when he said to you in Markses' Café that he was sorry about today and was going to make it up to you soon? He meant he was sorry you got fired from the Museum. He'd help you get revenge by killing off Zaydee, who he was laying for, anyway. And when you met him about half-past six—"

"No, no," I broke in. "It isn't true. I never met him. He had no way of knowing about Mrs. Proutman and me."

"No? Can you prove it?"

"Yes, yes, I can," I went on carefully. "Mrs. Proutman came into the laboratory about five o'clock. Dr. Gordon was there when she told me to leave. And Esquire Williams, the janitor. Mr. Harvey came in, and Mrs. Proutman said it again. They were all in the Museum building when I left at quarter of six. When I got to the restaurant Mr. Bill was inside. I had no time to tell him anything. He just spoke to me and went out."

"Uhhuh," said the Sheriff, "I can check all that. But there's somebody could have told Randy Bill you were fired. Zaydee Proutman could have told him. Before she did it."

"Yes, I— she could have." I took a deep breath. "But they weren't on good terms."

"Well," said the Sheriff, "they were on good enough terms so that she drove out to Lovers' Point with him on Saturday night. That is, most likely she did."

I gasped. "You mean that she got into the car with Randy Bill? Drunk as he was on Saturday night?"

The Sheriff smiled. "You don't like drunks very well, do you? You keep harping on that one thing about Bill. Trying to make me think he wasn't responsible for what he did? Trying to protect him?"

"I'm not trying to do anything. He really was drunk and— I'm not used to people like that."

"Uh? Well, it wouldn't jar Zaydee much. She could've done the driving, you know. Or you could have."

"I don't know how to drive."

"That might take proving, too. Now suppose Randy didn't know about your being fired." His tone had suddenly become conciliatory, and I was more frightened than ever. "If he didn't know anything about it from Mrs. Proutman or from anybody else, if nobody'd telephoned him"—he eyed me sharply—"well, what did he mean when he said to you he was sorry about what happened Saturday? What was he going to make up to you?"

I knew I had to answer. "I have no idea what he thought he could do for me. I think he was ...just talking vaguely about something that happened Saturday morning. After he found his car in front of the Museum, he came down to the laboratory and accused Dr. Gordon of stealing it. He said I was mixed up in it, too. That's all. Mr. and Mrs. Marks heard him apologizing."

The Sheriff pulled the red walrus mustache. "So he said he was sorry he spoke that way to you, and would you meet him later in the evening and, er ... make up?"

The insult was clear. "What can I do," I said wearily, "to make you believe me?"

"Right now"—he stood up—"you'd better get your wraps on and come with me."

The silver fox jacket lay on my bed beside the hat, gloves and purse, ready for the trip I was evidently not to begin that day. They did not seem altogether suitable for a jaunt to jail, but everything else was packed. I put them on and went into the hallway where Mrs. Hawks, red with anger, was saying, "You may think you're awful smart today, Bart Brown, but just you wait till 'lection."

The Sheriff's hand was on the doorknob when the bell rang. He pulled the door open and started to shove me before him onto the porch.

Miss Alice Barton, very straight and aloof, was standing there, as she had promised. "Good morning," she said quietly. "I have come to call on Miss Ellis. Were you escorting her somewhere, Barton?"

He was in a hurry to get away from her gentle stare. "Just over to my office for a few minutes, Cousin Alice." His arm propelled me more lightly toward the top step.

"Barton," asked Miss Alice, "are you being wise?"

He hesitated, thinking perhaps about the fatal date mentioned by Mrs. Hawks. "I think so. You've probably heard the news that's going round. Not much is kept quiet long in this town."

"I have heard something," said Miss Barton. "I have heard that poor worthless young Mr. Bill has been killed in a motor accident. I have heard that he is accused of throwing Zaydee Proutman over the cliff at Lovers' Point. I haven't heard any reason why you should be taking Miss Ellis over to your office. She would have no concern with people of that sort."

"Well, Alice," said the Sheriff defiantly, lifting and lowering a large flat foot, "she worked for one of them."

"So did I," replied Miss Barton. "Shall I accompany you?"

"Don't get riled, Alice. I'm not suspecting Miss Ellis of anything; she's just a witness."

"And the only one you have so far," guessed Miss Barton. "You would do well to leave her here with me, rather than to drag her through the town where every nose is at a windowpane." She nodded toward the parlor window, where Mrs. Hawks was descending in hasty confusion from her morning devotions. "I assure you, Barton, that I will not let her out of my sight, if you insist, but it is unnecessary to make a show to the town either of her or of yourself until you have more against her than I think you have at present."

It was a way out, and the Sheriff took it quickly. "All right. I'll trust her to your care, Cousin Alice. I'm getting together the staff of the Museum and that nigger girl out at Zaydee's house. Everybody to meet at the Museum at ten o'clock. You bring Miss Ellis without fail."

"We shall be there," she said. "Neither of us would want to miss the excitement. Since we are otherwise in no way concerned with Mr. Bill and Mrs. Proutman." She held his eye firmly as he backed down the steps.

As he climbed into his car, she went on, "Come in, my dear. Have you had your breakfast?"

Mrs. Hawks swooped upon us. "No she ain't, Miss Barton. Sheriff couldn't wait. No wonder she's so white, without a thing in her stomach. Land sakes, what's Bart Brown blowing off about where she was last Saturday night? There, I shouldn't have spoken that way. I forgot he was your cousin."

"My second cousin," corrected Miss Barton. "And I think we all know Barton. Could you get Miss Ellis a cup of coffee right away?"

Sitting at the table, drinking the hot reviving coffee, soothed by the murmur of happy horror in Mrs. Hawks's voice, I began to lose the numbness in which the accumulated shocks of the last few days had frozen me. That Randy Bill was dead by accident seemed an acceptable ending to his bitter, brief career. But Zaydee Proutman, blazing, vital, tough—it was hard to believe that she was not alive.

"She's really dead?" I questioned aloud.

"It isn't entirely certain," Miss Barton told me and the avid Mrs. Hawks. "They have not found the body, or at least, they had not found it early this morning; but Elmer Anderson, the constable, told Mrs. Watson's niece that they had the weapon and some important clues."

"What weapon?" demanded Mrs. Hawks, her usual deference to Miss Barton diminished in her greed for gore. "What'd he do? Bang her over the head before he threw her over the cliff? How'd they know all that, anyway?"

Miss Barton had little to add, and the reiterated story came briefly to this: On Sunday evening the weather along the lake had cleared, and in the moonlight a young Warrenton couple driving out on the Point had come upon the ghastly wreck of a car and its driver. They had at once telephoned the Sheriff's office, and at dawn officers had identified the charred body of Randy Bill lying beneath the pine uprooted by the impact of his now-burned car. The tree was some distance from the cliff, which dropped down twenty feet to the stormy waves. At the edge of the cliff the bushes in one spot were matted and trampled as if something heavy had been dragged through them. All footprints had been washed away by the long rain. Either in Randy's pockets or in the debris of his car the officers had "found something."

That was all Miss Barton knew, except that the Sheriff, going to the Proutman house at seven o'clock to inform Zaydee of Randy's death and to ask her to identify what was left of the body, had learned from Isabelle that Zaydee had been missing since Saturday afternoon. How the important clues pointed to Zaydee's presence at Lovers' Point and what they could possibly be, was a rich mystery.

"But why did he come here to question me?" I asked. "What could Isabelle have said to make him do that?"

"I'll bet 'twas the Markses," decided Mrs. Hawks. "Probably he sent Elmer or Deputy Guild round there to see what they knew, and they told him about—" She turned scarlet.

About what you heard at the keyhole, I finished to myself with the first smile of the day. I rose and went into the bedroom to freshen my face before our ordeal at the Museum. It seemed hours since I had dressed that morning. Miss Barton, saying, "I suppose I must keep my word to the Sheriff and watch you every minute," followed me into the room and shut the door.

I ran the comb slowly through my hair. "Do you really think Mrs. Proutman can be dead?" I asked her.

"Yes, I do." She sat very straight with folded hands and, between precise words, a folded mouth. "She was a violent woman, and she came to a violent end. I believe that we shall never be troubled by her again."

"And Randy Bill did it."

"Miss Ellis," said Miss Barton, "he was the instrument, but I believe he was in God's hand."

I didn't. Randy Bill may have saved the staff of the William Henry Proutman Museum a lot of trouble, but for this minor achievement, not much had been done for poor broken Randy.

CHAPTER XII

Over the porch and steps of the Proutman Museum were scattered jagged pieces of glass, under the custody of Constable Anderson. Someone had smashed the case around the sacred redwood, and I couldn't see the bridal doll. The Constable opened the door for us, and there was the smell, the all-too-familiar odor of simmered chimpanzee, stronger than ever for its two-day confinement in the unaired Museum.

Alpheus Harvey stood in his office doorway. He gave me a look no more suspicious than usual and said, "Everyone is here now except the Sheriff and Dr. Gordon, who is still in his laboratory. Will you kindly ask him to join us, Miss Ellis?"

I said, of course, that I would. With no light heart, I moved off through the Corset Room to summon the man who, in what I had optimistically thought was the low point of my life, had kept as far from me as possible.

I was halfway down the room when I saw the gleam. As usual outside of visiting hours, the window curtains were nearly drawn, and the sun never found much to light up among the misty, musty draperies of Esquire's favorite ladies. That was why I noticed the reflection from a fluffy bosom. It was well across the room from my shortest path to the basement stairs, a flat diffused phosphorescence. Mainly to delay the dreaded meeting, I was detouring to find the source when John Gordon entered at the opposite end of the hall.

He saw me and cried out harshly, "Kay!" In a bound he was at my side.

"For God's sake, are you still in town?"

"Unfortunately," I replied as coolly as I could. "And I shall probably be here for some time. Here, that is, or in the Warrenton jail."

He seized my arms roughly. "What are you talking about?" he demanded.

I shook myself free. "Mr. Harvey sent me to bring you to his office," I said. "The Sheriff will be delighted to tell you all about it."

He was hurrying after me and, almost at the hallway, his hand caught my shoulder. "I know about the Sheriff," he said. "And Bill. But I've got to know how you come into it. Kay, has anything happened to you?"

I stood facing him. He looked tight-faced and tired, and his hair needed brushing. For one weak moment I almost stood on tiptoe to push the black lock off his forehead, but I had not forgotten that on Saturday night he had let me leave the Museum alone, that he had made no gesture of kindness during that long, empty Sunday of waiting. "Your concern for me," I said steadily, "has come a little late." I turned, and he followed me into the director's office.

Mr. Harvey sat at his desk behind the weasel, and beside his clenched marbled hand I saw with a shock the big bunch of keys he had handed to Zaydee on Saturday evening. Well, why not? She wouldn't be likely to take them out for an evening's drive. In the farthest corner between desk and bookcases Jensen crouched on a chair, twirling his black, visored cap between his knees. I had never seen him bare-headed before, and his pale flat face looked less aggressive. Beside a pinched Esquire, Isabelle pressed a fur collar against trembling gray lips. Miss Barton's precise little profile under the square black silk toque stood out against the window. Beyond her were two empty chairs, and there was a third near Isabelle, into which I slipped. John Gordon slumped into one of the remaining chairs and looked at the floor. We were all too quiet.

Barton Brown stamped in, followed by Guild, his cheerful little deputy, and big Elmer Anderson, who had talked too much to Mrs. Watson's niece.

"Good morning, good morning," blustered the Sheriff with pre-election heartiness. "Sorry to have to bother all you people about this mess, but we've got to get to the bottom of it." His eye fell upon me, and his tone changed. "And *you're* here, too," he added.

I winced as he turned away to accept Mr. Harvey's offer of the official seat at the desk.

"Got to find out what you all know," Brown went on. "About times, about places. What you know about Randy Bill. When you last saw Mrs. Proutman. Anyone know shorthand here?"

No one answered, so after a moment I said, "I do."

He looked undecided. "It's irregular, considering your possible interest in the case." He was avoiding his Cousin Alice's eye. "But I want to clean this up. I don't want to wait till they send somebody over from Warrenton. I'll be obliged if you'll take the testimony, Miss Ellis. But I'll have to ask you to take oath to record the full truth to the best of your ability."

John's chair scraped noisily, and Alpheus Harvey cleared his throat.

"Yes, sir," I said, and moved to the Sheriff's side at the desk. Taking testimony would be nervous work, but infinitely better than sitting idle, aware of the Sheriff's suspicion and of John's desertion.

Sheriff Brown was assuring everyone that they were there as helpful citizens, that no one was suspected of anything, but, owing to certain ... er ... complications in the case which he had otherwise well in hand, it would be of the greatest service to him and to the county to inform him of er ... etc., etc.

"And while we're talking it over, Guild, you and Elmer take all that broken glass over to the office and fingerprint it. It isn't likely anybody broke it with his fingers—ha, ha—but you never know. Guild, here," he informed us, "went to the State Police School this summer and can do a professional job." Guild beamed and trotted out, followed by big, red-necked Elmer.

There was, however, nothing informal about the "talking it over." Each person in turn was asked five identical questions: How long have you known Randy Bill? When did you see him last? How long have you known Zaydee Proutman? When did you see her last? Where were you on Saturday evening, November 4, between 5:30 and 8:00 P.M.? Why 8:00 P.M.? I wondered. And then concentration on my rusty shorthand filled all the mind I had.

Alpheus Harvey's answers were slow and clear. He had never really known Randy Bill, although he had seen him at the Museum several times with Mrs. Proutman. He had last seen him on the morning of November 4. Bill had said to him, "You've locked my car keys in your safe because you think it's your duty to do it. If I just get my hands on Zaydee Proutman, wish me luck."

Mrs. Proutman he had last seen soon after quarter to six on Saturday evening. He had left her sitting at his desk with the Museum account books before her. She dropped in to go over them now and then, particularly near the first of a month. All accounts were in order, as the Sheriff could see. Alpheus had reached home, five blocks from the Museum, at six o'clock, had had supper with his wife, and at eight o'clock had been engrossed in a game of anagrams with Mr. Jim Watson.

Miss Barton was next.

"Bart Brown," she told her cousin plainly, "I am quite willing to co-operate with you in your official capacity, but I do not think that need include questions to which you already know the answers. You must be aware that I would not *know* a person of Mr. Bill's caliber. As for Zaydee Proutman, I heard her voice in the basement and in Mr. Harvey's office on Saturday afternoon. Mrs. Proutman has a strong voice."

"She had," said the Sheriff.

Miss Alice nodded stiffly. "I left the library a little before six. There was a light in Mr. Harvey's office. I did not see anyone there. I do not pass the door directly. You know quite well where I was between six and eight-thirty."

"With my wife and all the other good ladies at Mrs. Jim Watson's. Was the car still in front of the Museum when you went out?"

It had been standing there, she said, and the glass case had not been broken. Mr. Harvey said the same thing. So did Esquire Williams, who had left the building a minute or so after Alpheus.

The Museum, Esquire was certain, was securely locked; the night catch was on the outer door to which he, Mr. Harvey, Dr. Gordon, Miss Barton, and Jensen had keys. His acquaintance with Mrs. Proutman was limited to the eighteen months he had been in Hinchdale, and he had seen Randy Bill for the first and last time on Saturday morning when Mr. Bill had been "a little high" and had "spoken against Mrs. Proutman like Mr. Harvey told you, suh."

"And where were you, Williams, between the time you left the Museum and eight that evening?"

"Well, suh"—the words came slow—"I went over to the Cash-and-Carry and bought me a couple o' pork chops for my supper. Then I went up to my place, up over Mr. Rogers's hardware store, and I cooked 'em an' ate 'em, and then I got me all shaved up and dressed up, and then I went out to visit with a friend."

"Who is this friend? Where does he live? When did all this happen?"

"Well, it was kind of far out in the country and an awful long way on a dark rainy night, suh, and ..."

"Come, Williams, snap into it. Where did you go and what time did you get there?"

The next voice was Isabelle's. "Please, sir, may I speak? He came out to Mrs. Proutman's house. He was visitin' me."

"Why didn't you say so in the first place, Williams? How did you get out to Mrs. Proutman's? Walk? Ride? What time did you get there? Any witness except the girl?"

"I walked. No, nobody was there but Miss Isabelle. Mrs. Proutman had dismissed the other folks that worked for her. I don't know what time I got there. Right soon after I came, Dr. Gordon rang up on the phone and wanted to speak to Miss Zaydee."

"I called first at eight o'clock." That was John.

"Did he call again while you were there?"

"Yes, suh, twice, suh."

"Well, that checks with what the night telephone operator says. O.K., Williams. Now you, Jensen."

Jensen knew the last time he'd seen Zaydee, all right. In the basement of the Museum, in this Dr. Gordon's part of it, and she'd just busted up a lot of glass and stuff and was yelling around the way she always used to, before she got married to old man Proutman.

"And I says to her, 'Bin throwin' dishes, Zaydee? Good old days come back, huh?' and she says, 'Get the hell out of here, you big Swede,' and I'm a Dane, so I says to her, 'I won't work for no one that ain't a lady. I'm quittin' this job for good. Dr. Gordon can run the furnace, because he's got an engineer's license and he's a real useful feller.' And then I quit and I ain't seen Zaydee since."

"And where were you between five-thirty and eight o'clock?"

"Well, I tell you, Sheriff, it was all right to be where I was, and I wasn't doin' anythin' I shouldn't. But wife's over to her mother's in Ioway, and it might sound kind of bad."

"All right. Where were you?"

"Well, you know old lady Riggins, her that was sister to Zaydee's mother and married Riggins's brother? Well, she likes a good laugh, and I yust dropped in to tell her about Zaydee throwin' things again. We sat round drinkin' coffee till nine, nine-thirty. Probably she'll know yust how long."

"Mrs. Riggins will know or her daughter will know?"

"What's Beryl got to do with it?"

"I don't care about your friendship with any of the Rigginses," said the Sheriff. "I'm investigating a case of violent death, most likely of murder. On Saturday morning I picked up that car, the one that was burned out on Lovers' Point the same night. And where did I pick it up? From in front of the house of your friends, the Rigginses. Now, was Beryl at home on Saturday night?"

"Well, I tell you she was," said Jensen. "She was home and she was alone. She was expectin' some ... someone, but he never showed up before I left like I told you, nine, nine-thirty."

"Who was she expecting?"

"I dunno. Beryl Riggins don't talk about her business. She ain't Zaydee."

"I'll do some checking up on all this. Now you, Isabelle, you've already told your story out at the house, and it checks so far as there's anything to check. Rogers's delivery man says, just like you did, that Zaydee was waiting to ride in on his truck when he came out to her place to bring the new clothes boiler, and she told him she was going to drive a car of

her own back home. He left her in front of the Museum about five o'-
clock, and he saw the car in front. You say you didn't see her again after she left on the truck and you haven't heard from her since, that she
hadn't talked about taking a trip or made any preparations. Well,
maybe so, maybe not. We'll have to wait and see. But there's one or two
questions I'd like to ask you right now. How long you been with Mrs.
Proutman?"

"Five years, sir."

"Must have got to know her pretty well in five years. Now, you're a
smart-looking girl. You tell me this: Everyone here says young Bill was
roaring around town, saying he'd get Zaydee Proutman for taking his
car. Do you think she'd be very likely to go off with him in that car the
very day she took it away from him and when he was drunk, too? Does
that make sense to you?"

It didn't to me; it hadn't all along.

"Please, sir," said Isabelle softly, "are you right sure Miss Zaydee is
dead?"

"Fairly sure."

"Well, I don't like to talk about her personality before strangers, but
if Mr. Randy has done her harm ..."

"We think he did."

"I really think, Mr. Sheriff, she would have gone with him. Mrs.
Proutman was a right—peculiar lady. She'd been mean to Mr. Randy,
and she was going to be meaner before the day was over; but on Saturday morning when I was fixing her hair, she showed a real hanker-
ing after him."

"Huh? How'd she hanker?"

"She kept tellin' me sweet little things he used to say to her. How much
he cared about her or he wouldn't be hanging around town and drinking himself to death. It seemed a kind of—of a monument to her."

"More like a tombstone." He picked up the telephone. "Marilyn, give
me my office. Hello, Elmer, come over with Guild and take the girl out
to Proutman's. She can show you the best places for fingerprints, while
I finish up with the rest of this. And, Elmer,"—he lowered his voice
mysteriously and uselessly, considering the size of the room—"when you
come back with the girl, bring me the ... er ... weapon and those things
in the safe. O.K."

Jensen got to his feet. "Sheriff, it's all right with you I should gust go
look at my fire? It ain't goin' so good. Seems kind of cold here."

John spoke. "I'm afraid, Jensen, I managed to mess things up thoroughly."

"Uhhuh, well, 'snothin' can't be fixed. You didn't do so bad. All right if
I go now, Sheriff? I got to get back to the bank soon."

"I'm through with you," said Brown, "but how come you're running this furnace, Jensen? I thought you quit on Saturday night."

"I quit Zaydee Proutman," said Jensen. "I didn't quit furnace. She's pretty good furnace. I like to work with."

He lumbered out the door, the cap back on his head. He looked like himself again. Isabelle slipped out after him, and I heard the constable's car drive away.

Sheriff Brown was looking hearty. "Now," he said, "this unpleasantness will soon be over. You're my last victim, Dr. Gordon. How long have you known Randy Bill?"

My fingers felt cramped as I took down the statements of his calm deep voice; I was listening for every tone now.

"I saw Randy Bill only twice. The first time was in the doorway of the Marks's restaurant on last Tuesday evening, October 31. He blocked my way. That's how I happened to notice him. He looked as if he had been drinking. After he went out, Mrs. Marks mentioned his name to her husband. That was how I knew it was he. Mr. Harvey and Williams have described the second meeting. On Saturday morning, when he found his car parked in front of the Museum, he came down to my laboratory and accused first me and then Miss Ellis of having the car keys. He had a good deal of liquor on board, and his talk was rather wild. Miss Ellis, who knew more about the car situation than I did, explained things to him and that calmed him down. Williams and I started him upstairs, and ran into Harvey. You've been told about what happened then."

"Let's have your version of it."

"As nearly as I can remember, Bill said that he knew Mr. Harvey had been given the keys to the car and would keep them because it was his duty. Bill then said, 'If I get my hands on Zaydee Proutman, wish her luck; she'll need it.' Or something close to that."

Close, yes, but Randy had said, "Wish *me* luck," and none of the three versions—Harvey's, Esquire's, John's—had included, "you'll have no good wishes for her, the lot of you."

"And then you and Williams trailed him to the Museum entrance," concluded Brown. "Dr. Gordon, how long have you known Mrs. Zaydee Proutman?"

John's voice was still calm. After all, he had known for an hour that this question was coming and that his answer could be checked. "I met Mrs. Proutman in March of last year. It was in New York. I was staying with a friend, Charles Newton, during the spring vacation. Mrs. Proutman was there, too. She had met Newton's parents on a Caribbean cruise a short time before."

I knew something about Chuck Newton. A cheerful soul who had played with a few terms of anthropology at Oldwick before he had gone home to the family brokerage business, a family said to be recently very rich, quite the friends for Zaydee Proutman.

"You met Mrs. Proutman in New York in March, so in August you came to Hinchdale," said the Sheriff.

"I came to Hinchdale"—John was keeping almost all of the anger from his voice—"in complete ignorance that the Mrs. Proutman whom I had met was in any way connected with the Museum or with the town. My dealings were entirely with Mr. Harvey. I hardly noticed the name of the Museum. I had known Mrs. Proutman very slightly. She had not mentioned the town or the Museum. She may have asked me about my work, but I don't really remember. A lot of women think anthropology is amusing."

"When you found her here as your employer," asked the Sheriff, "were you pleased?"

"Not entirely."

"You didn't like her?"

"It wasn't that. I prefer to keep my work quite apart from my social life. Most men feel the same."

After which, to me, completely offensive speech, the Sheriff put the fourth question. "When did you last see Mrs. Proutman?"

"In my laboratory on Saturday afternoon, I should say between five and five-thirty."

"And," the Sheriff cut in, "we'll go into that meeting later. Mrs. Proutman, so they all say, went upstairs with Harvey. Miss Ellis followed, and almost behind her, Williams. What did you do?"

"I went back to my work," said John Gordon.

Probably he did; he could. He hadn't lost his work, he hadn't been deserted by a so-called sweetheart.

"About six o'clock," John went on, "I stopped typing and thought I had better have a look at Jensen's fire. I wasn't sure whether he had gone off without banking it for the night. When I was in the basement passage, just at the foot of the stairs, I heard the outer door of the Museum close. I assumed that Mrs. Proutman was leaving. Almost immediately, I should say, a car drove away from the front of the building. I went on working and struggling with the fire, which Jensen had not banked, until two in the morning. I telephoned Mrs. Proutman's house three times during the evening. The first, you say, was at eight o'clock; I didn't notice. The others were later. Isabelle answered each time."

"Doctor, why were you so anxious to get in touch with Mrs. Proutman? Did you want to warn her of Randy Bill's threats? Or had you already told her about them when she was at the Museum?"

"No. I didn't take the threat seriously. Bill was almost certainly drunk when he made it. I wanted to talk to Mrs. Proutman about a hasty and,

I felt, unfair decision she had made regarding my laboratory assistant."

"I was coming to that," the Sheriff said, "so if you will leave us for a while, Miss Ellis. Miss Barton will be kind enough to make any notes we need in longhand."

I got up then and, with eyes straight front walked to the door, which Esquire held open for me.

"You go along, too, Williams," ordered the Sheriff, "and get on with your work. Miss Ellis, in the library if you please." The door closed again.

Esquire, his eyes soft with pity, shook his head at me and scuttled off to his coat closet. I sat down in the library, which still smelled like cold Sunday dinner, and stared out across the shadowy hall at the closed door behind which my fate might soon be sealed.

If the Sheriff heard Zaydee's exact words to me, or even a transcription refined for Miss Barton's ladylike ears, what would he think? That I had really been "necking" with Randy Bill, that I was his accomplice and his dame? Or that to me "promiscuous" was the fighting word that had joined outraged virtue to Randy's drunken rage to send Zaydee Proutman to her death? What would they say about the brandished umbrella and the broken measuring tube?

Mr. Harvey merely knew that I had been dismissed for laziness and insolence. Only John Gordon had heard the full attack. For his own benefit and for Mr. Harvey's, he had done some neat editing of evidence. He could do as much for me. But would he? Could I trust John?

CHAPTER XIII

I couldn't sit still. I had to do something, anything—track down that unexpected gleam in the musty exhibition hall.

All the curtains in the Corset Room were rolled to the top of windows open wide to let out the last of the chimpanzee. In wind and sun the garments on the dummies looked more fragile than ever and a little more mussed, particularly the ruffled bodice of Esquire's pink chiffon pet.

"Isn't it kind of cold in here for you, Miss?" Esquire, in a clean brown linen coat and his uniform cap with the gold-lettered "Proutman," had approached with mop and pail. "Excuse me, but don't you think maybe Sheriff Brown intended you should sit right still in the library?"

"Probably," I agreed. "But almost anything I could do would seem wrong to him. Esquire, he thinks I helped Randy Bill do—whatever he did."

"Oh, Miss Kay, I hope not. But even so, don't you worry too much. I expect he'll decide Mr. Randy did it all by himself. It'll be the easiest thing for *him*."

"Why will that be easier for the Sheriff?"

"Miss Ellis"—Esquire's tone was almost an order—"you go right back in the library if you don't want to be suspected of nothin'."

It was good advice and given none too soon. I had scarcely been at the magazine table, hat off, long enough to look really settled, when the Director's door opened and the Sheriff came out. The staff of the William Henry Proutman Museum followed him. The sight of the three together across the hall from me typified the change in my position which Zaydee's decree and the Sheriff's suspicion had brought about.

I was sure that no one had told Brown about Alpheus Harvey's dismissal. The little gray and yellow man was standing almost straight this morning, looking positively chipper. And why not? For the first time in many years he was really the director of the William Henry Proutman Museum. I wondered if he would send a nice wreath to Randy Bill's funeral. If one held funerals for all that seemed to be left of Randy. Which was more than they had of Zaydee Proutman. Why were they so sure that she was dead?

Miss Barton smiled at me, but I couldn't tell whether it was in encouragement or pity. John, who came out last, did not look in my direction.

"In here, Miss Ellis," commanded the Sheriff. As I crossed the hall John was close to me, whispering:

"As soon as this is over, go home and stay. Swear you will."

It seemed an odd thing to be so vehement about, particularly since I had no other place to go.

I sat beside Alpheus's desk and stroked the weasel. Through the half-open door I could see Guild ushering Isabelle into the library and handing a long newspaper parcel to his superior. Then the Sheriff closed the door and laid the bundle on the desk. His heavy-lidded eyes were fixed on my face. For all I knew, that bundle might contain an arm or a leg of Randy Bill. Bones are nice clean things, but only in the end. I was afraid of being sick.

He unwound the paper slowly, saying, "I want just a little help from you, Miss Ellis, just a little help."

Inside the newspaper were three packages wrapped in paper towels, two very small, the third the length of the original bundle.

"So you just tell me if you ever saw any of these things before." His heavy fingers pulled the rubber band from a small lump of a parcel and laid back the paper. It was a china doll, naked, hairless, sooty.

"You know what this is?" he stated.

At first I didn't.

"Think hard, Miss Ellis," he said unpleasantly.

"It could be from the broken case on the Museum porch, the ... bridal doll."

"It could. Image of Zaydee Proutman set up on her wedding day by her loving husband, William Henry. He was her loving husband. People haven't loved her much in the last ten years. Zaydee didn't have such a good life, maybe. Ever think of that, Miss Ellis?"

I was thinking that, when away from the electorate, Mr. Barton Brown was a rather smart man.

"So when she thought this poor creature Bill loved her in spite of the way she'd treated him, it might have been easy to persuade her to go off with him in the death car. She probably was tired of people who just wanted to get things out of her." Did he mean John? Did he want me to think so? "Where do you think we found this doll, Miss Ellis?"

"I don't know."

"Miss Ellis, when you came back from the café along Broadway about six-twenty on Saturday night, you say the car was gone from in front of the Museum."

"It was."

"Miss Ellis, was the glass case broken then?"

"I don't know. I was on the other side of this great wide street."

"You didn't, a little later in the evening, see Randy Bill break that case?"

"I never saw him after that moment in the restaurant. I've told you the truth."

"This little doll"—the Sheriff balanced it horribly on his palm—"was found a long ways from here. About sixty miles. Out on that long point you remember, running out into the Lake. Under the pine tree the car knocked down. It had been burned out of what used to be Randy Bill's overcoat pocket."

I did feel a little sick.

He put down the doll and opened the smallest parcel. On the white paper lay three bronze bobby pins. I had seen pins like that Saturday morning in Randy's car, while the Sheriff watched me through the Museum door.

"Are these yours?"

"No," I said definitely. "I don't wear that kind or that color."

"But you've seen these before?"

"They're the commonest kind. You can buy them in every dime store."

"You think that almost any woman could've left them in Randy Bill's car?"

"If she was in the car. And if her hair was red or brown."

"They could have been Mrs. Proutman's?"

"Yes, so far as the color is concerned. I don't know whether she wore that type of pin."

He put them aside and began to unroll the paper around the long parcel. It was the Holtzerman umbrella, muddy on one side and with a deeper patina on the ape's grinning ivory head. "You've seen this before?"

"Oh, yes."

"Yes. But perhaps it looked a little different when you saw it last?"

"Yes."

"Well, since then we've scraped the blood off the handle and sent it to the state police laboratory. The blood and the hair."

I gasped at the horror he pictured, and at my descent into his trap.

He got up, opened the door, and called, "Isabelle, bring a glass of water for Miss Ellis. Now"—coming back to the desk—"where did you last see this umbrella? It's a funny-looking thing. Can you tell me anything about it?"

I had told him before Isabelle arrived with the water. He ordered her to sit down and pointed to the three objects on the desk. Isabelle's face could not pale revealingly, but her brown hands squeezed hard together, and the quivering of her wide lips showed recognition and horror. The doll she did not identify but agreed to the Sheriff's statement that it was the former bridal figure from the redwood section. She added that Miss Zaydee was right vain of it, and that it would hurt her to have it insulted. Yes, she was sure Mr. Randy Bill would have known this.

She hesitated about the ownership of the pins. Ladies ought not to wear those cheap, ugly little things, and Mrs. Proutman knew it; but she thought they were useful and, then, she loved to shop in the dime store. Whether she wore such pins on Saturday, Isabelle didn't know.

"Well, they were wedged down back of the seat in Bill's car. They could have been there earlier than Saturday. Do you know any other time lately she might have been out with him?"

Isabelle could name only one likely time. Early Friday evening Miss Zaydee had gone out alone for a while in the sedan.

"So they could have been Mrs. Proutman's pins. Couldn't they have been Miss Ellis's, just as well?"

"Oh, no, sir, not that color, and not Miss Ellis."

"Why not? Women's stuff don't always match. My daughter wears blue and green fancy pins in her hair."

Whereupon Isabelle favored him with a soft dissertation on use versus adornment, style in haircuts, and personal taste. The Sheriff grinned. "If I get you right, Miss Ellis isn't the type to own these pins, but lots of people are, and one of them could've been Zaydee Proutman."

"Yes, sir."

He picked up the gruesome umbrella. "Do you think Mrs. Proutman would have gone around carrying an old-fashioned thing like this?"

"Oh, yes, sir." Isabelle was sure. "That's just what Miss Zaydee would do. There was a little story about it that she could tell eve'ybody. And, no matter how old it was, the silk would still turn the rain. Lots of rich people are practical about little things, particularly Miss Zaydee. Like she rode in town on Rogers's truck. Like the dime-store hair pins."

"You say she had this umbrella in her hand when she left her home? Dr. Gordon says she knocked over some glass laboratory stuff with the end of it. By mistake." He watched me carefully as he said the last two words. "When she went upstairs ahead of you, Miss Ellis, was she carrying the umbrella?"

I tried to see it and I couldn't. "I honestly don't know."

He turned back to Isabelle. "Just what was Mrs. Proutman wearing when she left her house last Saturday afternoon? Miss Ellis can take down the list."

A red tweed skirt, a gold metal-cloth blouse with high neck and long sleeves, a belt, a brooch, a ring and earrings of heavy Mexican silver, little sombreros, all matching, and on her feet old beige leather pumps. You could tell the fastidious Isabelle's feeling about this combination in each terse word. No hat, no rubbers, and her raincoat of red oiled silk without fastenings, except ties at throat and breast.

"Wasn't she cold?"

"She was too mad," said Isabelle. "She'd just had a telephone call, and she ran after Rogers's man and left with him in a hurry."

"Who called her?"

"I'm not sure. I don't like to say."

"Didn't you answer the phone?"

She had, and she finally admitted that it was undoubtedly a man's voice, maybe Mr. Randy's after he had been drinking a while. It couldn't, she was certain under pressure, have been Dr. Gordon's. That I also could have proved, but my word at this point was worth little to anyone.

However, the Sheriff chose to dismiss me with a polite show. He appreciated my co-operation, and everyone seemed to think I was a nice kind of girl and I wasn't to believe he thought I had anything to do with the alleged death of Mrs. Proutman, but if I could remember anything useful Randy Bill had said to me, I was to let him know. And I was not to leave town. I went home, not reassured.

Two men were in Mrs. Hawks's parlor, and Mrs. Hawks was excited.

"We got company," she said. "You have, but they've been settin' with me." John got up from the sofa. Rocking furiously was my first acquaintance in Hinchdale. "Mr. Marks here's been over to the lake to identify the body."

"Mrs. Proutman?" I sank into the chair John brought up for me.

"Naw, naw, ain't found her last I heard. Ain't likely to till spring. Next spring, some spring, maybe never. They say Great Lake never gives up its dead. Naw, I been out to identify Randy Bill's remains. Remains is a lot better word than body for what's left of that feller. Why, there wasn't hardly ..."

"How much," broke in John, to and for my relief, "was left of the car?"

Mr. Marks relished the details of that, too. "Funny thing," he concluded, "what escapes and what perishes. Instrument board not hurt a bit. Keys in the ignition. You could even see that he'd had the lights turned on. Clock was broken and stopped at just exactly eight. Gives the time he hit the tree, and the lights switched on shows 'twarn't morning. The neckers from Warrenton phoned Bart Brown at seven-thirty Sunday evening, so Randy musta turned over in the rain at eight o'clock Saturday night."

That explained a lot, and there was more. The keys in the ignition suggested strongly that Zaydee Proutman and Randy had at least met after she had received them along with the Museum keys from Alpheus Harvey.

What he had come around for, Epp Marks explained, was to say to me that he and Mrs. Marks was both real sorry they'd had to tell the Sheriff anything 'bout me and that Randy Bill. They hadn't ought to've let him bother me that Friday night, and then he wouldn't 've talked to me on Saturday night and then they wouldn't 've had to tell the Sheriff something that didn't mean nothing but might make trouble for me. This was no town for a nice girl like me. He'd told me on the first day I wouldn't be here long.

He went at last; and so, at John's order of food for me, did Mrs. Hawks.

"Kay," John said abruptly, "there are some things we've got to get together on." I looked skeptical and he added, "if I'm going to be able to help you."

"What do you want to know?"

"Have you told Brown that Zaydee fired Harvey as well as you?"

"Of course not."

"Good. No one else has or will. So the Museum goes on all right. Whatever has happened to her. Now, what about you and Bill?"

"You can take my word or Mrs. Proutman's."

"Don't be a fool, Kay. What did she think happened between you? And why did she think it?"

His eyes held mine, cold, insistent, and I answered as coldly, telling him about my one talk with Randy and his attribution of a ruined life to Zaydee, our farewell handshake as the car was passing the house.

"It was probably Zaydee in the car."

"Or it could have been you."

"And I could have told Zaydee? You're thinking that?" I have never seen a man so white.

"John," I said weakly, "I'm not thinking anything. I'm too … tired."

"We've both been through a bad time," he said. "Here comes your lunch."

I tried to eat, while John laid a plan before the too-acquiescent Mrs. Hawks. She would give me my meals until the case was settled, and keep me away from the Greasy Spoon, where reporters from city and county papers might soon be added to the local curious. He didn't want them presented with a beautiful blond menace. I was too nice a girl for that.

"And not beautiful enough," I revived sufficiently to comment. "If one other person in this town calls me a nice girl I shall kill—" I stopped. It wasn't a word to use carelessly today.

"Shall I come over and help you on the Holtzerman Collection tomorrow?" I went on quickly. "As a volunteer. I've got to stay in town until the Sheriff lets me go, and I'd rather have something to do."

His answer was stiff and a blow. "No, it would not be suitable."

"She couldn't have come tomorrow anyway," interposed Mrs. Hawks. "It's the day of the fall D.A.R. luncheon. I've been telling you about it, Kay, all day Sunday, but I guess you didn't hear a word I said. Ev'rybody's goin'. It's at the Spirit Falls Inn."

CHAPTER XIV

It was close and crowded in the sedan; but, wedged in the rear seat between the overflowing warmth of Mrs. Hawks and the superimposed dumplings that composed Mrs. Barton Brown, I felt as cold and gray as the world through which we passed. There was no black, vast mystery about the road that bleak morning. The sky, heavy with leaden clouds, pressed down on the poor fields of stump country, on blackened houses by little cattle ponds skimmed with ice. It was a devastated land from which the trees had been wrenched, taking almost all life with them.

But nothing outside the car windows weakened the vitality of Mrs. Phillips. As she sat at the wheel, her big red face under a purple velvet beret loomed far above Miss Barton's neat black turban, and her voice boomed out heartily for sixty miles about those aspects of the Proutman-Bill case which seemed suitable for discussion before the wife of the Sheriff, a young unmarried girl, and Miss Alice Barton. I felt that, left alone, she and Mrs. Hawks could have had a better time.

However, there was still plenty to talk about, and the others encouraged the flow with interjections, surmises, and, in the case of Mrs. Brown, a bit of inside information which I was not sorry to hear. But didn't any of them really feel, I wondered, that someone was dead? That people we had known and seen and touched had suddenly, violently, ceased to be? In the middle of the night, lying in the ghostly Hawks bedroom, it had struck me for the first time, that reality of death. My father had been far away, and it was a long time since I had seen him; but one moment Randy Bill had been telling me he'd be seeing me, and two hours later he had crashed to death. Sometime before that, Zaydee Proutman's blazing, intense life had ended. Of all the people whom she had made to suffer on that Saturday afternoon, none had met disaster; only Zaydee, to quote Alpheus Harvey's words to her, had had reason to regret the day. No, not regret, not to remember with dissatisfaction or shame or fear. There had been no time.

"Well, I guess we've seen the last of Zaydee," said Mrs. Phillips cheerfully. "Lake never gives up its dead, as they say. 'Twouldn't be very good for my husband's business if everyone was thrown off Lovers' Point but, any way she went, Zaydee Proutman isn't exactly a loss to Hinchdale. Carrying on the way she did! However much you believe, it was enough. It was funny the way Providence decided it all. That it was one of her boy friends who killed Zaydee."

"And him gone, too," agreed Mrs. Hawks. "They're real sure she's dead?"

"They must be. Zaydee wouldn't skip out of town when she had two young men right here all stirred up about her, one way or 'nother. At least it looks like that to me. But Mary Brown is more of an authority than I am."

Mrs. Brown's curves swelled nervously into my right side. Her cheeks puffed. She seemed in an agony of indecision between discretion and desire to prove Mrs. Phillips's compliment.

"Well, Barton seems pretty sure," she finally said in a small voice, "with the blood group and the fingerprints and all. 'Twas funny that another of Zaydee's boy friends, as you call 'em, Addie, was the cause of our having real official fingerprints of Zaydee."

She had an audience. I could hear avid intakes of breath.

"Barton found out about the blood type all by himself," announced Barton's wife proudly. "Seems he'd heard from Doc Cummings Zaydee gave some of her blood when old William Henry was having his last sickness. He wired the hospital in Florida, where William Henry died, and the blood was the same as the blood on the uh,"—she stopped in time. "On the weapon," she added in a lower tone. "That colored girl told Bart about the fingerprints. He was questionin' her pretty hard, I should think." So should I.

"She told him Zaydee's fingerprints were registered in Washington, D. C."

"Was she a Public Enemy?" asked Mrs. Phillips hopefully.

"No, no, not the kind the government means, anyway. But they're trying to get all good citizens to be fingerprinted, too, and keep their records in a separate file in Washington. Bart made me do it, a year ago. It made me feel awful, just like a criminal, but Guild was learning then, and Bart wanted him to have practice. Besides, he thought it was the right thing to do."

"How 'bout Zaydee's prints?" demanded Mrs. Phillips. "Don't tell me Guild was her boy friend, too."

"Not that I know of. Zaydee was somewheres in the East, and she met this FBI man. You know, they're college graduates and meet the public well. I guess Zaydee was quite taken with him, and the colored girl said she sent in her prints to please him."

"What else she do to please him?"

"Mary," interrupted Miss Barton gently, "did the prints help your husband?"

"With several things," said Mrs. Brown, "but I'm not free to speak about them."

"Zaydee had some pretty unusual friends," went on the undaunted Mrs. Phillips, "an FBI man and a musician and a missionary and an anthropologist."

There was a sudden silence. In deference to Miss Barton or to me?

"I wouldn't put him with the rest, Addie," said Mrs. Brown. "Dr. Gordon came here to do a real job, not because of her, didn't he, Alice?"

"Yes, he did, Mary."

"Everyone thinks he's a good resident for the town," agreed Mrs. Phillips. "He belongs to Kiwanis and is friends with the Harveys and the Watsons. Of course, there was talk that he might marry Zaydee, and we thought maybe it would be a good thing for Hinchdale if he did. She might give more to local things."

I could feel Mrs. Hawks turning anxiously toward me.

"That's why we accepted her invitation to dinner," said Mrs. Brown. She added indignantly, "Bart was mad about that hairy old something-choke she gave us to eat. I was scared stiff when he began to cough so at the table. Zaydee Riggins half-killing people just to show off with foreign food."

"Well, Frank wasn't mad that night," Mrs. Phillips remembered. "He was pretty tickled with everything, the food and Zaydee putting him at her right-hand and telling him how much she respected his attitude toward liquor. So the next day I just told him about the brandy in the pudding and the sherry in the soup, and now he's off her for life. Or death,

I should say. Not that he'll have much to do about Zaydee's death. With no body to hold an inquest on or lay out or buy a casket for, there isn't much need for a coroner, an undertaker, or a furniture dealer."

"Randy Bill's folks doin' some business with Mr. Phillips?" inquired Mrs. Hawks.

Randy Bill's folks. It was the first time I had thought of his having any. He had seemed so utterly alone.

"Eyah, a brother wired Frank to go ahead and he'd be up here today. It's to be simple but good. The father is a druggist in a little town in Iowa."

Randy Bill, like John, the son of a small-town druggist—two boys going out from similar backgrounds and in the development of their careers, attracting strong, rich Zaydee Proutman. But from then on the story was different. Randy had said of John: "He has all the luck."

"I guess Rigginses wouldn't spend much on a funeral for Zaydee," suggested Mrs. Hawks.

"Zaydee's relatives," said Miss Barton, "had nothing to gain by her death and nothing to lose. Mr. Proutman provided for her parents with the understanding that they would leave town when he married Zaydee. They are both dead, I believe, and there's no one left except the aunt and her daughter. I understand that Zaydee established a small trust fund that takes care of the aunt for life, as well as she cares to live."

Her tone implied that we wouldn't talk any more about the Riggins family.

Mrs. Phillips, accepting this point of view cheerfully, tried another approach. "Does Zaydee's disappearing or dying—or whatever, make things hard for you people at the Museum, Alice?"

"Not for the moment, Addie," Miss Barton replied. "Zaydee has been away three-quarters of the time in the last ten years, and it's arranged when she's away that Jim Watson at the bank countersigns all routine checks for salaries and supplies with Alpheus Harvey. It is a standing order that doesn't have to be renewed each time she leaves Hinchdale. Alpheus will have to apply to court, I guess, before he can carry on other things legally; but, with William Henry Proutman's will as we all know it was, there will be no trouble. Zaydee's personal estate can't be settled, of course, but the Museum is all right."

The Museum was all right—with Mr. Harvey really the director at last, Miss Barton without the insults of the vulgar Zaydee, John secure to study the Holtzerman Collection to its ultimate conclusion without having to play Joseph or become Potiphar in person.

And what about Kay Ellis? I can go East, I thought, if the Sheriff lets me and if his wife doesn't accidentally crush the life out of me with her right-hand bulges. I can go East without scandal. I can say to Professor Alden, "My employer was killed. Finances in part were held up at the Museum (John will probably think that's a good explanation) and that is why I have no job." I would never have to say, it would never leak out, that I was fired because I played around with my employer's—my employer's what? Her fiancé? Her lover? Well, let's just say her boy friend. Anyway, it's something that doesn't have to be explained now, and that won't keep me from getting another job before my money is gone. John, I'm not being fair to you. Were you fair to me? I don't know. If you ask me to stay on, shall I stay? I don't know.

"It takes three years to get a person declared dead in this state," the Sheriff's wife was saying.

It will take three years, I went on thinking in sheer association, to finish the study of the Holtzerman Collection. Why wouldn't John let me help him today? He was so eager to have me finish the ape and get back to his work. That was only three days ago. Three again.

Things go in threes. Randy is dead. If Zaydee is dead, who will be the third? If the Sheriff continues to think I was Randy's accomplice, I shall be the third. If he thought so, would I be allowed on this jolly little outing? Am I here because I am above suspicion, a Daughter of the American Revolution, or am I in protective custody? It feels like the latter. But John thought it was the most respectable, the safest, way for me to spend the day. He was kind yesterday. I am kind of crowded. I am in protective custody ... I was asleep.

When I woke up they were saying, "Here's the lake."

I struggled upright, clutching my falling hat and my aching neck, and apologizing to Mrs. Brown, on whose shoulder my head had evidently been imposing.

"I was glad to see you got a cat nap," she said. "You must have lost a lot of sleep lately."

Who had said that to me? Not someone with the kind little round eyes of the Sheriff's wife. Zaydee Proutman had said it to me. That or something like it. I shivered and looked out at the lake. But it was not there. Fog lay thick to the land's edge and beyond, almost to the scrub pine by the roadside.

"It may be perfectly clear when we're through eating," somebody said. "Or we may get snow. Snow's late this year."

The car turned away from the lake and up the gravel trail to Spirit Falls. Mrs. Phillips had opened a window, and the air, smelling of damp cedar, seemed sweet and fresh after my sleep. There were two other cars in front of the red-roofed log inn, enough to have carried the rest of the Amanda Adams Barton Chapter, the group from Warrenton, and Mrs. Jim Watson's car with the other Hinchdale members and their guest, Mrs. Alpheus Harvey. Mrs. Harvey's family had missed the last boat before 1781, but as a member of the State Daughters of the War of 1812, she was invited each year to the Autumn Luncheon.

With the Amanda Adams Barton Chapter humming and purring and fluttering around the fire, there was literally no room for phantom figures of romance. Nobody was under forty, and all of them were carefully and too-tightly waved, neatly dressed in prints and dark silks and sensible shoes. Tired and cold, shivering from nervous fatigue more than the winter fog, I could have used the martini of the previous visit, but I would have been almost equally grateful for hot soup. But, like all ladies at luncheon, we ate chilly fruit cup, and for what seemed hours went on through fried chicken and gelatin salad and a lot of talk about the Christmas party for school children and the January regular meeting and, of course, the Washington's Birthday pageant.

"Lucky we wasn't planning to hold it at Zaydee Proutman's house," Mrs. Phillips shouted across the chattering table. "Mary Brown and I fixed *that* offer."

At the sound of Zaydee's name, the eyes of every woman from Warrenton looked hungrily at every woman from Hinchdale. One or two also glanced hesitantly at Miss Barton and at me, and all of them fixed hopefully on the wives of the Sheriff, the Coroner and the Director of the William Henry Proutman Museum.

Mrs. Alpheus Harvey was sitting directly opposite me across the yellow chrysanthemums and star-spangled banners in the center of the luncheon table. She was a thin, tall woman with a long upper lip, who always seemed to be scuttling around town alone. She and Mrs. Hawks were members of the small Primitive Methodist chapel, the others of the steepled Community Church. I had never before met her, and her greeting today had been vague and frightened. At the mention of Zaydee Proutman, and with all faces now turned to hers, she nervously licked at the long lip, and her pale green eyes wavered in the terror of the very shy.

The Daughters of the American Revolution were politely mouthing, "Yes, indeed. Of course. Better so"; but their eyes were begging, pleading: Tell us. Tell us all about murder.

And in response, the robust Mrs. Phillips said, "She was thrown over the cliff just three miles from here."

They gasped. They glowed. A lady sucked in her coffee in forgetful sound. This was exciting.

"Could we ..." someone began. "Do you suppose ..." went on another. "As near as that ..." a third was almost suggesting, and Mrs. Phillips finished it, "How about it, girls, shall we drive out and view the scene of the crime?"

There was a gasp and hesitation. Did they really want to? Ought they?

Then one voice was sure.

"I want to go," said Mrs. Alpheus Harvey. Her cheeks were flushed, the hand holding her bead bag trembling.

"Isn't somebody on guard? Will they let us near?" The questions were aimed at Mrs. Brown and, fluttered, she said, "Well, I think Mr. Lawson from the Inn is out there, acting as Bart's deputy. I guess he'd let us pretty near if I asked him."

"Let's all go." More than one said it, and there was a movement toward coats.

I can't, I thought. I can't go there. Not where Randy Bill and Zaydee Proutman died; not where two people I know met violent death. Not to that place of hate and murder where I was once happy. I looked at Miss Barton, and she came over to me at once.

"You must go," she said. "It will not be wise to let Mrs. Brown see you hang back. I am sorry that our Chapter wishes to do anything so ill-bred."

I nodded agreement with it all and turned away to get my coat. Mrs. Hawks was holding it. "Go into the kitchen a minute," she said. "My cousin Sigrid Lawson has something she wants to say to you."

I went through the swing door where Mrs. Lawson, a flushed blond, was waiting anxiously. "Listen, Miss Ellis, I hate to bother you, but there's a favor I want to ask you. Have you told the Sheriff you were out here having dinner Wednesday night?"

"No," I said. "He didn't ask me."

"Well, he didn't ask us about people out here, and we didn't tell him, see? And we forgot to ask you to register, and we don't want to get mixed up in this anyway."

"Of course," I said. "But neither Dr. Gordon nor I had anything to do with it."

"No, no. I know you aren't that kind of people, but we don't want a reputation for the house. We don't want any investigation."

"I don't see," I said, "that it makes much difference whether we mention it or not. You had already told a friend of Mrs. Proutman's that we were here—as you were perfectly free to do."

"Mrs. Garrett." Mrs. Lawson's face grew redder. "How'd you ... Excuse me, would you mind telling me how you knew that?"

"From Mrs. Proutman. Why shouldn't Mrs. Garrett tell the Sheriff, too?"

"Oh, no, Miss Ellis." Mrs. Lawson twisted her handkerchief between her fingers. "She won't tell anybody."

"Why not?" What was this all about? I wondered. "She was a friend of Mrs. Proutman's. I should think Mrs. Garrett would tell anything that might help to find the person who killed her. However mistaken she might be."

I thought of what she might have added to Brown's original suspicion of me. So it was protective custody.

"No, no," Mrs. Lawson repeated, "she won't. She won't do a thing. She's worse afraid of being mixed up in this than Lawson and I are. She don't want her husband to know she was ever here. The girl that works for her called me today and told me as soon as she heard about Mrs. Proutman being killed out near here, she pulled a nervous breakdown and left for Florida this morning."

"Oh," I said, "so that's it."

"Miss Ellis, please." She grabbed my arm with hands that had worked hard. "We've never done a thing like that before, but business has been awful bad, and so that Thursday night we let them stay—her and her friend. But the inn isn't that kind of a place. We don't want it to get known. We want just nice people here—like you and Dr. Gordon—and run a decent place. If the Sheriff once started investigating us ..." Her words tumbled on and on.

The logic seemed to be that if you harbored murderers, you might easily take in breakers of the next commandment or vice versa. But from all her fog, one thing emerged with comforting clarity: neither she nor her husband nor Mrs. Evelyn Garrett would tell Sheriff Brown that John Gordon and I had taken the way to Lovers' Point three nights before the death of Zaydee Proutman and Randy Bill.

So I reassured her and even suggested that John and I would come again to dine with her in the spring and, with the first relief of the day, went out to visit the scene of the crime.

The Scene of the Crime—so it was capitalized on the excited faces of the fourteen Daughters. Even Miss Barton looked a little eager. The general aspect was of fourteen tongues hanging out, although only the tip of Mrs. Harvey's was actually visible. I felt more than a little sick, and the deep thank-you-marms in the gravel road combined with the way I always feel after carrots and marshmallows sunk in lime jello.

And then the road came out on the lake. The fog had rolled far back to the cold horizon, and I saw the great expanse of stormy water and felt the breeze and knew that only to the hypocritical Easterner did the Great Lake lack the vast freedom of the sea. A mile or more ahead, a rocky cape sprang out from the shore, proud with the white shaft of a lighthouse. Nearer to us ran a shorter promontory with a deep graceful curve, faced with jagged cliffs. Above the cliffs a man stood out against the sky.

"That must be Lawson," said Mrs. Brown and ended the beauty for me.

The cars bumped out along the narrow trail, hardly a road, between ground pine and granite. I could see now ahead the limbs of the fallen pine and the man running, waving his arms to stop us.

"I'm not real sure whether Bart would like our coming here," murmured Mrs. Brown.

"Oh, he wouldn't mind, Mary," Mrs. Phillips assured her. "We're a kind of committee of responsible constituents, aren't we, come out to admire his work?"

"I … guess so," said Mrs. Brown. "Good afternoon, Mr. Lawson. We'd like to get out a little and look around."

"I'm not supposed to let anybody on the Point, Mrs. Brown." Lanky Mr. Lawson bore the perplexed look of mine host who is most reluctantly deputized by his Sheriff, and very cold to boot. "Not anybody at all. Unless you've got a note maybe from the Sheriff?"

"Mary Brown," exclaimed the ready Mrs. Phillips, "so that's the paper you were fussing about leaving on the table back at the Inn. Shall I run you back to get it?" She turned and stared hard at Mrs. Brown's round little face. "I don't know as I can turn around now. The other cars are right behind me."

"Well, if you had a note …" I am sure Mr. Lawson did not believe her, but it offered an escape from insult to his patrons.

Miss Barton sat rigid, and Mrs. Hawks was poking me in the ribs with delight and vigor. Mrs. Phillips was already opening the door of the car. "All right, girls," she called to the following group, and got out.

But it was not Mrs. Phillips who first reached the scene of the tragedy. Scuttling ahead of them all, Mrs. Harvey came to the fallen pine and passed beyond, where torn and matted bushes lay over the edge of the cliff. I could see the water seething white far below her and beating against the rock. Not far behind her, the other thirteen straggled and bunched. Only I remained near the cars, trying not to see the broken pieces of gray hood and red leather seats, the splintered tree trunk uprooted from the shallow soil. I saw the women's arms waving and pointing, and Lawson pointing in reply, and the wind brought me occasional words. They formed a thicker cluster around the broken bushes, and Lawson's arm held up to them a long pointed stick with which he had apparently been searching the ground. I turned toward the lighthouse, the clean gray eternity of the water, and tried to lose everything else.

"Kay Ellis, come, come quick," I heard someone shouting—Mrs. Hawks, I think. I ran forward toward the group, expecting to see that someone had gone over into that shattering sea. It seemed most probably Mrs. Harvey.

They were standing in a disorderly semicircle around Lawson, and no one was looking over the cliff. They were all looking at his outstretched palm on which lay a crushed, blackened bit of metal.

"What is it? What is it?" they were chorusing.

I looked again, saw the beaded, embossed edge, a tiny broken clasp, and I knew.

"It's silver," Mrs. Phillips said, "a piece of silver jewelry."

"It's an earring." I saw the wild light in Mrs. Harvey's eye. "It's one of Zaydee Proutman's Mexican earrings. Now I believe that she's dead."

Miss Barton turned to me. "Do you recognize it, Miss Ellis?" she asked.

"Yes." They were all looking at me. "She wore them on Saturday. I heard her maid tell the Sheriff. How— Where did you find it?"

"We were all standing around here," Mrs. Phillips said, "and Mr. Lawson was just showing some of us how he poked around, going over and over the ground for blood on the moss or hair or other clues. And wedged down between two little chinks in that rock where they think Randy threw her over, there was this."

"Almost right under my foot." Mrs. Jim Watson was shaken.

"I've been over that place a dozen times, I swear," declared Lawson, "but it was crushed and dulled and just about like the rock. And," he continued, "that's about what happened to Anderson when he found the doll."

"The doll?"

"Listen, I can't talk about this. This is a crime case. This is murder."

"I guess," said Mrs. Brown nervously, "we'd better be going. I'll tell Barton about your finding Zaydee's earring. He'll be real pleased."

With which conventional if inappropriate speech, the Amanda Adams Barton Chapter climbed into their cars. They no longer looked like ghouls on the scent of blood. That broken bit of junk jewelry had brought the reality of death to them at last. I do not think that anyone in our car spoke during the drive home. Long before we reached Hinchdale, the snow began to fall.

CHAPTER XV

By Saturday morning the snow covering William Henry Proutman Park was thin and grimy, and so was I. A four-day struggle with Mrs. Hawks's soft coal had done it to us both. Mrs. Hawks had caught cold on Lovers' Point and taken to her bed. I had done my best with her furnace, the quality of my performance being just what those words usually imply.

Through long hours of storm, I had alternated between the grimy basement and Mrs. Hawks's watching post, often wondering, as I looked out on empty whiteness, how it must seem to Isabelle alone in the Proutman house. I hoped that Esquire managed to struggle out in the evenings to see her.

I had only one visitor, and that in answer to my call. On Thursday night the fire went out, apparently forever, and I telephoned to John. It had seemed perfectly natural when I gave the number, but, waiting for him to answer, the practical reason got all clouded up with my wanting to see him and his very probably not caring if he ever saw me. So I said with heavy humor:

"Dr. Gordon, I've heard you have a neat hand with a furnace."

After silence he rapped out, "What have you got on your mind?"

I stammered hastily and explained.

In a few minutes he was stamping in snow and cold, and being technical and clear about the problems of a central heating system that was practically a museum piece.

After we had scrubbed off soot together at the kitchen sink, things were more natural. I made coffee and John sat down on the kitchen stool to wait till the fire was surely going. I told him about my talk with Mrs. Lawson.

"It's a break," he said, not smiling, "a real break for both of us. You haven't had many in this town, have you, Kay?"

"One or two," I said, but he didn't return my smile, and I went on hastily. "At least it will be easier to explain my return to Professor Alden, if he reads the papers."

Wouldn't he say he wanted me to stay, that he was sorry, that he would miss me?

He said, "I've brought along these to show you. The joke is rather on us."

He spread the newspaper pages out on the kitchen table, and we bent over them together. And they were a surprise. For, unlike our little local world, Zaydee Proutman was in every account a minor figure. The tragedy was focused on Randy Bill. Randy, who for us existed only as an appendage to Zaydee, owed his newspaper space largely to a very different connection. He had been, at the time Zaydee spied him, accompanist for Giolotti, one of the world's great singers, and it was in this role that he appeared in most accounts. The *New York Times* of Tuesday morning, to a dignified and correct outline of the case, added:

Three years ago in his first and only New York concert in the Carnegie Chamber Music Hall, he was considered by critics to be unusually endowed with vibrant musical understanding, combined with a technique which, while in need of further development, already placed him far beyond the stage of mere promise.

To other journals Randy was rejected suitor, alleged murderer, suicide, accident victim, recently unemployed. There were smeared, theatrical pictures in evening dress.

"John, it's just as he said; she ruined his life."

"I talked to the AP man from Chicago," was John's answer. "He says there won't be much more about it. The discarded lover theme is always good for something, but not too much, because there's sure to be another in a day or two. And Zaydee wasn't well-known nor rich enough to make a lot of copy. Also, the papers have been asked to soft-pedal Randy's connection with Giolotti, who has just signed a Hollywood contract."

There were, he explained further, to be syndicated stories in the Sunday magazines. Young musical genius, protégé of the great Giolotti, gives up all for rich older beauty who casts him off. Murder and suicide from heartbreak. Pictures of Randy, of Giolotti, of Zaydee (smaller), of the Lake, and (very small) of Sheriff Barton Brown, who solves crime by sturdy intellect and the latest scientific methods now available in the most remote districts of our enlightened country.

The sob sister, who was a gentleman of middle age, and the AP correspondent had left town, apparently with no interest in visiting the Museum they listed among the civic enterprises of the late Zaydee's late husband, between the bank and the park. Yes, it was all rather a grim joke on us.

"The Sheriff didn't tell them about me? That I was his chief suspect, next to Randy?"

John put the papers back in his pocket and rose to go.

"No, he's quite pleased, I hear, with the angle the papers have given the whole thing. His name is in every account, and Mrs. Watson tells me she met Mrs. Brown in the dime store, buying a scrap book. I think the whole thing will be settled in a day or two. He never really had any evidence of conspiracy between you and Bill."

"He thought he did. And so did you. Didn't you?"

He came back to the table. "For God's sake, Kay, no. Never for one minute did I think you had the slightest connection with the whole dirty business."

"But you did." My misery would not yield to the white, stricken face. "Here in this house, last Monday afternoon. You demanded what there was between me and Randy Bill."

"I knew it was not murder," he said. "This isn't the time for personal feelings, but if the truth will help you at all, I was—jealous."

His arms around me and his kisses seemed all the help I would need, but after he had gone I realized that he had said nothing about my returning to work at the Proutman Museum.

When the summons came for me to appear there on Saturday morning, it was issued by Sheriff Brown. Not a legal document, just a curt word by telephone, telling me to be there in half an hour.

I was there, we were all there again in the director's office. The desk was cleared of all Alpheus Harvey's impedimenta, including the weasel, and on heavy brown paper were laid out the exhibits. There was the umbrella with the ape's heavy grinning head still not quite cleaned of blood, the bobby pins, the naked doll, the crushed earring. A pile of what looked like laboratory reports, photographs with water in the background and some horrible fragments to the fore, and a white card to which was fixed clotted strands of henna-red hair.

We sat around this feast, Alpheus, John, Miss Barton, Esquire and Isabelle, Jensen and I; and at the festive board beamed Sheriff Brown. It was evident that a little publicity had turned his bald head almost as pink as his mustache.

"On the evening of Saturday, November 4," he began in a sepulchral voice, "at six o'clock or shortly thereafter, Mrs. Zaydee Proutman disappeared."

No one seemed much interested. After all, it was only a week ago, and we had every reason to remember.

Why did Zaydee Proutman disappear? The Sheriff explored all possibilities, and we explored them with him. Her cars, the common carriers, the descriptions sent out on the teletype of fourteen states, his examination of her correspondence for clues to a sudden departure (there were none, but he must have had fun if she had many letters similar to the one from the Swedish attaché).

Nothing of her wardrobe was missing except the clothes she had worn when she departed on Rogers's delivery truck. She had drawn no extraordinary sums from the bank. Nothing pointed to a planned departure or to anyone outside the immediate environment who might be involved in it for good or ill. The answer, then, the motive, the means and the opportunity must be found in Hinchdale.

"That last afternoon"—Barton Brown warmed to his subject—"Mrs. Proutman came here to the Museum to do a couple of things. She wanted the keys to the car Randy Bill claimed was his. And she wanted to—ahem—do some business with Miss Ellis."

Motive for Miss Ellis, I thought. Also for Mr. Bill.

"Well, she got both jobs done before 5:45 P.M. when you all began going home for the night. Jensen, I guess you went out a little earlier. Then, between 5:45 and 5:58, Miss Ellis, Mr. Harvey, Williams and Miss Barton left separately. Mrs. Proutman was alone right here in this room. Dr. Gordon, you were in the basement. You say you heard the front door close again about six o'clock and a car drive away from in front."

"I did," John was definite.

"Now, none of you good people are the kind that go around committing crimes. And only one of you had a motive for killing Zaydee Proutman."

"None of us had," said Miss Alice Barton.

"But this Randy Bill. He was a drunkard who never did a good day's work in his life. He'd been threatening all day to finish off Zaydee. And he had plenty of time to get to the Museum before she came out at six o'clock.

"We know he got here. His fingerprints were on some of the pieces of that glass case. Lucky for us, Esquire had washed it off that afternoon. There were cuts from the glass on Bill's hand. We only found one hand.

"So when Zaydee came out the door carrying this"—the Sheriff raised the ape-head umbrella from the desk—"she met Randy Bill carrying this. Only it looked fancier then." He picked up and replaced the dirty naked doll.

Isabelle covered trembling lips with her hand. Esquire bent close, whispering, "Never mind, honey."

"Nothing to be upset about, Isabelle," Brown assured her. "You've been a real help to me. If you hadn't told me Zaydee still was talking about her weakness for Bill, it would have been hard to believe she got into the car and drove away with him that night. It's not hard to explain why they drove out to Lovers' Point. Lawsons at Spirit Falls say they used to park out there pretty regular a while back. I guess I don't have to tell you what we found out there on the following Monday morning."

And none of us, I was sure, wanted to hear it again. Broken bushes, burned car, bits of Randy Bill. And the exhibits spread out before us.

"There was one clear set of fingerprints on the umbrella"—the Sheriff brandished it—"right here under the handle. They were Zaydee's, all right. Her hair, too. Matched what we found on the brushes out to her house. Anybody that used this for a weapon wouldn't leave prints. He'd grab it here around the cloth."

"Wouldn't it take a pretty hefty feller to knock anybody out with that thing?" Jensen wanted to know.

"Nope," said the Sheriff. "That ivory handle is real heavy. It's hardly got a dent even now. Randy Bill could have done it all right.

"And it seems pretty clear he did. We don't know just what happened. We never will. If he murdered Zaydee, he may have deliberately driven his car into the tree to commit suicide. Or he may have hit it by accident. Anyway, he died there at eight o'clock or soon after, and left behind the weapon used to knock out Mrs. Proutman."

I drew a deep breath. I was free? Barton Brown was looking at me hard.

"Randy Bill could have had help," he said.

"Not," I murmured, "from me."

"You were the person he confided in, Miss Ellis," he reminded me. "If

Mrs. Proutman was killed in Hinchdale and then put into the car—on the Museum steps, for instance—you had the opportunity. No one actually saw you between six-thirty and eight-thirty that night. You had a motive. I thought for a while you had two."

I stared straight at his red mustache. Everything else in the room was a waving background.

"Miss Ellis, you were a stranger in town. We hear a lot of talk in a place the size of Hinchdale. You're a young girl, and you were working for a young man. You could have a reason for hating Zaydee Proutman that would ride right along with Randy Bill's."

Even the mustache was fading before my eyes.

"As I say, they talk a lot in this town. Mostly, it does harm. This time it did somebody some good. Because the most respected people in Hinchdale agree that you and Dr. Gordon have never had anything to do with each other outside working hours. Unless," he grinned, "you count one trip to the movies."

The most respected people—Miss Alice Barton, Mrs. Barton Brown, and the rest of the D.A.R. Mrs. Hawks, who would lie for me and for the Lawsons. Zaydee Proutman had been a better detective.

"And," he added, "there was the circumstantial evidence of the time you must have spent packing."

Things were clearing. I could see Isabelle's hopeful look, Miss Alice's triumphant smile, the black lock fallen across John's bent face.

"The case," said Sheriff Brown slowly, "is closed. Closed unless Zaydee Proutman returns. Or unless her body is recovered from the Great Lake, which never gives up its dead. Probable death by misadventure."

He had finished. His reasoning seemed to me as full of holes as a sieve, yet was probably the true as well as the simplest solution. Evil had destroyed evil, and all the good people would vote for the good, smart Sheriff who had tracked down the truth so quickly.

I was free to leave Hinchdale now, but since it was again Saturday afternoon, there would have to follow another long weekend until trains began to run and banks opened on Monday morning. I sat on the hard chair, looking at the floor. Around me I could hear sounds of people rising, and then Mr. Harvey's voice in my ear. "Come into the library, please."

He closed the door and said, "I will not keep you a moment longer than necessary. Miss Ellis, as director of the Proutman Museum, I ask you to remain on our staff at the salary originally offered, that is, one hundred and fifty dollars a month."

I looked at him, and then he was a blur through tears. "Come, come," he said. "You have gone through a great deal. This isn't anything."

"It's—it's so ... decent of you."

"Well, you'll accept, won't you?"

I started to say yes, and then I remembered, "Will Dr. Gordon agree?"

"Of course. Why not?"

"Does he know you're asking me to stay?"

"Of course," he snapped. "Good night. We'll be glad to see you back at work on Monday."

It was Saturday night, the eleventh of November. At the Harvey home a special extra session of anagrams was being held with Dr. Gordon and Miss Alice Barton. Jensen, sitting in his kitchen, drank coffee and told his recently returned wife about how Zaydee Riggins had broken things for the last time. Esquire Williams and Isabelle borrowed Dr. Gordon's car and drove over to Warrenton and got married, and Kay Ellis ate her dinner at the Greasy Spoon and came home and unpacked her trunk.

CHAPTER XVI

When I arrived at the laboratory on Monday, the bridegroom was standing before his broom and coat closet in the basement passage, taking off his overcoat. He explained, beaming at my congratulations, that he and Isabelle had just driven back from his cousin's house near Warrenton.

"I think you've got a very lovely wife," I said shaking hands.

"Yes, I have, Miss Ellis." His smile was solemn. "Isabelle could've married lots of men with long cars and sharp clothes. It's kinda funny, her wantin' me."

In his best suit of oxford gray and his smart bright tie, Esquire did not look unworthy of his more worldly wife, and I told him so.

"Thank you, Miss Ellis, thank you, thank ..." His tone suddenly became absent. He had been feeling through the side pockets of his suit coat before taking it off, man-fashion, and his fingers seemed to have encountered something surprising.

The laboratory looked just the same—not the same as it had on that last terrible evening, but as it had on my first morning in Hinchdale. The clothes boiler was gone, and the smell was gone. The room once more was dedicated to the Holtzerman Collection. And almost as soon as my hat was off, work was under way, for John, coming in from his office with his arms full of instruments, announced that we were now going to fall to and measure every single skeleton.

It was nice to get back to the bones, clean bones without resistant cartilage or slimy tendons. Our recent encounter with double death in no way lessened my pleasure in the work; at no point in the investigation had it been suggested that either Randy or Zaydee ever had a bone.

As for my feeling toward John Gordon, I was back on the old footing of work and work only that had been broken ten days ago. He had telephoned to me on Saturday evening, saying briefly, "Kay, I'm glad about the Museum arrangement," and after the Sheriff's suggestion that only our mutual indifference cleared me of suspicion, it seemed wise to support the opinion of Mrs. Watson and Mrs. Hawks (real or not) for some time to come. The ugliness and fear of the last week hadn't left room for many other emotions.

I don't know how John felt; I just know how he worked. Quietly, with economy of motion, no extra word, as if he were trying to make up for something lost, something more than time. For the self-respect he had given up to Zaydee's service? To satisfy his professional pride? But had he really given up anything? I didn't think it was the loss of Zaydee herself.

Toward noon, Mr. Harvey, looking normally suspicious and yellow-blue, interrupted us and took Dr. Gordon into the office. A few moments later they were back, and the director, with a glance that accused me of listening at the keyhole—apparently in my astral body—went quickly upstairs. John, sitting down again at the work table, spoke for the first time in a relaxed voice. He seemed amused and completely natural.

"Should you mind telling me what Alpheus did about your salary, Kay?"

I told him about the restored figure.

"Good for the old boy. That's exactly like him. He isn't any too fond of having young women around the Museum. He thinks they're natural trouble-breeders, but he's done what he thinks is right. And now he's done the same thing to me, only in reverse. I have just been informed that my salary is to be reduced each month to the extent of eighty-eight dollars and thirty-three cents."

"Why on earth?"

"Because he feels that for what he calls 'er ... personal reasons' my wages were set too high. As yours were cut too low. He's not only right, he's damned right, this time. He's done a lot of writing around to museums and universities this fall, and he says, and correctly, that my pay was out of line. To be honest, it still is. Good old Alpheus, my hero; he never lets me down."

"Meaning you can always count on him to be himself?"

"That's it."

Then I said a foolish thing. "John, can you count on me?"

The strain came back into his face and into his voice. "If I can count on you for the kind of teamwork we've had this morning, we'll be getting some place fast."

So we went on until, hungry and tired, I reminded him that it was long past lunch hour. "What," I asked as I gathered up my purse and gloves, "did you do with the clothes boiler?"

"I returned it," he said shortly.

"Returned it to?"

"To the Proutman house. I kept knocking into the blasted thing. I was sick of seeing it around, so I took it out in my car and hunted for the town dump. Which I didn't find. I didn't want to lug it back, so I took it out to Lake Laurel and left it on the back porch."

"That was smart," I said with my back to him as I reached for hat and coat. "Considering Mrs. Proutman's practical uses for old objects, her ghost might have come back to haunt you if you'd thrown that boiler away."

I turned around, and he had gone into his office and shut the door. It seemed a just comment on bad taste. All through lunch and errands, I had twinges of shame. I was feeling that if Zaydee Proutman's shade returned, it would be to hound and haunt me out of the Museum, as I entered that most mundane of institutions, the dime store.

And there she was. I saw Zaydee Proutman. The deep rich color of her hair, the deep strong curves of her body in marigold wool, the handsome nose, the chin a little weak, a little old. A long white hand with fingernails stained henna was extended across the counter. She was holding a card of bronze bobby pins.

CHAPTER XVII

She was not a ghost. In my black whirling mind, that was the one clear thing. Zaydee Proutman was alive. And now it would all begin again—the fear and uncertainty, lost jobs, lost love, violence, and all that hate. Irrationally but just as vividly I saw it all end, too. For if Zaydee Proutman lived again, Zaydee Proutman would have to die again. Around me I smelled the miasma of oil cloth, cheap perfume, and varnish which is the dime store, as I stared and stared at the profile of that woman and realized how gladly I had believed her dead.

I don't know how long it was before she spoke, but it was before she turned and saw me. The voice prepared me a little, but not enough. It was loud, but thinner than I had expected, nasal and undernourished in comparison with the brazen clang or the honeyed flow we knew too well in the Proutman Museum. She said, "These all you got?" and looked toward the counter where I leaned for support.

Her eyes were not deep brown beneath the stiffly blackened lashes but a watery blue, eyes that looked at me without recognition. There was no reason why she should have recognized me. For I had never seen her before. She was not Zaydee Proutman.

Everything inside me seemed to turn completely over and right itself once more. With returning sanity I knew who she was. Who she was and what she was.

"'Sall we got, Burl," the thin little salesgirl told her, and in the righteous way she shifted the gum beneath her acned cheek, she managed to convey all the scorn of the working girl for the village prostitute.

Beryl Riggins, with the beaded lashes and crudely brushed eyeshadow, in front of whose house Randy Bill's death car had stood all night; Beryl, daughter of "old lady Riggins, her that was sister to Zaydee's mother and married Riggins's brother," and to whom her double cousin had given her marigold wool dress. She was younger than Zaydee, by perhaps ten harder years that had left her softer or, rather, flabbier. And however hypothetical Zaydee Proutman's selection of hair fastening might be, there was no doubt that Beryl used that variety of bronze bobby pin so emphasized by Sheriff Brown. While I still sagged weakly against the next counter, she bought the only two cards remaining in stock, pulled on the shabby beaver-cloth coat that had hung on her arm, and went out of the store. Too exhausted by emotional shock to remember my own intended purchases, I dragged out after her and back to the Museum.

I suppose it was the effect of the highly emotional moment that freed from my unconscious the memory of the first morning I entered the Museum after the murder. Whatever the cause, without conscious plan I found myself crossing the darkened Corset Room in the direction from which, on the fatal morning, I had caught the illusion of faintly gleaming metal. I was standing beside a wax lady, my hand wandering vaguely among the ruffles of her bodice, much as one moves in a dream.

With all the sick horror of too sharp awakening I heard: "What are you doing here, Miss Ellis?"

The voice, querulous and low, was Mr. Harvey's, and the gleam I had not found on the dummy's clothes was playing weirdly on his pince-nez. My gasp was more like a small squeal.

"Nothing," I said inanely.

"That material is extremely delicate," he said. "No one is supposed to touch it. Have you ever done so before?"

"Oh, no, Mr. Harvey, never."

"Are you sure?"

"Of course. Is it torn or anything?"

"No," he said, and his tone was something I could not understand. "It is not torn." It was as if he thought I should read some meaning into the commonplace statement.

"I assure you I won't come near the figure again," I said. "I don't know why I did it now, really."

At the moment I didn't, but I was sure that Mr. Harvey believed I had a motive of the most sinister. Of course he had always felt that way about me, more or less.

At the foot of the basement stairs I ran against a chair outside Esquire's broom closet. Esquire was on the chair, leaning into the closet and poking something far back on the shelf.

"Ouch," I said, rubbing my insulted flank. "Whatever are you doing? Hiding the family jewels?"

"'Fore the Lord, Miss," he began, looking down at me, and his hands, now free from their task, were trembling, "you sure did scare me."

"You did the same to me," I said, but it wasn't true. I had been frightened, that day, but not by Esquire. He looked as I had felt when I saw the ghost of Zaydee Proutman.

First I, then Alpheus Harvey, now Esquire all seemed to be going mad on this day of return to normality. Who next?

Obviously not Miss Barton, who was talking cheerfully to John at my laboratory table.

"Come in," she said, "and close the door. We are planning a little wedding gift for Esquire and Isabelle. Isn't it nice they are married? I understand they have wished to do so for some time, but Mrs. Proutman did not approve, and had told Esquire she would dismiss both of them at once if they did so."

I did not look at John. I wondered if he had been told the same thing. Probably not. Probably John hadn't wanted to get married to—well, to anybody. Not even to Zaydee.

So we talked about dishes versus Community Plate. After she had gone, the long afternoon of comforting routine steadied me, and I thought all my feeling of queerness was over.

But at night, lying under the depression of Mrs. Hawks's padded patchwork, it all came back to me. When I closed my eyes there stretched across dull background those long, henna-tipped fingers of Beryl's, holding out the card of hair pins—pins like those I had once found with relief were the only occupants of Randy Bill's car, pins I had seen with horror lying beside the blood-stained umbrella and the burned and naked doll. Beryl's pins, not Zaydee Proutman's. Why should that thought make me shudder in the cold sheets? I had always been scornful of the Sheriff's regard for the bobby pins as evidence; as a matter of fact, hadn't I said to myself in the course of his summary of the crime that it was as full of holes as a sieve? And added that it was, in spite of this, true? Evil had destroyed evil; but in Hinchdale, Beryl was evil, too. She represented the Social Evil, probably the Necessary

Evil with which sheriffs elected by the people do not like to grapple.

If you were really looking for an accessory to the murder of Zaydee Proutman, if you believed that Randy Bill might have had an accomplice, wouldn't Beryl Riggins fit the roles better than Kay Ellis? She knew Randy. She had obvious reasons for hating the cousin whose luck had exceeded her own, and whose family feeling was expressed in handing down clothes. If she happened to be fond of Randy and aware that his association with her was a bitter substitute for Zaydee, her jealousy and hatred could have been great indeed. And supposing that, in spite of Miss Barton's contrary statement, Beryl thought that she or her mother were Zaydee's heirs? Might she not have urged on broken Randy, infuriated him to action, even if she had not assisted in the actual murder? According to Jensen, Beryl had been at home with him and her mother at the fatal hour of eight on Saturday night, the fourth, and therefore could not have been present when Zaydee's body was pushed over the cliff. That is, if Jensen was telling the truth.

If Jensen was telling the truth. On that rested the Sheriff's entire case: that we were all telling the truth, all the Good People—Mr. Harvey, Miss Barton, John Gordon, Esquire, Isabelle, and I. If any of us had lied, any of us could have been implicated in the crime or had some knowledge or suspicion of it. That is, anyone but me.

So why pick on Jensen's testimony? He was less concerned with the Museum's troubles than any of us and had for Zaydee a more superficial aversion which he got out of his system periodically. Nor was Beryl's problematical part in Randy's violent act really important, even if proved. The bobby pins were no more a clue to her than they had been to Zaydee; and, whoever the loser, they had been left in the car some twenty-four hours before the murder.

What a flimsy tower of black nonsense I had built from my fright in the dime store. Thank heaven I had toppled it now and could go to sleep.

I couldn't, of course. I had dismissed Beryl Riggins from my mind, I had decided Jensen told the truth, but I could not get rid of the dreadful possibility that someone had lied and that his lie filled the holes in the Sheriff's sieve.

For, contrary to the Sheriff's statement, the staff members of the William Henry Proutman Museum did have motives for killing their one-woman board of trustees, and they could all have lied about the time they left the Museum. Everyone had an alibi for eight o'clock, but would that alibi stand?

Fuzzy in the head after the night my imagination had given me, I sat by John's side the next morning and stared out the door at Esquire's broom closet. Esquire, who wanted to marry Isabelle and keep his job. Hard pressed, what would he do? I would guess that, with the patience of despair forced on generations of his people, he would simply have taken it. But did I really know?

"Kay, wake up." John's tone struck. "You're recording pelvis measurements in the column for foot bones."

Why was Esquire frightened when I found him rummaging on the shelf of his broom closet? Why had he almost ordered me out of the Corset Room when, on the morning of the investigation, I had gone to hunt for the metal gleam? Why had he so hastily married Isabelle? Because a wife, loving and loyal as Isabelle was, would never testify against her fleecy lamb?

His wool shining with hymeneal oil, Esquire padded into the room with his brush. He shook his head ruefully at the trays piled with skeletons. Which was what he always had done.

"Since you're more interested in watching Esquire's work than mine," said John, with mean justice, "I'm quitting until after lunch."

I went out of the laboratory fast, but not to lunch. Shivering along Broadway with nerves and cold, I tried to shake off this new obsession. I didn't want Esquire to have anything to do with Randy and his murder. He was too decent.

Well, why did anyone but Randy have to be involved? The Sheriff had considered everyone and eliminated them. Why can't you? Are you smarter than the Sheriff?

The answer could be yes.

Esquire said he left the Museum immediately after Alpheus Harvey, at about 5:48 P.M. on Saturday night, a few minutes before he was followed by Miss Barton. He was seen in the chain grocery between 6:00 and 6:15, and at 8 P.M. Isabelle said he was at the house on Lake Laurel. It wasn't much of an alibi for a man who had a key to the Proutman Museum and a motive for killing Zaydee. He could have gone back to the Museum after everyone but John had left—everyone except Zaydee—and killed or stunned her with her umbrella. Or he could have met Randy and Zaydee outside the Museum and somehow mixed in their quarrel in the dark and empty street, made noisy by the rain. Then he could have helped Randy Bill to dispose of the body and the weapon at the Lake and escaped injury in the accident, as the Sheriff had suggested I had done. In that case, of course, he hadn't reached Mrs. Proutman's house until long past eight o'clock, but Isabelle could have lied for him.

But part of this involved time schedule was contradicted by John Gordon's statement that he had heard the front door of the Museum close for the last time at six o'clock, at which time Esquire was seen in the Cash-and-Carry Store. Only did it really close after Zaydee Proutman? And was John's watch exactly right? It wasn't, I remembered, a good watch, nor was he very particular about setting it. And everyone had left within ten or twelve minutes of the hour. He had said a car drove away almost at once. But whose car? It need not have been Zaydee and Randy. Their car, I knew, was gone at six-thirty, but it could easily have been driven off later than six while John was in the furnace room.

I had to get back to the broom closet and see what Esquire had plowed under.

There was no one in the laboratory. Dragging a chair to the closet, I mounted and peered along the shelf. It held the usual conglomerate of such places, rather neater than usual—ammonia bottles, oil cans, furniture polish and scrub brushes, with rags and rubber sponges piled in the farthest corner. I was at this at once, fingers digging under the pile, and was just closing over some alien substance when I heard feet descending the stairs. There was no escape, for the stairs were short. For a horrible moment I wondered what would be the result of being discovered by a murderer, unearthing the evidence.

It was not, however, Esquire, but John Gordon who came blindly down the stairs and into my chair, just as I had struck Esquire's on the previous day. In my relief, I laughed, thereby contributing as much as the bruise to the flow of minor profanity from the victim, all centering about why the this-and-that I was poking into places where I didn't belong. I suppose I looked much as Esquire had in the same position, if not the same situation; but I was not going to descend without seeing the object my fingers held beneath the rags. Mumbling something about typewriter oil, I buried my head in the closet and pulled out close to my eyes the little metal links I had almost identified. Even in the dim light, it was obvious what that circle of miniature sombreros formed. It was a bracelet, part of the set of Mexican junk jewelry that Zaydee Proutman had worn on the day of her death.

Poking it back under the rags, I got down in a hurry.

"You've forgotten the oil," said John Gordon. He was holding the can from my typewriter table. "Don't bother to climb up there again. This is full." He was quite justified in looking as unpleasant as he did.

And after all, when I thought it over that night, the Mexican bracelet didn't clear up a thing; it didn't accuse Esquire and it didn't absolve him of implication in the murder. For, try as I would, I could not see it in my remembered image of Zaydee Proutman on that last afternoon. I merely saw her with a lot of that cheap stuff hanging about her and over the gold tissue blouse. It was as it had been when Barton Brown asked me where I had last seen the umbrella. Was it in Zaydee's hand as she climbed the basement stairs with Alpheus Harvey? Was the bracelet on the wrist that had raised the umbrella toward me in the laboratory? Or on the other hand, which I had later seen smoothing her heavy red hair?

I didn't know. It could have been. I was sure, however, that a bracelet had not been included in the list of ornaments I had made for the Sheriff from Isabelle's dictation. Of course, if she knew that it had come off in a struggle, that it was in Esquire's possession, she would have omitted it. But the bracelet was not broken, and it rather seemed that Esquire had not confided its location to his wife. Nor did it appear that I had solved the mystery of the gleam in the Corset Room which Esquire had not wished me to investigate.

For who would ever place for safekeeping a small link bracelet on the sloping bosom of an Edwardian dummy? Only one thing, then, had been made certain by my prowling: Esquire Williams was hiding some knowledge, suspicion, or fear along with Zaydee Proutman's Mexican bracelet.

CHAPTER XVIII

That year, winter came down early on the prairies. It's a sentence in every novel of the sturdy pioneers, and it ran through my chilly mind as I crossed bleak Broadway in the November dusk. A wind that had been practicing how to blow all the two thousand flat miles from the Arctic Circle showed its proficiency by sweeping me off my feet and up the steps of the Primitive Methodist Chapel, an assistance really, since that was my destination.

On each side of the porch bright yellow windows glowed with the hot light of gas and airtight stove round which the Ladies Aid Society were packing their annual barrel for the heathen. This year, however, was an occasion of extraordinary interest. In addition to the honorable purpose, the layer cakes and salads and coffee, there were to be two added attractions: the first visit of a colored member and, as guest star, a young woman who had almost been arrested for murder.

Mrs. Hawks, breathless with eagerness, had asked me to come. She had asked it proudly as President of the Ladies Aid, and humbly because hers was not the Community Church dominated by Miss Barton, the Phillipses and the Browns, with a regular full-time preacher and a gray stone tower. Six weeks of Hinchdale had made me more aware of social gradations than had twenty-one urban years. To exhibit one so closely connected with Zaydee Proutman's murder would add something to Mrs. Hawks's prestige, and there was little that I would have refused to her after the kindly protection she had given me throughout my week of fear.

I was the last arrival, John having released me from work reluctantly and with a wry smile at my sarcastic allusion to missionary societies rating close to the D.A.R. as conductors of respectability. "Or don't I need that anymore?"

He answered me far too seriously, "It is a wise thing for you to do."

"What," I demanded, "is so wise about it? Do you mean that I'm still under suspicion?"

"No, no, Kay." He was impatient. "I don't mean anything. We're perfectly safe now."

There could scarcely have been a snugger, warmer haven against the prairie cold than was the chapel parlor. Twelve women were grouped around the stove and an open packing box, against the background of a long table set with tapers and red paper roses; cakes splendid with chocolate, cocoanut, and orange icing; and great blue bowls of green lettuce and pink shrimp. The air was full of gossip and good coffee.

There was an awkward moment of silence when I entered. Then Mrs. Hawks came over to me and said, "I guess most of you know Miss Kay Ellis, who rooms at my house. I asked her to come today, partly because she's such a fine packer."

Someone said, "We heard about your packing"; and I said, "Yes, wasn't it lucky for me that Mrs. Hawks came home when she did that night?"

And then almost naturally I was telling them what they wanted to know about the Proutman case. Almost but not quite; for, while they really didn't ask the questions to which there was no answer, I was made self-conscious by two of my audience—by Mrs. Harvey, her long lip pressed hard against her teeth, and by the nervous black eyes of Isabelle Williams. Or was I reading into their faces my own uneasiness? Perhaps, but I was almost sure that Isabelle would have preferred not to have me come.

She sat quietly at the edge of the circle, her coat with the red fur collar wrapped around her, although I thought it was too hot in the room, her softly dark face without the animated attention marking the other women's. Naturally, my story was not news to her. Even if she knew no different version which perhaps horribly included her husband, she may well have felt the elements of bad taste.

But all the others loved it. Their cheeks were a deeper pink than the stove could have produced; and, like the Amanda Adams Barton Chapter, they dwelt lovingly on the blood. To them the big moment was the scene at the cliff when Zaydee's earring was discovered, and I gladly resigned my recital at that point to the real expert, Mrs. Hawks.

"Right while you was standing there he found it, Sarah," they breathed. "Right by Mrs. Jim Watson's feet."

"Eyah." Mrs. Hawks was properly modest. "But the person who got the best view was Mrs. Harvey. She got to the bushes first, before the rest of us had kind of kicked around all over them. You tell us about it, Mrs. Harvey."

I had thought at our first meeting that Mrs. Harvey was shy. It was painful now to see the fear in her pale eyes before she dropped her gaze to her twisting fingers. Her lips opened and closed. "I saw—" She began and stopped—at what memory of horror? "I saw," she went on, "just what the others saw."

Her fellow members were not watching her as I was.

"What kind of earring was it, Sarah? Was it all stamped out of shape? Was it valuable? Was there any blood on it?"

"There wasn't any blood, so's I could see," she told them. "'Twas kind of flattened out, but you could still tell the shape all right—one of those cowboy hats with ball fringe sewed round them, like what cattle thieves wear in the movies. Came from Mexico, didn't it, Mrs. Williams?"

Isabelle spoke gently, but there was no hesitation. "Yes. It was part of a set of silver costume jewelry. It wasn't valuable, but Mrs. Proutman liked to wear it sometimes, 'cause a young man she met in Monterey gave it to her. She had the earrings and a pin and a ring and a big ugly belt. They looked sort of silly all together."

I looked steadily at Isabelle. "Wasn't there a bracelet, too?" I asked.

She returned my look directly, her brows raised as if puzzled by my interest, but not embarrassed, not afraid. "Yes there was," she said.

Mrs. Hawks rose and bustled over to the table. "Now our work's all done 'cept a few things to tuck in the top of the box, what say we eat?"

It was, as I had seen, a feast so bounteous that the Greasy Spoon would lose my patronage that evening. While we all consumed it with honest pleasure, the talk still hovered round Zaydee Proutman's death, with interlarded satisfactions concerning the amount and type of donations to be sent to the conference mission in Sierra Leone.

An anthropologist would wonder a long time about what would be suitable to send to the natives of West Africa, what would supplement without destroying the best in their own way of life; but the ladies of Hinchdale had not a moment's hesitation. The thing to send was silk dresses, just as good as new, just swell, only out of style, and you can't wear them forever, here where everybody knows you. Mrs. Steinhardt, their conference missionary, had said on her last furlough that nothing brought the heathen into the church as silk dresses did. This year they were sending seven. The good ladies were, however, somewhat checked in their expressions concerning the African pagans by the presence of Isabelle. They cast quick little glances of embarrassment at her. Of course, being a member of their church, she was obviously not a heathen but a good Christian woman. But was she an American or an African? Should they apologize to her?

Isabelle Williams, with the tact of the lady she was, put them at their ease. "I've brought the eighth dress," she said. "It's very gay, but I think wild people would like it." She took from one of the large patch pockets of her coat a folded square of cloth and unrolled it. It was brocade, gold, green and purple, very rich, the gold a little tarnished. "It belonged to Mrs. Proutman."

It was a sensation. They left their chairs and crowded close, touching it.

"She gave it to me, a year ago," Isabelle explained. "It isn't the kind of thing I wear. I was saving it for a rug I'm going to make."

They all thought she was generous and it was just wonderful and 'most too good to send; and Isabelle from that moment was one of them. There was more synthetic enthusiasm for the tiny Brownie camera I had decided some youngster with Mission-school training might have fun pulling to pieces.

"That makes everything, then," said Mrs. Hawks. "We'll tuck these right in on top and sing our closing hymn."

Mrs. Harvey stopped fingering the brocade which had been Zaydee Proutman's. "There's mine, too. I'd forgotten." She scurried toward the box. "It really isn't anything. I guess I won't unwrap it."

The parcel she brought and tucked into the packing case was also flat and soft, wrapped in tissue paper, quite possibly another silk dress. Her fellow members, evidently respecting her pathological shyness, did not press her to show her contribution, merely murmuring that they knew everything she gave was always just fine. Beside her angular form, Isabelle, her soft full coat about her, stooped to add her offering.

We stood in a semicircle around the box and sang "From Greenland's icy mountain to India's coral strand," and then gathered up our outer garments to combat the first-mentioned clime.

"You wait just a minute for me," Mrs. Hawks suggested. "I'm going to turn out the kitchen light. Will you just see that the top layer in the box is perfectly level? The janitor's going to nail on the lid when he gets through his work at the Cash-and-Carry tonight."

She was not in the room when I knelt by the packing case to rearrange slightly the last three packages, my own hard square and the two soft, flat bundles. There were four bundles—my own, Isabelle's, hastily wrapped with the brocade showing through, Mrs. Harvey's tissue around what seemed to be a man's gray sweater, and between these another of the same size and shape, of brown paper tied with plain string. Curious, I slipped my finger under a loose edge and pried back the paper. Something bright came to view, sparkling under the light—gold tissue, fresh, untarnished.

I knew where I had last seen material like that. Again, before my sick eyes blazed Zaydee Proutman, silly silver hats swinging in her ears, another larger hat pinned on a blouse of gorgeous tissue-of-gold.

Before Mrs. Hawks could see it, I pushed the package far down under a lower layer of the box. Which one, I was wondering, which one had done it? Was it Mrs. Alpheus Harvey, wife of the director of the William Henry Proutman Museum, or Mrs. Esquire Williams, wife of the janitor, who was sending to convert the heathen of Sierre Leone the gold blouse in which Zaydee Proutman had gone to her death?

CHAPTER XIX

How did I know the sparkling gold cloth was really Zaydee's blouse? I didn't know it. For all my prying had revealed, the package in the missionary barrel had contained a skirt, jacket, dress; perhaps extra cloth from the blouse of my obsession, which Zaydee had given to Isabelle for her rug. Or material bought by Mrs. Harvey to satisfy some lack in her dull life and then not used. The tissue had been bright, blatantly rich and new—of that only I was certain.

But why, if Isabelle was the donor, had she troubled to wrap separately and conceal from the Ladies Aid a second gift so acceptable to them and to Mrs. Steinhardt of the Mission? Shy Mrs. Harvey might hide anything from the curious; but, again, why two packages? Kay Ellis, detective. What was the beginning of all this stupid sleuthing?

It had begun, I decided, on the Monday morning after the murder, with that odd, light-catching object in the Corset Room, and it came back to that now. For, while the sombrero bracelet was an improbable object to hang on the chest of the wax figure, a gold tissue blouse could easily be draped across its shoulders. The horror this possibility invoked stunned me. A bracelet could slip off, an earring be torn free in a struggle; but a blouse would have to be taken from a body. Unless, macabre thought, the last hours of Zaydee's life had included a love scene in the Proutman Corset Room. With mad Randy or— Go back to the safer horror: if the blouse was in the Museum on Monday after the murder, who knew it, who took it away, whose wife put it in the missionary box? If it was the blouse in the Museum or in the box.

Twice I had tried to verify my suspicion about an unfamiliar object in the exhibition hall; twice I had been warned away—by Esquire, by Mr. Harvey. Esquire, on leaving the Sheriff's meeting before the others, had had the best opportunity to remove the blouse from the dummy; but Mr. Harvey had been the most insistent that I leave the vicinity of suspicion, had probed into any former visits to that particular mannequin. And nothing in his Museum could be out of place for long before it caught the director's eye. Between Saturday night and Monday morning he had not had access to the building; but early on Monday he would have seen the gleam of the gold tissue. Why, then, had he not removed it at once? Because he himself, with all the drawers and cupboards of the Museum at his exclusive disposal, had chosen so obvious a hiding place? Because he preferred to watch and wait for the guilty person to retrieve it? In which case, did I figure as the criminal in his mind?

Either Esquire or Harvey, having discovered by chance an object likely to bring scandal on the Museum, might well have removed it and, in consultation with his wife, hit upon this unique means of concealment. Which did not involve either man in the murder of Zaydee Proutman. Concealing further evidence of Randy's crime was no business of mine. Particularly since I did not know whether the gold cloth I had seen had ever been remotely connected with Zaydee.

On that night of November 5, four days had passed since the Sheriff had pronounced Zaydee Proutman dead by misadventure on Lovers' Point; and I had found two clues, the bracelet and the blouse, pointing dubiously in different directions. Beryl's bobby pins were not a clue, but Beryl herself, raising the ghost of her murdered cousin, had touched off suspicion in my oversensitized mind.

Mind or soul or nerves, whatever you want to call the spot where suspicion lies like a cold lump; from before Thanksgiving until Christmas, it seemed to sit mainly in the pit of my stomach. For six long weeks of confusion, insecurity, fear, I added nothing, no real knowledge to those two ambiguous objects. Clues they remained, clues to what? That was all, except for the smell.

I was alone in the basement when I first smelled it. The day was mild and sunny, and as I labeled bones in the welcome rays, I became aware of an odor foreign to the laboratory. It seemed to come and go in mild waves. I would stop work and sniff, and it would not be there. I took up my drawing pen, and there it was again. It was not bad, but there was something unnatural about it, a sort of mixture of roses and chimpanzee soup.

After a while I got up and began a systematic prowl around the room, snuffing along the shelves of bone trays. From the bottom shelf adjoining the Holtzerman miscellany I pulled out the newly cleaned chimpanzee, which might well be the offender. Nothing, not even dust. Reaching the door to the basement, I laid my nose to the crack of Esquire's broom closet. Furniture polish.

I came back to my work room and closed the door, leaning against it. There was a strong, short wave of *pot pourri*, especially *pourri*. Opposite me was another closed door, leading to John Gordon's office. I crossed to it, smelled nothing, dropped on my knees and, like a spaniel, laid my nose on the sill and snuffed under the door. First cold air, then a draft laden with the sickly sweetness, then clean cold again. I got up and opened the door on the elegance that Zaydee Proutman had selected. "My pansy office," had been John's grunt about it when I first came to Hinchdale. It was all red and green leather, and bookcases with glass doors, beneath which were built deep storage cupboards. There were window draperies with a pattern of apes and cocoanuts, and the cupboard handles were brass skulls. From door to window the floor was covered with a Chinese rug of deep blue pile with high raised garlands in pink and tan.

Wind puffed through the half-opened window, and I caught the smell again. It was definitely stronger here, but it took a lot of methodical hounding to locate it. Since it came and went, it had to be in the path of the breeze, in a line with the window and the door into the laboratory. And in John's office that was an empty space. Desk and chair well to the right, bookcases built into the left wall, clear passage between. Passage across the rug. I stooped, and the smell was steady. Heavy, full of old meat overlaid with Chanel No. 5. Feeling slightly sick, I went on my knees again and found it.

On the rug was a stain so small and so almost blended with a garland that only canine zeal could discover it; but, once located, a dog would never have left it. Whereas I was on my feet at once and breathing deep of the sunny air that had revealed this hidden decay. For decay it was. The deep whiff had made its origin clear to me. I remembered the day in an Oldwick classroom, sun like this on my notebook as I wrote down Dr. Alden's words: "In the early stages of putrefaction the odor is sweet, and this has given rise to legends of the perfume of roses emanating from the corpses of dead saints and martyrs."

It wasn't hard to account for such an odor in a laboratory where we had recently sacrificed a primate martyr to science, particularly since I hadn't emptied the clothes boiler when I finished the cooking. In the ten days of my absence from the laboratory, the fluid thick with membrane and cartilage and muscle could have distilled considerable perfume before John remembered to pour it out. So that explained everything. Except why it lingered only on the office rug. The ape kettle could never have stood on that Chinese elegance. However, it was not unlikely that the liquid had slopped on the laboratory floor and over John's shoes and been tramped into the one surface not mopped up by Esquire's daily industry. He had certainly been assiduous in his efforts to get the anthropoid aroma out of the Museum as quickly as possible. The strange thing wasn't that it lingered in this one spot, but that it wasn't all over the place. Still, this was an odd spot, on the rich rug just in front of the biggest floor-cupboard door.

It was then I heard the cough and whirled around, heart hammering, hands cold. Through the door I saw Alpheus Harvey standing in the center of the laboratory. How long he had been there I never knew, but the lips rolled back, the silent shaking, the eyes nearly closed in the yellow face—all the signs of his laughter seemed to indicate too clearly that he had witnessed my canine progress. There was, since I didn't want to mention the smell which might imply carelessness on the part of Esquire, nothing I could say. I closed the office door and came wretchedly toward him. The laughter stopped abruptly.

"Miss Ellis." He motioned me to a chair and sat down at the opposite side of the table. "Will you tell me just how you catalogue the Holtzerman Collection?"

I couldn't have been more surprised. "Certainly." I rose to get card-index box and accessions register. There was no answer to the question of my lifted eyebrows.

The system was very simple. From the individual measurement cards certain data were transferred to the big register of the entire collection, the number, degree of completeness of the skeleton, sex, approximate age, and any pathological condition of special interest. It would then be easy, I told him, if we wanted to study all young males, or all conditions of osteoporosis, or only those skeletons with a complete set of foot bones.

He read off the line I indicated. "'HU 48, Skull and long bones, male, old, healed fracture of left tibia.' What is HU? Holtzerman what?"

"Holtzerman Upper, the older cemetery above the village. HL stands for the newer burial ground nearer the valley."

"And those are all the classifications you have? Everything fits into those two classes?" His eyes were beads, holding mine.

"Everything we've catalogued so far. And all the skeletons from the community came from one of the two burial grounds. We have a third classification, but we haven't used it yet. I am not sure that we shall need it for any skeletal material."

"Explain yourself." It seemed such a heavy way to deal with routine method that it made me uncomfortable.

"HMisc," I said, "for the Miscellanea. The things Frau Holtzerman packed up and sent along with the collection."

"Ah, I hadn't heard of them."

"You have seen one," I told him, "the umbrella."

"The umbrella, hum—what else?"

"I've never really looked at them. We've been too busy with the main collection. I looked them over hastily once. There are a few animal bones and household things, like tacks, and some anatomy student material."

"But you will catalogue them some day?"

"Well, I intend to list them and then ask Dr. Gordon—and you—what you want kept for the Museum. Some of it is just plain trash."

"That," he said, "will be for me to decide. I want to see it all. All."

"Certainly, Mr. Harvey."

He went. And because his visit didn't quite make sense, the spot of suspicion felt sore in my middle. What, if anything, had he hidden in the Holtzerman Collection? Did I want to know? But from Mr. Harvey's manner it seemed that I, not he, was trying to get away with—I was going to say murder.

I should have asked John why Alpheus Harvey was so concerned about the Holtzerman oddments if he had come to the laboratory alone. But Esquire preceded him with his brush and his old refrain, "Very many bones and very dry."

John's voice cut like a whip. "We've had enough of that nonsense, Williams."

Esquire's eyes fell, his voice shook. "Yes, suh. Excuse me, suh." He slipped out like a shadow.

Trembling with anger, I kept my eyes on my work and did not move until John sat down beside me at the work table and picked up a skull from the tray of newly labeled bones I had set out ready for him. Even then, I did not look toward him. I tried to keep my voice flat and expressionless as I read figures back to him, holding myself as remote and stiff as possible. We seemed to go on like that for hours.

"73 point five."

"73 point five."

"56 point three."

"56 point six."

"Point three."

"Sorry. Point *three*. Next."

Because I didn't look at him, as hours went by I became cumulatively aware of him as I had not been since our earliest days together—of the scent of tweeds and pipe, of the touch of his hand or shoulder when we measured a pelvis together. Weakness crept through me, but I didn't know I had showed it until he said, "Kay, love me."

It was warm and sweet, and more exciting than it had ever been before; but when I reached up and pushed the black lock from his forehead, our eyes did not meet. It was as if love were good, but not good enough to bridge the chasm of doubt and misunderstanding cut between us by Zaydee Proutman, living and dead. I kissed him again and pulled away from his arms, saying in a poor imitation of a blithe spirit, "To be continued. I'm going to supper at Miss Alice Barton's, and I need to get into the mood."

Actually it wasn't hard to adjust from the strained emotion of my last hour with John to the staid peace of Miss Barton's home. I liked the fire on the hearth, the orthodox cat on the braided rug, and the *Atlantic* and *Harper's* in the magazine rack. I liked being admitted to her slowly given friendship, but most of all I enjoyed the perfectly natural manner of Miss Alice. She was just as I had expected all the Museum staff to be after the death of Zaydee Proutman, as soon as the first shock was over— soberly relieved, quietly realizing their release from hate and fear. But Alpheus Harvey and Esquire Williams were not like that, and certainly John Gordon was not. From their repression and strain I had felt my own spontaneous feeling of freedom die within me. Only when I was with Miss Alice did I feel that Randy's violent act should have made things all right for the rest of us. We didn't talk very much about Zaydee, but we didn't avoid mentioning her; that really was the difference.

Tonight for the first time she took me into her bedroom to show me her treasure, the murky little portrait of Amanda Adams at sixteen, done by a journeyman painter in Connecticut before the long trek west.

"There is some baby linen she wove for her first child," said Miss Barton. "I keep it on the top closet shelf. Do you think you can reach it, my dear? I am so ridiculously short."

As she opened the closet door, an odor met me, sickly sweet. Recalling that other, I drew back for a moment and then explained laughing, "Ever since the days of the chimpanzee I smell corpses everywhere I go. But I know what this smell is. It's dye for shoes."

"Or for straw hats," said Miss Barton. "I blackened my last summer's turban just the other day. People who live alone have odd times for doing all sorts of small jobs; it keeps them from being lonely."

As I stood on tiptoe to reach the box of ancestral treasures, I noted the neat little row of black hats, silk and straw and velvet, on the middle shelf and below it a neat little row of black oxfords and pumps.

After supper we sat before the fire and read poetry aloud. Miss Alice did most of the reading in a precise but spirited style. Her taste ran to the bellicose and, for a daughter of revolution, not always on the side of democracy. She loved to beat time to the rhythm of:

> Kentish Sir Byng
> Stood for his king,
> Bidding the crop-headed Parliament swing ...

And to attempt to follow the less-jiggling

> King Charles, and who'll do him right now?

From there, her eyes wandering across the page of her carefully mended Browning, she began "The Lost Leader." Her voice softened, and suddenly this less-than-just accusation of old Wordsworth became something else to me:

> Life's night begins; let him never come back to us!
> There would be doubt, hesitation and pain,
> Forced praise on our part—the glimmer of twilight,
> Never glad, confident morning again!

That first afternoon when John and I had looked at each other had seemed the beginning of a fine life; this afternoon we had kissed and avoided each other's eyes—because doubt had taken the place of confidence. Luxurious tears filled my eyes, and I didn't hear the last stanzas of the poem. The voice stopped and I swallowed hard.

"Miss Ellis," said Miss Alice, sitting very straight, "have you made a plan for your life?"

"I had," I answered in surprise, "have."

"And sometimes you are more eager to carry it out than you are at other times."

"Yes."

"Would you care to tell me about it?"

So I told her about my ambition to be a research anthropologist and, as a first step, to go back to Oldwick and take my doctorate under Professor Alden's direction.

"You had that in mind before you came to Hinchdale?"

"Oh, yes. That was why I was so glad to come. It was a wonderful chance to work with the Holtzerman Collection, and I could save toward my graduate work."

"And after you came, you meant to get through here as quickly as possible and return to develop your profession?"

"Ye-es. At first. Then I did think, for a little while, that it would be fun to stay for the three years until the work on the Holtzerman Collection was finished. To see how it turned out." I wasn't quite meeting her gaze until I concluded. "But after Mrs. Proutman told me my salary would be so much less than I had expected, I thought it would take three years, anyway, to save enough to go back to Oldwick."

"How soon," said Miss Barton, "will you be going now?"

I answered honestly, "I hadn't thought."

"You must," she said, and a gentle flush came into her old cheeks. "You must. While you are young, you mustn't let go of your ideals. You mustn't just drift and stay on, because from day to day it is pleasant."

I was silent.

"Is it," she asked, "pleasant for you?"

It was hard to answer, harder still to know, so again I did not speak, and again she went on, precise, low-voiced, vehement. "Go. Go as soon as you can. You will always be glad that you have done it. When you carry out your own plans, then and only then you are free."

"It would take a year here," I said, "if I live very carefully, to save enough for a year at Oldwick. I have only two hundred dollars left from my father's insurance, so really I ought to stay longer if Mr. Harvey wants me."

"Couldn't you get a scholarship?"

I met her firm gaze. "I think I might."

She stood up, the cold little old figure of a college graduate that, twenty-five years ago, Mr. W. H. Proutman had merely admired. "No woman," she said, "should permit her happiness to depend upon a man."

"I could write about the scholarship," I said.

"My dear," she laid her dry hand on mine, "I do not want you to leave Hinchdale. I shall miss you greatly. But there is nothing worthy of you here. Remember always what I say. There is nothing."

CHAPTER XX

In William Henry Proutman Park they had wired the municipal Christmas tree. All day children had run and stumbled up the stairs of the Proutman Museum and giggled to pageant rehearsals on the third floor. At four o'clock Esquire departed in great dignity for the final workout of the carol singers.

I took out my mirror, and my wrists felt weak. Powder smooth, hair smooth—Kay, what are you waiting for? For courage. Courage to— You fool. For courage to give your boss a Christmas present. Your boss or your boy friend? Guess which.

It was quiet behind the closed door to the office he had seldom used since Zaydee Proutman died. Whenever I was in the laboratory, he had been there, too. If we weren't measuring bones, he read or wrote at a table by the window. It might have been because of Zaydee's interior decorating, or because he, too, was aware of the smell on the carpet. Or it might have been because of me.

In the mood of Christmas Eve I was inclined to the last view, and hoped I could hold it until I had made my presentation. I hadn't intended to buy a gift for John, but in the catalogue of the smart Fifth Avenue shop from which I was selecting something for Professor and Mrs. Alden and for my college roommate, I saw pictured a cigarette box of beautifully grained walnut, an austere rebuke to Zaydee Proutman's taste in art. Now it lay on my desk "in a plain wrapper," as the classified advertisements promise. No compromising bells and wreaths and ribbons and "Merry Christmas from Kay" for Esquire to find in the office wastebasket. I turned off my desk light and put on my camel's-hair reefer—a quick getaway from embarrassment seemed indicated—and with purse under arm, hat in hand, I picked up the white package. The big, low room, bright beneath the swinging central bulb, shadowy in the corners, and the closed door was as it had been when I sat waiting for Zaydee Proutman to come and discharge me. Beside the strain of that day leading to death, the apprehension of hurt from giving a Christmas present to a man who probably wasn't going to give one to me seemed very Junior Miss. I pushed the box into my coat pocket (as Isabelle had concealed the gold tissue blouse?) and crossed to John's door.

The grunt that answered my knock was not full of Christmas cheer. He sat behind his desk, emanating good grooming—fresh haircut, close shave, clean white linen, new tie, best suit, unruly hair brushed and oiled into place. He put down a book and looked toward me, not at me.

"Did you want something?"

The answer to that should have been: No, never again from you, darling. But instead I murmured, "I ... well ... I was just about to carry out a quaint old English custom for December 25." My hand met the package and pushed it to the bottom of the pocket. "I just came to wish you a Merry Christmas."

"Thanks, Kay." He got up. "I'm driving to Warrenton in about an hour and taking the Chicago night plane. One of my brothers is there. I'm going to spend Christmas Day with him and fly back tomorrow night."

"It sounds ... fun."

"Sometimes I feel as if I couldn't stand it in this town." The words he spoke echoed back from the day of our first encounter. He still had not met my eyes.

"That," I said, "is easy to understand."

He was looking straight at me now, and his words came sharp. "What do you mean by that?"

I took a step nearer the door. "Nothing, John, except that ... Hinchdale isn't ... wouldn't be the favorite holiday spot for lots of people."

He looked down at the high polish of his shoe. "What are you doing for the holiday?"

Did he, at that late moment, think of taking me with him? Cover the hope, quick. "The high point of celebration," I said, "is dinner tomorrow at three with Sheriff and Mrs. Brown and their cousin, Miss Alice Barton."

His face flushed, and a thumb pressed against tight knuckles. So he didn't think maybe this was an ideal Christmas for the girl he liked to kiss, but he wasn't going to do anything about it.

"Of course," I went on, "that won't fill quite the whole day, and in the interstices I thought I might come over here and do a spot of work. Particularly if I could find something to cook into a nice meat soup. To make the place smell like home to you when you come back."

He stiffened as if he were going to spring at me. "What the hell are you trying to do? You're to keep out of this place while I'm away."

"I undoubtedly shall," I blazed. "I haven't got a key. Nor," I added, "a wash boiler."

At that moment I hoped he would fire me; it would have been a pleasure to us both. But he didn't; he pulled himself together, and did it fast. "Kay, I'm sorry," he said. "I don't know what got into me. Christmas spirit in reverse. I meant that you're to spend your holiday in rest at least. This winter has been hard for you, as well as the rest of us. Take a few days off—a week if you like." His eyes met mine, glazed and remote. "May I drive you home?"

"No," I said, my fingers hard against the box in my pocket. "Thanks. I'm going just a little way, and I'd like the walk. I'm going to take a Christmas present to Isabelle Williams."

"That's awfully decent of you, when you gave so generously to the Museum's fund for Esquire." He looked almost like himself, and there was a humorous twist to the mouth that said, "Well, Kay, Merry Christmas."

"Thank *you*, sir," I managed, and left.

Out on Broadway, Christmas was everywhere. Cars parked double by both curbs were being loaded with turkeys and trees. Christmas trees blinked blue and red on the stone porch of the Proutman Bank, before the Odd Fellows Building, the Legion Hall, in seasonal competition with the chiropractor's neon sign. The dark, unimproved street leading to the Williams cottage was more in my mood. I felt deflated and banned, and all that was needed to flatten me forever was to find that Isabelle had left for the tree-lighting ceremonies in Proutman Park.

There were lights in her windows, white candles pyramided in iron holders, looking so like Christmas Eve on Beacon Hill that I was almost in tears when she opened the door and stood in a white dress and gay peasant apron.

"Why, Miss Ellis, Merry Christmas." There was no doubt that Isabelle was glad to see me. "Come in and rest you'self by our fire."

"Merry Christmas, Isabelle." I stepped into the glowing little kitchen where hand-woven rugs, bright curtains, and blue and gold pottery on the shelves transformed the kind of place that landlords rent to colored people, into Esquire and Isabelle's home. "Won't you be going out right away to the carols?"

"No." She shook her head, the gold earrings swinging against dark cheeks that were softer and fuller than in the days of Zaydee Proutman. "Esquire's there, representing the household. I thought I wouldn't go. It seemed a little far to walk in the cold. I guess marriage has made me kind of lazy." She giggled and took my package. "For me, Miss Kay, after what you all did for our wedding, and with Esquire's Christmas gift! Oh, I just have to open it right now." The white paper that I now wished had been sprigged with holly fell away from the box. "Oh, Miss Kay!" She held it up in the lamplight with fingers as exquisitely brown as the walnut. "This is real elegance."

"It—I thought you'd like it," I stammered. "It came from New York. I thought it looked like you ... like the way you wear your clothes."

"Yes." She put the box gently on the table, a finger caressing the grain. "I learned taste, being with Miss Zaydee, but not from her. I owe her a lot. I owed her a lot when she was alive. Maybe I owe her more because she's dead."

The motive, the bracelet, the blouse. "Yes?" I said.

"Miss Zaydee didn't think very much of marriage, especially not for me and Esquire. Maybe you heard she was going to discharge us both if we got married?"

I nodded.

"I thought maybe she'd change her mind after a while and let Esquire stay, but there didn't seem to be much hope, and we was going to Chicago where he was 'most sure to get work in the stockyards. It would have been hard, but we could have stood it all right. I can sew and do a lot of handy things, but a tenement district in the Negro section of Chicago isn't a nice place for children."

"No."

"Miss Ellis, don't you know why Esquire and I got married in such a hurry?" She stood up, untying the full peasant apron. "I'm going to have a baby."

Well, Isabelle's was a pretty ordinary accomplishment, I know, but on Christmas Eve and all that, I got up with tears in my eyes and patted her shoulder. "Are you glad?"

"I'm just terribly happy. Except about one thing. It's coming in June."

"What do you care? You and Esquire were in love, and Mrs. Proutman wouldn't let you get married, and—"

"If it was you"—Isabelle put me in my spinster place—"you'd care. Not for yourself. For *it*. You'd want everything perfect for your baby. I don't want people saying about its birthday that it's just like colored folks."

"Did Mrs. Proutman know about the baby?"

"Yes." The kindliness went out of Isabelle's face. "She knew. She told me she would do anything in the world, spend any amount of money, take the finest medical care of me. Anything to get rid of it. She said ... she said I was a fool, young and with looks and training for good steady work, to marry a laboring man like Esquire and live with him all my life. She couldn't see that was the one thing I wanted—to live all my life with a good man who wouldn't deceive me. You see"—she raised her solemn dark eyes—"I'd known lots of flashy men, traveling around with Miss Zaydee, entertainers and doormen in big clubs in New York and Paris, and I'd had wonderful fun." She laughed a little. "But getting married to Esquire was *real*."

"But I don't quite know why Mrs. Proutman was so determined to stop you. Except that she was like that about everything."

"No, Miss Ellis, you wrong her, really you do. She wasn't always that mean, particularly not to me. But she was lonely, and I was the person she'd always thought she'd be able to depend on if—" She stopped. "If things she had in mind didn't turn out very well."

This was the day to end illusion. "You mean, her marriage to Dr. Gordon?"

"I ... guess maybe I did, but it was all in her own mind, Miss Kay." She wanted me to believe it.

"Then she wasn't really so dreadfully against marriage, just against yours?"

"Yes, she was, Miss Kay. I know maybe I shouldn't be talking about my employer, particularly now she's dead. But I want you to know about her, Miss Kay, now we've started this talk. It would be fairer to her. And to you, too. After old Mr. Proutman died, I'm 'most sure Miss Zaydee never expected to marry again. She liked to have interesting friends among young men. And she did, Miss Kay. Every single one I ever saw was something, a writer or a painter or a musician, like poor Mr. Randy Bill. And in the beginning Dr. Gordon was going to be another friend like the others. That's what Miss Zaydee thought. But when they got here to Hinchdale, he wasn't so much fun as she expected. It was then, I think, she had the other idea, about getting married. Miss Zaydee was a smart woman. She knew she was getting old. And Hinchdale was her home. She was feeling she'd like to stay here for the rest of her days and be queen of the town. The best folks were starting to come to her house and asking her to theirs. But she didn't want to settle down here yet, without a young man, and if she wanted to be any queen of Hinchdale she'd have to be married to him. You see?"

"Yes."

"And Dr. John Gordon was very pleasing to her. And everybody thought so well of him that if he married her, Miss Zaydee's place in town would be real good."

"It had everything."

"Not quite. Like I told you, Miss Zaydee was smart. She didn't believe she could hold a young man all her life. Particularly not Dr. Gordon. But she did feel she could maybe get him to do it through business influence and his being a little lonely here. That was before you come."

I had to know the rest. "Isabelle, tell me, did you think things were going well for her?"

"Not too well. I'd say he hadn't been absolutely discouraging. But Miss Zaydee's dead now, and it's all over. All our trouble."

"Is it?"

Her eyes widened with fright; her dark hands tightened against her white dress. "You know something?"

"Do you?"

She shook her head defiantly, but the stress of a word tripped her. "*I* don't."

"But Esquire does."

Her face looked suddenly old. "He's never told. I don't think he knows very much, but he's afraid. He's done nothing, nothing, I swear to God, Miss Kay, nothing no more than you have. But he's afraid of his knowledge. Miss Kay, aren't *you* afraid?"

Suddenly I was. If Zaydee Proutman had been killed in the Museum, that person other than Randy Bill who had aided in her death or disposal would not be likely to meet discovery with benevolence. If the person were Esquire—Esquire and Isabelle—I had very neatly done myself in.

"Not really afraid," I answered her, "because I don't know anything. It's just that—Oh, people around the Museum didn't seem to be as relieved after Mrs. Proutman's death as I thought they would be. Things seemed strained. But I don't know that anything is different from the Sheriff's case."

That was her chance to try to turn my suspicions, but she didn't. "I think it's the same with Esquire," she said. "That, or maybe something he saw when he was workin' around. Whatever it is, he's terribly upset. He can't sleep or eat like he should. Oh, Miss Kay, if it only could be straightened out before the baby gets born!"

Tears were in her voice, on her cheeks, and I forgot caution.

"Perhaps," I said, "it was the bracelet."

"What bracelet?" Her eyes were so innocent, and I wanted so much to calm her for her sake and for the baby's, that without a qualm I told her the story of the linked Mexican hats, from the pocket of Esquire's wedding suit to the interment among the cleaning rags. To my complete surprise she laughed.

"Oh, my poor honey lamb!" She giggled in evident relief. "He must have been upset. That bracelet didn't have anything to do with Miss Zaydee."

"It wasn't hers?" I doubted.

"It was hers, Miss Kay, but she wasn't wearing it when she was killed. I was."

"You?"

"Yes, she went off that afternoon in a terrible rush when the grocery truck came, you remember, and she left the bracelet on her dressing table. And when I was clearing up and waiting for Esquire to come out and see me, I thought he'd think it was kind of cute and funny, and I slipped it on. After he came, we were fooling around, and he took it off me and slipped it in his pocket. And forgot. He didn't have his good suit on again till the wedding. And that next morning at the Museum when he found it, with you standing right there, and it being like all those other pieces of jewelry I described to the Sheriff, and like the earring, he must have felt he was in an awful fix."

"I'm so glad I know about it," I said as heartily as possible, but caution was awake again and I didn't mention the blouse. Neither did Isabelle. The bracelet story was almost too good for spontaneous creation, but not quite. Isabelle and Mrs. Harvey were equally able to put the blouse in the mission box. It would be well to curb confidences with the wife of Esquire Williams. I rose to go.

"If we only knew the truth, Miss Kay"—her eyes as well as her voice pleaded—"then we wouldn't be afraid. I feel sometimes I'd give anything to know what really happened to Miss Zaydee."

I took a chance, a long one.

"I want to know as much as you do, Isabelle. It might just be possible that there's still some clue in the Museum. On an ordinary day I never could find out." There was Alpheus Harvey at my elbow in the Corset Room, at my files in the laboratory—the laboratory, where it suddenly seemed sinister that John Gordon never left me alone. "Tomorrow, Christmas Day, I'd have my one chance. Dr. Gordon has flown to Chicago. Mrs. Hawks, with whom I live, is leaving on the early bus for Spirit Falls. I'm free until three o'clock. But I have no key."

"No key," she repeated. "You need a key to the Museum?"

"Yes."

"Wait." She slipped back the curtain from the wardrobe, and there was a soft clink as she drew out of the pocket of Esquire's work trousers the bunch of keys to the William Henry Proutman Museum.

"Can you pick out the master key?"

I nodded, and together we wrenched it off the thick ring.

"We're going tomorrow morning to his cousin's in Warrenton. He'll still be wearing his good suit. When you're through with the key, slip it into the Christmas greens in the window box at the right of the door. I can pick it up when we come in, without his seeing. And if I can't find a time for putting it back on the ring, I'll drop it on the closet floor and find it later."

"All right," I said. "Remember, I don't promise anything. There probably won't be a thing to find, and if there is, I won't know what to look for."

"You can try, Miss Kay," she said. "Merry Christmas!"
Merry Christmas!

CHAPTER XXI

Fog drifted far down from the Great Lake, crowded about the door of the Proutman Museum. The brass knob clung to my hand. I closed the door and fumbled for the light switch. It was too dark in the hall, too still.

It had been darker, I thought, on that November night of rain when a body had been carried out over the checkered tiles and begun its journey toward the lake that never gives up its dead. Was there any greater chance that, after seven weeks, the cluttered Museum would yield a clue to the spot where that body had fallen, to the hand that had struck the blow? After all, the hand was probably Randy's, and the spot the edge of the cliff on Lovers' Point. To imagine otherwise was inexpedient; to discover otherwise was danger. Today, however, I was to act on the suspicion that Zaydee Proutman had been killed within the Proutman Museum. If this was so, there seemed to be only two clues to look for: first, blood stains which might mark the spot where she fell; second, any jewelry or clothing that might have been removed as, I thought, the gold tissue blouse had been. If the murder had taken place in the Museum, it would have needed collaboration at least as far as concealing clues was concerned. Randy Bill, drunk and wild, would never have stopped to clean up details. No member of the staff had reported anything in disorder, anything added or missing; so, if Randy had received help, it was from a habitual resident of the William Henry Proutman Museum.

Where had Zaydee Proutman died? In this hall, on these checkered tiles, the head crashing beneath the chandelier? Impossible to search for bloodstains in that weird light, impossible that they should be there. Esquire was too careful to have missed them. Was that what Esquire knew?

Had it all happened in the Corset Room? Had Zaydee fled there from Randy, or had she, deceived by his greeting at the door, led him there herself? Something was wrong about that room. Best begin there.

Although it was a long time since I had shivered at the ghostly wax ladies, too much had happened in their abode to make it an inviting place. The room had never been wired for electricity, and I was forced to pass between their twilit ranks to the far side and raise a window blind. Since it overlooked the blank wall of the hardware store, there was little chance of anyone's noticing a raised shade at eight o'clock on Christmas morning.

The light that came in was not great, but it was a comfort. I went up to Esquire's favorite lady, the pink chiffon "like ashes" billowing above and below the armor of whalebone and steel and satin, her fragile pink smile a little dirty at the corners. A "right nice lady," and I wished I knew her well enough to ask her what she knew. Around the shoulders of this dame or that of her nearest neighbor, someone, in crude attempt at concealment or cruder jest, had draped a blouse of gleaming gold tissue. I went over every inch of the pink lady, a lady in velvet and button boots, a red-head in purple and ermine. I lifted their ruffles, lifted their skirts, poked down their sawdust bosoms. Not a thread of gold, nothing.

But once there had been something alien in this room. Esquire knew it, Alpheus Harvey knew it. And John? He had stopped my one chance of knowing the truth. On that Monday morning after the murder my first few steps toward the strange gleam had been checked by his cry, "Kay, for God's sake, are you still in town?" A few hours later Esquire was telling me to "go right back in the library if you don't want to be suspected of nothin'." Either of these interruptions could have different interpretation, but Mr. Harvey's "What are you doing here?" was less easy to divert to other causes. Particularly since it happened a week later, and there was nothing to see. No more than now. I pulled down the shade and recrossed the hall, tiptoeing because it made less echo, discouraged and uneasy in the empty dusk.

What to do now? Follow up every suspicious thing I could remember from that first visit to the Museum after the murder. I had seen the gleam, I had smelled the stale fumes of chimpanzee soup; that was all. And since then I had, perhaps, seen the gold blouse packed off to Africa, and I had smelled another smell—another and the same. Go down and look once more at that rug. Look and sniff like a dumb terrier pup.

The stairs cracked far too loudly, but once in the laboratory I felt calmer. It was getting lighter outside and, thanks to a children's party on the third floor following the Christmas Tree celebration, it was fairly warm. Through the open door of John's office I saw the blue Chinese rug. I went over and knelt beside it. There was still a small spot close to the pink garland, but it was no longer darker than the surrounding area; it was distinctly lighter. I raised it to my nose, and there was a smell of wool and dust and, faintly, of soap. Someone besides myself had known about that particular spot on the rug.

If that person had been Alpheus Harvey, he was well aware of my olfactory investigation, and if it was he who was somehow involved in Randy's violence against Zaydee, it seemed useless to hunt further for clues. Mr. Harvey would never forget anything, and if he chose to hide odd objects, he had the whole Museum at his disposal. It wasn't like him to hang large, bright evidence of guilt in his most prominent exhibition hall; and all that questioning about the Holtzerman Collection and the catalogue system, while it might have been a red herring for me after he caught me snuffing the rug, could also mean that he thought someone was hiding something from him. If they were, our laboratory would be the safest place, the one spot in the Museum not directly under his eye. And of all places in the laboratory, the most obvious for concealing Zaydeeana would be the big carton which we called "Holtzerman Miscellaneous." It was of this midden that Mr. Harvey had said to me, "I want to see it all. All."

The carton stood under the shelves built to hold the main skeletal collection. I lifted it out into the center of the room and saw from the outline in light dust that it had not been moved very recently. In case anyone had a guilty interest in its contents, snoopers had better replace it with precision. I laid a newspaper on the floor beside the container and took out the contents, one by one. They seemed to be just as I remembered them. First, the bones, white shiny specimens sold to medical students by anatomical supply houses—two half-skulls, two humeri, two tibiae, two femora; then the skeleton of a nonhuman mammal, probably canine, possibly the Holtzerman's pet dog. A copy of *Karl Heinrich* with illustrations and without cover; scientific reports in three sizes by Professor Holtzerman, none of which dealt with his famous brigandage; a three-legged iron object with holes bored in each foot, easy at this season to identify as a Christmas-tree standard, of early type but hardly a museum piece. In the bottom three nails, rusty and slightly bent, fitting the holes, and a lot of thin steel bars with rounded ends. There were twelve, all about fourteen inches long and a half-inch wide, except for two which were nearly an inch across. I looked at them and grinned. Of all superfluous trade goods that ever came into Newcastle Harbor, these were the tops. Frau Holtzerman, evidently one of the heavier figures, had unwittingly presented the anthropological department of the William Henry Proutman Museum with the so-called bones of her old corset.

I put the things back in the box and set it in the frame of dust. Insignificant as it was, there was no use in leaving traces of meddling. I straightened up and faced the shelves, a little stiff from the cold, a little weak from nervous strain. On those shelves stood the wooden boxes, two deep, which contained the measured skeletons of the Holtzerman

Collection. Across the room were ranged the cartons of material still to be studied. During the past six weeks of concentrated work, when John had measured almost constantly with me in the laboratory, the proportion of boxes to cartons had increased enormously. I looked, not without pride, at the rows of wooden containers, each bearing a clear black HU or HL, followed by a number, all in my hand. After all, the work in Hinchdale had been good; perhaps when I was older, that would be enough.

One box was not labeled. That would be the chimpanzee, put away by me in preparation for Zaydee's last visit. I had never wanted to see it again; but, now that my detecting had failed, I might as well lay my last ghost and inspect my laundry work. I lifted the box to the laboratory counter; behind it, on the wide shelf, was a second box like the first. Just like it. It also was without a number. With all my pride in "domestic science" I had put away the jam without a label. I'd right that wrong at once, forget the ape, and go home to prepare to dine with the Sheriff.

I put the box beside the ape container and reached inside for any earth-browned Holtzerman bone, the number of which I would paint on its coffin. I brought out a thigh, slender, slightly curved, and strong, not brown and not numbered. It was white, the dead white of fresh bone. Along a third of the shaft ran a crack. This bone had not been prepared for a medical supply house, carefully macerated and then varnished. This had undergone a crude boiling like our chimpanzee skeleton. It must be the chimpanzee. Even while I knew this was not true, I turned to the first box and saw the prognathous jaw, the small brain, the long flat nose I knew so well. I lifted out the two thigh bones, short, smooth, almost straight, of an animal who depends mainly on his upper limbs, and dropped them back again.

In the box concealed behind the chimpanzee's, there seemed to be a complete human skeleton, all of the same dead white. I began to lay it out on the table, bone by bone, in approximate anatomical position. I had laid out a hundred skeletons thus, in preparation for marking and cataloguing. It was work I particularly liked. Now my hands trembled. The limb bones were at the top of the box. I laid them in order, arms, legs. They were all fairly slender but strong. The person would have been five feet nine or ten. Then the graceful S-curve of the collarbones, and, between, the poignard of the breastbone. Below them, the two wings of the shoulder blades. I piled the ribs and vertebrae at the side, and well below the end of the breastbone I laid the thick, wide wedge of the sacrum, the keystone of the pelvic girdle. Before I put one on each side of the sacrum, I looked carefully at the two pelvic bones, the *ossa innominata*, the nameless bones. The circle they formed with the sacrum would be wide, and they met in front in a deep angle. The surfaces where they joined were rimmed with slight lips on the margins. I took out the skull and the separate lower jaw, leaving in the box only the knee caps and the bones of hands and feet.

I held up the skull. It was fairly large, with smooth, full forehead, wide cheekbones, but relatively small arches and mastoid processes. The teeth were remarkable. White, even, complete, without a single cavity. Yet the cusps showed the wear from use that would correspond with that rim on the pubic symphysis, both indicating someone between forty-five and fifty years of age. The teeth of the lower jaw were equally perfect. It was a wide jaw. Held in profile, it showed a slight development of the mental eminence; in other words, a weak chin. I dropped the jaw and looked at the skull, at the right side where, along the region of the temple, there was a depression in the bone, very shallow, rather wide. I couldn't touch it. I pressed my quivering hands to my face, and from them came a faint aroma not otherwise noticeable in the cold room, the smell that had risen from the rug. And in a sick mind, I added up what lay before me. The skeleton, freshly cleaned by someone with a knowledge of anatomy, belonging to a tall woman of middle age, with a weak chin and perfect teeth—and a lesion of the skull, possibly caused by a blow.

But that's all you know, I was saying to myself. That's all you know. I turned from the skeleton to the box from which it had come; I forced my fingers to take out the bones of wrist and ankle, of foot and hand. There was nothing else among them.

In a state of shock, when one is conscious of neither thought nor feeling, habit can still go on. I took out those small white bones one by one. I laid them out in the anatomical pattern I had followed so many times on that same table—the bones of each wrist, the bones of each ankle, the five metacarpals of each hand, the fourteen phalanges of its fingers. Last the feet, the five metatarsals and their phalanges. It should have ended there, like a jigsaw puzzle completed. But there was something wrong with the picture. Out of daze, I struggled to awareness. There were too many bones. Not ten metatarsals, five slender bones to each foot. There were twelve.

I took up twelve short shafts with knoblike heads, carried them to the adjoining counter, examined them slowly one by one. They blurred and danced before my eyes, but I could see well enough that two were different. The same fresh white bone, the same form; but two were more slender than the other ten, sharper at the points of articulation.

And I knew what it meant. Knew it, but would not quite admit it without proof. The proof was under my hand. Out of its box I tumbled the skeleton of the chimpanzee, seized, unsteadily, metacarpals and metatarsals, not stopping to sort them, dropping a few, dropping more when I stooped to retrieve. Count them, count them slowly and carefully, again and again and again. Every time the number was the same. Five to each hand, five to each foot, makes twenty; but the sum of the chimpanzee's bones was always eighteen. Eighteen plus two equals twenty. Two slender bones of a young animal.

Two metatarsal bones of the chimpanzee left carelessly in the wash boiler after the simmering of the last remaining part, the left leg and foot. Later, in that kettle, the bones of a middle-aged woman with a weak chin and a wound on the side of her head.

Too many bones.

CHAPTER XXII

Everything must be put back just as I found it. To leave no trace, no sign of illicit activity, meant the difference between life and death. My life and her death. At that time I hadn't consciously given those white female bones a name. Everything back as it was, and quick. Out of the cold and the silence as soon as possible, but make no mistakes.

I didn't have to be too careful about replacing the chimpanzee's bones, for I had packed that box myself, and probably no one had touched the contents since. They went in fast, the convicting foot bones, pelvis, shoulder blades, limbs, the skull with the long muzzle that made him look as if he were about to weep and the canine teeth contradicting with a grin not unlike that of Alpheus Harvey.

It wasn't altogether easy to remember the exact order in which I had found those other bones, and it wasn't pleasant to touch them. I wondered if I ought to wipe my fingerprints off each one. No, don't waste time. Police look for fingerprints. Murderers don't. Was the skull lying on the right side, covering the depression that had once been red? I think so. Psychologically it is indicated. Now, the two boxes, unmarked, identical, side by side. And still in my hand two small white bones. Best put them where they belong, with the chimpanzee. I leaned over a box, pushed back the upper layers of limbs, and in the cavity thrust the two ape metatarsals down to the bottom among the other foot bones of—the woman.

Three times after I had started up the basement stairs, I went back again to check the order in which I had placed the boxes on the shelf, to be sure I had left the door open into John's office, to retrieve a face tissue from the otherwise empty wastebasket. After that, I seem to have lost all sense of anything except the desire for escape. I walked out of the Museum without the slightest attempt at reconnoitering, and straight on to the Williams cottage, where I openly dropped the key into the window box. The murderers of the woman had temporarily left my mind when I fled the scene of the crime. And it was a pretty empty place, my mind, for the rest of the day. I know I went home, took a hot bath, dressed and went to the Browns' for dinner. I know I ate the dinner, because I know I lost it. That was late in the afternoon, after I had seen, while saying good-by to my hostess, her red china umbrella-stand shaped like a giant tulip and, sticking out of it, Exhibit A of the Zaydee Proutman murder case. I got as far as a quiet corner of Proutman Park before I was completely stricken. I don't know what Miss Alice Barton must have thought of me.

For a long time after I got home, I lay on my bed and slept. Still my shocked consciousness pushed away the truth, put off the moment to face horror. At last, terribly cold, I got up, put the kettle on to boil, and went down to the cellar to struggle with the furnace. Beside the coal-bin stood the basket of old papers and crushed cartons for kindling, and adjoining it the box for things that didn't burn well—tin cans and hair pins, which left too much residue to be cleaned out in the spring. I opened the furnace door. It was a capacious old firebox, not a quarter the size of Jensen's, but you could get a lot in there. Flesh would burn quickly; so would cloth and hair; but you can never be sure about bones.

I threw in a shovel of soft coal, coughing in the dust. John Gordon had stoked this furnace a lot more neatly than I could. What was it I had said to him on the telephone that night? "Dr. Gordon, I hear you have a neat hand with a furnace." Silence. "What have you got on your mind?" I had nothing—then.

Another shovel of coal on the fire. Some things about clothing wouldn't burn well. Zippers, jewelry. And the dozen corset steels that confine a woman of fuller figure.

I slammed the furnace door and ran upstairs and turned on every light in kitchen, dining room, and parlor. Tea and toast helped. I ate slowly, sitting on the couch by the window. Through the lace curtains the lights of the Municipal Christmas Tree glowed blue and red. It was a moment of precarious peace. I felt the way you do when you think maybe you haven't really got a headache, but you'd better not move your head to test it. I opened the book Miss Alice Barton had given me for Christmas, the *Complete Poetical Works of Rudyard Kipling*, and the first work I tackled began:

> Smells are surer than sounds or sights
> To make your heartstrings crack—
> They start those awful voices o' nights
> That whisper ...

Effluvium of anthropoid ape, filtering through the registers of the Museum, creeping, clinging, sickening. The cold stale smell of an unknown stew, not chimpanzee, on Monday morning, November 6.

I dropped Rudyard Kipling on the table beside another book, Mrs. Hawks's family Bible. Something about bones in that—too many, too dry. Jeremiah, Lamentations—here was Ezekiel:

> There were very many in the open valley, and, lo they were very dry.
> And he said unto me, Son of Man, can these bones live?
> And I answered, O Lord God, thou knowest.

Live! They had almost come alive under my hands. In just a moment I might see the sinews and flesh come upon them and the skin cover them. But no breath in them. That went out with the blow on the right temple.

Did a blow in the temporal region leave beneath hair and skin and flesh a dent like the one I had seen in that dead white skull? An anthropologist ought to know. I was the beginnings of a scientist, and I was through with fantasy. I went into my room and looked for relevant literature. There wasn't much, probably nothing. I gathered up the last number of the *American Journal of Physical Anthropology* and the pamphlet by Weidenreich I had been intending to read since my first visit to the Museum library. It was called "Did Sinanthropus Practice Cannibalism?" and was a cold scientific account of how you got your man in China two hundred thousand years ago. There were illustrations, photographs of human skulls in a condition I recognized; and Dr. Weidenreich said about them:

> There is not the slightest doubt that these depressions were caused by blows on the bone still covered by its soft parts. Some of the depressions have the characteristic appearance of so-called depressed and comminuted fractures which, in the practice of forensic medicine, are considered the results of heavy blows with more or less pointed instruments. The long cuts seem to be the effect of sharply edged tools, and the larger and more shallow lesions the results of blows with rounded stones or clubs.

There was no use to dodge the horror, the truth that Isabelle and I had sought—the knowledge of what happened to Zaydee Proutman. I knew that Zaydee Proutman was not thrown into the lake, either dead or alive. She was killed in the William Henry Proutman Museum by a blow on the head from the ivory handle of the Holtzerman umbrella. I had seen the matted red hair, the blood, the depression on the skull. The body had been macerated there. I had smelled it in process, and I had gruesome evidence that it had been soaked in the wash boiler sent by Zaydee herself for cleaning the chimpanzee. Later, the bones had been picked and trimmed clean, as I had done for the anthropoid, probably with the same dissecting kit. ("God," John had said, "I hate to see you digging out that fellow's filthy nose." How much had someone enjoyed excavating Zaydee's?) Now, the clean bones were boxed and filed among the items of the Holtzerman Collection for which she had paid fifty thousand dollars. For that, and for the interesting friendship of Dr. John Gordon. She would be near him now for a long time.

There was not in my mind the slightest doubt that the skeleton was that of Zaydee Proutman. The age and sex were clearly marked; the teeth were as remarkable as she had boasted; the height, as reconstructed from the limb bones, corresponded to hers; the forehead was full and rounded, the cheeks wide, the chin weak. If I had been a member of the FBI, with their laboratory behind me, I would have sent in a sample of the spongy bone from the vertebral column, and after it had been ground, immersed in A and B sera, refrigerated, and tested, I would know whether or not this woman belonged to the same blood group as did Zaydee. I didn't want to know any more than I did right now.

All this, I was fully aware, might have been done to her body, done with the facilities present in the Museum, and in the time free to carry out the whole process. Done not easily, not pleasantly, but thoroughly. If you have spent much time around the odds and ends of economic life in an American graduate school, you can't have missed knowing at least one medic or premedic who was paying his way by working in a morgue. Theirs are the best stories, and they tell them most often, and so you learn all you need to know about rigor mortis. First it isn't there, and then it is, and then it isn't; and this last limp stage would have been reached in Zaydee Proutman's body sometime in the first night. After that, it could be undressed and the body bent double to fill the ape kettle. Flesh cut off and burned, with clothing, in the furnace. Slow cooking and simmering all Saturday night, all day Sunday, all Sunday night. The bones piled in trays, hidden in locked cupboards, picked and cleaned when no one could see. I had been away from the laboratory from the fourth until the thirteenth of November—for eight days, for nine nights.

Of the accessories to the body, two had turned up, certainly—the corset steels, the earring—one at the place of Zaydee's death, the other, along with the probable weapon, near the corpse of Randy Bill. The gold blouse may have been in the Corset Room or in the missionary barrel, in either or in neither. And there was still a question about the Mexican bracelet in Esquire's pocket. It looked as if someone, after going to enormous trouble to conceal the body, had been a little careless or a little mixed.

Someone. Face it. Who? By person or persons known. By Randy Bill; but not alone, and possibly not at all. Very little pointed to him now—the umbrella, easily thrown into Zaydee's car which the murderer could not expect Randy to drive off, and the earring. I had been present when the earring was found, crushed and blackened, at the edge of the cliff. A dozen women and one man were standing huddled over the spot, and all of them might well have stepped on it during the four or five minutes preceding Lawson's discovery. But just before, one woman had stood there alone, her thin stooped figure silhouetted against the wild lake, a pathologically timid woman who had scuttled ahead of all the others. Mrs. Alpheus Harvey could easily have planted Zaydee Proutman's earring.

So back again to the staff of the William Henry Proutman Museum, to the six who, through varying motives and intensities, all disliked Zaydee: to Jensen, Esquire, and Isabelle; to Miss Barton, Alpheus Harvey, and John. Between the moment when, hurt, angry, frightened of the future, I had gone out of the Museum to the moment when I had returned up rain-swept Broadway and seen that the car no longer stood before the door, thirty-five minutes had passed. Alpheus, Esquire, Miss Barton had each told the Sheriff of leaving separately within the first five minutes. John said he heard the car drive off at six o'clock. Any one of them could have lied; any two could have collaborated; all six could have worked together. For Jensen could have returned to the Museum and Isabelle joined Esquire. Not any two; one would have to be Jensen or John, the only person qualified to run that affair at the furnace well enough to deceive the engineer. And one had to be the only person who could macerate and dissect, who controlled the means of destruction and the method of concealment. One person had to be John Gordon. Perhaps one person was enough.

CHAPTER XXIII

They were laughing in the laboratory, a guffaw, a deep chuckle. Two men. I was on the stairs, tiptoeing, mouth dry, wrists weak, knowing that, for my safety, I must behave as if nothing had happened, wondering how I could.

"*He, he*, sure is a good one, Doctor Gordon."

"Did you ever hear the one about ..."

I leaned on the door frame as Randy had done. Esquire was grinning over his broom handle, John sprawling at my desk, pipe hanging from his mouth. Suppose I said, "You dirty murderers—"

I said, "Good morning."

I mustn't—ever—look at the shelves on the north wall. I must look straight at John. He was on his feet, coming toward me, holding out his hands for my coat. He looked, as I hadn't seen him since the murder, perfectly at ease. I couldn't prevent him from helping me out of the coat, because I had never wanted to before. He hung up the coat and bent his head down to my hair; and Esquire, still grinning, withdrew. John's hand touched my cheek.

"You're pale, Kay. Was it a rotten Christmas?"

I mustn't cringe. "Yes."

"So was mine." (I'd better let my head down against his shoulder.) "But all the others will be different. We'll have fun."

I tried to pull out of his arms. "John, isn't it as bad to make love in the morning as to ... to drink before noon?"

The arms tightened. "No, it's good." His mouth met mine, hard. And it *was* good. For the moment, I did not have to fear that I was not behaving as usual.

"John, remember, we work here!"

He released me, laughing. "I'll try to remember until 5 P.M. But not after that. You aren't pale right now, Kay."

But I would be again. I felt cold already as I moved toward the cartons of unmeasured skeletons on the south shelves. He stopped me.

"Let's lay off that today. I've had enough bones for a while."

"Yes," I said. "Then what?"

"We'll go over the measurement cards to date and sort them according to age, sex, and condition of teeth."

"Yes." Was he looking at me queerly, testing my reaction, or was he just as usual? I couldn't tell. I'd never be sure again.

"I want," he said, "to get together all the dope for my paper on dental condition. I never saw worse. Did you?"

"I've seen better." Wasn't that a dangerous remark? It didn't seem to be, but he could be a better actor than I, and more experienced.

I got out the card file and tabulating sheets, and began sorting cards into two piles, males and females. My hands were awkward, and I made a lot of mistakes. John, dividing the male cards into age groups, jeered gently, "Can't you tell the difference between a man and a woman? Darling, I've always thought you were quite aware of it."

He held out three female cards in the long brown fingers I had loved to watch in their fine control of small, precise instruments. How had they looked, grasping the scalpel throughout a night of horror? This place must have been a shambles, and this man, my lover, the presiding butcher. My stomach muscles contracted, and I had an almost un-controllable desire to stare at the unmarked skeleton box on the north wall.

Miss Alice Barton saved me. She came in so very straight and prim that I was sure she had heard John's delicate bit. And he thought so, too, for he rose, stiff and flushed when she spoke to him.

"Since I was on my way here to ask Miss Ellis to lunch at my home, I am also bearing you a message from Mr. Harvey. He wishes to see you about the budget for laboratory supplies as soon as it is convenient."

"I'll go now, of course. And thank you very much, Miss Barton."

"You are welcome, Dr. Gordon. You will meet me in the library at twelve, Miss Ellis."

It was a statement, and I agreed. Then they left me alone. John need have no fear of leaving me unguarded: I had no further desire to explore his grisly domain. But he didn't know that. Why did he think it safer to leave me here than on all the previous days? Why was he cocky, amorous? Was it all an act? And would he report a successful perform-ance to his fellow murderer abovestairs?

During the night before, after I had put Mrs. Hawks to bed, too full of turkey and aqua vit' and a cold in the head to notice my strangeness, I had eliminated two of the six possibilities from co-operative murder. Jensen was definitely out. If he had killed Zaydee, he would have needed no elaborate assistance from John in the disposal of the corpse. He could have dumped her in his furnace and cleared out the residue at his leisure, before Sheriff Barton Brown thought of looking inside. Al-though I knew my liking for her softened my judgment, I removed Is-abelle Williams from the list. She could not drive a car, and on the night of the murder it would have been a long hard walk from Lake Laurel in the rain, particularly in her condition. And I was sure her concern for the truth, her fear, and her ignorance of what troubled her husband were real. Esquire knew something. He had found something or seen something—or smelled it—and that, I was almost sure, was all. He was-n't telling what he knew. Probably, like me, he was afraid of what the killers might do to him. If Esquire had been the murderer, I did not be-lieve that John Gordon would have gone through all that hell to help him. Esquire as a murderer would have been as good a solution to all the Museum's troubles as was Randy Bill. John would have turned him in without compunction, which one shouldn't have for murderers, any-way. Miss Barton just might have helped someone else, but I couldn't see her doing much laboratory work, but jewelry could be hidden in her house, or other noncombustibles. You couldn't hide anything from Mrs. Jim Watson, and if Randy Bill's co-operation had failed, and the law had begun to prowl, it would not have been through the bureau drawers of his cousin, Miss Alice. Most probably she was not involved at all. She had been the one calm, natural person throughout the whole affair.

Things could be hidden at the Harvey home, and probably had; e.g., the earring. "You don't like the old bitch any better than I do," Randy Bill had said to Alpheus Harvey, and the Museum meant more to him than to anyone else. "You will regret this," he had told Zaydee Proutman, but she had not been given time for that. If Alpheus had killed her, had returned to the Museum after Miss Barton and Esquire were gone, and John had come upon him with the body, then, knowing John's estimate of his own character and his feeling for the old man's very different qualities, I felt he would have done everything to conceal the evidence. The career of John Gordon and the life of his friend would thus be secure. And Alpheus Harvey, accepting the maximum in human collaboration, would have behaved just as he did—cut the salary of his savior and retained the potential danger of me in the laboratory, because both were the right things to do. John had no reason to kill Zaydee Proutman. What was needed to consolidate his position was not murder, but marriage, as per tentative schedule.

If I were to swallow any lunch at all under the eyes of a shrewd hostess who had witnessed my condition of the day before, I knew I mustn't see either of the potential killers. I took my coat and went to the library, leafing through journals until Miss Barton put on her rubbers and summoned me at one minute of twelve. There was no terror for me in her home, but there was a lot to deal with. For Miss Alice asked me if I had applied for a scholarship, and I blurted out that I'd like to go right away.

"Why don't you?" she asked. Scholarships, I told her, were not open until September, and application for a loan from the Graduate School would bring to Professor Alden's attention the fact that I was quitting my job. It was the best job he had had to offer anyone that fall. He had given me the chance, and he would not give me another soon if I left this place for no apparent reason. With no family to back my future, it was a terrible risk to take.

"For no apparent reason." Miss Alice repeated my words without stress. The silence lay heavy upon us, and then she went on, "There is your great-aunt. She is a woman of very considerable means?"

"Yes."

"Ask her to help you."

"It would be no use. Aunt Jane only helps those who have helped themselves. She sent me her first present when I wrote her that I had a good job. She would do nothing for me if I were leaving it."

"She has no family feeling?"

"No, and after all she doesn't know very much about me. My mother died when I was born. She was the daughter of Aunt Jane's sister, who had been dead a long time. Aunt Jane didn't know Mother well, and of course my father was alive then to look after me more or less. One summer when he was in Peru, and I had whooping cough and no camp would take me, I went to her summer home with a nurse. We stayed in a caretaker's cottage almost on the beach, with rambler roses growing over brown shingles, and I had a white rabbit. I saw Aunt Jane only in the distance, because of the whooping cough, and perhaps because I look like my father. He was good company, but not very reliable about money. Anyway, she gave me the rabbit and, when I came here, the handwoven homespuns and the silver fox jacket. There was twelve years between gifts. No, Miss Barton, I couldn't ask her to help me now."

Miss Barton sat straight and still. Then she raised her eyes and said, "Miss Ellis, I will gladly give you five hundred dollars whenever you wish it."

I gasped, "Oh." I felt gratitude mounting pink to my cheeks, and I felt something else. Fear. This could be a bribe, hush money because I knew too much. It could also be a trap. A few days ago I had been reluctant to consider leaving my work even in the following September; if I agreed eagerly to go at once, it would show that I knew at least a part of the secret of the Proutman Museum. Revealing that, I might never be allowed to go anywhere again, except into a wooden box without a label.

"No," I said breathlessly. "It's the kindest thing I ever knew, but I couldn't. I'm almost sure to get some sort of scholarship in September, and I can save the rest of the money by that time. If I left in the middle of the year, I couldn't tell Professor Alden why. Could I?"

My eyes couldn't meet hers.

"No," she said. "No. I hadn't thought of that. There are so many things to think of."

The moment was soon to come when I could no longer avoid Mr. Harvey. He stood in his office door as I passed, after the disconcerting lunch. In the dim hall light his hair looked like rolls of dust, his face more gray than yellow.

"You," he croaked, waving a limp claw, "come in here, please."

There was no pleasure about the room where Sheriff Brown had separated good from evil, and a weasel still mounted fitting guard over yellow old newspaper pages spread on the desk. Mr. Harvey lowered himself to the desk chair, indicating a seat for me with an upthrust of his chin. He scratched the ear with the gold chain and the hearing-aid, and stared at the paper. The type was gothic, the newsprint broken by three smudged and faded halftones. Up came the head with the question. "You know about this?"

"I don't think so."

"Huh. Sure you don't?"

"May I look at it closer?"

Nodding, he pushed the paper toward me. "*Carpathische Anzeiger*, Mai 1897," I read across the top. "Oh, yes, the missionary story about the people in the Holtzerman Collection. I haven't seen this paper, but we have copies of the photographs downstairs. They aren't very good, are they?"

"So you have photographs, but you don't think they are good." This with the yellow tooth showing. "I'm sorry, because I find them interesting, most interesting."

"Do you, Mr. Harvey?"

"Yes, Miss Ellis, I do." He leaned back in his chair and smiled. "It is rare, isn't it, to have photographs of anthropological specimens? You must often wish you had more of them. Don't you?"

"Yes, Mr. Harvey, of course we could be more sure about the race type if we knew something about—well, pigmentation, for example."

"Um. Miss Ellis, suppose these two men and the woman whose pictures are printed here were dead and buried in the cemetery you call H Lower, and suppose their skulls are in those boxes downstairs. Some day you will be labeling those skulls, and you and Dr. Gordon will be observing them very carefully. I have great respect for you both as thorough workers, Miss Ellis."

"Thank you," I responded, with more apprehension than gratitude.

"Um. Now, then, if you saw the skull of one of these people whom you are already acquainted with from those photographs downstairs, would you recognize the original?"

Here was danger, not in the answer to his question, which was an unequivocal no, but in the way I gave it. He mustn't guess that I understood why it had been asked.

"I couldn't recognize it," I said quickly, "and I'm sure no other anthropologist could. So many of the contours of the living are gone in the dead. The hair covers the shape of the skull, and layers of fat change a face from its sheer bony structure. And the nose would be particularly hard to recognize because the part that sticks out from the face is cartilage, not bone. That's one of the most characteristic things about the appearance of a person, and none of it remains on the skull." Had my voice come steadily to the end? Everything I had said was true, and that should have helped me.

"Um." He sat up straight, and the horrible silent laugh shook him briefly. "Disappointing, isn't it? Scientific truth. Useful sometimes. Good day."

A bad day, and the end still to be faced when John, overcoat on, stood over me and said, "Kay, it's 5 P.M. You have been warned."

"Is that supposed to be funny?" I tried to turn a gasp into a giggle and pulled on my coat and hat before he could take them.

"No, darling, just fun."

"Not here."

"Right. Away from interruptions. Come on."

We walked through the hall, his arm holding me close to his side. Through open doors Alpheus Harvey watched us, and so did Miss Barton, but my glazed eyes could not read their expressions.

"We'll go to the garage and pick up the car," he said.

"No." I pulled us to a halt on the sidewalk. "I can't. I'd love to. You know. But I can't."

"Why?" His tone cut.

"Because Mrs. Hawks has a dreadful cold, and I've promised to get her supper. You know how awfully good she has been to me, John."

"Yes," he said, "better than the rest of us. All right. We'll walk down to your house and I'll wait while you feed the old girl, and then we're off for the evening."

I didn't say no. I mustn't pull away from him. I must smile up at his face. In silence, very close, we passed along the dark, almost empty street. I was trembling a bit, but I knew how he would probably interpret that. The last block now. We were at the gateway to William Henry Proutman Park; it was time to cross the street. The arm through mine drew out and closed around my waist, and I was pulled through the gate and against the inner surface of the stone wall.

"We're going to settle this now." I was held tight against him. The other hand was reaching for my throat. Mad thoughts in my head. This is like movies, *Love from a Stranger*, *Night Must Fall*.

"Settle what?" I breathed.

The face came down toward mine, the hand had my chin, gripping it. "You're my girl," he said.

"Am I?"

"Of course. Ever since you walked into my office the first day. You know it as well as I do."

"Y-yes."

His mouth was on mine, choking a rising cry.

He raised his head a little, still holding me immovable against him. "Then what," he said, "are we waiting for? Let's get married."

For a moment I could not speak. If he meant it, it was a reprieve—of sorts. "We, get married?"

"Yes. Now."

"Now?"

"How about tonight?"

So I was not to die. There was another role for me. The girl who can't be forced to testify against her husband if anything ever goes wrong.

"Are you crazy?"

"Crazy about you." It did not ring true.

"Oh, John, I can't." I hoped fear sounded like girlish confusion.

"Why?"

"I can't leave Mrs. Hawks like this, when she's sick. I can't ..."

"Can't leave your work for fear the boss will scold?"

"Silly. We'd be going right on together at the Museum whether we got married or not."

There was iron in the arm across my shoulder. "We would not. I don't want you around the laboratory, Kay, after we're married. I want you in our home. There's a pretty decent little bungalow for rent on the Lake Laurel road. We could build in the spring."

He was kissing me again, and I was coldly editing that speech, stripping it to the core. "I don't want you around the laboratory" was the text. Footnote one: I am prepared to pay a high price to keep you out.

"You think of everything, don't you?"

"*Mmm hmm*. O.K.?"

Fool him, do your best. You still could die here. "Darling." I put my hand on his cheek, my cheek on his coat, pressing hard. I giggled. "Darling, no."

"Did you say no?" It was not a lover's voice.

Neither was mine. "John, listen to some sense. You and I have worked hard to build up a good reputation in this town. Kiwanis, D.A.R., Missionary Societies. You—we're going on living here, and we want to keep that up. We nearly lost it over ... over Randy Bill's mess. Let's not spoil everything by eloping tonight."

We went out the park gate just as the lights blinked on in the Christmas tree and were reflected in Mrs. Hawks's windowpanes. But on her porch he said, "You haven't told me when you *will* marry me, so I'm coming in and wait until you do. If it takes all night. And if Mrs. Hawks is already in bed, I wouldn't be too mad if you didn't tell me until tomorrow morning."

I unlocked the door. There was nothing else to do. I crossed the entry, John close behind, and flung open the parlor door. One glance, and I knew that for one night, at least, I was safe from death or a fate that was worse than death.

"Good night, John," I said, and held out a polite hand.

"Good night," he said, and the humorous twist to his mouth admitted defeat. Not many murderers and seducers, however practiced, would care to meet, in the course of their work, a fat uncorseted old lady with straggling carrot hair, sitting in the middle foreground and soaking her feet in a hot mustard bath.

CHAPTER XXIV

"Kay, do you have to leave me?" Mrs. Hawks was feverish in the morning, really ill.

I kissed her, hoping I would catch whatever she had, and promised to stay with her all day and quietly thanked heaven for a respite. So I was at home when the mail came and saw the letter before the neighborhood knew about it. It was covered with foreign airmail stamps, and it had a West African postmark only ten days old, all of which I hoped wouldn't raise Mrs. Hawks's temperature to a dangerous degree. I took it up to her room. When I returned later, arms numb from bearing what she would doubtless consider a light breakfast, I was prepared for the flood of detail about Mrs. Steinhardt and the heathen and the silk dresses and the airmail, but not for what she handed me, saying, "This is for you."

It was a snapshot, made with a small Brownie, skewed, hazy, but unmistakable, the image of a black girl with bare legs, full calico skirt, peppercorn knobs on her head and, from neck to waist, straining across her generous breasts, the gold tissue blouse of Zaydee Proutman.

"There's writing on the back," prompted Mrs. Hawks. "Ain't it wonderful!"

I read aloud to her, "'Deborah Mary Akasanti, a good Christian. Taken, developed, printed by her brother, Isaiah David Akasanti, December 20, Gombo Mission Camera Club. God bless the kind ladies.' It's wonderful to say the least. Eat your breakfast while it's nice and hot."

I went to the phone and called John. Better deal with this myself than have to meet his voice at an unexpected moment.

"John?" soft, faintly amorous.

"Yes. Oh, Kay."

"I'm terribly sorry I can't come to the laboratory today. Of all days. Mrs. Hawks is really sick. She looks as contagious as the devil, but we'll hope for the best. Don't you dare come near this pest house."

"Is there something I can do?"

"No, really. Thanks a lot. I'll be seeing you pretty soon."

"O.K. Still love me?"

"You should know, but I don't think the operator needs to."

"You win."

This round, yes. But not the next. Not the final decision. I dressed to go out, and went upstairs for the breakfast tray, telling Mrs. Hawks that I was going to the drugstore for aspirin and a thermometer. I managed to knock the African letter off the quilt and to pursue it under the edge of the bed. The snapshot went downstairs on the tray.

Ten minutes later, Isabelle Williams was letting me in at her door. She looked sleepy, but she and her house were neat enough for a party.

"Miss Kay, I got the key. You found out something. Is it very bad?"

I shook my head. "It doesn't have to be. It's something not directly from the Museum. Maybe you could help."

"I'd like to."

"Isabelle, you remember the day at the Missionary Society. I brought a camera. You brought a dress."

Her lids lowered ever so little. "Yes, I remember, Miss Kay."

"Mrs. Hawks, the president of the Missionary Society got this by air-mail today."

She did not need to turn the picture over; she studied it a long time.

"Mrs. Harvey," I suggested, "could have put the blouse in the box, just before we went home."

Isabelle sighed. "You know I did."

"Not till you told me. I saw a piece of it when I was helping Mrs. Hawks, after the others had gone home."

"Miss Kay"—Isabelle was crying—"what you must think of me for holding out on you on Christmas Eve! I didn't think the blouse had any-thing to do with Miss Zaydee's being killed. Not anything different than what we all know. It was hanging on that wax lady in the Museum, the one whose dress I mended, draped round her shoulders. Esquire saw it there the morning the Sheriff had us all come to the building. He thought Miss Zaydee and Mr. Randy had been fooling around in that room before she went off with him, and she put on her coat and forgot the blouse. Miss Zaydee had been killed, and Esquire didn't see why she should be shamed, too. Neither did I. That's all, Miss Kay. Except, later, I kind of hated to see it around the house, and I kind of hated to waste it. When you walked into the Missionary meeting I was sure you would recognize all that gold cloth, so I hid it in my pocket. But I was-n't very smart about it, was I?"

"I think you were very kind, Isabelle. I'm glad you and Esquire did it for Mrs. Proutman. If that's all Esquire had on his mind, he should rest easy."

"It isn't all. Miss Kay, didn't you find out one single thing on Christ-mas day?"

"A little." I didn't look straight at her. "I think I know what Esquire knows. He may have found something, as I did, that seems to mean that Mrs. Proutman was killed before Mr. Randy drove away. Somebody at the Museum may have known it and helped him to get away. Since she was dead, they might have felt it was better that the body shouldn't be found in the Museum."

"Yes, it could be. Finding Mr. Randy with the body. Helping him tote it to his car. They wouldn't know he'd get killed himself."

"No, they couldn't."

"You don't think"—panic was in her voice—"that it was Esquire who helped Mr. Randy?"

"I know it wasn't. Forget all the rest. It's most of it guessing. Everyone trusts and likes Esquire. If he has stumbled on some of this, he'll forget it soon. It needn't touch you or the baby. Good-by. I must run."

The worst thing about housework is that it gives you so much time to think about yourself. Dishes, dusting, meals, and furnace all can be attacked and conquered to an unbroken refrain of How I Suffer. Fact and fantasy jumbled my mind all day, where in a haze, words, looks, gestures of John, Miss Alice, and Mr. Harvey clutched like malevolent arms to drag me down to death. It would be so easy, after a little while, to get rid of a girl who was all alone in the world. Name three easy ways, said what was left of sense. Well, here's one: They could bring in some man—John's Chicago brother—and see that I went out few times, and, after he went away, say I had eloped and had written Miss Alice to send on my things. No one in Hinchdale would question that authority. Aunt Jane would not communicate with me for years nor worry about a letter returned with "address unknown." Sometime at an anthropological conference, Professor Alden would say to Dr. John Gordon, "So that little secretary of mine eloped with your brother, and it didn't last. Too bad."

In my better moments, just after carrying up meals and shifting my attention to Mrs. Hawks for a bit, I saw clear alternatives for the future. I could go or I could stay. I could take Miss Alice Barton's five hundred dollars, with its tacit agreement to silence, add the two hundred of my father's insurance, plus my own savings in the Proutman Bank, and walk into Professor Alden's office at Oldwick, announcing that my boss had wanted to marry me and I couldn't take it. It was the sensible though humiliating course, the one I should probably be forced to choose. If I were permitted. It was Miss Alice's idea, and I could apportion no more than a little guilty knowledge as her share in the crime, but how would it suit John Gordon to have me and my suspicions transferred to the office of the head of his avidly pursued profession?

I could stay in Hinchdale and marry him. Even now, after the horror and the fear, there was warmth in the idea, and in his arms I might forget; but, pushing a vacuum cleaner around that little bungalow on the road to Zaydee's house, I would have time to remember everything. And some day John would know it. He might not kill me, but after even the frankest conversation about it all, what would our married life be worth?

It was the chicken that ended that argument. I found it in the pantry, a big bird that had to be cleaned at once, lungs, gizzard, guts, a little blood, and then long, slow simmering. "Smells are surer than sounds or sights." I dined on hot milk, but Mrs. Hawks smacked her lips over the second drumstick and said she aimed to get up 'round noon tomorrow, and I was to go to work same as usual.

Tomorrow. Another day of straining concealment to the danger point; and, with or without sleep, I had got to take it. In the heavy dream that finally came near dawn, a dynamo whirred in my stomach, shaking me, I thought, for hours before it became a sound toward which I was struggling. I stumbled into the living room, picked up the telephone receiver, and heard:

"New York is calling Miss Kay-thrine Ellis. All right, New York, here is your party."

"Yes," I said to the clipped masculine voice, and "Yes," again. After that, "I want to do whatever is right, but in my circumstances it would be difficult ..."

He explained my circumstances. Everything went black before my eyes. There was nothing in the world but that sure, improbable voice.

"I don't understand why," I gasped at last.

He told me why.

"Yes, I ... guess I understand now," I repeated slowly after him, "I am to leave here on the eleven-o'clock train and take the plane from Chicago." I scribbled an address. "Someone from your office will meet me at La Guardia Field."

I dropped the receiver into place and put my head down on my arm. When lights no longer shot at crazy angles before closed eyes, I raised my head.

The clock on the mantel showed just past seven; eight o'clock in New York. I was important enough for a man like that to get up early. For a few moments I sat and thought, but not for many; it must all be action now. I called the drugstore and asked them to send word to Esquire Williams to come to Mrs. Hawks's house at once. That should take half an hour. I zipped on my housecoat. I packed a small bag—a sweater, a dark plain dress, night things. I opened my typewriter and wrote two letters, one to Mrs. Sarah Hawks, one to the address in New York, hoping it was legal. I stamped them and put them in my purse, together with my bank book. I had the coffeepot on the stove when Esquire's soft knock came on the kitchen door.

He listened, submission in his bearing, hope in his eyes. "You're sure that Isabelle ..."

"Miss Ellis, you can count on me and Isabelle right through to the end of eternity."

I gave him the bag I didn't wish to be seen carrying through town. Epp

Marks would flag the Chicago express. Esquire would meet me at the bank at nine o'clock, and then I had a job to do. He went, and I got breakfast for Mrs. Hawks and took it upstairs. She was asleep, her mouth open, the forehead beneath the rutabaga hair moist and cool. I put the tray down softly on her bureau and tiptoed out. She had been awfully good to me.

Tidy the kitchen, straighten the bedroom, drink a cup of tepid coffee. I could eat a large lunch on the train. If I took the train. Dress with care, though fingers shook which shaped curls and zipper caught in violet skirt. Wipe off smeared lipstick, and this time, steady hand. Hat at pert angle. Silver fox soft around a face now flushed and thin. Straight stocking seams. No slip showing. Off.

CHAPTER XXV

I came down the steps of the Proutman Savings and Trust Company, facing, across Broadway, the red twin mausoleum with the name of the deceased cut in gritty sandstone. On the stone porch before the glass-encased redwood, I stopped openly to straighten my hat. This was my last visit to the William Henry Proutman Museum, and it no longer mattered what anyone thought of me. I went in, thinking about a girl with red hair who had been a bride twenty-five years ago.

Mr. Harvey and Miss Barton followed me down to the laboratory as soon as I said I had to see them there: that part was easy. The look on John's face when he came forward to meet me in the laboratory door was the hardest. He fell back when the old people appeared behind me, and I knew I should never again see that look for me. He got chairs from his office, and they sat in front of me, Miss Barton very straight and looking directly into my eyes, Mr. Harvey hunched and fidgeting with his watch chain, John under the window by the gas stove where the ape had simmered, sun falling on the lock of black hair, on the brown briar of the empty pipe between his lips.

I leaned against the laboratory counter. "I'm going away." My breath came a little hard. "I am not coming back. I could have gone without coming here, but before I go, there is something I have to know. If I don't, I'll never have peace."

I paused. No one spoke or moved. John was trying to light his pipe.

I went on, "I know what happened to Mrs. Proutman. I know you can all do the same thing to me. But it might not be quite so safe. Before I came here, I mailed two letters. One of them to Mrs. Hawks, telling her I shall write to her from New York in three days. She talks a lot. The other letter is to a lawyer. It tells him to look after Esquire and Isabelle

Williams if anything happens to me. The Williams are on their way to New York now. The lawyer expects to meet me at La Guardia Field late tonight. If I am not on that plane, he'll go to a lot of trouble to find me. My great-aunt Jane is dead, and she has left me her estate, the house in Westchester, the house on Cape Cod, and a lot of money. So they'll hunt for me."

It was a cheap, ostentatious speech, but it might save me.

Miss Barton spoke. "Didn't you tell me, a day or two ago, that your aunt would never do anything for you?"

I nodded. "It was you who changed that. Aunt Jane stated in her will that everything was left to me because I was the kind of person who joins the D.A.R."

Even in this moment John's mouth responded to my cynical smile.

Mr. Harvey thrust his deaf gray head forward. He asked hoarsely, "What did you say you knew about Mrs. Proutman?"

I went over to the north wall and picked up the ape's box and put it on the counter. Then the box behind it. I opened the second box, looked in, felt deep, and from beneath Zaydee's skeleton, drew out the two metatarsals. I looked steadily at Mr. Harvey while I held them toward John Gordon.

"There were too many bones," I said. "These belong to the chimpanzee."

"You ..." said John. He did not take the bones.

"It was careless of me to leave them in the wash boiler. You see, I know how it was done. There was a smell from your Chinese rug, the one in front of your cupboards. I was gone from the laboratory for eight days."

Silence. Then I had to go on. "But I don't know who killed Zaydee Proutman, or exactly why she was killed. I can't go on puzzling about it all my life. I'd go mad. I'd rather die."

I covered my burning face with my hands, pressing back tears.

"You thought we were all three involved in Mrs. Proutman's death." At Miss Barton's quiet voice I turned to meet her level gaze. "Alpheus Harvey thought you and Dr. Gordon did it together."

I saw Mr. Harvey's slight nod.

"Dr. Gordon," she continued, "thought Alpheus Harvey killed her. But I *knew*.

"I knew, of course, because I did it. You see, Miss Ellis. They are as surprised as you are. Yet it was quite simple. Everything Mr. Harvey and Esquire told Barton Brown was true. So was almost everything I told him, but I left out a few details. Mrs. Proutman came into the hall of the Museum as I was about to leave. She opened the door and made a remark about the amount of rain. It was a vulgar remark. She had left the umbrella in this room and she wanted it, but because she had recently appeared to Dr. Gordon in a rather unpleasant light, she did not wish to return to his laboratory at the moment." A new note came into the quiet voice, stiffened it. "She sent me.

"I went. Dr. Gordon was in his private office, typing. He neither saw nor heard me. I went up behind Mrs. Proutman. She was standing under the chandelier. She fell on the floor. I took the keys out of her purse, put back the Museum keys on their usual hook in the director's office. Then I looked at her. She was dead. It seemed a good thing for us all.

"I had to hurry, then, to get to Mrs. Watson's at six. I unlocked her car and put the keys in the ignition. There was always the chance that some car thief would drive it off. It seemed a good place to put the umbrella, too. Then I went to the D.A.R. meeting.

"I had a pleasant evening, but I was a little anxious, so at half-past eight, after Mrs. Hawks and Mrs. Phillips had left me at my door, I came back. I unlocked the Museum door, and I was just stooping over Mrs. Proutman when Dr. Gordon came through the exhibition hall. He said, 'She's been dead for some time. Poor old boy, what can we do for him?' In that way I knew he thought Mr. Harvey responsible.

"You know what was done. I took the hair pins and jewelry, and went home. You know what I did with the earring. And her beige pumps."

"You dyed them."

"Yes. All of mine are black. I had forgotten how strong the sense of smell is in youth. In age it is almost gone." Her eyes were not kind. "Everything was all settled quite nicely. And then you did not go away."

"But Randy Bill ..." I said. "You couldn't have counted on him. He saved you. You let him die—a murderer."

Miss Barton smiled, serene. "Mr. Bill was the instrument sent to serve. It had to be, for the good of us all."

"It did not have to be." John was on his feet, pipe clattering to the floor, eyes blazing at Miss Alice. "If you had let things alone, it would have been all straightened out in a day or two. Mrs. Proutman—I had obligations to her. I was ready to fulfill them. No one needed to die. That's why I called her house at eight o'clock. When I supposed she was still alive. The later calls, of course, were bluff. We would have been married, and Harvey would have been right back at the Museum."

He took a long breath. "But she was dead, and you deliberately made me believe Harvey had done it. That could have been bad for all of us. Proutman's will made no plan for the Museum beyond Harvey's lifetime. And anyway, I couldn't see him burn for a woman like Zaydee. You"— he took a step nearer her chair—"you tricked me into all that hell. You knew I wouldn't have done one damned thing to save you."

She said to him, "But you have done it." She was still smiling.

He turned to me, his eyes a black smolder. "When did you suspect?"

"I don't quite know. Soon after the Sheriff dismissed the case."

"You made some queer remarks," he said, "but you made them so ... innocently."

"I was innocent when I made them, John."

"Kay"—his voice was dead—"I tried to keep you out of the bloody mess. Always. Since Christmas, I thought maybe we could forget it all."

"Perhaps you could," I said.

"Miss Ellis"—Mr. Harvey took command—"I don't understand what aroused your suspicions."

"You did," I told him. "You and John. Everything was so strained. The funny thing is that Miss Barton was the one person who seemed perfectly natural." The complacency in her face deepened at my words. "Even she urged me to leave town. John never left me alone in the laboratory. You seemed always to be spying on me. And there was the blouse."

"What blouse?" It came shrill from Miss Alice, a growl from John. He had, I thought, looking at him, almost all he could take. He wouldn't enjoy boiling my bones for Miss Alice Barton, and I shouldn't like it, either.

"The gold tissue blouse," I replied. "The one you left hanging on the dummy in the Corset Room. It was there on Monday morning after the murder."

Mr. Harvey stirred, and on his yellow face there was the faint beginning of a smile. "I hung it there," he said. "I thought it would be interesting to see who took it down. But the Sheriff interrupted my observations."

"Where," Miss Barton demanded, "did you find it, Alpheus Harvey?"

"In the library," he said. "Monday morning, on the floor under your coat hook. Hadn't you planned to burn it, too, because of the metal threads?"

Her face looked crumpled. "Yes," she said, "I had. I must have dropped it and forgotten. There were so many things to remember."

"I washed the rug, too, Miss Ellis," Mr. Harvey explained. "I thought it might confuse you. What called my attention to the whole affair was that the laboratory was much too clean for Monday morning. There had been a lot of washing up in here. Are you through with your speech, Miss Ellis?"

I nodded, waiting.

He stood up, straighter than I had ever seen him. He seemed taller than John, towering over Miss Alice. "I have something to say to you. You were right. We are all involved in the murder of Mrs. Proutman. Miss Barton is the murderer. Dr. Gordon is accessory to the murder. It would be difficult to prove my complete innocence, since I am the person who most obviously profited by her death. Miss Ellis"—the sharp eyes behind the pince-nez held me motionless—"you are safe. No one"—

he turned for an instant toward the others and back to me—"no one is going to do you any harm. But we are in your hands. There is a telephone at your disposal. What are you going to do?"

I knew then what John had meant about the integrity of this old man. I looked at Miss Alice's horrible sure smile, and I thought of what she had been willing to do to us all; and then I remembered that unwittingly through her, I was rich and free, and Isabelle's baby could play on a Cape Cod beach. I did not look at John Gordon. I knew too well how he looked, how he could make me feel, and, basically, what he was like.

I turned away from them all and took up the accessions register and opened it to a fresh page. Uncapping my fountain pen I wrote, slowly because my hand was not quite steady:

"Holtz. Misc. No. 1. Complete Skeleton. Female. Middle-aged. Depressed fracture of right temporal region, possibly caused by a blow."

I handed the open book to Mr. Harvey. I went out of the room.

THE END

BLOOD FROM A STONE

RUTH SAWTELL WALLIS

To
Sally, Nancy and Kay
None of Them Can Read

CHAPTER I

THE FEAR

Between the darkening hills it was utterly quiet until the boys came. Two lean farm boys on their way home from the fair at St. Fiacre, with oversized caps and red cummerbunds above their dusty corduroys. They had left the highway for the path along the stream. The older boy slashed at the bordering alders with a short ox goad and boasted, hoarse and happy.

"You know, kid, there's not a thing in the world I'm afraid of."

"Not anything?" the younger boy croaked. "Not even ... of ... of The Fear?"

The other took a sharp cut at a bush before he said less loudly, "No. I tell you, old man, I'm a modern type."

They had reached the spot where a narrow gap opened between the alders. They could see the early evening light on the water, on rough boulders and on something white at the water's edge.

The boy's words died in a noisy gasp. Sharp wooden click of sabots, flash of scarlet sashes, and all again was still.

The first sound in the silence was small and cold. Hands lifted from the water of the stream. White hands placing something whiter on the rock.

There was no sound when the man entered the lane. The tall shadow of a man stepping light and noiseless in rope-soled sandals, a Basque beret tight above dark brows. The rest of his clothing was careless and urban, tweed trousers, a leather jacket. The man's hand was in the right pocket of the jacket. With wary eyes he watched what the boys had seen.

Suddenly he relaxed. The hand came out of the pocket. He smiled.

"The White Woman," he said.

A very young woman in a stiff white garment was kneeling by the stream, holding a jagged strip of jawbone filled with squat, gleaming teeth. Even in the pale light under the trees, her hair was an extraordinary red.

Startled by the man's voice, she looked up.

"Mademoiselle," he said in a quiet, friendly tone, "I am sorry that I disturbed you. I was passing by when two boys dashed out onto the road. I was curious to see what had frightened them."

"I haven't the slightest idea, Monsieur," she said. "I'm curious, too."

"Well, I can explain that." The tall young man smiled down at her. "They were running away from you."

"From me?" the girl sat back on her heels, regarding him with suspicion. "I find that hard to believe."

He came down to the water's edge. "Mademoiselle," he said, "you are not from this part of the country?"

"Obviously not. Every word I speak tells you plainly where I come from."

"I like the American accent."

"That I doubt." She did not look displeased.

"Believe me," he told her pleasantly, "you frightened those boys terribly. They fled, certain that the devil was literally at their heels."

"I am the devil, Monsieur?"

"Does that surprise you? Look at what you are doing!"

For answer she picked up a brush from the rock beside her, dipped it in the river, and applied it vigorously to the broken jaw.

"Is it fiendish," she asked, "to clean the teeth of a pig that hasn't squealed for fifteen thousand years?"

"It's unusual, let's say. But quite normal, I'm sure. In a laboratory ... preferably in full daylight."

He came down to the rock where she knelt. Through the thick screen of leaves late sun crept in to burnish her copper-colored hair. Water made a quiet gurgle around the rock.

"Mademoiselle," he rallied, "won't your scientific mind admit that you are an astonishing sight to come upon at twilight and in a country like this?"

"The light is a little eerie," she admitted, "but I shouldn't think it would be very strange to find someone playing with bones and teeth in a country that's practically rotten with caves."

"Not to you and me," he said, "but don't think the peasants put in much time underground. Caves are where the spirits live and spirits are real—in Aston."

"You mean it?" she put down her work and gazed at him steadily. Her eyes, set in a creamy oval face, were gray with black lashes.

"I do," he returned her look, half-smiling. "Mademoiselle, in this country men live under the shadow of two fears, the fear of want and the fear of the supernatural. The fear of The Fear. *La Peur*. Ghosts, fairies, werewolves, unnamed shapes. And the greatest of these is the White Woman."

"The White Woman? You think that's why those boys ran away?"

"I know it. She appears in many guises, but the one you hope you'll never meet is when she sits by the river, washing shrouds."

"You're teasing me," she said.

"Not altogether." His eyes mocked her, "And perhaps I should add that the White Woman is reputed to be twice as deadly when she has—hair like yours."

She said briskly, "Too bad the boys came along today. I shan't be mistaken for anything white hereafter. Once I start crawling around every day in cave mud, this will be a different coverall." She wrinkled a delicate nose at the stiff newness of the garment which masked, but could not conceal, a foundation young and curvilinear.

Not from this man, anyway. He said, "You can't, thank heaven, so easily change the color of your hair. But tell me, Mademoiselle, you are planning systematic excavation of a cave?"

"Yes, Monsieur." She studied his face for incredulity and found none. "I'm so lucky to have the chance to dig here in France. I've been trained, of course, in America but I've never been on my own. I didn't dream it would be so easy to arrange."

"I doubt that it would be easy for everyone," he said. He was looking at her intently. It was not a look that merely added: easy for a beautiful girl. "You've already been at work, I see. May I look at your finds?"

"Of course," she moved over on her rock, and he slipped down beside her, touching the objects spread out on her knees. Two coarse gray fragments of a Stone Age pot, a few chips of blue flint, and a long shaft of bone, split and blackened by fire.

"These are just things I grubbed up on the surface," she explained. "I couldn't resist poking about a bit with my hands, but I don't want to do anything that will spoil the site. As soon as I can find a workman, I want to do everything absolutely right."

He looked at her curiously. "You are very serious about this—digging, Mademoiselle?"

Her answer was curt. "Yes, Monsieur."

"Bravo," the dark, intelligent face approved for a moment. Then he said carefully, "I can understand quite well that you have work to do here."

She did not seem to catch the slight shift in tone. "You know the caves of St. Fiacre, don't you?" she asked.

"Only as a boy knows them. I haven't lived here for some years, but when I was a kid, the village school-teacher used to do a bit of digging, and I tagged along. In the days before the last war, things weren't done in any very scientific fashion. The teacher used to hunt for nice-looking tools of stone and bone and not bother very much about what other objects he might destroy with his pick. Then once or twice a year some bearded scholar from Paris or Toulouse would make the tour of Aston and gather up the 'handsome pieces' the local amateurs had collected. Archaeology in St. Fiacre used to be called 'collecting stones' and that's about all it was. Later on, when I might really have learned something about the caves, I was more interested in hunting." He paused, then added slowly, "I am still a hunter."

The girl studied the face now in profile. Lean, mobile and dark, a high fine nose, deeply arched brows. The rock on which they sat was small. Something hard in his right-hand pocket pressed against her thigh. She spoke to break a silence growing too long, "I am in love with your country, even if I don't yet understand it."

His smile was now all warm friendship. "It isn't hard to get to know."

"I should have known so old a land would be full of superstition. I was awfully dumb about the boys."

The man rose lightly to his feet, still smiling. "Mademoiselle, I do not, perhaps, understand you better than you understand my country but of one thing I am sure: you are not dumb."

She, too, was standing now. He held out his hand. For a moment they were close together. A tall dark man, a girl with red hair. Their fingers clasped light and warm.

"*Au revoir*, Mademoiselle," he said and turned up the little lane that led to the highway, and disappeared behind the screen of trees.

Alone in pale gold light by the swift water, the girl gathered up the stones and bones and stowed them in the deep pockets of the white coverall. A sound came from up the road, the purr of a little Citroën getting underway.

The girl stood listening and remembering. *Au revoir*, he had said. Until we meet again. She had forgotten the gun in his pocket. She had forgotten the boys who fled from The Fear.

CHAPTER II

THE CATINE

The hard white road lay flat beside the river. But a yard beyond its farther edge the land began to climb. Lanes, gardens, pastures rose higher and higher to the ridge and the sky.

The house stood beyond a mounting lane of apple trees and quince bushes. A two-storied house of warm stone chinked with earth. A deep roof of purple tiles slanted over the white shuttered windows, and over the cool dark cavern of the barn. The shutters were of white wood; the brown door carried a hand-wrought iron knocker. Above the door and windows of the ground floor, the slim festoon of a grapevine was doubled by its shadow on the stone. Between the lane and the soft, worn stone of the doorstep, grass lay close and green. It was like a house in a book called *Picturesque France*.

To every farmer in the valley of Saint Fiacre it stank. Because it had become a house without a smell. No healthy steam of beans, corn and potatoes from a big iron pot where a pig's soup should be cooking in the dooryard. No rich fumes from a manure pile outside the kitchen window. From the kitchen itself no stomach-warming whiffs of garlic frying in olive oil. Foreigners ate pale, unwholesome food, and what was a farm without poultry droppings on the doorstep and cattle living comfortably under the same roof with the family? This house did not even have a man in it—yet.

The name of the house was La Catine. The house of a woman of bad habits. In this summer of 1935, it was the residence of an American girl with red hair.

The girl now coming out of the lane was mainly aware of one thing about her house. One window. Second floor, right. Through it she could see the black *armoire* sharp against her whitewashed bedroom wall. All the other windows were lightly hazed with gray. No other windows in the department of Aston were like that—screened against the hungry southern flies. Those screens represented a triumph for the girl. That one window was defeat.

Through the kitchen window came the clank and clunk that meant Moise was washing dishes or breaking dishes. There was no sound at all of Neva.

The girl hesitated a moment before the door, then turned away sharply to the right and rounded the house toward the back where the roof extended wide to make a deep hangar for storing crops or ploughs. A hammock swung from the rafters and two bright-striped camp chairs were empty, except for Neva's crumpled yellow novel and a piece of green linen on which someone had been lying heavily.

She slipped out of the clumsy coverall, taking care that no cave treasure should fall from the buttoned pocket. The man she had encountered by the river would have liked to see her now. Smoothly tanned legs and arms were as well-tailored as the aquamarine shorts and sleeveless shirt. She shook out the green linen skirt from the hammock. As she put it on, a quick pucker of the forehead beneath the parted amber hair matched the deep wrinkles in the cloth, but her faintly smiling mouth insisted that such things were not important.

In the quiet of the country evening, faint approaching sounds were clear. The tinkle, tinkle like a bell on a toy lamb, the swish of quick little feet in close-cropped grass.

"Seppel!" The red-haired girl's warm tone indicated she had met a friend.

But friendship seemed too intimate a relationship for the independent little brown personality that trotted to her feet, gave her ankle a darting, civil lick of its black tongue, and trotted off again.

His mistress laughed and followed. Mistress in name only. You can buy, feed, beat a dachshund but you cannot own him. He climbed past a half-acre of corn, skirted the farmer's patch of *sain foin*, the dainty shoots of the season's second crop of "healthy hay," as if he knew it was sacrilege to trample it, and turned to look back at his human companion. His keen little snout, perfect tool for insertion into the burrows of the badger, the *dachs* for which his breed was named, quivered toward her to say she was welcome to take a walk with him if it gave her any pleasure.

Soft as a water color the fields rose to a sharp ridge. Against the sky a farmhouse, purple-roofed like the Catine, with three golden haycocks and byres strung out beside it, looked like a tiny village overpowered by one giant poplar tree. Halfway up the hill, the girl dropped to the ground and looked down on the place she had left. The road, like a white slit between hills as green and smooth as golf links, turned to the right a quarter-mile beyond the Catine, to enter the town of St. Fiacre, and on the left made the first of the many hairpin curves around cave-studded cliffs that led to the provincial capital of Foix. Poplars like plumes and clumps of alders marked the riverbank where the boys had fled in fear. And where the tall, dark young man had stayed to talk. Seppel's harness bell tinkled in the grass, accompanied by his noisy snuffing for departed beast or bird. From the farmhouse on the ridge a little shepherdess was singing a plaintive air not quite on key.

"Seppel," his owner said to the dog's deaf brown rear, "this is a lovely spot."

And added to herself: this is a lonely spot. She had not found it so until that moment. The moment that she saw a man coming toward her up the hill. He was a short man in a waistcoat and white shirt sleeves, his face shaded by a large-visored cap and a heavy mustache. Although his steps were directed toward the spot in the otherwise empty field where the girl was sitting, he did not look toward her. He simply came on. There was something disturbing about his straight, dour progress.

The girl sat up straight and looked around her. The purple roof of the Catine was far below, and there was no one else on the hill. No one except a very small brown dog suddenly come to attention. Seppel, drawn up to his full height of twelve inches, was a dignified animal, but even with nose and tail strained out at opposite ends of his elongated trunk, he did not look formidable. He looked like a brave little dog ready for the selfless protection of a threatened mistress. Touching, if true. Actually Seppel had never been more unaware of red-headed girls in all his egocentric life. For the man climbing the hill was not alone.

The girl, also egocentric, had failed to notice a second oncomer, less purposeful but still coming right along. This dog was high-built, rough-coated in mixed brown and gray, uncouth, unkempt, and with the general air of one whose grandmother had, in the Biblical sense, known a wolf. He had been attending strictly to personal problems until Seppel spoke.

"Woof!" said Seppel.

In the Pyrenees dogs are not fed by their masters, and the hungry look in their eyes is not an anthropomorphic figure of speech. This gaunt dog looked ravenous.

"Seppel," the girl cried out, "come here!"

It has been said that every dachshund thinks he is a greyhound. Seppel trotted ahead.

The man with the black mustache did not call off his dog. He did not look at the girl who sprang to her feet and ran forward. He stood completely still and stared at Seppel. So did his dog, one wild, torn ear twitching as the little monster barked up into his battle-scarred snout. His yellow wolf eyes were glazed with the horror of one who sees a ghost. Pyrenean canines may well have their own particular Fear.

"Nom de Dieu, it's a dog."

Just as the girl's right hand grabbed the harness crossed in the middle of Seppel's stiff little back, the man spoke. He did not laugh or smile. He had merely stated a fact of which he had been doubtful. His question answered, he ignored the somewhat unusual sight of Seppel dangling from what seemed to be the neck. No more than his hound who was now far to the rear, pretending he had never left the corn patch, would this man have thought of saying, "Poor little doggie!"

He said, "Mademoiselle Suzanne Khant," and for the first time looked hard at the girl.

A drooping eyelid should always be diagnosed as a physical affliction quite devoid of sinister psychic connotations, but this is not the common view, particularly when it is set in a hostile face.

"Yes," said the girl, "I am Susan Kent."

The man nodded impatiently and held out an envelope. The turn of his thin brown wrist had unconscious grace.

The small, slightly glazed envelope bore the inscription, "Mlle. Suzanne Kent, à La Catine, près de Saint Fiacre, Aston."

The girl tucked Seppel under her arm and read the letter. If one could trust the dim light, the spider-web writing, the language of almost antique formality, someone named Gaston de l'Arize seemed to be inviting her to lunch on the following day.

She folded the note and looked straight into the eyes of the inauspicious messenger. Beneath the visor of the cap he had not removed, he returned the look with an intensity that had nothing to do with beauty or sex. Even the droop of the left eyelid did not suggest a leer. It merely added to the disconcerting quality of his concentration.

"If you please," asked Susan Kent, "who is Monsieur de l'Arize?"

"Mademoiselle is certain that she does not know M. le Comte de l'Arize?"

"Quite certain," she spoke sharply. Then she colored faintly. "I am a stranger."

The bearer of the letter said with meaning, "The Englishman is acquainted with M. de l'Arize."

The girl was again looking at the letter. His words might have had no significance for her or she might not have heard them.

Might one, too firmly fixed in the habit of resting always by his own fireside to pay his respects in person at the domicile of youth and beauty, might he not dare to hope that she would do him the honor to take a simple country lunch with him and tell him of the work she proposed to undertake in his beloved countryside?

Over the squirming armful of sausages that made up Seppel, she said, "Monsieur le Comte is not in good health?"

"On the contrary, he's quite well."

"He is, perhaps, an old man?"

If anything could amuse the man, this seemed to be it. "Yes, Mademoiselle, he is old."

"Is it far to his house?"

"It is about seven kilometers to the Chateau de l'Arize. Ten minutes in a car."

"I have a bicycle," said Susan. "Come down to the house and I'll write a reply."

During their uncompanionable descent through darkening fields, the man spoke once. "The Englishman has a car."

Susan Kent made no answer.

Windowless at back and sides, the Catine was a black block. Even the front looked none too bright. Firelight flickered from the kitchen, and in the window above two candles burned dangerously near blowing curtains.

Susan Kent pushed open the door and set Seppel on the stone-paved hall. "Come into the kitchen," she said. "Moise will give you something to drink."

On each side of the tiny hallway the house had one room. On the left the glowing hearth outlined an old iron crane and a young girl with the exquisite profile and the great knot of hair of a Grecian goddess.

"Moise."

"Mademoiselle." It was not a lovely voice; hoarse and loud, it had long had good effect on her father's cattle. Her name, rhyming with "Louise," sounded pleasantly feminine to Susan Kent. Actually it was the French equivalent of Moses. "Mademoiselle," she repeated, "I was afraid."

Then she saw the man and turned her head aside, her cheeks a brighter pink than from the hearth fire. The man stood in shadow.

"He has come from the Comte de l'Arize," Susan told her. "Please give him a glass of wine."

She went into the small room across from the kitchen and lighted the lamp on a massive black wood table. There were books in a row on the table, and two crude chairs of oak and leather were drawn up on each side. Across the back wall was the blue-covered cot where Moise slept. Seppel leaped upon it and went efficiently to sleep. Susan found pen and paper and sat down. She wrote slowly and correctly, pausing now and then to push back a lock of her bright hair or to check a word in the *Nouveau Petit Larousse*.

"Please receive favorably my most respectful sentiments," she finished and put the portly pink volume back in its place next to a thin green pamphlet.

Now she was ready to seal her letter. The house was queer and still. No one could be as soundless as Neva when she chose. And in the kitchen the man with the squint might have murdered Moise. Susan held her breath, listening.

After a moment she heard across the hallway another's breath released, a shuffle of heavy shoes, and—as she strained her ears for a moan—a quite definite giggle. Susan got up and scraped her chair loudly before she crossed the hall. Moise was again standing by the hearth. The man took the letter from her and went with a curt, *"Bon Soir."* Whatever refreshment he had received in her house, it had not brightened his social manner.

When the girls were alone, Moise turned toward Susan. "Mademoiselle, I pray you," she slurred the old formal phrase of the countryside, "may I take your bicycle this evening? It is so much better than mine. I want to go to my father's."

"You don't mind riding up a mountainside at night?" Susan asked.

"Mademoiselle, I pray you."

"Of course, Moise."

A dimple appeared at the corner of the girl's soft mouth. "Thank you, Mademoiselle."

"Any time you like, take it. Moise ..." she hesitated.

"Yes, Mademoiselle?"

"Have you ever seen the White Woman?"

The girl was frozen before her. The stiff lips said, "No. Oh, no! You—you haven't seen her, Mademoiselle?"

Susan laughed, "Of course not, Moise."

Moise had not moved. "How do you know about ... secret things?"

"I don't," Susan told her. "It was just something that happened this afternoon by the river."

"Yes, Mademoiselle?" Moise's voice was a croak.

"Two boys saw me in my coveralls and ran away. I ... I was told that they had mistaken me for the White Woman."

Moise drew a normal breath. She came toward Susan, speaking earnestly. "No, Mademoiselle. Oh, no, I hope they didn't really think that! It would be so bad for you. People have said so much ... about the screens and going into caves and why you haven't a husband."

Susan smiled. "Why do the people of St. Fiacre say I haven't a husband?"

"They say—" Moise stopped, crimson. "They know nothing. People!"

"And the White Woman? What do people say about her?"

Moise edged to the door, looking out fearfully into the night. She lowered her voice. "My grandfather saw her long ago," she said. "She held up the stagecoach one night when he was a boy. She was dressed like a bride. And once my father," her voice was hardly audible, "once my father met her right in the middle of the road when he was coming home from the fair. Mademoiselle, she was stark naked and she had red hair. Oh!"

Susan laughed. "Thanks, Moise. Take the bicycle and run along home."

Again the dimple hovered, "Thank you, Mademoiselle."

Susan Kent went up the short steep stairs and stood in the doorway of Neva's room. There was not much in the room except a big low bed heaped with cushions, but the way Neva lay somehow labeled it boudoir.

Neva was looking at the ceiling as if she had been looking at it for hours with perfect content. Her bandeau, her pants and her bangs were dead black. Everything else about her was pale, soft, relaxed. Very slowly her eyes left contemplation of the ceiling for a long look at Susan. They were wonderful eyes, slumberous yet alive. Her voice was like them.

"Moise has departed on your bicycle to meet her lover."

"She called it her father," Susan smiled.

"Really, Susan," Neva was wholly serious, "you must remember it is normal to have a lover."

"I remember," Susan's laughter had a slight edge. "I remember, and I believe you, Neva. But you should remember that it is also normal to visit one's parents. Now and then."

Neva's eyes were superior and sorrowful.

Susan said quickly, pleasantly, "Come in my room and talk to me while I get ready for bed."

The room across the hall was smaller than Neva's and barer. White walls, black wardrobe, hard chair, and an austere bed on which Neva sank with an abandon that turned it into a harem divan.

Susan opened the wardrobe filled with the homespuns and seer-suckers best suited to country living. One garment hung apart. In the candlelight it shone soft and sensuous. Susan took down the hanger and looked at the house coat of sheer white velvet over satin the exact tint of her own skin.

"I wonder why I brought that with me," she said.

"It seems to me," said Neva in her low, refined voice, "the sort of garment a woman should take everywhere with her. Because one never knows."

Susan jerked down a tailored wool bathrobe while Neva went on, "Of course, one doesn't really need anything of the sort. It's not what one wears— However, there are men to whom such things are a stimulus. I have an idea, Susan, you would appeal to that type."

Susan, pulling on plaid butcher boy pajamas, said briskly, "I would-n't know, Neva."

"No," sighed Neva, "you wouldn't know. Susan, when any man sees you in a beautiful white garment and nothing else, that garment will be your shroud."

CHAPTER III

THE CAVE

The old woman stood like a watchtower on the mountain. Dark, massive, and still. Black dress, black knotted coif, a face earth-brown with wrinkles deepened by hearth smoke, and the hard eyes that looked down to the road through the valley.

In the morning sun the road was clear-cut and empty. Toward Foix smoke rose where the gables of the Chateau de l'Arize poked through the chestnut grove. The old woman's back was broad to the chateau. The offensive power of her eyes was trained along the poplar-bordered way from St. Fiacre, heavy artillery for the one human object advancing on her stronghold. A single bicycle, a female rider with green dress and bright hair.

The old woman gave a snort such as cattle make. She turned to the slope behind her, where over crags and boulders rough country linen had been bleaching in the dew. Easily she lifted to her head a dozen folded sheets and stepped down the mountain like a caryatid on holiday.

When the bicycle coasted down the slope to the hamlet at the foot of the mountain, the old woman was in her doorway, roaring "Good day, Mademoiselle."

Susan Kent slipped lightly from the saddle. "Good day, Madame," she said with respect. "You are well?"

"Yes, thank you. And you, Mademoiselle? You're going to climb up and gather stones?"

"Yes, Madame," the girl flung back her head to look high above her, where a hill rose sudden and dramatic, topped by the purple and gray of crowding medieval walls. Christian steeple at one end, Saracen gate at the other, and cliffs falling away from each. There was excitement in Susan Kent's gaze, not for the village, but for something far older. Below the town ran a limestone ridge shaded by bushes and brambles. And there were deeper shadows. Black chinks in the soft white stone, crevices, rock shelters, holes in which men had lived thousands of years ago. One black mouth opened wide. That was Susan's cave.

Reluctantly, she turned to the giantess. "Yes, Madame," she repeated, "I'm going to 'gather stones.'"

"Huh! You're doing that all by yourself? A young girl like you?"

"Yes, Madame."

For a moment they stood measuring strengths. "*Eh bien,*" the old woman conceded something, "Mademoiselle, you'll need help in your work."

"Indeed I shall, Madame." Susan came nearer, explaining with a serious smile, "There are heavy stones, small rocks to remove from the cave floor, a trench to be dug, and refuse to be dumped."

"Huh." The smoky wrinkles between the old woman's eyes deepened. "Mademoiselle, you will find that at this season every man, woman, and child in Volvestre is needed in the fields."

"I know," Susan's tone was humble. "But there might by chance be someone. I need only one man."

"Huh."

"I am on my way now to ask about a workman."

"Mademoiselle," the roar became conspiratorial, "what wages are you thinking of paying?"

Susan studied a face hostile but interested. "I want to pay what is right," she said carefully. "Not too much so that a worker might be tempted to leave the crops. Not too little. What would you say to the same rate as the farmers pay, Madame?"

It was the right answer.

"Where are you going to ask about a workman?"

Susan nodded toward two standard governmental structures on the opposite side of the highway. "At the post office and the schoolhouse. Or," she indicated the village on the hill, "at the mayor's house."

"Imbeciles, all of them," the old woman stated. "What could they do? Listen, Mademoiselle, I'll find you a workman. A good one."

"Thank you, Madame," Susan's tone was noncommittal. "I should be glad to talk with this man. If you will be good enough to tell me where to find him."

"He's out." The old voice was louder and brisk. "You won't need to see him till he comes to work. I give you my word he'll come. It is my son."

Hands on great washtub hips, she stared hard at the girl. "You think my son might not suit you, huh? Well, don't you like the Catine? Don't you like Moise?"

"Yes, certainly, Madame."

"*Eh bien*," Madame drew a logical conclusion, "you will find my son good for your job."

Susan's inquiring eyebrows did not fall.

"Mademoiselle," bellow became bawl. Foreigners, the giantess had just remembered, don't understand French very well. She knew foreigners, people from Toulouse and far places like that, fifty miles away. "*I* found your house. *I* ordered Moise to work for you. I will send my son to gather stones in your cave."

There was no doubt that she would. "Madame, I had no idea you had done so much for me. And why did you take such great trouble?"

The meaty shoulders shrugged. "I get things done around here. I am 'Ri. This is my inn."

"Yes, Madame," said Susan weakly. "How lucky I am to have a place to 'eat *la soupe*' when I'm digging up there." She began to move toward the mountain path. "*Au re ...*"

"Wait a minute!" The bassoon voice stopped her. "You're taking lunch at the chateau today."

The woman knew everything! "Yes, Madame 'Ri."

Craft returned to the leathery face. "You are well acquainted with the Comte, Mademoiselle? You have met in foreign parts? Perhaps in Paris?"

"Madame," Susan was emphatic, "I have never met M. de l'Arize."

"You know nothing at all about him?" It was the light irony of an ox.

"Nothing, Madame. He seems to be an old man."

Unexpectedly a broad grin creased the leather of 'Ri's cheeks. "Yes, he's old. He never was much of a man."

"And Madame de l'Arize?"

"She's dead."

"There are children?"

"Children?" from the depths of 'Ri's strong vitals a hearty laugh blared forth and died. Black eyes again probed Susan's unanswering face. "He has a son."

"Good-bye, Madame," said Susan, "and thank you for the promise of a workman."

"Wait a minute," 'Ri roared after her again. "There is a message for you.

From the chateau. I was to tell you if you went this way. The Comte will send for you at half an hour after noon. He will send—" the grin was back again, "he is going to send—an equipage. *Au'voir*, Mademoiselle," and she marched into the black maw of the inn.

Free at last, Susan Kent sped lightly up the steep slope to the white line of limestone, unaware that official Volvestre was at its government-standardized doors to censure her progress.

"What ravishing legs!" said the postmaster. "What ugly hair!" said his wife. "She'll die of a heart attack from running uphill," hoped the yellow-faced school-mistress from the bed behind her lace-curtained window.

Before the half-cleared opening of the cave Susan pushed back thick bushes still dense around a central pillar of stone. Beyond the arched entrance she stepped into a high gray chamber. The jagged vault, sometimes dipping low, sometimes rising into black infinity, was crossed by streaks shadowy blue and mauve. The floor was hard-packed earth and stone with now and then a streak of vivid green where a fern sprang from a damp spot. Just inside the entrance the floor was gashed by the little trench where Susan had scratched up the first bits of flint and bone.

She moved softly across to the rear wall. Under her feet lay the remains of a life long dead, perhaps even the bones of men and women themselves who had lived and died here when reindeer and woolly mammoths roamed the Pyrenees. Against the wall something white lay on the ground, a substance alien to the cave way of life. Susan stooped to pick it up and just above her head loud wings whirred and a little rat body flew away.

"I don't *really* mind bats," Susan said aloud to herself in English and looked at the thick, irregular piece of plaster on her palm.

"Ah, Mademoiselle," a voice replied in French, "I see you have found my cave."

A curious figure had noiselessly entered. An enormous sun hat like a straw umbrella, a dusty, rusty black gown. There was also a face, round, pink and timid, and a clerical collar not very clean.

Susan identified him somewhat more slowly than she had the bat. "Good day, *Monsieur le Curé*," she said holding out her hand. "You were excavating this cave? I regret that I didn't know. Of course I can find another ..."

"No, no, Mademoiselle," he explained sadly. "Continue. I do not go in for archaeology. Only, this cave is the scene of a sad event in my pastorate."

"Oh," Susan was sorry. "You have been at Volvestre for many years?"

"No, Mademoiselle, two only. Before, I was quite content. But you know, the Bishop ... Well, here I am and here are you with my Virgin."

"With your ...?"

"Yes, with the last little bit of my Virgin of Lourdes. You know, Mademoiselle, when I came to Volvestre, here was this cave. *Tutto Biouletto*, the Violet Hole. You see the color in the rock. Everyone knew the spot. A good many came here. Not many came to church. And I said to myself, 'Why shouldn't this old heathen cave become a great center of miracles just like Lourdes in the very same mountains?'"

"Why not?"

"Why not, indeed! Because this is a country of savages, I tell you. I bought the statue, I set it up, I consecrated the cave, and look! You have all that is left."

"Some impious person destroyed the statue?"

"Mademoiselle," the nice little face grew redder, "it was far worse. They ignored it. Look, up over the spot where you picked up the plaster. The cave is very high. They say around here this cave belonged to the fairies. Children throw stones high into the upper gallery and believe that the fairies throw them back."

"Perhaps the Virgin understood," Susan suggested kindly, "that there are things too old to change quickly. I'm sure she forgave the children."

"Our Lady is ever kind," the priest agreed sadly, "but there are other things that go on in this cave that will take a lot of forgiveness."

"That's too bad," said Susan.

"It is terrible. It is ... Mademoiselle, it is growing very dark in here."

Susan moved forward. "I think it is because we have ... a visitor standing in the light."

The little curé whirled around and faced the long black figure. Broad black hat, black beard outlining hollowed cheeks, shiny black suit, black rubbers.

"*Bon jour*, M. Dumas," the priest was barely polite. "And how is Madame Dumas?"

"'*Jour*, Père Bigorre. She's always the same." The teacher was clearly rude. "Mademoiselle Khant? I come to pay my respects. I am only a poor schoolteacher but a humble and devoted worker in the field to which you doubtless bring great scholarship." An unpleasant red lip slid out beneath his beard.

Susan took his awkwardly extended hand. "Monsieur," she said, "everyone knows what the world of prehistoric archaeology owes to the work of French teachers and," she smiled at the little cure, "of French priests."

M. Dumas bowed without grace.

"I hope," said Susan, "that I haven't been assigned a cave where you had planned to dig? If so ..."

"No, no, no, Mademoiselle," he waved a pallid claw. "Do not think of it. I would never spend a day in this cave. It is much too damp. Look at those ferns. And when you turn up the soil, you will certainly find mud below. You would do well to do as I and wear rubbers whenever you enter it."

"Thank you," said Susan.

"But," M. Dumas went on, "there is a certain cave not far from here. Very wholesome. Very dry. Of that I have been totally dispossessed." He looked at Susan balefully. "By the Englishman. You doubtless know him well."

"Not at all," said Susan.

"But, M. Dumas," suggested Père Bigorre brightly, "everything is not lost to you by having the Englishman established in the Cave of the Cross. They say that he pays your youngest boy a nice little wage for clearing away the dirt."

A frown as lowering as the beard appeared on M. Dumas's face, and Susan said hastily, "Monsieur, were you ever fortunate enough to meet the late Professor Capitan and the late Professor Carthaillac?"

"Yes, Mademoiselle," the frown lightened slightly, "those were great days when the savants made their annual visits to local collectors. Of course, I was only a poor schoolteacher, *but ...*"

"And is there something comparable now? Is there some field supervision from the Ministry of Beaux Arts, for example?"

It was little Father Bigorre who answered. "Oh, yes, Mademoiselle. There is a monsieur who comes quite often, isn't there, M. Dumas?"

The hollows in the teacher's cheeks looked dark and ill. "Now and then," he said nervously. "Not a well-qualified man." His eyes were glued on Susan Kent.

She looked quickly at her wrist watch. "You must excuse me, gentlemen," she said, pushing aside the screen of bushes that made the cave so gray. "I must hurry home. I have an engagement for lunch." She looked from one to the other of the intruders. "With M. de l'Arize."

Père Bigorre bowed low. M. Dumas still stood and stared. The hand she shook was quite cold.

Outside the cave the summer air was fresh and warm. Across the narrow valley, above the next dark range of mountains, rose the great peaks of the Pyrenees, centered by the white summit of Mt. Valier. Susan drew one deep breath. And then M. Dumas was at her side. He did not turn his head toward her; he did not seem to speak. But there were words. Hissed? Or sighed?

"Mademoiselle, remember that this work you are about to do is full of danger."

Then his long black spine followed the curé's little round rump down the mountain.

CHAPTER IV

THE CHATEAU

The equipage of the Comte de l'Arize was approaching the chateau.

An equipage, "a carriage of state or of pleasure, with its horses, liveried servants, et cetera": so it is defined in English, so also in French. The title of the count was ancient and proud; to a certain degree the victoria conformed. The horse was slow, not young, not proud of his assignment. The livery of the servant was a shepherd's beret and a short black smock.

For five rocking and lumbering miles Susan Kent had concentrated on holding the position most calculated to preserve the elegance of her appearance. She had succeeded, and with just enough margin left for appreciation of Madame 'Ri's sense of humor. Her white linen suit was without crease, the wide white hat sat straight and low above decorously brushed amber hair, and now the towers of the chateau were before her. There was a tangle of towers; two of them old. In the Fifteenth Century the family de l'Arize had had wealth and power; unfortunately, in the mid-Nineteenth they had again acquired a little, and the result was a structure which would have made Susan's grandfather Kent nostalgic for his house in Cleveland.

A faded maidservant with a black coif like Madame 'Ri's came out upon the porch, jerked a curtsy, and took Susan up cold stairs to a high bedroom chiefly remarkable for the enormous size of the painted pitcher and bowl on the washstand. Susan removed her hat, dropped it beside her gloves on an ugly red eiderdown, and descended to meet the lord of the castle.

A lord, indeed. Small, slender, elegant hands and feet, a proud thick fluff of white hair, features cut sharp and rubbed soft by age and indolence.

"Mademoiselle, this is an honor," the hand he gave her was exquisite and firm. "It is a great pleasure." The blue eyes looking at her face and throat could justly appraise beauty and also pearls.

"On the contrary, Monsieur," the girl's voice was poised and low, "I know how great an honor you are doing me. Such hospitality is rare in this country."

"Please take that chair. The view wherever one looks in this room is regrettable, perhaps a little less at this angle." His small gesture indicated that he and Susan had seen the world.

She took the stuffed chair and leaned her head against a little square of linen embroidered with stiff flowers. The room was spotted with such minor housecraft on piano cover, tablecloth, footstools, all very clean with the flora beginning to fade. Above the iron grate, where cannel coal burned small and blue, shone two magnificent urns of Sèvres ware. The air smelled of roses and jasmine in bowls and vases, and of the coal oil that had been rubbed into the floor as preventive against the summer invasion of fleas.

"Yes, Mademoiselle," the Comte sat precise on an opposite chair, "we are an egocentric people, we French. Few foreigners enter the sacred family circle. A misfortune, but not for the foreigners."

Beyond his right shoulder hung the portrait of a dark lady in a purple dress. It could have been achieved only by a painter without talent and a subject without joy.

"May I offer you a cigarette, Mademoiselle? Alas, on short notice I could obtain only our dreadful native brand." He held out the ubiquitous yellow package. "But perhaps you have something preferable with you?"

Susan, smiling into his hopeful eyes, opened her bag of soft gold leather and drew out a second yellow pack. "When in France ..." she said. "In the beginning it was a matter of principle. Now I like them."

"Truly?" He struck the government match, waited for the sulphur fumes to die.

"Absolutely."

"Mademoiselle," he held the light to her cigarette, "you are a formidable character."

"Do I say 'thank you?'"

"As you like." He settled back in his chair. "Seriously, it takes a great deal of courage for a young girl to come to a strange country alone and to do what you are doing."

She returned the bright intensity of his stare. "I am not alone. A friend is with me."

"Ah, the young Russian. Pardon me, Mademoiselle, one can't help hearing gossip in a place the size of Volvestre. You know the two most terrible words in the French language? *On dit*, 'They say.'"

"I know what Neva would say if she heard anyone call her a Russian. She's a Latvian."

"A fierce patriot, this young lady who is not Russian?"

"No," said Susan, "I wouldn't call Neva fiercely anything." She made one silent reservation. "Of course her people are Russian but they've lived in Riga since the Revolution."

"Mademoiselle Neva is also an archaeologist?"

"Not at all." She added, "She has been ill. She is here to rest."

The Comte's smile was acid. "She is a wise young lady. There is nothing else to do in Aston. Unless ..."

"Unless," said Susan, "one happens to be mad about it. As I am."

"Ah, Mademoiselle," a gleam rose to the blue eyes bright in the old face, "you, also? You already love this country of mine? And what do you love? Ruined towers, ghosts, caves?"

"Everything."

"I, too, Mademoiselle. And do you know our folk songs?"

"No, Monsieur."

"They are not really very lovely. But they have a certain charm. Listen. They are always sung like this."

His eyes danced. He threw back his white head and sang in a small nasal falsetto:

> *I always vowed when I was young*
> *That I would never marry;*
> *And now today I leave my father,*
> *My tender mother with regret.*
> *Adieu, the flower of my youth ...*

"The marriage song," he explained. "All that is most falsely demure. A proper Aston marriage is arranged, you understand, with all formality some three months before the child is born.—You will forgive an old man. That is not a correct subject for discussion with a young girl."

"I have studied biology," Susan's tone was cool.

"And rightly. But tell me, how did you find your way to this quiet corner of the old Comté de Foix? I know we owe your visit to the fascination, not of ourselves, the living, but of our forebears, the dead, in the great caves above us. But why *our* caves, Mademoiselle? We are a poor country today: we were a poor country thirty thousand years ago. You cannot hope to make rich finds in this valley."

"Perhaps," said Susan, "that's why I am here. When I took my letters of recommendation to Professor Boulanger in Paris, I told him that I didn't want to undertake a job that was too big for my experience, or one that would have to be continued for many seasons. I might come to France every summer. Or the first year might be the last."

"You are prudent," said the Comte. "One can easily see why you were—recommended."

"I am only a beginner. I shall try to be careful. And thorough."

"Mademoiselle," the old gentleman's light eyes were opaque, "I admire both qualities."

The girl's fair skin colored slightly.

The eyes brightened again. "Mademoiselle, in spite of the great distance of our years, I hope we may be friends. We have, I think, certain things in common. Your fondness for this countryside. A certain acquaintance with the world. You will not find much intellectual companionship here, since your friend is not in sympathy with your work ... I myself am entirely alone."

Susan said quickly, filling the pause, "Your son, Monsieur? He does not live with you?"

The Comte de l'Arize stiffened in spine and voice. "My son," he said, "deserted this countryside five years ago. There seems to be little possibility of his return."

To their mutual relief a sound broke the outdoor silence, the purr of an advancing motor.

"Ah," said the Comte, rising, "your fellow guest arrives."

There was no suggestion that this guest was tardy. The little wizened servant opened the door and in stepped a man who had probably never been late. He was tall, ruddy, gray, close-clipped, correct.

"Mademoiselle Khant," said his host, "permit me to present to you your British colleague, Sir Cyril Brrrooks-Brrrr-ooks. Or have you met before?"

"Miss Kent," Sir Cyril Brooks-Brooks's bow to Susan was wooden, but his handshake was not without appreciation. "I have not before had the pleasure."

The Comte de l'Arize said dryly, "Mademoiselle has a different air."

"Oh, I've never seen Sir Cyril," Susan explained. "But of course I've read his book."

"Very few have done so," said modest Sir Cyril.

"Lots of anthropologists have." She turned to the Comte, "It's about the KuKuKuKu clan. In New Guinea. It was a fine job and awfully hard to do because they were always in the middle of a feud."

"Ah," murmured the Comte, "I was not aware of that aspect of Sir Cyril's activities."

"Only a little monograph," the author explained. "A little job I did when I was district commissioner."

"It's first-rate," insisted Susan.

"The English are always so thorough. Shall we," said the Comte, "go to lunch?"

They sat down in a dark, narrow room with a bay window looking out on a garden wall. The sideboard was laden with silver, old, weighty, ornate. The little old servant brought in a steaming platter of Lilliputian lobsters.

"Oh," Susan's eyes were sparkling, "*écrivisses!*"

"You know them, Mademoiselle?"

"Oh, yes. They're the most epicurean things in the world. I adore them. And I've never eaten them except in Paris."

Sir Cyril said, "Crawfish in Paris come too high for my purse. We don't touch them in England."

"Nor in America, either. It's a wicked waste." Susan was busy, pulling off shells. "What perfect sauce."

"You hear, Titine?" the Comte said to the smiling servant.

Susan said to Sir Cyril, struggling politely with the British distaste for taking food in fingers, "I didn't know you were also a prehistoric archaeologist."

"In a very small way, Miss Kent. A pastime. Serious, of course."

"It certainly must be," Susan went on, "if you are willing to work in the Cave of the Cross."

"Eh?" Sir Cyril applied a large napkin to a small drip of sauce from his stiff mustache. Obviously he lacked technique for the sport.

"Every archaeologist knows the flint scrapers found in the Cave of the Cross are unique," Susan went on, "but it must be the hardest site you could have chosen to excavate. Everything incased in solid breccia as hard as stone. Don't you have to hack them out with a cold chisel?"

"And a mallet," agreed Sir Cyril sadly. "But it is ... a very interesting cave. Monsieur de l'Arize selected it for me. I ... naturally, was delighted to obtain such a famous site. Ah, chicken!" Warming to civilized food, he launched a long, dry description of a recent expedition to the great mountain cavern of the Cerf.

"Most remarkable spot I ever saw. Tunnel must be a mile long. Like crossing a desert with a roof."

"Oh," Susan was again enthusiastic, "you've seen the mural paintings? How I should love to! Aren't they marvelous?"

Sir Cyril, setting down his third glass of a wine far less distinguished than the food, admired Susan in a nice elderly way.

"I'll take you there. In my car. You," he turned to the Comte, "probably know every inch of the place by heart."

"I have never been there," replied the Comte.

"I should be delighted to have you accompany the ..." he bowed to Susan, now rapturous over a green salad delicately dressed with herbs, "the archaeological expedition."

"Alas," M. de l'Arize spread his hands lightly, "the climb I hear is steep. I am an old man." His tone lacked regret. "I hope you received proper attention from the forest ranger who, I understand, acts as guide to the cave."

"He did his work well," said Sir Cyril. "And it was thanks to him that I had the most remarkable experience of the trip ... Ah, we have trifle."

A purée of chestnuts, light as thistledown had just been set before him. "Sacrilege!" cried Susan.

"What is that you called the purée ... treefle?" inquired the Comte.

"A British dessert," Susan explained, "slightly indescribable. Old sponge cake soaked in wine and laced with jam and whipped cream. In the interests of international relations, I will not discuss flavor and consistency."

"I thank you for that, Mademoiselle. A fellow epicure. What else shall we discover in common?"

Susan turned from the appreciative eye of the old Frenchman to Sir Cyril who was emptying his plate with stolid Anglo-Saxon sense. "Tell us," she said placatingly, "about your big moment in the Cerf."

Sir Cyril was willing. "Strangest thing I ever saw. It gave me quite a turn. You come to a place on that white cave wall where there is a row of red spots. Seven of them. Been there thousands of years. All covered with stalagmite ... Well, you take just seven steps from that spot and where are you? Just turning a corner that leads to a big high gallery. Signpost someone put up in the year 18,000 B.C. Extraordinary."

"Fun," agreed Susan.

"Very interesting," murmured their host.

That seemed about to end it.

After a moment Susan said, "It is remarkable luck for me to have two experts available for consultation if I find something of importance in my cave."

"Experts?" Sir Cyril demanded. "Two of them? Oh, I see. A nice compliment to you and me, Comte."

"I pose as nothing I am not." M. de l'Arize looked curiously at the speaker. "I suggest that Mademoiselle name your colleague."

"I meant," said Susan hastily, "Sir Cyril, of course, and the field supervisor from the Ministry of Beaux Arts. I understand he comes here frequently."

There was a deep silence. Sir Cyril in an apologetic sort of way seemed to be trying to look like an Englishman who looks as if nothing has been said. The Comte de l'Arize gazed steadily at Sir Cyril. Susan made another try.

"I met a local archaeologist today."

Sir Cyril did not look up from his dessert. The Comte said, "An archaeologist working in the valley?"

"Yes," said Susan. "He called on me in the *Tutto Biouletto* this morning. The schoolteacher, M. Dumas."

"Really, and did he give you any valuable assistance?" There was a small bite in the old man's voice.

"He told me to wear my rubbers."

"I believe you. No other advice?"

She hesitated. "No, Monsieur. His son is your workman, isn't he, Sir Cyril?"

"Not a bad boy," Sir Cyril set down his coffee cup. "Not good, either."

"The Dumas family is a glum lot," smiled M. de l'Arize. "Have you secured a workman, Mademoiselle?"

"Apparently. This morning I met a remarkable old woman named Madame 'Ri. You know her, doubtless?"

"Without the shadow of a doubt. And has old 'Ri undertaken to find a man for you?"

"She has succeeded."

"Who?" His interest was real.

"Her son."

He was silent a moment. "Jean-Marie. That surprises me a little. I would not have expected him to undertake it."

"Will he be reliable?" she asked anxiously.

"Perfectly. What Jean-Marie starts, he finishes. Shall we return to the salon?"

Sir Cyril, seating Susan in her former chair, produced Muratti cigarettes. The Comte gave a voluptuous sigh and inhaled deeply. "Mademoiselle, I am not as good a Frenchman as you."

"That's an odd name for a man—Jean-Marie," said Sir Cyril, offering his *briquet* to Susan.

"It is very common for boys in the valley," the Comte explained. "John, son of Mary."

"'Ri short for Maria?" asked Susan.

"Exactly."

"Isn't the name," Susan wondered, "a French version of one of the most usual masculine names on the other side of the Pyrenees? Jesus-Maria?"

"Very probably. Mademoiselle, you know Spain well?"

"Not really. I've been there two or three times. Not long stays and not for several years."

"Not," he asked, "since the Revolution of 1931?"

"No, not since then."

"Poor Spain," he said.

"Frightful mess," said Sir Cyril.

"You find it so? And you, Mademoiselle?" His interest was weak.

"I'm not a political animal ... yet," Susan said slowly. "Probably I will be some day. Sometimes I feel it coming on. What feelings I have for any side lean to the left, but I don't think my reasons are worth much. If my father weren't such an old royalist ..."

She stopped abruptly.

The Comte looked mildly bewildered. "Your father is a royalist? Is there such a party in the United States of America?"

Sir Cyril laughed. "I think Miss Kent simply means that all the old are conservative and all the young are radicals. Isn't that true?"

"Partly," said Susan.

The door of the salon opened abruptly and a man stepped in. He was dressed like a peasant workman, rope-soled sandals, corduroys and red sash. His hair rose in black waves above his forehead. He held letters in his hand and seemed surprisingly at home.

The Comte accepted his presence with a lifted eyebrow. "Ah, Jean-Marie, thanks for bringing up the mail. Mademoiselle Khant tells me that you are about to become an archaeologist."

In bright light and without the sullen cap, the messenger of the previous night seemed younger, less sinister, but the drooping lid veiled the look he turned on Susan. "So they tell me," he said.

Susan looked steadily at him. "So they tell *me*. Will you come tomorrow?"

"Day after tomorrow. Good day, Messieurs, 'Dame." He went out.

The Comte smiled at Susan. "Jean-Marie is full of character. You will get accustomed to his ways." His hands were turning over the little pile of letters on the table at his side. All the envelopes were addressed in spidery writing similar to the Comte's own hand.

Susan rose. "Thank you for a most delightful lunch."

Sir Cyril followed suit. "We'll leave you to your letters," he said. "Miss Kent, may I have the pleasure of driving you home?"

"It has been a remarkable day for me," said the Comte. "These letters are of no importance when I have real companions. They are, one might say, a survival of the Eighteenth Century. Like the correspondence," he bowed to Sir Cyril, "of your Horace Walpole and Madame du Deffand. Old cronies of my youth, of my middle years in Paris. We meet seldom now, but always the letters go on. Plays, books, fashions, gossip, a little philosophy. In a way, it is all the life we have." His smile was sweetly sad. He looked at Susan. "But I, Mademoiselle, also have my love of Aston."

They had reached the front door. The Comte swung it open and stepped out with an abrupt exclamation. Up the driveway between the poplar trees a little Citroën was putt-putting. It stopped beside Sir Cyril's low green motor.

With unbelievable ease a tall dark young man unsheathed himself from his form-fitting car and sauntered up to the stone step on which the Comte was standing.

"Good afternoon," he said, "my father."

"Marc!"

"The prodigal son. Shall we let it go with a handshake?" His long fingers covered the old man's small ones. "And don't be alarmed. Nothing will be required. I've brought *you* a calf."

He waved toward the little car where bundles overflowed into the driver's seat.

"My son," said the Comte de l'Arize, "you are evidently unaware that we have guests."

He stood aside, revealing Sir Cyril Brooks-Brooks, correct and blank. Susan Kent, just taking hat and gloves from the old maidservant, looked up at the man who twenty-four hours earlier had told her they would meet again.

She and Sir Cyril went down the steps. As she passed close to Marc de l'Arize, he spoke.

"The White Woman," he said and looked down at her with a hard, sardonic smile.

CHAPTER V

THE WATCH

Sir Cyril Brooks-Brooks was stalking game.

In pearl gray hat and blue serge suit he crept along the side of the Catine with a stealthy cinema tread. Sir Cyril would have preferred to call it a quiet approach. To stalk, he felt, was not sporting except, of course, in the case of natives who often, unfortunately, turned out to be the better stalkers. The pretty little peasant maid had told him that Miss Kent was breakfasting under the hangar. When people were caught unaware, one often learned things. And Sir Cyril needed to know quite a few things about Susan Kent.

That beautiful red-haired young woman could, he feared, ruin his summer. Perhaps at the worst, she could only make a fool of him. He wouldn't like that. Nor did he want her around if that quiet little plan behind his plan should mature. The plan meant a great deal to Sir Cyril; he had worked toward it for a long time. If only the girl were a different type. With all that youth and beauty, she could be just what he needed. No, she was too well brought up, too remote to be used in that sort of game. And too hard to persuade. Still, one never knew. Sir Cyril continued to stalk.

"Bow-wow-wow," it was Seppel who had done the catching unaware.

"Fine little fellow," said Sir Cyril, rounding the corner by the hangar.

"Woof," said Seppel. He took a heavy sniff of Sir Cyril's boot polish and sneezed.

"Sir Cyril, we apologize," the Kent girl, looking tantalizing and cool in a navy blue halter and shorts, rose from the table and came forward to scoop up her pet. "Bad little Nazi," she said. "Neva, may I present Sir Cyril Brooks-Brooks? Miss Borodin."

Ha, this was different. This was a girl it was easy to place. But what was she doing with a type like Susan Kent? They must be up to something here in remote Aston. They would bear watching. Sir Cyril would watch.

"No, no, thank you," he refused a yellow bowl of *café au lait* and a tartine spread with heather honey. "It is *I* who come with offerings. Or rather, a humble petition. The day is fine. No work for Miss Kent till tomorrow. I have already made an engagement with the forester-guide. Won't you both give me the pleasure of escorting you to the cavern of the Cerf?"

"How would you like it, Neva?" Susan asked.

Neva raised her great eyes to Sir Cyril. "Perhaps not greatly," she said.

"You might," he smiled at her, "if you tried. It is a beautiful cave full of magnificent paintings made by paleolithic man. It is also a very easy cave to visit. No climbing about, no rough spots. And," he added, "we can obtain an excellent lunch at Foix. My car is at the foot of your lane. Will you come?"

She looked him over from head to foot with the same animal regard for detail that a dog would show. He felt his face grow warm.

"I will go," she said.

She rose, gathering about her slowly a black silk kimono. It was full and long, but she looked more naked than Susan Kent did in her shorts.

"Swell," said Susan. "We'll dress fast. Seppel, where are you going, beast?"

The dachshund twisted free from her arms, tore to the corner of the house. A man came around the corner, and Seppel wriggled agreeably over his ankles.

"The sort of dog who would hold the lantern for a burglar," Sir Cyril observed. Not original but, he felt, true.

"*Quel drôle de chien!* Good morning!" said Marc de l'Arize.

He was a handsome fellow, if you cared for the French type. Susan Kent did, Sir Cyril could see that. Miss Borodin looked stunned. Better keep matters well in hand.

"Ah, M. de l'Arize," he said, "a beautiful day, indeed. I have just persuaded these young ladies to accompany me on a little expedition to the cavern of the Cerf."

"Really?"

Sir Cyril knew he could count on breeding. A gentleman always knew when to refuse. "You wouldn't care to go along?"

"I shall be delighted," said Marc de l'Arize.

As the breeze roused by the open car blew over her neck, Neva smiled.

She was just where she wanted to be, in the place of honor with Sir Cyril beside her, and on the back seat, Marc de l'Arize in a position to evaluate the white nape that had received tangible admiration from every country in Europe. Well, almost every country. In secret Neva sometimes admitted—to Neva—that she had never had a lover from Liechtenstein.

Through a wisp of veil she studied Sir Cyril Brooks-Brooks, another item lacking from her list: pearl gray hat, long face, flat florid cheeks, clipped white mustache, blue eyes whose pure courtesy, only slightly tainted by a just appraisal of herself, in no way betrayed what he intended to do about it. He looked at her now and stopped the car.

"I hope you will forgive the delay," he said. "I should like to ask if the post office here has received a telegram for me."

Marc de l'Arize followed him out of the car. "That gives me a chance to send word that I won't be at home for lunch," he said and strode across the road to the inn where a dark man with a drooping eyelid lounged in the doorway. Neva saw Marc put his hand on the peasant's shoulder in the gesture of a Comrade—but Marc de l'Arize walked like a Lord.

"Look, Neva," Susan spoke behind her, "this is Volvestre. My cave is up there."

Neva tilted her head politely, then turned and gazed at her friend. "I think I shall become quite interested in archaeology," she said slowly, and meant it.

In archaeology and in what else? Was the whole Pyrenees affair a scheme to bring this correct and frigid girl to the arms of the savory M. de l'Arize? Or were they both engaged in some dark impersonal intrigue under cover of bones and caves? Neva shuddered with pleasure and with something else. There were ways in which it was unwise to be entangled just now. But at this moment she could not afford to depart. She must stay—and watch Susan.

On the summit of a castled rock, his back to a crumbling wall, Marc de l'Arize sat close to Susan Kent. Behind them rose the three romantic towers of the ancient Counts of Foix. The air was sweet with eglantine and bright with sun. Susan's head was bare and she was humming a little song.

There was only one reason why Marc did not take her in his arms. A certain small scruple about making love to a girl he might presently shoot to kill.... Regretfully he moved his shoulder away from Susan's, offered her a cigarette, and asked with a smile, "You like Foix?"

For a moment of silence they both looked far down over huddled tiled roofs, over the color and noise of the market place, to the mountain stream that cut coldly through the town. The farther bank was lined with cafés; behind them dark mountains walled out the world.

"Marvelous," said Susan, "and a bit grim."

"It was the largest town I had seen until I was sixteen. I still like it the best."

"Then why did you desert it?"

Marc de l'Arize did not like the verb. "Mademoiselle, what do Americans do when they have no money?"

"They go out and earn some."

"Exactly. It is also a French custom."

Susan said gently, "I was rude. Please ..."

He placed forgiving fingers on the soft nape of her neck. Dangerous, perhaps, to touch her, but coolness between them was not wise.

"Look around you," he said. "Observe the possibilities for earning a living in Foix."

Close to their left a hill, higher than the castle rock bore tier after tier of vineyards; stone walls defined rectangles of green gold.

"Every spring," Susan said, "most of that earth must be swept down the hillside along with the snow. You could get a nice job carrying it back. In a basket on your head."

"Unfortunately, my dear young lady, that is locally considered women's work."

She pointed up the narrowing valley where two tall chimneys were black against the sky. "You could work in a steel mill."

He stared at the blast furnaces, waiting for her to go on.

"Haven't the Germans owned those iron mines," she asked, "since before 1914?"

"Mademoiselle," he said, "is this the fruit of a typical American education?"

"My father ..." she began quickly and stopped. He regretted the pause. "Oh, in a course in economics, one heard about the Comité des Forges. We'll assume, then, you wouldn't be eager to help your enemies rearm. —How about being a waiter in one of those cafés by the river where our friends are sitting in sloth? That's my final suggestion."

"An able occupational survey of Foix."

She looked at him with the smile that seemed so frank and charming. "Yes, you really had to go away. I can't see you mixing a salad for Sir Cyril and Neva."

He said, "That's a rather extraordinary companion for you, that Mademoiselle Borodin."

"She is, isn't she?" the answer seemed natural and spontaneous. "I suppose we rather attract each other because we are so utterly different. At first, she mainly amused me. And, also," the tone grew bitter, "she had a new kind of flattery."

Marc did not doubt that she had been offered them all. "There is actually a new one? For example?"

"Oh, well, the first time we met—in Paris, you know—she asked me, quite parenthetically and in that low, well-bred voice of hers, 'have you never had an abortion?'"

"You said 'flattery?'"

"Of course. I was so obviously a young girl very well brought up. Neva delicately suggested that she was accepting me as a member of her society at, one might say, the third stage."

Marc thought—and said—"You, too, are rather extraordinary."

"I?" She looked quite astonished. "But it wasn't for things like that, that I admire Neva. She has a kind of courage and generosity that I've never met before. She has a small income from an unnamed source. Three days after its arrival she hasn't a sou. It has all been spent on poor compatriots in Paris. And when she has no money and she finds someone homeless, she lets him sleep on the floor of her room."

"On the floor?"

"I know," she smiled, "but I also know that she has repeatedly offered such hospitality to a sick and dirty old man and to a woman with two children. It is what I would want to do. It is something I know I would evade."

"But aren't you doing something rather like that now? I mean, your hospitality to Mademoiselle Borodin?"

"Not at all. It is true that I might have found things here simpler if I had been alone and that she was tired and ill and needed a change. But the equality that makes Neva so fine is quite absent. You see, before I made arrangements, I took her to an American doctor to be certain that she didn't have tuberculosis or ... other contagion."

"That was only sensible, Mademoiselle."

"That," said Susan, "is what I mean."

"She doesn't seem particularly ill."

"No," Susan agreed. "I sometimes wonder why she came." She rose lightly to her feet. "We mustn't keep them waiting longer. Neva and Sir Cyril with his seven red steps. One last look at this lovely spot."

They leaned on the wall, Susan gazing up at the three strong towers that were the last remnant of the fortress of Foix. Marc looked at the girl. Clever? Naïve? Honest? Anyway, lovely and warm and sweet. If only he had not chosen to follow this dark path, or if he were sure she was traveling the same road ... She was humming again the little song.

Marc's deep voice joined her in the tune. And then he sang:

> *Aquelos montagnos qué tan aouti sount*
> *M'empatchon de bese*
> *Mais amous oun sount.*

Susan's eyes and mouth were soft when he finished. "The little shepherdess on the hill behind the Catine sings the air. The words are ...?"

"The old patois. 'These mountains so high forbid me to see the place where my love may be.'"

"Oh."

"The man whom legend says wrote that song was a comte of Foix who lived up here in the Fourteenth Century when that square central tower was built. Gaston Phoebus, they called him. Gaston, the Sun, because of his hair. A bit like yours, I imagine." Very lightly he touched her head. "We had better start down."

As they descended over grass-grown cobbles to the porter's lodge, Susan said, "I've now heard two folk songs of Aston."

"Who sang you the other?"

"Your father."

"That would have been the Marriage Song."

"Yes, it was. How did you guess?"

"Because, Mademoiselle," he could not keep the irony from his voice, "it is the only one he knows."

CHAPTER VI

THE SEVEN RED STEPS

Five people stood by a crevice in the mountain. Above them the summit was bare rock; below them a waste of stones and brambles fell to the white road from Foix. Everywhere in the gaunt, rust-stained limestone of the valley were black holes, holes for badgers, holes for giants, holes for men. Twenty, forty, sixty, one could count the caves in one sweep of the panel of cliffs.

The mink-faced man in the green uniform of the forestry service was adjusting acetylene lamps.

"The treasure is guarded well." Sir Cyril parted bushes that nearly concealed the entrance to the great cavern of the Cerf.

"Yes," Susan spoke softly, sniffing the breath of cave adventure, the sweet choke of water poured on calcium carbon.

"Must one," inquired Neva, "be afflicted with these graceless sandals?" She looked down woefully at brown canvas desecrating black lace hose.

"One must," said Susan, "and one might tie the tapes tighter."

"Oh," said Neva and spilled the contents of her purse at the feet of Marc de l'Arize. A comb, a cake of rouge and a fat lipstick rolled into the cracks in the rock on which the forester bent over his lamps. Marc silently retrieved; on a flat palm he offered the intimate impedimenta to Neva who, with a slow smile, let them linger there.

"Miss Borodin, we are about to enter the Cerf," Sir Cyril announced with impatience.

Marc scooped the cosmetics in his fist and dropped them into Neva's open purse.

The forester-guide had already disappeared into the mountain. Now each one slipped after him for a moment's swift, dark descent. The guide handed each a lamp which revealed a white-walled corridor, thick underfoot with granular yellow loam. Two hundred yards and they came to a locked gate. They passed through and on between walls of red and gray marble, water-cut in deep facets. Suddenly a lamp flashed forward. On the wall there appeared a row of small red hands.

Neva gasped. "Blood!"

"No, no," Sir Cyril soothed her, "red paint."

"I am certain," said Neva, "that it is blood. And dripping from those fingers. One can see that they were cut off at the joint."

"Paint," Susan walked over to the wall. "Dry twenty thousand years ago." She ran her finger over the print of a stubby little hand, over the hard, glistening surface through which it shone. "Stalagmite covered it long ago."

"How observing of you to notice the mutilated fingers," Sir Cyril said to Neva. "One reads, you know, that the cave men cut off a joint or two as a sacrifice to their gods."

"One could get the same effect," Marc's voice came through the dark, "by simply bending one's finger underneath."

"Er ... yes," said Sir Cyril.

"I am about to take you to the Lake," the guide broke in.

"What about the seven red steps?" Sir Cyril wanted to know.

"I always do that last," the forester replied gruffly.

They crossed a sandy waste. "Like a desert with a roof," Sir Cyril repeated for Neva and Marc.

"Have you, Sir Cyril," Neva asked sweetly, "been much in prison?"

"Er ... no," said Sir Cyril.

"It is a pity. If one has been, one finds many similes."

Marc's hand touched Susan's as he bent to whisper, "Flattery?" Her fingers closed lightly over his.

More corridors of marble, gray and red. Then lamps flickered over water.

"The Lake," announced the guide.

"According to the *Guides Bleus*." Marc surveyed ten wet square feet.

"I admit it is not large, Monsieur," agreed the forester, "but it is rare. I shall now lead you to the Black Hall of the Bisons."

They moved on. There was a hushed excitement of drawing near something supernatural, vaguely hostile, waiting for them in the dark.

They came to the final chamber of the cave. Light touched on the first edge of wall. From a gleaming white ground the black outlines of a bison leaped out. For a moment they stood speechless before this image, which, perfect beneath its ancient varnish of stalagmite and guarded by a half-mile of mountain from wind and rain and sun, had lived on long ages after the hunter-artist had vanished forever from the Pyrenees.

Neva spoke first, "It is really rather good."

"You like bison, Mademoiselle?" the forester picked up the cue to his routine. "Well, take your choice." His lamp swept in a swinging semi-circle around the chamber. "There are thirty more."

The path of light swarmed with beasts—little Celtic horses, wild goats, a herd of bison. Drawn in black oxide of manganese, the brilliant profiles fitted into each other and into each vagary of the rock. Wild goat, horns curving back and eyes wide with terror; bison, head down and tail raised to charge, mad from the arrow in his flank; beasts as a hunter saw them twenty thousand years ago.

Neva began to comment and question, but Susan stood apart and still. Marc's low voice close to her ear seemed loud in the dark. "And how do these compare with the beasts of Spain?"

"Spain?" she repeated vaguely. "Oh, in the caves at Altimira? They're too different to compare. The technique, you know. The Altimira bison are polychrome paintings. They ..."

Marc had wandered off, and Sir Cyril, very spritely, had taken his place at her side.

"And now," he proclaimed, "we're off for the adventure of the Seven Red Steps of the Cerf."

Susan sighed faintly. "I am ready." There was always a tourist stunt in every great cave, usually an "organ" of stalactites to be whacked with a stone. Now this.

The forester started briskly over the sand, Marc close behind, Sir Cyril trotting to keep up with them. Neva called out, "We must wait a moment. There is sand in my shoe. It is, moreover, untied."

"I'll take care of it," Susan sat down and grasped Neva's foot. "We'll catch up with you," and began to untie knots and dump sand.

Neva spoke once, "You can, when you like, be quite coldly efficient, my dear Susan."

Susan continued to dump. The men's voices were lost in the black cavern.

"Come on," said Susan brusquely. They stumbled along through the loam between the marble walls. Light waved ahead, and Sir Cyril's lamp joined them.

"Now for our little game."

The forester stood ready beside a gray stretch of rock. A few feet away Marc de l'Arize leaned slim and dark against the cave wall. Between the men gleamed seven horizontal spots of red.

Sir Cyril and the two girls faced them.

"Just seven steps beyond this first dot," the guide's mink nose twitched, his voice was solemn, "just seven steps beyond, a gallery begins. It is a high gallery. You must be ready to look up and up."

He walked to the spot nearest to de l'Arize. "This is the first step. One," he placed his feet with precision, "two, three ..." he relaxed and stepped aside, "and so on. Who will try it first? Will you demonstrate for us, Sir Br-rooks?"

Sir Cyril shook his head. "I have already had that thrill. I suggest that we give first place to our distinguished and charming archaeologist."

Susan, raising an eyebrow to Marc's unresponsive face, replaced the forester in front of the first red blot. In the flicker of the lamps it looked like blood. For such a childish performance everything seemed too tense and still.

She took the first step, short of the second red spot, lengthened it for the third, and the fourth. At the fifth she came even with the mark. Two more. Her lamp began to splutter and she raised it.

"Play fair," called Sir Cyril. "Mustn't peep ahead."

She took the sixth step. The lamp flickered low. She could not see to judge the distance. She felt ahead cautiously with her foot. Her toe began to slip. There was darkness, one sobbing cry, a slow crash on rocks far below.

Four lamps flashed forward on the gray wall, blazed on the seven spots of red. Below the last spot, clinging desperately to a sharp cornice, Susan lay flat on the cave floor. Marc de l'Arize grasped her around the waist and pulled her to safe ground. Then he strode forward and swung his lantern around the sharp corner that should have opened upon a high gallery. Instead, there was a black well down which Susan's lamp had plunged to a depth unknown. The forester was trembling. Sir Cyril Brooks-Brooks stood guard over Susan. Neva knelt at her side.

"I'm all right." Susan was on her feet, staring at the signs pointing the way to death. Marc de l'Arize's hand fell on the forester's shaking shoulder. "Explain. Fast."

"Yes, yes, Monsieur. If I can."

He crept along the wall, past the spots from the fatal seventh to the first, and on past twenty feet of blank gray wall. His light crept slowly ahead, found a sharp turn to a gallery. Beyond it they could see another horizontal band of red dots. "There, Monsieur." His breath came deep and hard.

Susan Kent, white and quiet, moved over to the wall where she had clung. She raised her hand to the nearest shining spot. Then she stood looking at her palm. Across it lay a broad red smear. She lifted her hand to her nose. Then she turned to the four who were watching: to the forester, a frightened animal in uniform, to Sir Cyril Brooks-Brooks frozen in correct horror, to Neva looking as tragic as she had ever tried to be, to the dark, expressionless face of Marc de l'Arize.

Susan spoke, "The flavor is raspberry."

The men looked blank, but Neva with a little cry sank down in the loam and began to tumble the contents of her purse into her lap, clawing frantically in the shadows. Finally, her hands were still. Her great eyes, full of fear, looked up at Susan.

"You are right," she breathed. "My lipstick is not here."

CHAPTER VII

AND SEVEN MORE

For a moment after Neva's cry died against marble, the cavern was still. The rough black rock ceiling, elongated by the lamps to giant teeth, seemed pressed down on the dwarfed human group. Four pairs of eyes, alarmed, surprised, stared at the girl on the ground. Then a voice spoke, quiet and cool.

"Haven't you chosen a rather damp spot for a seat, Mlle. Borodin?" asked Marc de l'Arize.

A nervous rasp of a laugh broke from the spot where the forester stood beside the second line of red spots over which black shadows washed from his quivering candle. Sir Cyril marched to Susan, took her hand in his, and examined the scarlet smirch. He sniffed at the daubs, greasy-bright on the cave wall. When he turned and faced the others, his eyes had a hard blue look that would have been interpreted correctly by a member of the KuKuKuKu clan.

"Put the things back in your purse and get up," he told Neva, who obeyed with angry eyes.

"You are telling me those smears are not made by lipstick?" she demanded. "I am to believe that no one laid a trap to kill Susan?"

Sir Cyril's tone was gentler. "One thing at a time, please."

"Those spots were drawn with lipstick," Susan Kent clenched her stained hand.

"But not Mlle. Borodin's," Marc de l'Arize spoke from the shadows.

"No," Susan, pale and composed, turned toward him, "no, unless ..."

"Unless what, Mademoiselle?"

"Miss Borodin," Sir Cyril cut in, "when did you last see your lipstick?"

"Outside the cave," she glanced quickly from face to face, "when I dropped it on the rock."

"And when M. de l'Arize picked it up?"

Her eyes behind the little veil were now fixed on Sir Cyril. "I—don't know."

"You don't know?"

She shook her head. "There were so many other things that I had dropped. You were urging me to hurry, you remember. And then, I was aware of ..." Her eyes shifted to Marc.

"You saw her lipstick?" Sir Cyril asked him coldly.

"I couldn't be sure. There were several bits of feminine goods. And I, too, perhaps found the episode—distracting."

"What did you notice, Miss Kent?"

Susan answered curtly. "Nothing."

"But I saw it all happen." The forester-guide came close to Sir Cyril. "I was kneeling by the lamps on the rock where Mademoiselle's little objects fell. I saw the lipstick roll toward a crack beside me. And Monsieur brushed my shoulder as he stooped to pick it up." He pointed a steady finger at de l'Arize.

Marc shrugged. "Perhaps. I tell you, I don't remember the exact details."

"And anyway," Susan said quietly, "they have no importance."

"No importance?" Neva lifted her veil and stared wide-eyed and tragic at Susan's tranquil face. "It is not important to you that you have just escaped horrible death?"

"That isn't what I meant, Neva. Somebody painted those spots on the cave wall with a lipstick, but not with yours. And not for me."

"You are sure?" Neva's voice was still a dramatic moan.

"Listen, Neva," Susan explained, "there is only one time since we entered this cave when we have not all been together. During those few minutes when you and I fell behind to tie your *espadrille*. Do you really think that these three men together painted the false signs on the wall and staged the ... accident?"

Neva clung stubbornly to melodrama. "It could have happened."

"It could," Sir Cyril agreed, "with the assistance of a fourth person."

"But there is no fourth!"

"Pardon me, there is," Marc de l'Arize came close to her, the light full on his faintly smiling face. "Yourself, Mademoiselle Neva."

"I? You are mad."

Again the guide gave a convulsive laugh.

"He means, Neva," Susan sounded matter-of-fact and kind, "that I would have been with them all the time if your sandal hadn't come untied."

Her back against the rock wall, Neva looked at the three men and Susan. "That is absurd," she said.

"Of course it is." Susan crossed through the loam to her side. "It just couldn't have happened while we were in the cave. And no one in the world would have planned to murder me."

Neva tilted back her head against the wall. "I do not find everything in the situation absurd." She paused, then added in her slow, elegant voice, "Susan, have you never had an enemy?"

"Let us assume she has none here," Sir Cyril Brooks-Brooks was still official, "and let us not forget that, while it was presumably not aimed at our party, some very dirty work has been done in this cave. You," he turned sharply on the forester-guide, "how do you explain what happened?"

The man's pinched face had regained a certain calm, and in a dull, steady tone he answered. "Boys, Monsieur, hoodlums. They've done plenty of other mischief in the cave, though nothing as bad as this."

"What kind of mischief?"

"Trampled ancient animals drawn in the clay on the floor. Written their initials all over the walls, and the dates they were here with their girls. That's why we put up the gate."

"A gate and a padlock."

"Yes, Monsieur."

"When were you last at the cave?"

"A week ago. With you, Sir Brrr-ooks."

"Were these red dots ... the false row pointing to the pit ... in place then, do you think?"

The man shook his head. "No, I think not, Monsieur. I would not be certain after every visit, but you will remember how great was your interest, your ... excitement. You had me show you every inch of this entire wall, you remember?"

"Perfectly," Sir Cyril's answer was stiff. "I wanted to be sure that the seven spots under the stalagmite were unique, a real prehistoric map, as one might say, not an isolated part of a more or less continuous decoration.... So that was your last visit to the cave? How do you account for the presence of this malicious trap today?"

The man's nose twitched slightly. "I do not know."

"Is there a second entrance to the Cerf?" Susan asked. "Many caves have two or three openings."

The guide shook his head. "Only the one locked and barred."

"Locked?" At Marc de l'Arize's low word, the man in uniform flushed. "Locked," Marc repeated, "today?"

The sharp rodent face turned toward the tall Frenchman. "You—saw, Monsieur?"

"I saw you," said Marc, "playing some sort of game with the lock and key. I had a glance at the gate as we passed through. That lock had been smashed, and it was no surprise to you."

"Y-y-you are right, Monsieur."

"Very well. Who did it and when?"

The man looked around him in fright. "If you tell anyone, it will cost me my job."

"Perhaps it should."

"No, no! What I know has nothing to do with those horrible red spots. I swear it."

"Continue."

"It was the Governor. The Prefect of Aston."

"Now we are *really* absurd," said Sir Cyril.

"I am not so sure." De l'Arize stared down at the forester. "When and how?"

"Two days ago. He had a guest from Marseilles. They had lunched well. And they decided that they wanted to see the Cerf. So they came along without me ... the prefect knows the cave well. And they also came without the key. *Alors*, the prefect smashed the lock with a stone."

"How do you know?"

"His clerk told me. It is easily proved. I should have written already to the Department of National Monuments for a new lock but I am a busy man and there are so many forms to fill." He spread out his hands in a gesture of futility.

"So," said Sir Cyril, "in the past two days the condition of the lock might have been known throughout the countryside and almost anyone could have entered the cave and painted with a crayon, or a lipstick, this series of red spots leading not to a high gallery but to a bottomless pit?"

"Anyone," said Susan, "who knew the procedure followed in showing the cave to visitors."

"Anyone," added Marc de l'Arize, "who had a criminal or an insane mind."

"That," Sir Cyril suggested, "should narrow the number of suspects and simplify the work for the police."

"Police?" the forester repeated. "Monsieur will report this affair to the gendarmes?"

"No," Sir Cyril told him, "*I* shall not. I am a foreigner and a stranger here. You will, I hope, forgive me," he bowed stiffly to the two Frenchmen, "for having fallen into ... old habits in the past few minutes. It is you who will make the report. I shall be glad to drive you to the *gendarmerie*."

"Certainly, Monsieur," the forester replied without hesitation.

"And I, Sir Cyril," Neva laid her hand on his arm, "will you drive me home?"

Sir Cyril looked down at the white hand, the dark, soft eyes, and assumed another old pattern. "Of course, my dear—young lady," he said in English.

"I will just check the lamps before we start," the guide suggested. He handed the first to Sir Cyril. "Plenty of carbide, thank God." The second lamp went to Neva, the third to Marc. He picked up the fourth and started ahead into the thick dark. "Follow me."

"Hold on," Marc de l'Arize called out. "Have you completely forgotten that Mademoiselle Suzanne is no longer equipped with a lantern?" He held out his own to Susan. "Take it. I'll go ahead with the guide."

"Thank you," Susan searched his eyes, obscure in the flickering light.

"You're bearing up well?" It was a question and a tribute.

"Of course. The guide is waiting."

He bowed formally. "Yes, Mademoiselle. I am off."

Off, past the black well down which the lamp had crashed, past the seven new red spots pointing to death, past the mounting shadow leading to the high gallery, past the seven innocent signs made twenty thousand years ago. Jagged blackness overhead, yielding blackness underfoot, between hard narrow blackness, lanterns dim. The two Frenchmen leading, Neva slipping along on Sir Cyril's courteous arm, and at the end, Susan alone.

CHAPTER VIII

THE SKELETON

Susan sat in the doorway of the Violet Hole. In the ten days since the trip to Foix, the cave had changed. Through two great archways curving from a crude central pillar of stone, one could now see the peak of the Vallier, beautiful and stern. Susan's eyes were only for the big round sieve on her knee. Around her the interior of the cave was no longer gray; in the strong light the walls, blue-green and soft, gave the air of a pleasant room. That same light reaching certain crude inscriptions and graffiti had made it quite plain that the *Tutto Biouletto* was not dedicated to the Virgin principle.

Across the rock wall at the back of the cave there ran a shadowy trench six feet deep. A brown cap rose suddenly above it.

"Mademoiselle, are you ready for more?" asked Jean-Marie.

"Just." Susan knocked out the last loose dirt against the side of the rock on which she sat and stretched.

Jean-Marie clambered out of the trench. The sieve he held was filled to the brim with a muddy mass of stones and snail shells. He set it at Susan's side and stood looking down at the little row of objects laid out on a potato sack.

"Not bad luck in the last lot," he commented, running the edge of a thick, short flint scraper against his finger. Beside it lay two or three animal bones split and burned in the hearth fire, a small bone spear point with the tip broken, and a beautiful curved stag horn.

"That's the morning's haul," said Susan, "unless you count this."

In a hand crisscrossed by tiny cuts from the snail shells, she held out a small blade of smoky blue flint. "Neat work," she complimented him, "but you overlooked the fact that after a few years of use and ten thousand years in the earth, the scars on flint shouldn't look fresh."

Jean-Marie's fierce mustache rose in the first smile his employer had seen. "Mademoiselle, I see you know your business."

"I learned it," she explained, "from a professor who used to teach his classes to chip flints, probably because it was easier for him than to lecture to us. Where did you learn?"

"At the Cave of the Cross," he gestured farther up the valley, "where the Englishman is now at work. Before the war a German dealer leased the site and sold the finds to museums in his country. He paid by the piece and didn't come around very often. Mademoiselle, those big blocks of breccia in the Cross are hard to work. So on a slow day the boys who worked for him did a little manufacture. The *Boche* didn't know the difference."

"I don't pay by the piece. Why did you bother?" Clear gray eyes, veiled black eyes measured each other.

"To find out how much you knew," he said with respect.

"And I've passed the test?"

For once he looked at her squarely. "Perfectly." The tone was gruff but as he dropped back into the trench, his hand lifted in salute.

Susan on her hard rock slowly rubbed mud from each bone and stone and chip, searching for the tools by which man had lived twenty thousand years ago. Once her hands closed around an irregular mass, red ochre. With such pigment as this, prehistoric men had painted the hands and the seven dots at the Cerf; with such color they often drenched the bones of their dead.

"Mademoiselle!" It was a quiet command from Jean-Marie. "Come down here, please."

She slipped down into the pit. Imbedded in the wall along the back of the cave lay several large fragments of rock.

"Put your hand in here," he pointed to a crevice between two rough blocks.

Susan thrust her hand through the chink, then her arm to the elbow. "There is a space behind here."

Jean-Marie nodded. "It looks as if someone in the old days wanted to wall off this space for some reason or other."

Susan's eyes were bright. That opening might lead anywhere. Perhaps to a great painted gallery like Niaux or Altimira or Font de Gaume.

Jean-Marie looked at the huge stone fragments without excitement. He picked up his crowbar and went to work.

During the next two hours the cave was still except for occasional taps as Susan emptied a sieve and for a few straining groans when Jean-Marie heaved another rock out of the trench.

"That's the last," he straightened, red and dripping.

Susan knelt by the edge of the excavation. Where the rocks had been piled so long ago, she could see a low rocky arch stretching across the back of the cave. At its highest point it did not clear the level of cave deposit by more than two feet. The opening beneath the arch sloped away to the unknown depths of the hill.

"You must be worn out, Jean-Marie." Susan was remorseful. "Give me just one more sieveful from under the arch, and we'll call it a day."

Jean-Marie drew a hand across his thick mustache. "As you wish, Mademoiselle."

She climbed back to her rock. Her eyes were still shining.

"Mademoiselle!" It was a cry.

A hand rose out of the pit. The hand waved a long shaft of bone.

Susan gave one look and flung herself into the trench. "Where did you find it?" she demanded. "Don't touch a thing. Show me the exact spot."

"Just under the last big stone I lifted." Jean-Marie crept with difficulty under the arch to place his hand where the rock had lain.

Stretched at full length beside him, Susan probed the wet black earth. Her fingers closed on something, lifted it cautiously. Another shaft, very slender.

"Is it—"

"Yes, they're human bones. The thigh bone, and now one of the leg bones, the fibula. Jean-Marie, we may have a complete skeleton here."

Jean-Marie reached for his pick.

"No, no," Susan cried, "nothing but our hands! It's terribly dark down here. Light a candle."

She took the light from his hand and bent close over the floor. "Here is the other leg ... and most of the spine. Oh, if I can only find the head!"

To the left where the stone had left a depression, the shafts of human leg bones now blanched, now gleamed red in the varying candle flame. In a line pointing toward the right base of the arch, the vertebrae Susan had uncovered gave the outline of a spine, mixed with animal bones and snail shells. Close beside the spine they now saw the bones of the arms. Then there was a black space of earth.

"Water must have washed the bones of the rest of the body away from the head," Susan murmured, her chin in mud. "It ought to be at the base of the arch. Here."

Just there. Her searching fingers, brushing back the earth, slipped over the contours of a human skull.

The skeleton lay on its right side facing the inner wall, the depths of the hillside. The head rested against the springstone of the arch. Fallen forward beneath it was the lower jaw.

"Jean-Marie," Susan lifted a large round stone from the earth, "this isn't just some old hunter who crept in here to die. He was carefully buried."

The stone was rounded, water-smoothed, a cobblestone carried up from some stream at the foot of the mountain. Other pebbles of many sizes outlined the rough grave. Beside the head lay a long smooth stone that had been dipped in red.

It was still at the bottom of the pit, and dark. The dead, with head turned away from the candlelight, lay unaware of the two behind him; Jean-Marie quietly concerned, Susan with a face streaked with mud and excited tears.

At the same moment mud and damp became paramount to both. They dragged themselves erect and out of the pit.

Susan stretched her arms high above her head. "Jean-Marie, this is the most thrilling moment of my life."

And it was the moment that the Père Bigorre chose to pay a call. "M-m-Mademoiselle," he gasped, his face a series of little round *o*'s. "I— Pardon me."

"Oh, good day," said Susan primly.

"You were engaged?"

"No, *Monsieur le Curè*. We had just finished, that is, for the day."

He looked sternly at Jean-Marie. "You would do well to."

Beneath the umbrage of his mustache, Jean-Marie's mouth was curving. "Mademoiselle is excited."

"Well?"

"She made a great discovery today."

Father Bigorre was red and stammering. "B ... B ... But ..."

"She has found a human skeleton in the cave."

Susan looked at him in horror. "Just a few bones," she said quickly.

"Where?" demanded Father Bigorre. Obviously his emotion had shrunk, either to relief or disappointment.

Jean-Marie pointed to the pit. "No farther, *M. le Curé*; there might be a cave-in."

Teetering at the rim of the trench, the little priest peered down where the light of the candle, stuck at the right of the arch, flickered over white bones. He did not linger.

He came slowly back to Susan and cleared his throat. "This isn't the first skeleton that has ever been dug up at Volvestre. Two years ago when they were repairing the church wall, they unearthed two individuals under the old fortifications."

"Interesting," agreed Susan.

"They brought them straight to me, Mademoiselle. Just as they should have done. I gave them Christian burial."

"Oh," said Susan. She looked at Jean-Marie.

"Yes," said Père Bigorre, "as was fitting."

Susan sank down on a rock, looking suddenly limp.

"Mademoiselle," he went on, "do you remember the man you were asking about? The scholar, the archaeologist who comes here sometimes to inspect the caves?"

She nodded.

"Well, Mademoiselle, he is here today."

"Saved," Susan spoke softly. "Oh, thank you, I should like to have him see the burial at once before anything is touched. Do you know where I can find him?"

For answer the priest trotted to the threshold of the Violet Hole. "Look, Mademoiselle." His fat finger pointed across the valley where a hillside of thorns and scrub oak led to a limestone cliff. Against the white rock a human figure, too small for individuality, moved slowly along. "Under that thick ivy at the top of the cliff, there are said to be rock shelters. I saw the professor climbing the hill."

"Was M. Dumas with him?"

"When I saw him, he was alone."

"I'm going right away to ask his advice about ... the removal of the bones. Thank you for telling me about him, *M. le Curé*." There was dismissal in her voice.

"Yes, Mademoiselle." He began to go, then turned. "I shall be back."

Susan turned on Jean-Marie. "Listen to me," she said. "Don't let anyone near that pit. That skeleton is an important find. I'm certain it's the first human being of its particular period ever found in France."

"I was only teasing the priest."

"And, as a result, we won't dare to leave the bones here till tomorrow when I could bring my equipment and photograph them in place. Well, thank goodness, there's an expert in the neighborhood to reinforce my word. I'm going to find him now."

Jean-Marie thrust himself in front of her. In a moment he had become the man of their first meeting, sullen, suspicious and dark.

"Mademoiselle, do you know this man?"

"No, I do not."

"You are sure?"

"Of course I am sure. What do you mean, Jean-Marie?"

"Mademoiselle," his eyelid seemed to increase its sinister fall, "you, yourself, are highly qualified for your work, aren't you?"

She looked at him questioningly, "I have had training."

"Yes, Mademoiselle. I have seen you. I have seen other archaeologists. You really know what you are about. It is not necessary to hunt up this man."

She explained patiently. "It is the custom in my profession. When you find something important, you call in another to check your findings. Particularly if you are young. And a woman."

He tried again. "Mademoiselle, consider this. If you call the professor here, he will perhaps bring M. Dumas with him. The schoolteacher is already jealous of you. He will certainly either say your skeleton is a fake or will steal all your glory."

She said firmly, "That is doubtless true. But I will have your evidence about the truth of the find, and in work like this, there is no question of personal glory. Well, I am going. Can I count on you to remain here every minute until I return?"

His tone was curt. "Perfectly, Mademoiselle," he said, and stood aside.

"Thanks, Jean-Marie. Let's hope I soon find this unknown expert."

He stood in the archway and watched her light progress down the hill. When she disappeared in the dense bushes by the stream, he sighed and sat down on the rock to wait.

When Susan came up the slope of the hill opposite the cave, everything was hot and still. Through the rough undergrowth, over boulders, she climbed to the limestone ridge indicated by Father Bigorre. No one was in sight, no one answered her calls. Slow and painful parting of overgrowth revealed rock shelters, but big enough only for badgers. There was nothing to do but go back.

She was halfway down the slope when she saw the stone. It was waterworn, long and slim. An ordinary sort of stone to be found in any stream. It should not have been lying beside a clump of blackberry bushes high above the little river.

Susan picked up the stone. It was about eight inches long and could be gripped nicely in the hand. She held it in the sunlight, looking at it idly, about to throw it down. Then she saw the color. A streak and a smear, dark brownish red.

Ochre? Long ago had some prehistoric man dipped this elongated stone in primitive red paint, the symbol of blood and life, like the cobbles placed round the burial in the cave? And quite recently had some modern archaeologist lost it in this empty field? Susan slipped it into the pocket of her coverall.

The climb back to the Violet Hole seemed long and hot, and there was not much but tedium in measuring the grave and removing the skeleton before Father Bigorre should pay his pastoral call.

They carried the precious bones down to the highway, wrapped in the potato sack. Jean-Marie loaded them carefully into the carrier on Susan's bicycle, and from window and doorway all official Volvestre watched.

"Tomorrow," Susan murmured, "I suppose they'll all be clambering up to see the spot marked X."

Jean-Marie did not smile. "No, Mademoiselle. When they know that you have dug up a dead man in your cave, they will not come near."

CHAPTER IX

DANSE MACABRE

"Champagne, of course," said Neva.

"Of course not," Susan pushed back her chair from the dinner table and lighted a cigarette. "Consider the standard obtainable in the local *bistro*. Consider the total absence of ice in this town. Sweet and ish. Anything else you demand for this party, but not champagne."

"Champagne," repeated Neva softly. Her heavy dark eyes focused across the lawn toward the Catine, scrutinized the green figs on the little tree over their heads. Her voice was conspiratorial. "We are having a ceremony, not a mere party. However bad the quality may be, champagne is the essential wine of ceremony. I feel, my dear Susan, that it might be well for you to be extremely conventional."

"For me?" Susan relaxed from the excitement of the day, smiled at her somber friend. "I thought you were mainly harried by my utter respectability."

"This is quite different," Neva's tone was grave. "People here do not understand you. As I do. There was, right at the first, that strange demand for window screens. Yes, I know it was because flies are not good for health. But they do not know. You see," she explained as to a child, "people in Europe have really lived a long time without them. Millions of people. Then, you are a woman alone, young and noticeable. It isn't strange, is it, that there was talk about the supernatural?"

"So you've heard about the White Woman," Susan's voice was constrained.

"Naturally," Neva returned her look with opaque eyes. "And you must know that there would be talk about your working alone in the cave with a man."

"Anything else?"

"Well," said Neva, watching blue smoke curl from her nostrils, "there is the skeleton."

"What about the skeleton?"

"Listen, Susan," Neva sat erect, "be sensible. Bones are nothing to you. But that is not the common view. A girl who rides off merrily with a dead man on her handle bars might well be a trifle suspect."

Susan poured a second cup of coffee. "You could be right. Then isn't it a little dumb to underline this final sin by giving a party for the skeleton?"

"I don't agree." Neva tapped a fresh cigarette on a gold case. "Everyone will see you—and the skeleton—in a normal setting. You will be a charming hostess; I have seen you do it in Paris. Everyone will have a good time— Whatever has that dog got?"

From the ditch bordering the dry brook that ran through the orchard, Seppel was struggling up the grass, his progress braked by the amount of breath necessary to utter gasps of excitement and retain a large object in his mouth. Susan fell upon him just as he attained the brink.

"Give."

He held tight. Susan, swinging him by the harness, came back to the table pulling at one end of a long, smooth stone.

"Good heavens!" She sat him on her knee and pried up his teeth. "What does he want with a thing like that? He'll wear off all his teeth."

Still gripping the leather strands that met on his sleek brown back, she hurled the stone far off into the orchard grass. A volcano of canine erupted in her lap. Bays, barks, sobs accompanied each writhe and leap.

"That stone might be a badger from the way he acts."

"Let him go and see what he does," suggested Neva. "He's been struggling in and out of the ditch all day."

"Beat it!" With the first relaxation of her fingers, Seppel was off Susan's knee, off toward the spot which his eyes had never left. The pants and yelps continued as he searched through the grass. His teeth closed happily and he bounded off, ears flying, to the farthest apple tree. There he lay down and licked his game. Susan strolled over to him. Seppel, wary, ready to spring up, kept his eyes on his mistress and his tongue on the stone between his paws. "Come here, Neva," she pointed to the ground beside the scrubby apple tree. "This is what our original young man has been doing today."

Close behind Seppel's beating tail rose a neat little cairn of cobbles and pebbles from the brook.

"*Mon Dieu*, what a dog for an archaeologist!"

"Isn't he!" Susan pulled at the stone between Seppel's black lips. He growled gently. "You're worth your weight in amusement.—Neva, I can't have a party tomorrow night. I've got to work at the cave all day, sifting the layer where the skeleton was lying. I can't let Seppel be a better worker than I am."

"Of course you will work in your cave. I will prepare for the party. I and Moise." She looked surprisingly energetic. "Tonight you and I will go into St. Fiacre to order the cakes and buy the champagne. Tomorrow I will do the rest."

She laid an arm about Susan's shoulder, guiding her toward the house.

"All right," Susan laughed, "we'll buy *napoléons* and *madeleines* and all the execrable champagne you want. And we will also purchase beer and lemon pop. You may know what the countryside thinks proper drink, but I know what it likes. A delectable mixture of the last two items, known as *panaché*."

Under the heavy beams of the kitchen, Moise, washing dishes, looked flower-pink and young. "*Oui, oui*, Mademoiselle Neevaire," she agreed in the voice so much more faunal than floral, "I will ride over to Volvestre to deliver notes for Mademoiselle Suzanne. And afterwards," she hesitated, looking at Susan, "I should like to spend the night at Madame Souquette's, at the farm just up on the hill."

"Why, Moise?"

The girl blushed, twisting the dishcloth.

"If I take the bones I found today up to my room ..." Susan saw her shudder, "then will you sleep here?"

Moise raised fearful eyes. "Mademoiselle, I pray you."

"Of course, go to Madame Souquette's. Moise, we're having a party tomorrow night. The Comte de l'Arize, Monsieur Marc, M. Dumas, Madame 'Ri and her son. Father Bigorre. And the Englishman. Mademoiselle Neva will want you to help her get things ready. Isn't there perhaps some friend you would like to invite? Or have me invite for you? This is to be your party, too."

Moise's delicate face flushed; the dimple appeared at the corner of her mouth. "Oh, no, Mademoiselle! Thank you."

Susan crossed the hall and sat down at the desk. "Thank goodness," she told Neva, "one note at least can be written in English."

"Your French is remarkably good." Neva relaxed opposite her, smoking with deep pleasure.

"It should be," said Susan absently as she wrote. "The investment was heavy, but yours is just as good and your English is much more elegant than mine."

"That, also, is not your native language," Neva stated.

"English isn't my ... Well, of course you're correct. American is something else, isn't it?"

"Quite," said Neva.

"To be as American as possible." Susan sealed the last note and rose. "O.K. Let's go. Let's go to St. Fiacre. But how? Do we walk or do I take you in the skeleton's place on my handle bars?"

"I will ride Moise's bicycle," Neva stated. "Only the brake is defective and on the level that does not matter."

Susan looked surprised. "I didn't know you could ..."

"I am ready," said Neva.

Together they rode down the lane and turned up the highway toward the white box of a market town. From the twin bell tower of the church of St. Fiacre the angelus tolled softly, and from the river side it was answered by a frog. On the outskirts of the village they met another pair of riders, two heavy men in khaki and square military caps.

"The gendarmes," murmured Susan. *"Bon soir, Messieurs."*

They nodded solemnly and the one who passed close to Susan warned, "Take care to light your bicycle lamp, Mesdemoiselles. It is sunset."

When they were gone, Neva spoke, "It should be an amusing party. To see all together at the Catine so many people who either hate you or fear you, Susan."

Before the vine-draped door of the Catine, Sir Cyril Brooks-Brooks was opening the first bottle of champagne. Wafting light of Chinese lanterns fell across his hair, silver but thick, and down the long British planes of his cheeks; bright patches of red danced over the table set under the kitchen window with plates of crusty and creamy cakes, thin bread spread with *pâté de fois gras*, wine glasses, and inelegant bottles of beer and pop. More lanterns swayed from the low apple trees bordering the steep lane where Neva's filmy black gown blew over the legs of Marc de l'Arize. At each side of the house door two tiny pine trees blossomed in rose and blue and gold.

"Wedding trees," Madame 'Ri seated at the guests' table to the right of the door, slapped a hand on each huge knee and nodded meaningly at her companions. M. Dumas, glum and silent, leaned forward over the handle of his umbrella, his wide hat pushed well down to ward off dangerous night air. The *curé* tittered nervously. Across the table the Comte de l'Arize smiled lightly at her fierce old face. "And not entirely without meaning, 'Ri," he suggested.

Pop! Very neatly went Sir Cyril's cork.

"Beautiful." Susan in crisp white held the first glass to be filled. "You've done your job for the evening. Now the three of us will take over.

Jean-Marie will pour, and Moise and I will be the waiters."

With a copper tray bearing four glasses of amber wine, she moved off smiling toward her older guests. Moise held out two glasses to Jean-Marie. Her bunchy blue dress was the color of her eyes; Jean-Marie, under the visor of his best and biggest cap, exchanged a dark look with her. The girl sighed softly and turned away to carry the wine to Neva and Marc.

"On your feet, everyone," roared old 'Ri. "We must drink to Mademoiselle Suzanne."

"Yes, yes!" everyone laughed, everyone clustered about Susan.

"No, no," she protested, laughing. "Not to me. We must drink to him. To the Man. To the Old Man of Volvestre." She raised her glass.

They drank. As the unfamiliar bubbles tickled nostrils, Moise giggled, 'Ri snorted.

"You will still have to respond to the toast, Miss Kent," Sir Cyril reminded her. "Dead men cannot speak for themselves."

"Speech, Susan." Neva's eyes looked large in the shadows where she leaned lightly on Marc's arm.

Susan Kent looked at her guests. They had drawn a little away and she stood alone. Intruder, foreigner, Woman in White. A young girl who, by chance or plan, had all but been dashed to death.

She spoke in the low-pitched voice they did not expect from an American, "I have to thank the Old Man of the Mountain for the most exciting moment of my life. I want to thank Jean-Marie for the thorough and understanding help that made the discovery possible."

In the shadow of the night and of his mustache, she could not tell whether or not he smiled, but his mother was pounding her knees with pleasure.

"I want," Susan went on, "to thank all of you for coming here to help celebrate what is for me an important scientific occasion." Sir Cyril was beaming at her; the Comte de l'Arize approved; only M. Dumas sat dark and suspicious.

Susan sent a special smile to Moise, holding a cream cake toward Jean-Marie. "I can't return the Old Man to his cave. But I can promise him and you that he shall have a future not entirely without honor. He has left forever his mountain tomb. But I can give him two further burials."

Little Father Bigorre's round eyes seemed to hold only childlike curiosity.

"The Man of Volvestre shall henceforth lie in state in a glass case in the Museum of Natural History in Paris. And he shall be forever embalmed in the pages of the *American Journal of Physical Anthropology*." She took a laughing breath. "There, that's over. Now, let's have a good time."

Only a little too consciously she passed Marc de l'Arize and went again to her older guests.

"Mademoiselle," M. Dumas spoke sternly, "there is just one small question I should like to ask you. Perhaps I have not the right. I am only a poor schoolteacher, *but ... Mon Dieu*, what is that?"

That was a sudden blare of music from the window above his head, harsh but still sweet in the night air, the Citronen waltz ground out by the portable phonograph that Neva set in motion.

"The machine of the butcher's daughter!" M. Dumas was astonished. "She lent it to you?"

"Not quite." Neva waltzed languidly over the doorstep. "She rented it."

"She could have afforded to give it to you." The schoolteacher was sour, "Her father made millions selling bad beef for German prisoners in the War."

"You were asking me, Monsieur ..." Susan began above the music.

"No, no, no, not now, Mademoiselle," roared Madame 'Ri. "Now is the moment to dance. You must choose your cavalier and open the ball."

As Susan set down her glass and rose, Neva's eyes mocked her. You will not have the courage, they seemed to say, to choose the man you want.

"Monsieur de l'Arize," Susan's smile was proud and sweet, "will you do me the honor?"

"Mademoiselle, it is my honor," on his feet, quick and graceful, the old Comte bowed low. "We shall see how a beautiful young barbarian can waltz."

He led Susan to the most nearly level space in the sloping yard, and laid a firm hand on her waist. His back to them, Marc leaned in the window and flipped over the record. It was waltzing in the grand old manner and as they glided and whirled, Susan's light feet scarcely touched the turf. Only the Comte's fluff of white hair rose above her head, but his back was as straight and his arm as strong as if he were his tall young son.

When the small record ended, he led Susan to the table and gave her a courtly bow.

"Don't sit down, Mademoiselle," Old 'Ri commanded. "You must keep on dancing." She raised her voice to conquer the ancient jazz now blasting her ear. "You are not the age that a little waltz leaves panting. Here, Jean-Marie," she bellowed at her son busy at the refreshment table filling Moise's glass with homelike *panaché*. "Come here and dance with Mademoiselle."

"Oh, Madame," began Susan, "let him ..."

"Jean-Marie!"

He came then and in sullen embarrassment put a stiff arm about her. Around the visor of his cap, which in correct peasant fashion remained on his head, she saw Sir Cyril advancing with a smile on Neva. Jean-Marie plodded around without rhythm, and Susan followed without joy. Presently another couple joined them, Neva draped over Marc's shoulder. Then Sir Cyril passed, formal and kind, piloting a blushing Moise.

A last horrible scratch of the needle freed Susan and Jean-Marie, and again she sought her guests. The little *curé* was rising from the table.

"Mademoiselle," his flushed face was anxiously polite, "it is rude to go but I must. Tomorrow morning, I have been summoned to meet the Bishop. It is, you understand, a long ride. I must leave right away."

"Of course I understand. It was so kind of you to come."

"Not at all, Mademoiselle. I thank you for your hospitality." He trotted over to his bicycle lying beneath a quince bush. "Mademoiselle, I shall ... consult the Bishop. Good night, Mademoiselle."

Susan slipped into the chair between the Comte and the schoolteacher. "There was something you wanted to ask me, M. Dumas," she said pleasantly.

The hollow eyes beneath the broad black brim eyed her with hate. "Yes, Mademoiselle. You mentioned the Museum of Natural History in Paris. May I assume," he grated his words against his yellow teeth, "that you have already arranged to sell this skeleton?"

"Sell?" Susan's face was white with anger. "What do you mean, Monsieur? One does not sell scientific material. Before I left Paris, I told Professor Boulanger that anything I might find in the caves of Aston would be presented to the museum for the people of France."

The schoolteacher did not change. "Perhaps," he suggested, "this is not a very important find. Who knows? You removed it very hastily, Mademoiselle."

She was controlling herself now. "Because Father Bigorre suggested immediate burial. But the grave is there for anyone to check. I have measurements and today I have made photographs. And yesterday I did my best to find the expert from ... the Ministry of Beaux Arts, isn't it?"

All three were looking at her.

"Yesterday you ... I don't quite understand," the Comte's voice was clear and kind.

"Yesterday soon after I found the skeleton, Father Bigorre told me that the archaeological supervisor was in the valley. He had seen him climbing the hill opposite Volvestre. He pointed out a man to me near the rock shelters at the top of the ridge. So I went there as fast as I could."

"You found him, Mademoiselle?" For 'Ri it was a low growl.

The schoolteacher twisted the ferrule of his umbrella in the turf.

Waiting to answer, Susan heard the moan of jazz, saw Moise, awkward and happy, dancing with Jean-Marie, noticed that Sir Cyril was opening another bottle of champagne.

"No," she said, "there was no one on the hill. I searched and searched. And all I found was a stone."

"Miss Kent, allow me," Sir Cyril's arm holding the bottle appeared over her glass. He filled the others', drew up a chair and sat down between the Comte and Madame 'Ri.

"Mademoiselle Khant," the Comte told him, "was describing a stone to us. As a colleague it should be of interest to you."

"Ha," Sir Cyril eyed the girl cautiously, "what kind of stone?"

"It was a water-worn stone, long and slim but quite heavy. Much the same sort of thing I've found outlining the burial in the *Tutto Biouletto*. There was nothing strange about it, except for the place where I found it."

She sipped from her glass.

"Well, Mademoiselle?" muttered M. Dumas.

"It was lying beside a clump of blackberry bushes halfway up the hill—Oh, Neva!"

Neva, arriving with Marc to adjust the phonograph, turned lazily to Susan.

"Neva, will you reach inside the window, please, and hand me that stone beside the lamp?"

"You want me to throw this for the dog?" Neva's white arm swept out the stained stone with grace but not neatness. In the wake paper clips skipped to the ground, and a small green pamphlet slid over the sill.

"Don't bother about the clips," Susan called to Sir Cyril's gallantry and Neva's nonchalance. "But, please, oh, please, spare the little green book that contains the dark secret of why I came to Aston!"

It was Marc who laid the stone in Susan's hand and then moved quietly away.

"You can see," Susan held it toward M. Dumas, "those brownish red stains are probably ochre, painted the way the gravestones were. It is believed," she explained to the polite question in the Comte's face, "that the red color represented to paleolithic man blood, the vital force."

No one took the stone. Susan pushing her chair slightly back from the table, laid it on her lap.

"M. Dumas," the Comte asked, "did you see yesterday this mysterious and illusive expert from Paris?"

"No, no, M. le Comte, of course not."

"He would hardly have come to Volvestre without visiting you. I fear," he smiled at Susan, "our good Father Bigorre is sadly in need of spectacles."

'Ri gave him a hard brown stare, "You think Mademoiselle needs them also, M. le Comte?" she challenged.

"I am sure of it," he was still looking at Susan. "What really horrible music, Mademoiselle. Not," he raised a deprecating hand, "that I blame you. One meets it everywhere nowadays. Alas! Last winter when I was in Paris ..."

He stopped.

"Last winter when you were in Paris ..." Marc de l'Arize, carrying a chair, had stepped quietly to the table. Very tall and still he stood looking down at his exquisite father. "Don't let me interrupt you. Last winter," he encouraged with a smile, "when you were in Paris ..."

A flush that was not entirely vinous rose in the Comte's cheeks. "My son," he explained in an acid voice, "is trying to tell you that during my last visit to the capital we did not meet. My dear boy, shall I apologize for being an unnatural parent to—an unnatural son?"

"Oh, no, my father," Marc's smile was all friendliness, "my interest didn't arise from filial reasons, but from, shall we say, considerations of the national debt? —What the devil ..."

Placing his chair close behind Susan's, he was tripped by an onrush of panting, throbbing dog. Like a brown bullet, Seppel leaped into Susan's lap. The gasps rose in anguish as he tried to pull the painted stone from her fingers.

"He sounds positively hysterical," said Sir Cyril.

Susan relaxed her fingers. "Take it and go. We're sick of you," she told the sobbing dog.

With a bound he was off her lap and racing across the lawn to his favorite apple tree.

"Are you in the habit," sneered M. Dumas, "of feeding valuable archaeological objects to the dog? What a carnival he will have with the bones of the famous Old Man of Volvestre."

"The stone is quite safe," Susan said quietly. "Watch him."

"Most extraordinary dog I ever saw in my life," Sir Cyril who had followed Seppel to his cairn returned to report. "Licked it and buried it under the pile— Ah, Miss Neva, sit here. One moment and I will have another chair beside you.... We seem to have finished even your generous supply of champagne, Miss Kent, so I have brought along beer. Whose glass may I fill?"

"I once," said Neva dreamily, "knew a dog even more unusual than this one. Have you," she asked the Comte delicately, "ever taken drugs? No? A friend of mine, a Russian officer, did not like to take them alone. When I was not there or any other companion, he gave them to his dog."

The schoolteacher asked Susan nervously, "Mademoiselle, where did you get a dog like that anyway?"

"In Germany. The Black Forest." Susan bent over the match Marc was holding to her cigarette.

'Ri's old head, heavy with age and wine, was nodding on her black bosom.

"You have traveled a great deal," the Comte said. "Germany, Spain, France. You speak all three languages well?"

"Fairly," Susan raised her head. "My father ..." she stopped.

"Quite the training for a diplomatic career," commented Sir Cyril.

Neva's great eyes contemplated him. She said in her deep, refined voice, "Have you never been a spy?"

There was a long silence. It was Marc de l'Arize who broke it, teasing. "To whom is that flattery directed?"

Neva looked back at him across the table. She did not speak. She rose from her chair, slipped a record on the phonograph, set the machine slowly in motion. She turned then and said to Marc, "You will now dance a tango with me."

Marc did not rise. "Unfortunately, I have enjoyed few social advantages, Mademoiselle. I have never learned the art to which you refer."

"But I have, Mlle. Neva," Sir Cyril, straight and gallant, was at her side. "Allow me to take the place of this lad."

The music brought 'Ri up with a start. She looked about her, then roared, "Jean-Marie!"

He came quite calmly from the kitchen. "Yes, mother."

"Huh, that's better." She grinned at Susan. "It's getting late. But we must drink one more toast." She shoved a beer bottle from her in disgust. "Not in that."

"In my car," offered Sir Cyril, "I have a little brandy."

"Good."

When he had filled her glass, she raised it solemnly. "That little girl," she gestured toward Susan, "is nice. We've got to keep her in France. There's only one way to do it. To the husband," she beamed, "the French husband we will find for Mademoiselle Suzanne."

There was an amused murmur as they drank. It ended in Neva's laughter. "And I," she said, "can name the man. Susan has found him already."

"Neva," Susan's knuckles were white around her glass.

"Oh, yes," Neva went on. "Again, we should drink to—the skeleton of Volvestre. The only man Susan will ever love will be a dead man." She held out her arms to Sir Cyril, "Shall we dance our tango?"

Susan Kent rose quietly. There was something in her white face that silenced even Madame 'Ri, as she walked to the window where the phonograph gave forth languid accompaniment to the tango danced under the waning lanterns by Sir Cyril, all accurate dignity, and Neva, all voluptuousness. Beyond the light Moise moved with Jean-Marie, her blue dress strained tight over her billowy little figure.

The tango died in mid-bar. Deliberately Susan slipped another record in place and came back to the group around the table. She went direct to the chair where Marc de l'Arize lounged, watching her with quizzical eyes. She laid her hand on his shoulder. Her voice was a quiet command.

"Dance with me."

Without a word he got up and followed her. When they had left the ring of light from the Chinese lanterns, they could see the stars. Again the music was the Citronen, but Marc did not take it in the grand manner. He moved very slowly, holding her close against his body. Susan's head slipped into the curve of his shoulder, her cheek found his warm cheek.

Two bicycles climbed the lane of the Catine, ridden by two heavy men in khaki and square military caps.

CHAPTER X

THE GENDARMES

A flat oval basket, smelling of earth, dominated the supper table. Pushed to the edge lay the decaying remnants of civilization—empty bottles, dirty glasses, cake crumbs mashed in souring cream. The Chinese lanterns had burned out and in darkness eight people watched the gendarmes and Susan Kent.

In the glare of electric torches the heaped brown knobs in the basket looked not unlike the mushrooms for which it had been made. Both gendarmes were bending over it. Fatigue had worn down the little individuality they had, and at midnight they were just two policeman in uniforms identical to the mustache. One was only a little taller, heavier, and not quite so slow.

Half an hour ago they had returned to the *gendarmerie* from a long, steep pursuit of a very petty smuggler bringing tobacco over the wild mountain passes from Spain. And instead of hot grog and a soft feather bed, they had found a note upon the floor. A note that could have been slipped under the door at any hour after noon. They had passed the note to each of the eight people. None had seen it before, none could guess its origin.

Susan Kent was the last to read the note. Across the table from the two officers, she held the dirty ruled paper in the light of their lamps. "The American girl," was printed in block letters, "has found a body in the *Tutto Biouletto*." She held it out to the gendarme who was examining somewhat gingerly an earth-encrusted vertebra of the Old Man of

Volvestre.

"But you can see," said Susan, "that this is not a body. This is a skeleton, a very old one."

The second gendarme without reluctance replaced the lower jaw in the basket. "Exactly how old, Mademoiselle?"

"That I can't tell you. But certainly more than ten thousand years."

"How do you know, Mademoiselle?"

"By different ways." Her face, as white as her gown, was tired, proud, and young. "We have dug a trench seven feet deep. Throughout that depth the remains have been the same. We've found bison bones, red deer, wild boar, and stone and bone tools. And these same tools and animal remains were found over the skeleton and in the earth where he was buried."

The smaller gendarme nodded heavily. The other asked, "Mademoiselle, you have proof?"

"I have my notebook kept from day to day. There is the cave itself. And there is my workman."

Someone stirred in the dark beyond them. From the doorstep where she huddled alone, Moise gave a small sob. Jean-Marie walked heavily into the beam around the table.

"Jean-Marie Clanet, do you agree that Mademoiselle has told the truth?"

He did not speak at once and in the silence Susan's hands tightened on the edge of the table. The sullen voice came slow and definite. "Willingly. In all details. Mademoiselle knows her trade."

"How can you be sure of that?" the taller gendarme demanded. "Are you an expert?"

"In a way," Jean-Marie was truculent. "Have you forgotten all the years the boys of Volvestre dug for the *Boche* in the Cave of the Cross?

"Well," he wheeled suddenly toward the shadowed audience, "Monsieur Dumas, you go in for digging in the caves. What can you say about this?"

Only the rasping voice of the schoolmaster advanced from the dark. "In all these matters one must be cautious. It is always possible for a body to slip down from the surface to an ancient level."

The policeman turned back to Susan, "Mademoiselle?"

"If the conditions in the *Tutto Biouletto*," Susan picked her way carefully through anger, "if they were as M. Dumas suggests, then the skeleton might be of recent origin. By recent," she held her bright head high, "I mean several hundred years."

No one spoke.

"Monsieur," Susan spoke again, "there is another archaeologist present who could give us an ... impartial opinion. Sir Cyril Brooks-Brooks."

"My dear Miss Kent," Sir Cyril, stepping out of the night, had never looked more thoroughly the courteous English gentleman, "I should dearly love to help. But unfortunately, it is not my place. I—I am a foreigner, working here only as a guest. Don't you agree, Monsieur?" he addressed the taller gendarme who nodded doubtfully.

His partner spoke respectfully into the shadows, "Would you give us your opinion of the age of Mademoiselle's discovery, Monsieur le Comte?"

It was now de l'Arize's turn to walk—and haughtily—to the bone-piled table. Behind him loomed the dark form of his son.

"I regret," he said formally, "that I can be of no real service to you. Personally, I find Mademoiselle Khant to be utterly charming. Unfortunately, I know nothing of archaeology. Anything I could say would not be evidence."

"Thank you, Monsieur le Comte. And you, M. le Vicomte?"

Marc de l'Arize barely glanced at Susan Kent. "As a lawyer," he said, "I am forced to agree with the statement made by my father."

Susan raised an arm and slowly brushed a lock of hair from her moist forehead.

"Yah." Power burst out of the dark. "Yah, you Georges Lamotte!" Old 'Ri lumbered up to the nearest gendarme and slapped his shoulder. "Yah, you Pierre Ouray! What's all this nonsense about the *Tutto Biouletto? Mon Dieu*, you two fellows know every inch of it as well as you know your own bedrooms. And for the same reason. You know the surface of that cave was packed down as hard as iron before my son began to dig. You ought to know. You've lain on it often enough—and not alone. You and every other kid who's grown up in the neighborhood in the last hundred years. There was never time enough to bury a dead body there. A good half of the village would have noticed any change, and somebody would have told. I tell you my son hasn't buried any dead men in that cave and you know it. Ain't it so? I ask you."

Before the strong black body, the angry face as brown and earthy as the bones, the two policemen quailed.

"You ... you may be right, Madame 'Ri," agreed the shorter gendarme.

"I *may* be ..." roared into his ear.

"It is," his colleague added, "quite possible."

"Huh."

He drew himself up in military dignity. "All the evidence ... the scientific evidence offered by Mademoiselle indicates an ancient burial. I think we need detain no one longer. We regret ... deeply ..."

He picked up his torch, and his partner followed suit.

"Mademoiselle," he turned the beam full on Susan, "is there perhaps someone in the neighborhood who would like to do you harm?"

Susan, eyes wide in the glare, hands clenched in the folds of her white skirt, answered him steadily, "I don't know. I don't ... know."

"Well, Mademoiselle. Good night, M. le Comte, Messieurs, 'Dames."
They wheeled their bicycles down the lane.

Left in pale starlight, figures groped, voices murmured. Susan bent
over the doorstep where Moise crouched, and slipped an arm about the
girl's shoulders.

"Jean-Marie, will you ride with her to Madame Souchette's?"

The answer was a laconic, "Good," as he reached for their bicycles leaning against the house wall.

One by one the guests of the strange party gave the hand of parting
to Susan Kent. Monsieur Dumas's clammy and cold, Sir Cyril's hearty
and kind, the rough, strong grasp of 'Ri, the Comte's elegant and dry.
Did Marc's long fingers linger a bit?

"Good luck," he said oddly, and followed his father down the pale path
between dark, huddled trees.

Susan standing alone on the doorstep of the Catine heard the powerful
snort of Sir Cyril's car, the putt-putt of the Citroën. She stood listening
to the last faint sound dying away toward Volvestre; stood on listening
to the croak of frogs by the stream; listening at last to silence.

A sound from overhead sent her hands to her leaping heart.

"Susan."

Her voice shook a little. "Yes, Neva?"

"Are you never coming in?"

"After a while. Where did you hide?"

"I did not hide," the tones spoke sorrowful reproach. "I merely went to
bed. I do not like entanglements with the police."

Susan's reply was cold. "There is no entanglement. Nothing happened."

"No," Neva's voice lingered over each syllable, "no, nothing happened—this time. Pleasant dreams, Susan."

CHAPTER XI

THE BODY

In the early morning air the Pyrenees stretched across the far highway, thin and blue. Close at hand the valley road ran through a deep
gorge between cave-pierced walls. On a huge rock strangled in green lay
blocks of gray stone that once formed a watchtower on a feudal bound-
ary line, and across the road a graveyard sloped to the river where a
great white Christ shivered beneath dolorous cypress trees.

Oxen came down the road, immaculate brown beasts with hand-woven nettings covering their faces from the flies. Their dark, dirty driver wielded his goad with a sharp, graceful turn of the wrist reminiscent of the Comte de l'Arize. Or of Jean-Marie. A coifed old woman hobbled after an unruly pig. A foreign girl braked her bicycle to a stop.

The dreams that Neva had wished for Susan had been few. Dawn at the Catine had revealed the littered dooryard below her window, the untidy kitchen below stairs. Along the road to Volvestre the air washed everything clean, and an hour before digging in the *Tutto Biouletto* was an hour for exploration. Numberless caves through the valley, through a dozen valleys leading to the high peaks, the bleak passes, another nation. Susan in cave coveralls and carrying a steel claw hid her bicycle in the alders and crossed the boulder-filled stream.

Behind the tower-crowned rock, she began an aimless zigzag climb which bore increasingly to the left of the hill. As she came out of the thickets, she could see above her the ridge where, two days ago, the figure of a man had seemed to move along the rock. Turning, she saw that she was now nearly opposite the cliff where Volvestre stood like a toy village on stilts. She must, then, be near the spot where she had stumbled upon that enigmatic stone smeared with red. Somewhere close by there might be a cave. Behind one of these rough boulders, under a tangle of bushes, perhaps some snakelike tunnel curled away to a paleolithic stronghold deep in the hill.

Susan dropped to her knees, creeping, probing around bruising rocks, through biting briers. And it was among the briers that she found the hole. The clump of blackberries at first looked like all the other isolated growths on the hillside, but something had touched these recently. Only a few were bent and torn, but enough to suggest a passage.

Her heart beating fast, Susan parted thorny stems and looked into blackness. Scratch and bruise were forgotten now as she wriggled forward and thrust head and shoulders into the hole. Through the gray light within she could see a tunnel partly filled with the wash of earth from the hill. The tunnel fell sharply down to a great white gleam, like a high gallery filled with candles.

Susan's eyes were shining. She was going down to that gallery. But how? Three feet ahead of her face, stones and earth were piled nearly to the roof of the tunnel, hiding the contours that might mean a simple, safe slide of a few feet or a drop to death. With a shove of her elbows she backed out of the hole, picked up the iron claw, and again slipped head and shoulders far into the darkness. With the little tool designed to grapple with garden weeds and called the "Hand of Death," she attacked the mound that lay between her and that far, beautiful glitter. Dirt and pebbles were flung past both sides of her slim body, into her nose, over cheeks and chin, as she struggled to reduce the hump.

A few minutes of dripping labor and she could see almost enough. There seemed to be a gentle drop to a white stalagmite floor and through the sloping earth ran a track as if a boulder might have washed down it in the spring. There were still many feet ahead, of which she had no knowledge; cutting rock, slippery clay, and below always the chance of a pit. It was not wise to go ahead. Susan went.

Not headfirst. Again she backed out of the cave and dropped her tool in the bushes. If one landed on those claws at the bottom of a well, it could be a veritable hand of death. She felt in the pocket of her coverall and found buttoned tight within a candle end and matches, usual companions in cave adventure. She took a deep breath and backed into the hill.

A hasty reconnoiter with her feet, a few vigorous shoves of the elbows, then head on arms, she shot down.

Shot for two body-lengths and sat up in darkness. Alone inside the mountain. Her hands reaching for candle and matches were over-eager. The light grew beneath her fingers and all around her other candles sprang to life. Hundreds of tapers, great Pascal candles, tiny waxes for birthday cakes—all slender points of stalagmite made by the drip of water long ages ago. Gallery walls were glistening white, the floor a polished rock.

Susan stood erect. Alone in such beauty that perhaps no one had ever seen before. No, long ago someone had known it well. Under her feet lay split and blackened bones of bison and deer, the remains of a hearth of paleolithic man.

It was then that she saw something else. At the left of the spot where she had landed, two delicate stalactite needles had been broken and the points lay between the cluster. The broken white points, the furrow through the wash of earth—had the same object marked them both? A boulder? But where was it?

Here at the left of the white gallery, a little low chamber was worn in the rock. In such modest spots as these archaeologists had sometimes found wall paintings, animals modeled in high relief. If she could find something like that all by herself!

She knelt by the arch, holding her candle at arm's length within the little room. And then she knew that she was not alone.

There were no bones this time to gleam white and red in the candle rays. The wax was dropping on the breast of a blue serge suit, but no skeleton could have been more dead.

Susan fell back on her heels, her head against the rock. The candle shaking in her hand went out. In the terrible dark she could hear strangling breaths that threatened to deafen her. What great animal ...?

No animal. Her own frightened breathing, the only living thing in black hell. She would not, would not go mad. The dead are nothing to be afraid of. In what way was a corpse different from a skeleton?

Shuddering, she relit the candle, leaned forward, and looked at the man. A body pushed into the chamber like a heap of trash swept under a bed, a stiff black beard from which the dead flesh had shrunk back, a sunken, softened spot in the right temple.

Strange things going through her head, words, phrases. "It is always possible for a body to slip down from the surface to an ancient level" ... "Give him Christian burial" ... "A dead man is the only man Susan will ever love."

She must get out of here quick. But suppose she couldn't? Suppose the wash was too steep to climb alone? Suppose she lost her grip and fell back, hitting her head, breaking her leg on rock, lying here waiting to die. With him.

That must never be. She sat still for a moment, taking deep breaths, counting them. Then steadily she blew out the candle, buttoned it into her pocket, and with elbows and knees began to drag herself up the earth-covered rock. Only two body-lengths, she reminded herself, only a little way toward that pale gray glimmer above which is bright morning. Up, slow and sure, and then off for help. Don't think of those whose help it is not wise to seek. Because one of them might be a murderer. Think only of two slow, steady men in khaki, the gendarmes whose job is to look after ... after things like the man below. Careful. Loose stones. No falling back now.

The gray light was getting clear; warm summer air was reaching her face. Then sun reached her fingertips.

Suddenly the fingers were grasped. Mixed with the racing of her heart was the thought: the murderer saw me enter the cave. She was too weak to pull her hands away.

"Take it easy, Mademoiselle."

She had heard the voice before, dull and steady and reliable. Mist cleared from her eyes, and she could see a khaki sleeve. She gave a gasp and her heart began to quiet. The help she sought was here.

"Thank you," she panted.

"Put your head on your arm and I'll pull you through." His hands gripped her shoulders as she gave a last shove with her knees.

A moment later she opened her eyes. The sky, green bushes living around her. She gave a sigh and looked up at the taller gendarme.

She said faintly, "There is a body ... a dead man down that hole."

The heavy face looked down at her, blank and implacable. "Yes, Mademoiselle, I thought there would be."

He was holding the Hand of Death.

CHAPTER XII

BLOOD FROM A STONE

The flies wanted to get out. Around and around the hot room they droned, with now and then a futile assault on the wooden shutters pulled tight to keep out the noonday sun and the rest of their kin. The door of the darkened room was shut to keep Susan in, and sometimes she broke her slow pacing to softly turn the knob. During the long morning it had not been locked, but an hour ago, when a new voice had spoken in the room beyond, she had heard the quiet click of the key.

Red tendrils clinging darkly to her forehead, neck chafing under the hot, rough collar of her coverall, it seemed to Susan that this steaming little box in the *gendarmerie* was as hostile as the rest of St. Fiacre. Hostile to a stranger, a foreigner, a girl who crawled through caves and played with bones, who might be a witch, who had a companion like Neva and lived in a house called The Woman of Bad Habits.

In the center of a table otherwise bare lay the things that should make everything right: the private papers that the police had brought in a brief case from her desk. A United States passport, a Parisian *carte d'identité*, both in perfect order; letters of introduction from the head of the anthropology department in the most distinguished American university and from Professor Boulanger at the Museum of Natural History in Paris; a letter of credit drawn on Lloyd's for twenty thousand dollars. All solid, respectable, legal. But the gendarmes had locked her in this stifling dark while they hunted for two objects without intrinsic value— a water-worn stone allegedly spotted with blood and a pamphlet with a green cover. Symbols of the two main trends of the long interrogation: why had Susan Kent come to Aston? why did a man lie dead in a cave?

The fat *maréchal des logis* behind the table, the thin, nervous brigadier with his shorthand notebook, and Susan on a hard chair had sat together for hours. Question and answer, on and on and on. Her name and her father's? His occupation? A manufacturer. Of ball bearings. At Cleveland, Ohio. Her mother?

Susan said without emotion, "She is dead."

Her education? Why had she become an archaeologist?

"Because I wanted to do it more than anything else."

He looked puzzled. "Mademoiselle, in the United States isn't it customary for a young lady with ..." he glanced at the blue leather case from Lloyd's, "... in your financial position to marry before the age of twenty-four?"

"No, Monsieur, there is no particular age for marriage in my country." Between the heavy, doubting man in khaki and Susan Kent, the Atlantic rolled deep and wide.

"Well ... you wanted to be an archaeologist. Why did you want to dig in France? Aren't there any old things you could uproot in North America?"

What could she tell this native of Aston who would never want to go farther than fifty miles from home? "Yes," she said, "there are mounds and caves to dig all over the United States but ... well, the remains in them are of Red Indians. Here in France one can dig up one's own ancestors."

"Good." His tone did not express more than acceptance. "Exactly how, Mademoiselle, did you happen to arrive in St. Fiacre?"

She told him as clearly as she could. "In Paris, I visited Professor Boulanger and gave him the letter you have in front of you. From a professor in America who knew him rather well."

On an April afternoon in the museum that hid such treasures in its dreary dust, Susan had been proud, confident, thrilled at the nearness of the great cave adventure. Professor Boulanger's sharp little eyes peered at her over the upward thrust of his beard, like a brown spade, which in his moments of excitement seemed to jump up and smack the tip of his blunt nose.

"So I suppose you want to dig in the Dordogne? 'The Capital,'" he mocked the phrase of the tourist agencies, "'the Capital of the Prehistoric World?'"

"I'd like something more provincial," Susan smiled at him, "and less overworked."

"Ah," his eyes narrowed, "a site farther south perhaps?"

She nodded. What was he being so crafty about? "How far south? As far as the Pyrenees? What section of the Pyrenees, Mademoiselle?"

He seemed to want a definite answer. After a moment, "Aston?" she had suggested.

"Ah! Ha!" he sounded like a vintage villain. "Now is there any little spot in Aston where you would particularly like to ah—dig?"

She did not answer at once, aware of the excited quiver of the beard. "Any cave would suit me perfectly, Professor Boulanger. I should be so grateful for the chance.... There is a small cave near St. Fiacre. I think it is called the Violet Hole. If no one is excavating there this summer ..."

He jumped out of his chair. "Good, Mademoiselle Come back tomorrow. Everything shall be arranged for you. Everything."

"But, Mademoiselle, I don't understand at all," the policeman rubbed his forehead. "How could you know in America about a little cave like the *Tutto Biouletto?* There are hundreds of caves in Aston."

Susan smiled confidently now. "It's all in a little green pamphlet on my desk at the Catine."

"Mademoiselle, I don't get you."

"I'm sorry." She explained slowly, "An American archaeologist, Dr. Austin, has made a sort of directory of every cave and rock shelter that has ever been excavated in France. He hunted through all the journals, even publications, of local archaeological societies that only continued for a year or two. Dr. Austin listed each site under the Department of France in which it was found and arranged the Departments in alphabetical order. In the pamphlet with the green cover. Before I went to call on Professor Boulanger, I studied this little book so that I would be familiar with the names of at least a few caves. I didn't get very far in the book, but *A* stands for *Aston.* The only cave name I could think of when Professor Boulanger asked me to name a definite place was the Violet Hole. Because, I suppose, it made a picture in my mind ... Later I found there was almost nothing known about the cave. The priest of Volvestre picked up some pottery on the surface and published a few lines about it in 1881."

The *maréchal* turned to the man with the notebook. "You've got that all down?" he asked anxiously. "Now, Mademoiselle, we'll agree that's the way you started digging at Volvestre. But," his steady gaze was on her tense face, "was the cave with the corpse in it also listed in the green book?"

A slight shudder passed over Susan Kent. "No, Monsieur."

"Well, then, what were you doing there?"

Susan said, "I was exploring."

"Exploring, eh? Looking for another skeleton?"

"No, just looking for ... a cave."

"Yes. Mademoiselle, there are five or six caves alongside the *Tutto Biouletto* at Volvestre that are easy to get at. Why were you wandering around what looks like an empty hillside? And at six-thirty A.M.?"

"I was awake early." Her eyes were wide and candid, her tired face flushed. A true story and a likely story are not quite the same. "I ... after the party and after your men came to the Catine ... I didn't sleep very well."

"Worried perhaps?"

"No, Monsieur. I reached Volvestre too early to ask Jean-Marie to go to work at once. And I have always planned to explore lots of caves in the valley."

"No particular reason to begin today?"

"None."

"And," he asked, "no particular reason to explore that certain cave?"

"Yes, Monsieur."

"What?" he was astonished. "You said 'yes?' All right. What was the reason?"

He did not interrupt her account of the discovery of the skeleton in the Violet Hole, the visit of Father Bigorre and the threat of burial, the figure of a man seen on the far ridge. She told him about her climb, the empty hillside and, at last, about the stone.

"So you thought it was painted by cave men? Do you think that now, Mademoiselle?"

"I haven't seen the stone since ... The spot where I found it was just outside the hidden mouth of the cave. I think it would have made a very handy weapon with which to break a skull." Again she shuddered.

"Yes, Mademoiselle. And so would the 'Hand of Death.'"

"I don't agree with you, Monsieur."

"So you don't agree, Mademoiselle?"

"No. I ... I have seen the wound. You have not."

"Where is this stone you have so much to say about?"

"At the Catine," she told him eagerly. "On my desk. No, it isn't there!"

"Have you, by chance, lost it?"

"No, no! It's at the Catine. But not in the house. It's under the third apple tree from the edge of the brook. There's a little pile of pebbles. It may be at the bottom of the heap."

"So you hid it?"

"No, Monsieur." This she knew was the most unlikely answer of all. "It was my dog."

"Oh, a trick dog. You trained him yourself?"

"No. Oh, no! It sounds absurd. But I have eight witnesses."

When she had finished her story, he said again, "You could have trained him. A *German* dog. Have you been in Germany often, Mademoiselle?"

"I was at school there for a year. In 1929. I've also been at school in France and Italy."

"You have visited other countries?"

"Yes, for a summer or two. England, Spain, Norway, the Dalmatian coast. My father ..."

He did not ask her to go on. "Mademoiselle, you recognized the corpse in the cave, didn't you?"

"No. Of course not. I never saw the man in my life."

"No?" He drummed with his fingers on the desk.

When Susan winced, he said, "But you are quite sure of his identity?"

"No. I have no idea."

"You wouldn't care to guess?"

"I couldn't, Monsieur. I am a stranger here."

"Mademoiselle, is he perhaps the man Father Bigorre thought he saw near the rock shelters? The archaeological expert from the Ministry of Beaux Arts?"

"I don't know."

"You had met this expert in Paris?"

"No, Monsieur."

"Professor Boulanger talked to you about him?"

"No. I heard about him only when I came here. And just as I have told you."

"Ah, yes. You are quite sure you have never met this man elsewhere? In some other country? You are quite a traveler, Mademoiselle."

She said firmly, "I tell you again, I have never seen this man."

He got up heavily from his chair and nodded to his subordinate— "That's all, Léon. Mademoiselle, if you will have the kindness to wait a little longer, we'll have a look around the Catine and check back with you."

Susan also was on her feet, standing white and brave between him and the door. "And why must I wait, Monsieur? I have told you all I know. I will gladly cooperate in any way. Surely I am not under arrest?"

"No, no," he assured her in awkward embarrassment. "We are just asking you to stay here with us for an hour or so longer until we find out if further questioning is needed."

"You could always find me," Susan told him coldly, "at my house."

"Wait, Mademoiselle. I will see." He followed the brigadier out of the room, closing the door behind him. A moment later the new, somewhat familiar, voice had come to Susan through the panels. It was then that the key turned in the lock.

The long hot hour of flies buzzing in the dark, of headache and hunger and the growing knowledge of a loneliness that would follow her from this room. When a gendarme came again, she would demand a lawyer, someone from the firm her father employed in Paris. Not Marc de l'Arize. She dropped down in the hard chair by the table and laid her head on her arms.

Heavy steps, the key rasped in the lock, the door opened, the shutters were pushed aside. In the glare of summer light on the white house walls beyond the window, Susan sat straight and cool, waiting the word of the *maréchal des logis*. He bowed to her agreeably and sat down at the table.

"Mademoiselle, just a question or two more."

Susan said, "I should like to consult my attorney."

"Of course, Mademoiselle," he replied stolidly, "it's your right. But this is just an informal inquiry. To help us out with a somewhat difficult case.

We're anxious to find out who that dead man is. The body has been taken from the cave but it has not yet been identified. Would you be kind enough to tell me all you can remember of the conversations you heard concerning this mysterious archaeologist from Paris?"

Susan said doubtfully, "I'll try to recall what was said."

"Good, Mademoiselle, and after that, perhaps— Well?"

"The first time was about ten days ago. In the cave at Volvestre. It was the first time I had met Father Bigorre and M. Dumas."

"Oh, M. Dumas?"

"Yes. I think we were talking about former times when the great archaeologists from Paris and Toulouse used to make an annual visit to all the caves. I asked if anything like that happened now."

"And what were you told, Mademoiselle?"

"Father Bigorre said that someone came often. M. Dumas didn't agree. He said, I think, 'Only now and then,' and that the man wasn't much of an expert. That ended the subject for the day."

"And later?"

"I've already told everything about Father Bigorre and the figure on the ridge. The next evening, at the party, no one seemed to believe such a man had been there. Everyone heard the talk."

The *maréchal* looked down at his hands spread flat on the table. "Mademoiselle, can you tell me exactly who suggested that the man under discussion came from the Ministry of Beaux Arts?"

Susan answered carefully. "It was not M. Dumas. It might have been Father Bigorre. Perhaps *I* did. I may have asked if anyone came from the Ministry, and Father Bigorre replied, 'there is a man who comes here,' and nothing more. But I can't be sure. It didn't seem important at the time."

"Mademoiselle," he was still looking at his hands, "in reading over your testimony, we got the impression that the professor in Paris was a little surprised that you knew so much about the caves in Aston."

"I don't think I said that."

"No? Oh, well ... Wouldn't the professor at the museum know all about the little book with the green cover? He would have been sure where you got your information."

"Quite by chance," Susan said, "that isn't true. Professor Boulanger and Dr. Austin, who wrote the 'little green book,' don't get along well. Everybody knows that. It's a famous academic quarrel. And Professor Boulanger has sworn that nothing Austin writes will ever appear in his library."

"So?" he smiled faintly, then again looked down at the table. "One final question, Mademoiselle, if you please. Your father is engaged in a business which has interests outside the United States, isn't it true? It is a business that operates on the cartel system?"

Susan studied the stubby fingers lying flat on the table. Between them a scrap of white paper was visible. So the unknown voice she had heard beyond the door had belonged to someone rather smart. She said guardedly, "That is common knowledge."

"You have traveled widely, Mademoiselle. You have been educated in many countries. You are interested in your father's business?"

She met his eyes squarely. "On the contrary. I find it an awful bore. You can tell your superior that although my father may have found my training in languages an asset in entertaining foreign business men, his motive for sending me to Continental schools was merely to dispose of a motherless brat at a good comfortable distance."

The *maréchal* turned slowly red. "Mademoiselle is joking."

"Mademoiselle is not," but she gave him a tired smile. It was then that Ouray, the tall gendarme, lumbered in.

Susan looked eagerly toward him. He shook his head. "I'm sorry," he said. "We've made a thorough hunt at the Catine. Neither of those things can be found. No book. No stone."

She looked very pale. "I find it hard to believe. You asked Mlle. Borodin? And Moise?"

"Oh, yes," he grinned heavily. "We do our job, Mademoiselle."

"Surely they told you what I told you?"

"Not quite." He looked almost sorry for Susan. "The dark young lady regrets deeply that she has never concerned herself with the books on your desk. And she doesn't remember the incident of any particular stone."

"And Moise?" She did not look hopeful.

"She says she's seen nothing."

He watched her white, silent face, her still, folded hands.

"You had, however, one good witness, Mademoiselle. Although one not easily used in court."

"Yes?" her voice was slightly hoarse.

"The little brown German dog, Mademoiselle. At the time we were there he was gathering and piling stones."

Her face was soft for a moment. "Seppel." Then she said sternly, "So it was worth someone's while to carry off a book and a stone. Well, I assume this is the point at which I wire for legal advice."

"As you like, Mademoiselle," the *maréchal des logis* was smiling uneasily; the private was holding open the door. "Not that it is necessary. You have been most helpful with your answers. Thank you for your assistance."

The tall gendarme at the door nodded stiffly. "It's finished, Mademoiselle. We shan't need to bother you anymore."

Susan Kent rose slowly to her feet. She pushed back the damp curls from her forehead and looked from one commonplace face to the other. The faces slowly reddened as she watched, but no expression marred their professional uniformity.

"Thank you," she said, skeptic and weary, and went out of the room.

CHAPTER XIII

ILL WIND

Under the heavy black beams of the Catine kitchen, Moise stood listening. To footsteps overhead, to the bubbling of milk on the blue-tiled charcoal table, to the clack of the grapevine in the hot wind. The delicate engraving of her profile seemed puffy and blurred, and as steps sounded down the stairs, she pushed back her thick knot of hair with a heavy hand.

Susan came into the kitchen, her thin white dress hanging limp, her red-gold hair pinned in a tight bun, and looking rather like a child who has been scrubbed too hard behind the ears. She dropped into a chair by the open window with the rattling vine, and said through a yawn, "I'm sorry, Moise. I never was as late as this before. That wind!"

"Yes, Mademoiselle. It's the *Vent d' Autan.*"

"The Wind of What?"

"The Wind of Autan."

Susan leaned her head on her bent arms and watched Moise's sullen progress to the charcoal table. "That blast of dead air. How long does it go on?"

Moise, pouring coffee into the hot milk, said huskily, "A very long time. If it gets worse, the crops and the cattle will die."

"And me, too," Susan said. She raised her head as Moise approached slowly with the yellow bowl of *café au lait.* "Thanks. This is probably all I really need."

The girl did not return Susan's smile. "You had better get used to the *Vent d'Autan* if you're going to live in St. Fiacre for the rest of your life."

Susan looked up, startled at the change in shy, friendly Moise. "I am not going to live in St. Fiacre," she said quietly. "I shall go home to the United States as soon as I finish digging in the Violet Hole."

Moise, chin pressed into neck, hands clutched on folded arms, muttered, "You will live here always when you get married."

"Married!" Susan stared at the girl's bent head. "Married! I am not going to be married. Here or anywhere else. Ever."

Milk swashed, loud and foul, on the blue tiles. Moise stumbled dumbly toward the saucepan, and Susan thrust her offended nose into the stifling wind. Neither girl turned when Neva swayed languidly into the room and came over to the table by the window.

"What are you looking at?" she asked curiously.

Susan glanced obliquely at Neva. "I'm looking for a gendarme."

"A gendarme?" Neva spoke sharply. "You expect to be watched by the police?"

"Of course."

"You told me the police were through with you."

"I told you that was what they said. It wasn't what I believed. They said much the same thing the night of the party. But at six-thirty the next morning, a gendarme was waiting for me outside the mouth of an almost unknown cave halfway up a mountainside. Obviously, I was watched even before I found that dead man."

Moise with unsteady hands put a second yellow bowl on the table. She opened her mouth, looked at Susan, and pressed her lips tightly together.

"So I don't trust the police," Susan went on, "nor anyone else."

Neva drew the bowl closer to her and picked up a spoon with elaboration. "I think you are right," she said.

Susan stood up. "I would be right, wouldn't I, about you and Moise?"

Neva did not lower her huge eyes. "Susan!" she breathed.

Moise, lurching as if her body were off balance, drew back from the table. Susan glanced at her and back at Neva. "I am thinking of what you two did and did not tell the gendarmes yesterday. About the green pamphlet that was on my desk. About the stone that Seppel hid in the orchard."

They stared back at her, Moise red, Neva very pale. Burned milk sickened the air.

"Moise isn't entirely to blame," Susan's voice was cold. "On the night of the party when we were teasing Seppel with the stone, she was off somewhere with Jean-Marie. But the little green book? Surely you had seen it on my desk when you were dusting?"

"There were so many books," Moise's murmur was barely audible. "Mademoiselle, I didn't mean ..."

Susan turned sharply from her. "But, Neva, it was you who knocked the green book off the window sill. It was you who took the stone from the desk. You heard the talk, and told that apt little anecdote about the dog who was a dope fiend. You saw Seppel race off to the apple tree with the stone in his mouth."

Neva said, "I told the gendarmes about Seppel's habit of building cairns."

Sharpness left Susan's voice as she continued, "Neva, I don't understand. You've always seemed so—generous and ... Are you afraid of something?"

Neva closed her eyes, opened them slowly, sighed. "Yes, I am afraid. A little. In everyone's life there is something implacable. Susan, I tell you, I *cannot* be involved with the police."

Susan laughed slightly. "I thought *I* was the one involved."

"Yes. And after all, Susan, what are you really doing here in Aston?"

"I told you. I have told you everything, always."

"Have you?" asked Neva. She drew a cigarette from the black lace pocket of her negligee. "You did not tell me—about Marc de l'Arize."

Watching the flood of color rising in Susan's face, she put the cigarette between her lips and turned toward Moise as if for applause, but the girl had retreated deep into the shadows by the hearth.

"There was nothing to tell you about him," Susan's tone shook.

"No?"

"No, Neva. I met him on the steps of his father's chateau the day before we all went to Foix."

"And on those steps you fell in love with him?" Neva held a match to her cigarette.

There was anger now in Susan. "What else are you thinking?"

The wind licked between them, extinguishing the match flame. "I do *not* think," said Neva, "that Marc is your lover." She was now smiling, cool and superior. "It is possible that he is a—colleague."

"Colleague?" Susan demanded. "Just what do you think we are doing together?"

Neva struck another match. "Perhaps it would be better if one did not know."

For a moment the only sound in the low, dark room was the wind and the heavy breathing of Moise. Then Susan, standing over Neva, asked quietly, "Were you thinking of murder?"

The blazing match fell into the lace over Neva's breast, as Susan called into the shadows, "Well, Moise, do *you* think I killed the man in the cave?"

The girl stumbled toward her crying out, "Mademoiselle, oh, no!"

Susan shrugged. "Whatever you think, either of you, you have done your best to send me to the guillotine. I'm going to take my gendarme for a ride."

As she left the house, she could hear Moise sobbing out, "*Le Vent d'Autan. La Peur*. The wind that brings The Fear."

Stiff and swift in her anger, Susan went to her bicycle beneath a quince bush at the head of the lane. No gendarme was in sight, only Seppel dancing around her tires. She stopped to dig a stone out of the path with her heel and fling it far into the orchard, and when he had bounded off, ears blown back like pink flags, she rode down to the empty highway.

Through five miles of rising and falling road, the wind pressed hot against her, weighed down her arms and legs, burned her bare forehead. The grain fields were as weary as the languid cows. Again and again she turned to look for a red-faced policeman pedaling behind her, but she was always alone. Not until the rock of Volvestre was in sight did she meet a human being. She had reached the spot where, on the previous morning, she had begun her disastrous climb. No dewy freshness today; alders drooped, ivy streamers hung flaccid, and in the swaying black shade of the cypresses the Christ seemed about to fall from His cross, limp and dead. Around a bend in the road came a bicycle ridden by a strawstack. The Sahara breeze struck it, whistled through the straw and revealed under an enormous sun hat the round red face of Father Bigorre. Breathless he put feet to ground, the skirt of his rusty cassock trailing from the seat of the woman's model into the blowing dirt of the road.

"Good day, *M. le Curé*," Susan alighted beside him, "isn't this a dreadful wind?"

The priest shook his head sadly. "Bad, Mademoiselle. If it goes on long enough, no one can tell what may happen. The people, you know. Right here in Volvestre, a few years ago, the *Vent d'Autun* blasted the valley one entire summer. Mademoiselle, people went back to old heathen ways. They said *La Peur* was flying over the country and they organized a hunt. With guns, Mademoiselle. Yes, truly. And they say," he whispered in the empty road, "that they shot down 'something like a bird.' Then the wind stopped. Such things are bad for the Church."

Susan nodded.

"Oh," his face brightened. "The Bishop told me he holds archaeology in high esteem. He gave me a little book about it. I will come up to your cave some day and show it to you." He stopped suddenly, the smile dying.

Susan spoke quickly, "You've heard about the dead man in the cave?"

"Yes, Mademoiselle." He raised his feet to the pedals.

"*Monsieur le Curé*, have you seen him?"

He did not look at her. "Yes, Mademoiselle." The pedals were turning.

Susan followed the slowly moving wheels. "Did you know him? Was it the archaeological expert? The man from the Ministry of Beaux Arts?"

The bicycle gathered speed. Still looking straight ahead, the priest stammered, "I ... I ... I'm sorry. I forgot. I have been told not to speak to you. I gave my word."

Susan was left alone in the clouding dust.

Slowly she righted her bicycle as if it had suddenly doubled its weight, then stood irresolute looking up and down the highway. Back to St. Fiacre, forward to Volvestre, neither way led to friends. Well, what way did? Brusquely she pushed the red curls from her forehead, shook the dust from her white skirt, mounted and rode slowly toward the inn of Madame 'Ri.

Blinded from sun and wind she stumbled over the threshold into a dark-shuttered room smelling of wine and old oil. From the depths of this dungeon a well-known voice roared, "Huh. It's the little American Mademoiselle. Quick, Jean-Marie!"

She ploughed forward to Susan's side. "How pale you are. All this way in the heat. No hat. And in a fine white dress. What's wrong, Mademoiselle?"

The rough old face peered down at the girl. "Come and eat the soup," she commanded. "We've no grand things to offer but it's food, just the same."

Across the rear of the room a long table was set with a coarse white cloth and a steaming tureen of green bean soup, thick with slices of floating bread. 'Ri motioned Susan to a chair, brushing aside thanks as she shooed flies from the table, and roared again, "Jean-Marie!"

"*Bon jour,* Mademoiselle," Jean-Marie quietly took his place opposite Susan. Madame 'Ri ladled out generous platefuls of soup for the two and then stood over them, hands on colossal hips. She might be the head of the house but she would no more have thought of eating with a man and a guest than her son would have thought of removing his big cap while he ate.

"Eat," she commanded. "Eat."

And until plates were cleaned, and a glass of the sharp wine of the country emptied, no other word was spoken. Color came back to Susan's cheeks and she no longer slumped in her chair when the second plate was put before her, containing potatoes and carrots that had been simmering all morning in the pot, and a bit of salt goose that flavors every peasant soup. "This is delicious," she told Madame 'Ri.

"Ha! You like plain everyday soup? You should stay here and eat it every day in the year. Soup and lots of bread. Make you strong. So you can have a fine son, Mademoiselle."

Jean-Marie's heavy mutter in patois took the place of Susan's answer, and although his mother's retort in the same language was as loud as ever, she stood glowering for a moment and then left the room.

Susan studied Jean-Marie, silently sopping bread in his plate. "About the dead man in the cave ..." she began.

He regarded her with the disconcerting intensity of their first meeting. "Yes, Mademoiselle?"

"Have you seen him?"

He nodded.

"Did you know him?"

He brushed his hand over his drooping lid. "Did you?"

"No. And no one has told me who he was."

"They say no one knows."

"Not the police?"

"I doubt it. Are they bothering you, Mademoiselle?"

"Not ... obviously. But they were following me before I found him. That tall gendarme was at the mouth of the cave when I crawled out."

"Pierre Ouray? Maybe he wasn't following you."

"At half-past six in the morning? You mean he was following the man who was murdered?"

Jean-Marie smiled. "No, Mademoiselle. Pierre has a sweetheart in Volvestre. He was on his way home. Moise could have told you that." He looked down at his plate.

"Moise is no longer my friend. —Could we have the shutters open?"

He got up and parted the wooden blinds behind his back. Immediately below the window a swift mountain stream ran over sharp rocks. A crude swinging footbridge led to a small vegetable plot.

"Look at that garden," 'Ri returning with a bottle and thick glasses, thrust her big dirty face toward the shutters. "The soil where those beans are growing wouldn't feed a blade of grass. My man and I carried up all the earth on our heads. Ten thousand baskets, they say in the village. *We* were too busy to count. Drink some of our own *eau-de-vie*, Mademoiselle. Very good for you."

"To your health," Susan touched her glass to Jean-Marie's.

"'Health,'" he murmured. "There is someone at the door."

As old 'Ri lumbered to meet two thirsty drovers, he spoke still lower. "You want to work in the cave?"

Susan looked down at her white silk dress. "I'm not prepared for a real dig, but I'd like to look the cave over and decide where we'll begin tomorrow if ..."

"Good. Before we go ... Mademoiselle, what do you think of these things?"

From the pocket of his wide corduroys he brought out a fistful of objects and laid them cautiously in front of Susan. A primitive hammerstone, a bronze bracelet, and half of a human leg bone. Susan-picked them up one by one. On the thin, ribbed bracelet were a few flecks of red, the enamel admired by men and women of Europe two thousand years ago—and eighteen thousand years later than the cave man of Volvestre. The stone, cruder than any found in the Violet Hole, had at some recent time been polished to make it shine. And the leg bone had been cut across with the neatness characteristic of modern steel.

"Where do you think these came from?" Jean-Marie's eyes were probing. Was he friend or foe?

Susan did not hesitate. "From a curio store."

Jean-Marie grunted and swept them into his fist. "Mademoiselle," his tone warned, "there is a visitor behind you and," warning became menace, "you will say nothing about these things."

A lugubrious greeting sounded above Susan's left ear; the black beard and the black suit of the schoolmaster rose up at her side.

"Mademoiselle, pardon me for interrupting your repast. My wife, who is always suffering, saw you enter the inn. We have dared to hope that you might do us the honor of taking coffee with us. Our home is only the village schoolhouse, but ..."

"Oh, that is kind of you." Susan saw the ugly red lip protrude beneath the beard. "We were just starting for the cave."

"Yes, Mademoiselle. I understand. We would not wish to alter your plans. You are always so busy. Could you perhaps visit us on your way back to the Catine?"

"Please tell Madame Dumas," said Susan rising, "that I shall be glad to come."

"It will be a great honor for my poor wife," the schoolmaster made his ungainly bow. "She has never met an American."

Nor, his tone implied, a murderess.

CHAPTER XIV

TOUT À FAIT INDIQUÉ

Marc de l'Arize, leaning against the great central pillar of the Violet Hole, stared into the depths of the cave. In dim gray light, framed by rough arches, and against a rock wall streaked with purple and green, stood Susan Kent. Burnished copper head down-bent, clasped hands pressing the white dress against her breasts, she seemed to be listening in ecstasy to the hollow tones of a primitive organ rising from the black pit at her feet.

"The Virgin of the *Tutto Biouletto*," Marc said, stepping toward her with outstretched hand.

"Hello," Susan laughed. "Come and see." Holding his hand she drew him to the edge of the deep trench cutting across the cave floor. In the far right corner Jean-Marie, his head well below the earthwork, hacked away at the rocky wall.

"What the devil are you trying to do?" Marc called down to him. "Planning to blow Volvestre off its rock?"

Jean-Marie straightened and grinned. "I've made a beginning." He stood aside, flashing a small torch against the spot where he had been at work. A black hole, about a foot high and two feet wide, broke the panel of rock, like the cathole in a kitchen door. "I've done all that this afternoon."

"Not with your pick and your chisel?"

"With nothing else. Come and see."

"Come on," Susan jumped lightly into the trench and Marc followed, kneeling down by the gap.

Susan handed him a chisel and pointed to the gray mass above the opening. "Give it a whack," she said, "and listen."

The iron brought forth a hollow tone. "Ha," Marc repeated the blow, "not rock at all. Stalactite?"

"Bright boy," Susan patted his Basque beret, now at the height of her knee. "Isn't it thrilling? We've always supposed all this was the final wall of the cave and we've gone on digging day after day in a nice, systematic manner. But today I didn't want to settle down. The wind and ..." For a moment brightness left her voice. "So we were just wandering around, Jean-Marie and I, exploring our own cave, tapping the wall here and there, and we found *this*." She knelt in the powdery earth beside the men, her fingers tracing the irregular outline at the upper end of the hole. "See, water dripped down over this little arch and made a stalagmite door, ages and ages ago, and now Jean-Marie has broken it down."

"And now Mademoiselle will crawl through it," Jean-Marie grunted.

"Through there?" asked Marc doubtfully.

"Of course." Susan crouched close to him, laughing excitedly. "Shall I do it now? It would be awfully hard on my dress, but if you won't believe me ..."

Marc de l'Arize's eyes, deep under the arched brows, looked intently at the girl. "I believe you capable of anything."

Her expression changed. "Let's get out of the dirt and the damp," she said briskly. "Jean-Marie, you've nearly killed yourself. Not another stroke today."

She scrambled out of the pit before Marc; Jean-Marie followed with pick and chisel, across the cave to the great double archway opening on valley and mountains. Susan shivered slightly in the warm air. "I had forgotten that wind." She dropped down on the talus, leaning her head against the central pillar of the cave. "Tomorrow morning," she said to Jean-Marie, "we can finish the Northwest passage and then—who knows? Monsieur de l'Arize, would you like to crawl with us to the Indies?"

"I'd like it," Marc smiled down into her upraised face, "but unfortunately it can't be done. I'm going away for a few days." He walked over to Jean-Marie and, as that day in the inn doorway, laid a hand on his shoulder. "When I come back, shall we have a talk, you and I?"

For a moment they looked fixedly at each other. Vicomte and peasant, tall man and short, handsome eyes and a squint, yet alike in fine Mediterranean delicacy of bone, in sensitivity of nostril and lips, and in their dark coloring. Jean-Marie shrugged and turned away.

"As you like," he said dully, and headed down the slope. "*Au 'voir*, Mademoiselle."

"Until tomorrow, Jean-Marie." She glanced at her wrist watch and started to rise. With a light touch on her arm, Marc sat down beside her on the rock. "Four-thirty."

"I've told you before that you are extraordinary. I should have waited for today," he said.

She looked straight ahead at the clouds above the peak of Mount Vallier. "What do you mean?"

"Partly," he said, "I mean your willingness to crawl through another cave, after what happened to you yesterday morning."

Her arms drew tight against her sides. "That was a bad quarter of an hour," she admitted, "but the Violet Hole is different from other caves. It's, in a way, my home."

"Suzanne."

"Yes?" she turned to him.

"Yesterday wasn't your lucky day."

"I think today is worse."

His brows went up, "What has happened?"

"Nothing. That's the trouble. Not a gendarme in sight, but I know they are watching me. Not a word about the dead man, though I'm certain people are thinking about him all the time. I don't know who he was. Or why he died."

"Or who killed him?"

Her horror-filled eyes might again have been gazing at flesh shrunken back from a black beard, at a soft spot above a shattered temple. "And I don't know who went to Seppel's cairn and took the stone."

"It will soon be over, I'm sure. The man's identity will be known, and his killer will be found. Volvestre is a little place. It would be impossible for a stranger to come here without the knowledge of—someone."

"Obviously. Someone killed him."

"Suzanne," his shoulder was warm behind hers, "when this is all over..."

"Yes,—Marc?" She did not move away, but he did, and took out cigarettes.

"After the crime is solved," he held them toward her, "everything will be exactly as it was before."

"Thank you. You know better than that," she faced him a little scornfully, "or perhaps things were never as good as I thought."

"There's still heat in that damned wind," he opened the collar of his sport shirt. "What 'things' do you mean?"

"People and the way they feel about me. It's all my own fault. I was a bad sociologist or psychologist or whatever you want to call me. I thought if I tried to conform to the customs—if I didn't parade in shorts, if I didn't swank around in a car, that I wouldn't seem foreign. But that was silly, wasn't it? I might better have been the complete cliché of the American girl."

"What do you think that is?"

"Vulgar and rich."

"You know quite well you aren't vulgar."

"But how rich! Have you heard the expression, 'Down to their last yacht?' It's been going around the United States ever since the Depression hit. Well, that's the kind of family I come from. Mr. Kent's *Susan III* is in dry dock, but he hasn't been forced to sell her."

"Poor little rich girl!" Marc teased. "After all, this isn't the only country to manufacture stereotypes for foreigners. What do people think about Frenchmen in little towns in the U.S.A.?"

"Oh, that—" Susan stopped, flushing, "—that Frenchmen go around everywhere kissing hands."

"*Quelle horreur!* Hands? What a waste!"

"Sir Cyril," Susan went on hastily, "is much smarter than I. He behaves just the way one would expect an Englishman to act. Terribly correct in all circumstances and a little lofty to the natives and despising any food but roast beef."

Marc looked at her through a cloud of smoke. "So you think Sir Cyril Brooks-Brooks is exactly what he seems to be."

Her eyes measured his. "I don't think he is an archaeologist."

"During the war," he said, "Sir Cyril was a very distinguished member of the British Secret Service."

"I didn't know that."

"No? Some of his exploits have been written up in a book about the secret services of all the countries. For a while I used to read everything that appeared about the war. That was as near as I came to it. In 1918 I was only a kid of thirteen." He lighted another cigarette. "Jean-Marie was eighteen, he had two years of the trenches." He blew out the match. "We'll both be in the next."

Susan made a sharp sound.

"Oh, come, you aren't too surprised at the idea of another war? A girl who has spent as much time in Europe as you have? You don't think we're all one happy family here?"

"No, but ... everything is quiet now." She looked down at the serene valley and back at the cynically smiling man beside her on the rock.

"Oh, yes, it's quiet everywhere. In the steel mills of the Saar that became German again last March, and Mussolini stopped shooting Ethiopians in May. Over there on the other side of the Vallier, the Spanish haven't let much of each other's blood since last October, when a couple of thousand died in Catalonia and the Asturias. The leaders of that act in the melodrama are all in prison and at the moment the Republic seems to be taking a nap under some sort of Center-Right bloc—probably a short one."

"But," she said, "there's France."

"Yes, Mademoiselle," there was a bitter edge to the voice. "What do you know about France?"

She drew a little away from him, "Nothing."

"As you say, it's also quiet. But you remember, don't you, what happened a year and a half ago outside the Chambre?"

"I remember. The *Croix de Feu*. But I thought that was all over. Weren't the fascist leagues dissolved?"

"Yes, Mademoiselle."

She said positively, "I don't see how anyone can be a fascist."

"No?" His face was completely skeptic. "When there are so many reasons? One might desire the power that a new form of government could give its disciples. Or one might follow the fashion; so many of the people with whom one dines are fascists, in Germany, Italy, Spain—and France. Or one might simply hope to put one's personal finances in order." He threw away his cigarette and leaned toward her. "Or one might just possibly be an idealist. One might believe that one's country needed to be saved and that only under the totalitarian state could salvation be found."

"I'm beginning to think that my father had a good idea four years ago, when he ordered me back to the United States."

He said, "But you didn't stay there."

"Practically. Curiously, this little jaunt is a part of my rather peculiar American education."

"Seriously?"

"Completely. My father sent me to a highly experimental college for girls. I suppose I really fitted better there than I would have anywhere else, because I'd been to so many European schools. But my father didn't think of that when he chose the college; only that it cost about three times what any other did. And one of the very expensive experimental methods was to send each girl out for a term on a self-financed project. This is part of mine."

Marc de l'Arize said after a moment, "And in such an institution you met no fascists? I should have thought you would be encircled."

Susan laughed. "On the contrary. It was overflowing with communists. We are all bent on being everything our parents are not."

"You, too?"

"I'm not exactly following in my father's footsteps!"

He moved nearer to offer a cigarette, cupping a match against the hot wind, his brown fingers close to her cheek. "We are not altogether lucky in the matter of fathers, you and I."

She raised her head. "I think your father is charming."

"I might think the same of yours."

"You really might," Susan said honestly. "A few people have. But *any-one* would like your father."

Again his tone was bitter. "My mother didn't ..."

Susan broke the awkward silence. "Is the portrait in the salon at the chateau ...?"

"Yes, that was *Maman* after she had spent a few years with my dear papa. Not that she was ever a pretty girl. She was tall and dark like me. She was a shy girl who had lived all her life on a big estate near Toulouse with a widowed father and an old aunt, friends of my late grandfather. My father didn't want to settle down until he was forty-five, and with a property as barren as ours, he could only hope to marry a girl as land-poor as himself. No doubt he tried to do better, but facts are facts. He had known my mother's people all his life, the families were similar, she had no other suitors ... *alors*, the marriage was *tout à fait indiqué*." He went on sadly, "So for ten years she lived in that ugly house while my father spent her modest *dot* in Paris. She did petit point and occasionally drove out in that comic carriage—and died."

"She also had a son."

He rose abruptly. "And that son should be on his way to Foix. Let's go."

"Of course," Susan's smile did not quite mask hurt.

Silent and quick they descended the mountain path, Susan leading, between bushes that flopped in the *Vent d'Autan*, now blowing stronger as they neared the trough of the valley. Just before the last steep descent to the highway, where a trail crossed their way leading to the narrow mountain stream and the little bridge, a short cut to 'Ri's inn, Marc's hands fell on Susan's shoulders, steering her toward a screen of alders. His arms turned her toward him, holding her so close that her lips lay against his bare throat. He lifted her chin, whispering, "Frenchmen kiss hands?" His mouth was on her forehead, her eyes, very lightly on her lips. Then, as his arms released her, he said, "*Adieu*, Suzanne," and left her.

When she had smoothed her hair and powdered a very pink nose, Susan went to call on Madame Dumas. The glum schoolmaster met her at the door and led her silently up bare, waxed stairs to a room where foul air fought to overpower a lustful display of homemade filet lace spread over red sateen. Still sleepwalking, Susan was immediately immune to either disease; with a smile of great courtesy, she went up to the hard sofa by the window, where all day a sick old woman watched the road through curtains as coarse and gray as her hair. Monsieur Dumas was far from young, but this yellow-faced woman with the sour eyes was at least ten years the older. He handed a small glass of grenadine to Susan and placed another on a taboret beside his wife. His joints creaked and he withdrew.

The woman said in a shrill voice, "The Vicomte de l'Arize has just driven off in his car. Toward Foix."

Susan did not speak, and Madame Dumas repeated her statement.

"The Vicomte? Oh, yes. I've never heard his title ..."

"I'm sure of that," Madame Dumas's disgust was complete. "That young man has no respect for the best things, the old things for which France should stand. His father has more respect for his position."

"The Comte is a charming old gentleman," Susan agreed.

Madame Dumas chose to differ. "You find him so? Well, a good many girls in these parts have thought the same to their sorrow. However, he's a little too old at last, let us hope. One hears that he used to make all his peasant mistresses sing the Marriage Song to him before he ruined them. But one never knows what is truth around here."

"You are from another part of the country, Madame?"

"I should say so," she raised herself on an elbow and reached for the pale syrup. "Sainte Claude, halfway to Foix. I came here when I married. I was a teacher, too, Mademoiselle. I had been teaching for twelve years. *He* was my cousin and had just finished his teacher's training. So it was *tout à fait indiqué*." She sighed and gulped syrup. "Thirty years ago. I've taught the girls, and he the boys, every year since. Till now. Taught and looked after the house and raised four children," resentment rasped her tone. "Four children, although I always had a chronic inflammation. And every one of those children had hand-embroidered dresses, Mademoiselle. I sat up in bed far into the night, sewing and sewing."

"That took courage, Madame."

"How right you are, Mademoiselle! I've always tried to be an example in this town where nobody has any morals. Have one child, to get the man to marry you, and then abortion after abortion, that's the way around here. What would become of France if it weren't for women like me? Tell me that!"

Susan told her. "It would perish."

"Yes, Mademoiselle, but does the Government care? I tell you the country is in dire peril. The weak and immoral rule everything. Listen carefully. Oh, yes, they have passed a law to give a pension to schoolteachers who raised four children. Yes," she sat up, quivering violently, the thick liquid slopping over her glass, "but this wonderful law is not retroactive. Nothing, absolutely nothing for me, a woman who has given her life for France. The Government!" She ended in a weak snarl.

"Madame," Susan rose, "you must not tire yourself."

A hand ridged with veins waved her back to her chair. "So I suffer, suffer, suffer, and a woman like that," she pointed through the curtains to the inn across the road, "that old whore prospers. Isn't it so, Mademoiselle?"

Susan stammered. "M-Madame 'Ri seems to be in good health, but she's old and poor."

"Poor! Do you think her savings were gotten from that inn? Yes, they were, but how? In the old days when every cattle dealer broke the journey through the valley with a night at Volvestre, there was plenty of business for Madame 'Ri and plenty of fights among her suitors. And that dead husband of hers working like a blind slave. —But just once she wasn't quite so smart. When she produced that son of hers, by God knows whom. Evidently she let things go on a little too long. A fine mother-in-law she'll make you, Mademoiselle."

Susan was on her feet. "Madame Dumas, if you please! You must be ..."

The sick old woman cackled. "Crazy? Oh, no, Mademoiselle. 'Ri has talked to everybody about the possibility of your marriage to Jean-Marie. After all, you are over twenty and obviously there is some reason why you have not married in your country." Insult looked out at Susan. "We are poor people here in Aston. Even a little money would suit us, and you must have something to be able to travel so far. And every girl wants a husband. Jean-Marie has the basic requirements, as Moise could tell you! Mademoiselle, don't go! Don't be foolish. This is not what *I* believe, I, a woman of education. I know you could do a little better than Jean-Marie. I am giving you the current talk, and entirely out of kindness."

"Thank you, Madame, but I must go." Susan went to the couch for the handshake without which, in France, no leave could decently be taken.

The sweaty fingers gripped hers, with nails digging down to her palm. "Mademoiselle, I lie here all day but I know what goes on. And I can do things, too. You told the gendarmes, didn't you, that the corpse they found you with yesterday was a friend of my husband's? Didn't you?"

"Madame, no, no!" She was sickened by the woman's breath, her greasy skin, the old pillows, the cloying grenadine. "On the contrary. I told them that when I asked if the man was from the Ministry of Beaux Arts, Monsieur Dumas denied it."

The grip on Susan's hand relaxed a bit. "*If* you did, you were wise." A horrid smile spread over the yellow cheeks. "We are only poor schoolteachers today, but there may come a time ... Good day, Mademoiselle."

Outside the schoolhouse the air had grown a little cooler and more quiet. It was now six o'clock, and with evening the *Vent d'Autan* was dying. A gangling boy in shrunken overalls caked with cave mud was ambling down the road toward Susan from the direction of Foix. He had the lank, unedible look of Monsieur Dumas and a slack mouth that one could imagine drooling on a bib embroidered with rosebuds fifteen years earlier. Susan walked slowly toward him.

"Good evening. Have you been digging with Sir Cyril Brooks-Brooks?"

"Yah," he admitted, leering at her in the way that leads one to wonder if human evolution is worthwhile—or has been accomplished.

"Is Sir Cyril in the Cave of the Cross now?"

"Yah. Up back of the farm." He waved a dirty thumb, then stuck it in his nose. "Want I should show you?"

"No, thank you." Susan left no chance of being misunderstood.

A quarter mile beyond the village of Volvestre a farmhouse stood among prosperous barns and rich manure piles. Parked between a wine press and a kettle for the pig's soup stood Sir Cyril's open green car. A woman scattering scraps to the hens picking about the tires pointed to the high pasture in answer to a question about the Cross. Susan dragged up the hill and to the rim of the narrow valley. Rocky field, coarse underbrush, no sign of a cave. She sighed and sank down at the top of the cliff, dislodging a stone that fell heavily on the far side. Almost at once she heard another sound, a muffled *toc-toc-toc* like iron on rock. It stopped, repeated, stopped again. Lying flat, Susan leaned over the edge of the cliff and almost cried out. Immediately below her, under a heavy wire grating, an English gentleman in blue denim was seated on a rock pile, breaking stone with a cold chisel. So that was the entrance to the Cave of the Cross, private enough, one would think, without the bars? She was about to call out to Sir Cyril when he spoke.

"You see, I was right. You didn't really hear anyone. You are too apprehensive."

Into Susan's vision two legs moved forward, full soft calves in beige silk, a black skirt swishing above them. Sir Cyril said rather sharply, "Can't you believe that all your worries are ended?"

"And all of yours, too." The voice was Neva's at its most suggestive.

Significance, heavy and obscure, was in his "Quite!"

Cowering close to the ground, Susan saw Neva emerge between the bars and drag Moise's clumsy old bicycle from under a clump of thorns.

Sir Cyril reached an arm toward her. "It might be well to take this along," he chuckled. "I'll stay here a minute or two and play *tic-toc*, just in case someone lurks. Good night." A small green pamphlet changed hands.

Before Neva could wheel her bicycle up the rough track leading over the ridge to the farm, Susan crept forward, edging well to the right of the mouth of the cave, and down inch by quiet inch on the opposite slope of the hill. As soon as Sir Cyril started his precautionary tapping, she got to her feet, ran down the slope, and flung herself behind the first thick growth, a thicket of thorns. Bruised, torn, she lay motionless until, long after the last *toc*, she heard the scrape and rattle of small stones denoting Sir Cyril's exit from the Cave of the Cross. There followed the very jaunty whistling of a Pyrenean ballad, wherein the youngest daughter of a shrewd family of financiers gained a good living with little effort. Then silence in the gathering dusk.

Susan crept out of the thorns, smoothed her snagged stockings, licked the bleeding scratches on her arms. She was free to go, but not back to the highway by the only way she knew. The woman at the farm might at this moment be telling Sir Cyril about the second foreign young lady who had come calling. She got up and moved cautiously down the hill, looking often behind her for signs of movement from the farm. A path of poor sorts led off to the left of Volvestre, and for lack of any other direction, she followed it in the hope that before night set in it might bring her to some other farm where she could perhaps hire the farmer to drive her back to the Catine. After dark the dogs of Aston were not to be trusted with strangers, nor would the men of Aston easily recognize many motives that might bring a woman alone into the spirit-filled night.

Some faint semblance of a path meandered, always to the left, for about half a mile, through scrubby pasture and thin, low bushes, until it reached a screen of tall poplars. There it stopped.

Farmyard smells drifted through the trees and a faint rustle of footsteps that might be human. Susan called out an uncertain, "Good evening." The footsteps halted, then came on. She called again. There was no answer, but between the nearest poplars appeared a torn ear and yellow wolf-eyes. With courage not quite equal to Seppel's, Susan faced the dog that had followed Jean-Marie to the Catine. He opened his mouth, showing ugly fangs as he barked with passion and intent to chew. Susan drew back a step and called once more, "The dog! Please he-elp me!" With a deep growl the dog sprang forward toward her swinging white skirt. His teeth closed just as two men came running through the trees. The first, swinging a heavy stick, was the stout old coachman of the Comte de l'Arize; close behind came his master. The stick cracked down on the dog's scarred snout, and with a werewolf howl the beast fled, cowering, across the fields.

"Mademoiselle Khant! I am deeply distressed. Your dress! And those painful scratches on your arms!"

"And those ugly snags in my stocking!" Susan's relief was close to a giggle. "I had no idea I was near the chateau. I—I was looking for the Cave of the Cross and got lost."

The old gentleman showed courteous surprise. "Indeed you did. But your misfortune is my gain. My devoted son has again left me alone. Mademoiselle, will you give me the pleasure of your company at dinner?"

"I'd like to, but I really ought to find the highway and get back to Volvestre. My bicycle is there. I'll have to hurry to get back to the Catine before dark."

"Mademoiselle, of course I would not allow you to go back to St. Fiacre alone. Firmin shall drive you in the victoria, and there will be room for the bicycle. Come, my child. Titine will be glad to see you again."

In the dining room, under a swinging lamp smelling faintly of oil, red head and white bent over a ragout of rabbit in rich prune gravy. The Comte, after a keen glance at Susan's drawn face, let her eat in a silence only now and then broken by casual talk.

"And today, to every other misfortune, Aston added the *Vent d'Autan.*"

"That's really something in the way of a breeze, isn't it?" Susan raised her glass of thin red wine. "Tell me, what does the name mean?"

The Comte shrugged delicately. "No one knows. Of course, Eighteenth Century etymologists had their easy explanations. *Autan* to them was *ab alto*, from the depths of the sea. There's a quaint old book I'll show you after dinner."

Over the compote of apples he asked, "You've been working with Jean-Marie today?"

"Yes. He's very thorough, as you said he would be. And really he knows quite a little about archaeology." She smiled. "Enough to set a number of tests for my ignorance. I'm proud to say I passed them all."

"Tests, Mademoiselle?" He raised amused white brows.

"Oh, he slipped in flint chips he had retouched with the real tools to see if I would detect them, and he's shown me some curio store things, as if they came from the caves around here, a copper bracelet and a hand ax obviously polished with steel."

"Amusing."

As they rose from the table, the Comte said, "Thank you again for brightening my first evening alone. I shall soon get used to the old way, but this evening, you understand ..."

Susan said, embarrassed, "You will have to resume your letter-writing, Monsieur."

"My letter-writing?" his tone was thin and old. "Pardon me, I don't quite understand ..."

"Oh, I'm sorry," Susan answered quickly. "I only meant ... you remember the day Sir Cyril and I were here for lunch ...?"

"Yes, Mademoiselle?" impatiently.

"You told us about the correspondence you had carried on for years with your old friends in Paris."

"Exactly. Ah, Titine has a fire for us in the salon. Draw up your chair to this little table and I will show you the old book I spoke of while you take your coffee. And perhaps a sip of brandy? And then I will send you safely home with Firmin."

The fire was too warm for anyone under seventy, and the plain, sad face of Marc's mother hanging above the table added little comfort to the ugly salon. But the book, printed in 1737 at Paris "near to the Fountain of Saint Severin, at the Golden Lily," brought a cry of delight from Susan. The Comte laid it open at a beautiful map of the "Mer Mediterranée," whence a series of long-tailed diamonds labeled the *Vent d' Autan* blew over mountains, like an army of sand piles made by children on a beach.

He turned a page and read, "'This wind is warm, heavy, oppressive; it benumbs and beats down man and beast; it makes the head heavy, removes the appetite, and seems to inflate the whole body.' You recognize it, Mademoiselle?"

"All except the loss of appetite. You noticed me at the table?"

"Ah, Mademoiselle, you are young! Here is something else for you," his blue-veined, delicate hands turned slowly through the pages. "This is the place. Permit me." He carried the book to his chair at the other side of the fire and began to read.

"'Fairies are women of an order superior to human nature, whose power, knowledge, talent exceed the bounds of possibility—free from any infirmities common to us, but subject to many needs, passions, hazards, and, finally, to death.'" He paused, seeking down the page. "'They like to show themselves dressed in white and are often called White Ladies.' My dear child, this might almost have been written about you."

"Not quite," Susan murmured, her foot kicking gently against the chair.

"Just one bit more. This was written by the *Maréchal* of Arles to the Emperor Othon the Fourth in the Thirteenth Century. If one of these fairy women chooses a human lover, he says, she does everything for him as long as he remains faithful, but if he acts otherwise, she heaps misfortune on him and even brings him to death.'" He closed the book slowly. "That is all."

"Thank you. I loved it," Susan finished her brandy.

"The Russian girl," the Comte said softly, "your friend, is quite beautiful. At least, so she evidently appears to my son. She is not at all to my taste."

The liqueur glass shook slightly in Susan's hand. "Neva is lovely," she said.

"And very susceptible. Forgive me, Mademoiselle, but your own imperviability astounds me. How is it possible that you remain adamant to men?"

Susan looked for mockery in a face made enigmatic by shadows. She answered with asperity. "My father saw to that."

"Your father? And by what strange device?"

"A very simple one." Susan Kent sat straight in her chair. "When I was sixteen years old, he told me that no man would marry me except for my money. At intervals he repeated it, with variations. I was young and pretty and men liked red hair, but money was what they loved. Of course he was right."

"He was not altogether wise," said the Comte de l'Arize.

"I don't know. Perhaps he was. It had happened to him." After a minute she went on. "In the United States we believe in marrying for love. Not that money isn't the most important thing to lots of people. But American men feel they're supposed to be in love, that marrying for wealth isn't quite the self-respecting thing to do. Those who do it don't make the kind of husbands I want. So unless there was someone with as much money as I have now and shall have later—and that wouldn't be likely—I don't want an American husband."

The Comte's fluff of white hair bent toward her in the lamplight. "Mademoiselle," he asked, "don't you see the solution? No, I was not thinking of a nunnery."

Susan looked back frankly at the father of Marc de l'Arize. "A European husband? A man used to the idea of founding a family, who could behave with dignity toward a wealthy wife? Yes, that may be the answer some day. But I don't want it now."

He rose from his chair and stood straight, old, and graceful by the fire. "Mademoiselle, I think you do not know your own mind. There are certain things you lack at this hour. A secure social position, understanding, respect. You are not happy with your father. You are not entirely at home in your country. You have lived a great deal in France. You recognize the depth of life in the Old World, the grace and beauty, the finesse. If you were offered all those things, you could wait a bit for—love."

She had leaned back in her chair, keeping her burning cheeks in the shadows, pressing her cold hands close together.

"Mademoiselle," the Comte's eyes were sharp and proud, "I am about to say something very delicate, something that in other circumstances might be almost against nature. But in our extraordinary case it is, I believe, *tout à fait indiqué*. Mademoiselle," he bowed low, "will you do me the great honor of becoming the Comtesse de l'Arize?"

For a moment Susan sat quite still. Then the clasped hands fell apart, caught at the arms of the chair. She rose slowly to her feet, white, and shaken.

"You asked me to marry—*you?*"

His second bow was brief and haughty. "Exactly, Mademoiselle."

She put up her hands to the face that Marc had kissed, holding them for a moment over her eyes, shutting out the sight of his father. When she lowered her hands, her face was pale but composed, her voice controlled and low. "Thank you for the honor, Monsieur. I cannot accept it."

He stepped toward her. "I have surprised you, even shocked you a little? Tomorrow you may have a different answer."

Susan looked at his icy eyes. Instinctively, she moved away from his slight advance. "Never," she said firmly. "Forgive me but—it is true."

Coldly, the Comte de l'Arize answered her. "The carriage is at the door." He turned his back and held out his old hands to the fire.

CHAPTER XV

THE WHITE WOMAN

"The rest is solid rock," Jean-Marie laid down his chisel and pushed his cap back on wet hair, "I can't make the hole any bigger."

Crouched beside him on the floor of the pit, where splinters and chips of stalagmite gleamed dully in the candlelight, Susan scrutinized the cathole which an entire day's labor had not enlarged to encouraging proportions.

"All right. I'm going through."

"Now? Mademoiselle, you look tired out."

"I'm not, really. And I can't wait till tomorrow to see what's behind that wall. There could be galleries covered with animal paintings, perhaps even sculpture. I'm going now." The air of adventure was in her nostrils, with something added. For three hours she had been squeezed in a pit with a conventional peasant of Aston where baths are proper only at the feast of the village saint, now eleven months past.

Belt tightened around her coveralls, blue shepherd's beret pulled down over hair and ears, Susan flattened herself in front of the gap which was a bare nine inches high. The arc from her flashlight shone through a little tunnel extending for two or three yards and with a fairly uniform width of two feet.

"Hang on to my ankles," she ordered Jean-Marie. "Tight. I may be heading for a pit."

She dug her elbows into the dirt and shoved forward, feeling slippery clay beneath her and rock grazing her shoulders. She fought down the sensation of a mountain crushing her into the earth during the long moment before her head came free of the cathole and she could extend her arm to click on her torch.

"Let go," she called back to Jean-Marie, wriggled clear, and stood up in a small, high chamber with water-stained walls and a chimney of rock and earth mounting like a spiral staircase to an upper corridor. "Come on. It's exciting."

Scuffing of earth, a groan, an oath, and Jean-Marie's face, very red, appeared in the opening, and stayed there.

"You can make it. Give one more shove," Susan encouraged.

"M-mademoiselle, I'm staying right here."

She said scornfully, "What are you afraid of?"

It was impossible to read all the emotions in his face. "*I* can make it through the hole," he stated, "but, Mademoiselle, you understand ... my pants ..."

Susan's lip began to quiver as she looked down at the outraged face framed like a coconut shy.

"I could go down to the village ... We've used our last candle, and if the battery in your torch burned out, things wouldn't be too famous. And I could get my coverall. It won't take more than half an hour."

Susan hesitated. "Isn't it rather late?"

"As you like. But I don't mind working for a while. My mother has gone to the fair at St. Fiacre and won't be home until night. I'll escort you to the Catine on my bicycle, Mademoiselle. I am going that way."

She looked up at the tantalizing shadows of the high gallery and back at Jean-Marie's not altogether comic face. "All right. Moise will have a good dinner for us both at the Catine. I'll prowl around the upper gallery while you're getting—the candles."

He scowled up at the twisting pillar. "That's a bad affair for climbing. Watch out."

"I'll be careful."

The sinister eyelid twitched. "I won't be away long." He backed out of the hole.

Alone, Susan quivered slightly in the hollow quiet. The chimney of rock and earth, made by debris fallen ages ago through some crack in the mountain, rose in an almost perpendicular slope covered with a thin layer of stalagmite. Susan took a deep breath and, torch in hand, began to climb. Underfoot the stalagmite crumbled ominously and every foot or so streaks of slippery clay sent her sliding to her knees. Over her head great blocks of breccia barely clung to the cave roof. She reached the top of the chimney and saw stretching before her a thin, narrow bridge smeared with clay. Beyond lay a firm, rocky gallery but underneath, the cave dropped suddenly to a black well.

Her heart beating painfully, Susan crept across the bridge and into a white chamber, into the world of prehistoric man and beast. Great cave-bears had clawed the walls. Shattered bones marked the spot where a reindeer had fallen through a hillside pit to die here in agony. Died in those days too far for human thought to pierce, before the long drip, drip of water had sealed the opening into the Violet Hole. Died when man could reach the beast and take what he wanted for his own. In the clay of the chamber, prints of small, bare human feet led to the skeleton of the deer, to the jawbone where hands had removed the canine teeth.

Susan caught her breath. She had seen hundreds of animal teeth, pierced for necklaces, heaped in museum showcases. Now she could almost see before her eyes a slender man of the Old Stone Age bending over the jawbone, loosening the booty with a flint knife. Fearful that she might destroy some human record, she hardly dared to move. Slow probing with the torch revealed much more. A small quartz tool; imprints of fingers that had let it fall; among the broader feet of men, the tiny heelprint of a child.

In the strange state of timelessness peculiar to cave exploration, Susan forgot the outer world, the fear, horror, meanness of the last few days, the ache for Marc de 1'Arize. She forgot Jean-Marie. Until the torch went out.

Went out and would not come on. There was horror in that first moment in the dark. From some far point in the cave she heard the drip of water she had not noticed before. She ran her hand up to her forehead, loosening the beret that suddenly seemed to bind her flesh. But then she remembered that everything was all right and laughed a little. Jean-Marie would be back in half an hour.

Half an hour? It could have been three hours since he backed his ugly face out of the cathole; it couldn't have been less than two. Jean-Marie was not coming back.

Melodrama. But a man had died in the Cave of the Candles on the day that Jean-Marie had warned her from the hillside. A deathtrap had been set in the Cerf, and Jean-Marie, lounging in the inn doorway across from the post office telephone, knew about the trip to Foix. Suppose he had also blocked the cathole? She must get out of here.

Through thick dark, across the greasy Brig o' Dread, over the bottomless pit? With great blocks of breccia swinging overhead? She would have to wait. She could wait, she could take it for a night. In the morning, when it got light ...

It would never get light. At no hour of any day could a single ray reach that remote spot in the cave.

But someone might come. Marc? He alone knew about the hole hacked in the wall of the *Tutto Biouletto*; under the strain of the day before there had been no confidences between Susan and the two girls at the Catine. Marc had said he would be back in a day or two, but the old Comte had implied that the departure was final. Which one could be trusted? Marc who, through Jean-Marie, could have engineered the accident at the Cerf? Yesterday she had been close in his arms, but the first time his body had touched hers she had felt a gun.

Surely Neva and Moise would search for her, and Neva would go direct to Sir Cyril Brooks-Brooks, late of the Secret Service. But was that really a combination advantageous to Susan Kent?

No one to count on. Hunger, the drip of water, the endless dark, the White Woman ... "subject to needs, passions, and, finally, to death." There are words you don't use—trite, embarrassing, not done. You say, "I'm that way about him," and "Someday my number will come up," and you laugh. Why not cry now—sob, scream, curse? No one to know you died badly.

Susan's lips formed words in the dark. "I shall know."

Arms before her, she felt for the wall, found it, and sat down close against it. One hand touching the ground beside her slipped into a small depression. Finger by finger she felt them fitting into the mold of a hand pressed into the clay twenty thousand years before.

CHAPTER XVI

THE SHROUD

The voice came struggling up. Like a voice in a nightmare strangling in the sleeper's throat, demanding agonized effort to produce feeble sound. Susan woke, trembling in the darkness smelling of earth. So she had slept—five minutes, five hours?—and waked with a cry. She would do that a hundred times before ...

The voice called out again. Not hers! Muffled, but articulate. Not her voice, but her name, "Suzanne! Suzanne!"

Her first response was too low and broken to carry far.

"Suzanne!" the cry was nearer, hoarse and insistent.

"Here Here!" she crept forward along the wall.

"Are you all right? Are you hurt? It's I, Marc. Marc de l'Arize."

"I'm all right."

"I can't hear you. Where are you?"

"Where are you?"

"At the cathole. I'm coming through."

She tried to stand erect, but cramp knocked her to her knees. Flat on her chest, arms reaching at full length ahead, she crawled through the clay. Even the thrill of deliverance had not destroyed the sense of the black pit ahead.

Marc was a long time coming through so short a tunnel. He didn't call again; she couldn't see a light. Deliverance? By a savior with a gun in his pocket? Someone had killed the bearded man in that other unvisited cave, someone might be coming back to finish the job begun by Jean-Marie.

"Where are you?" Marc's voice rang out strong. "Answer me, Suzanne!"

"Up here," she cried, forgetting caution, "above the chimney."

Then she saw light, and wanted to cry. It came nearer; he started to climb.

"Be careful! It's terribly slippery."

"And how! You're really all right?"

"Of course." Her groping hands felt the edge of the rock; shuddering, she pushed herself back a foot. Now the light was no longer a mere glow on the ceiling. It was broadening to a path across the top of the chimney. She could see the wet gleam of the clay on the thin bridge, then a full, steady glare.

"Marc," she shrieked, "look out! There's a well in front of you!"

He answered her coolly. "I can see it clearly." The beam reached a few inches from the spot where she was lying. "I can see the bridge to the gallery. I can't see you."

She tried to rise again.

"Got a cramp in your leg muscles?" The inquiry was matter-of-fact. "Is there room enough to stand up? Keep stretching out your legs, then walk around a bit."

"All—right. I'm—doing it—now."

He ignored the catch in her breath as the numb muscles came to life. "You got up there pretty neatly all by yourself. I see you're a good climber," he said conversationally. "When you're ready, we'll go down. No hurry."

She walked to the edge of the pit. "I'm ready now." She could see him now, sitting astride the bridge, his face blotted by shadow, his steady brown hand holding the torch toward her.

"The flashlight battery! Are you sure it will last? Mine—didn't?"

"My pockets are full of candles. And matches."

She slipped to her knees, ready to crawl across the rocky span which looked as shiny as wire and about as wide. She paused.

"You did it before with one hand," he told her, "But this time you have two. *I'm* holding the light."

It made her mad and it carried her over the bridge. She could never afterward recall the crossing, the descent of the chimney, the passage through the tight, bruising cathole. In the Violet Hole, familiar even in darkness, things came clear again. "That was really something!" she laughed.

Marc de l'Arize stood over her. "You damned little idiot! Playing a trick like that. Trying to kill yourself off for no reason in the world except—"

"Playing!" she burst out. "You think I do archaeology just to amuse myself? I found simply wonderful things in that gallery, and I'm going back there tomorrow to find more!" She saw his face clearly for the first time, darkened by fatigue and by the beginnings of a beard. "Oh, Marc, what am I saying? You saved me!"

He put his arm around her shoulders and propelled her roughly out of the cave. "You are to come back here only with me. You understand?"

Reaction caught Susan and within Marc's strong grip, half-carried, half-sliding down the mountain, she shook with cold. The night was moonless and gray. No light showed in the windows of Volvestre.

"What t-time is it?" she chattered.

"Around one. Here's the car." He lifted her into the seat and wrapped his leather jacket around her. "We'll be at the Catine in a few minutes, and get you a drink and to bed." He slipped behind the wheel. "Sit close to me. You'll get a little warmth."

Her head against his shoulder, Susan asked, "Marc, how did you find me?"

"I got back from Foix at ten. Moise was in the kitchen at the Catine, evidently waiting for someone. She didn't know where you were. Mademoiselle Borodin didn't seem to be around. I couldn't find anyone who knew you. Finally, I brought myself to call upon that assiduous window-watcher, Madame Dumas. She had seen you go up to the cave with Jean-Marie and she hadn't seen either of you come down."

"I never thought I could be grateful to that woman. But Marc ..."

"Yes, Suzanne?"

"Why were you looking for me tonight?"

He said without a trace of feeling, "Because I felt like kissing you."

After a bit she asked, "And Madame Dumas didn't see Jean-Marie come down to the highway?"

"He probably took the short cut to the inn. Do you want to tell me what happened?"

She was still telling him, rather jerkily, when he stopped the car at the entrance to the Catine lane. "We'll wake up Moise and get you a bowl of soup."

"Moise isn't here. She won't sleep in the house since the skeleton moved in."

He flashed his torch on the upper windows of the house. "Then Mademoiselle Neva will have to get to work. Ah, I hear the voice of your colleague."

Seppel's barks came sharp from behind the door, and when Marc lifted the latch, he hurled himself against Susan's still uncertain knees. Marc's foot sent him skidding in astonishment across the kitchen. "Get in by the fire," he ordered Susan.

At that late hour embers were still red on the hearth. Marc swept his torch about the room, seized a stool, and set it within the deep, wide fireplace. "In with you." He led Susan to the stool. "I'll see if I can't raise that damned girl."

Seppel's reproachful eyes censured him from the top of the kitchen table. Marc scooped him up and dropped him in Susan's lap. "Here. You can get a little heat out of him, too."

He started up the stairs shouting, "Mademoiselle! Mademoiselle Borodin!" His steps were loud overhead, and light came through the boards of the rough ceiling. For a moment there was no further sound; then Marc came down the stairs slowly carrying an eiderdown quilt. Without speaking he crossed the kitchen to the hearth, wrapped the quilt around Susan, lighted two candles standing on the mantelshelf, and without a word set about building the fire.

Susan and Seppel, in eiderdown to the eyes, looked down on his kneeling figure with apprehension. She said hoarsely, "Neva is dead."

He sat back on his heels and lifted his face to hers. "She is in bed." He was grinning widely. "No, not upstairs." He put his hand in his pocket and drew out a folded paper. "She left this note for you which, under the circumstances, I took the liberty of reading. Here."

Neva's French flowed large and black across Susan's best paper:

> Obviously, my dear Susan, I have gone away. As I have already told you, there are things in life one cannot afford to ignore. Also, a lover, elderly and English, might be an extremely amusing experience.

Under the deep arches of his brows, Marc watched Susan as she read. She held the letter out to him. "Have a bit of kindling," she said, her disdain slightly impaired by the streak of clay across her nose.

Marc dropped the paper on the blaze and stood up. "Is the wine in that cupboard? And the spices?"

"Yes, Marc." Susan peered anxiously over the huddle of yellow sateen. "Couldn't this mean more than she says? I know Neva is always insinuating that she's involved in some dark deeds, but really she has known quite a few political plotters, and I rather think her friend with the sympathetic pup was a dope smuggler. Sir Cyril may be a silly old piece of senility but, after all, he's a distinguished man. You told me he's been a member of the Secret Service. Isn't it possible that he has found more than one use for Neva?"

Marc came back to the hearth, carrying a small copper saucepan filled with red wine. "It could be," he said in a noncommittal tone and placed the pan close to the fire. "That will be warm in a few minutes and then you'll begin to feel better."

She said softly, "You're nice to me, Marc."

"You think so?" He laid his hand on the mussed red hair.

"G-r-r-r woof," said Seppel.

"You have it exactly, old man," agreed Marc de l'Arize. "Woof to you also, Monsieur the Archaeologist."

An animated cheroot, Seppel plopped off Susan's knee and trotted into the middle of the kitchen, stood square on his bowed legs, and barked into Marc's face.

"Suzanne, shall I apologize to my rival?"

"No, kick him out. Your wine is beginning to sizzle."

Marc filled two cups and brought another stool near to Susan's. They sipped, not talking, shut in together by the night, warmed by fire and the wine and by the exotic stimulus of homely intimacy. Susan pushed back the eiderdown, a faint flush coloring cheeks that had been too pale.

"When I was alone in the cave," she spoke without a shudder, "I did a little thinking. Marc, I've been looking at things all my life from just my own point of view. Especially here in Aston. It's a perfect way of being dumb. I thought all the people around me were my enemies—Jean-Marie and his mother, the priest and the two Dumas; and Sir Cyril because he never invited me to his cave. Sometimes I felt that way toward Neva, and I was even suspicious of your father and you. But now I know what it all means."

"Really?" he had chilled.

She emptied her cup and held it out to Marc. "Something is going on here in Aston, in Volvestre and St. Fiacre. Something dangerous and pretty bad, but it isn't centered in *me*. I was important only when I happened quite ignorantly to get in the way."

"What sort of bad things are you talking about?" Marc very neatly refilled her cup. "This will help you to sleep."

"Thank you. I don't know what sort of schemes people have. Up there in the cave, when I thought I might ... stay there for a week or two, it seemed valuable to get myself into the right perspective in relation to the rest of the world. Isn't it called 'growing up?'"

"With your hair hanging on your shoulders and that smut on the end of your nose? No, no, leave it. I love it. Suzanne, you are an adorable little girl."

Wine and fatigue let her say something she had not planned, "Would you have found me an adorable stepmother?"

He got up, his face suddenly blank with anger. He demanded through tight jaws, "The old man suggested that?"

"Yes, last night."

He crossed to the window and stood stiffly looking at darkness. When he turned back to Susan, he spoke quietly, "It's time you were in bed. I'll carry the light for you."

In Susan's austere room he put the candle on the bedside table. "Have you got some sort of hot water bottle? Good. I'll heat some water and fill it for you." At the door he added in a fatherly voice, "Get into bed as quick as you can or you may have a chill."

When he had closed the door and gone, Susan pulled off her dank coveralls, and kneeling at the bottom of the *armoire*, drew from beneath a pile of broadcloth pajamas a silk gown. She stood up, slipping it over her head, and leaned far back into the cupboard. Her fingers searched for the texture of velvet as fine as skin, for the sort of garment a woman should take with her everywhere. She found a hanger, padded softly, smelling of mignonette, quite empty. The white house coat was gone and Susan knew where.

Her lips smiled as she said aloud, "Well, anyway, it won't be my shroud." She thought of what else it might have been; what at this very moment it might be to the leering old eyes of Sir Cyril Brooks-Brooks. "Really f-f-funny," and burst into sobs.

"Suzanne, what's wrong? Suzanne!"

She was a white shadow in the middle of the room. "Neva stole—stole my house coat."

Marc de l'Arize closed the door, and came close to Susan. "*Chérie*," he said, "you don't need it."

CHAPTER XVII

THE BLOOD

For a weary time he had been standing outside the closed bedroom door, the sun warm on his brown back, his long aristocratic nose quivering. The beam of sunlight moved forward and tickled his nose. The moment had come for speech. He spoke, loud and long.

From behind the door came an answer drowsy and vague. "Shut up!" He went on.

"*Tais-toi!*" the command was definite.

He raised his voice.

Through the panels came a plea and a prayer, "*Sei still! Still!*"

In triumphant repudiation of international understanding, he waved his tail and produced a prolonged howl. And then from the stairs behind him he heard something entirely comprehensible.

"*Seppe-le-ou!*" The hoarse flow of patois smelling richly of the stable, though designed for Aston cattle, was quite clear to a Swartzwälder hound. Meek and still, Seppel pattered into the room in the wake of Moise and a breakfast tray.

"Good morning, Mademoiselle. It's a beautiful day."

Susan sat up suddenly in the wide bed, pushing back the brilliant tangle of hair falling over her face and shoulders. "Moise, breakfast in bed! What luxury!"

Quickly she slipped a second crumpled pillow beneath the one on which her head had lain.

The dimple showed at the corner of Moise's pretty mouth. "I carried up a tray for Mlle. Neva every morning. Two hours after you had gone off to gather stones."

"Poor Moise! And after all the service we gave her, you and I, she has most ungratefully left us."

"Perhaps this morning," Moise suggested with a gruff little chuckle, "the Englishman will bring Mlle. Neva her breakfast."

"*This* morning, possibly. But in the course of time, I think Sir Cyril may tend to identify Neva with certain members of the KuKuKuKu clan." She took a big bite of toast, "I'm starving."

Moise looked blank. "Mademoiselle Neva is a bad girl," she pronounced.

"Bad?" Susan looked slightly astonished.

"Yes," Moise passed the moral judgment of Aston. "She didn't work."

Susan put a morsel of honey-smeared bread in Seppel's open mouth.

"Neither do I, Moise."

"But you do, Mademoiselle. Gathering stones, that's hard," she recited defensively as if from long practice. "Jean-Marie does it, too."

Susan stopped playing. "Sit down, Moise." Her tone was grave, "Yes, here, please." She leaned back on the pillows, studying the face of the girl perched self-consciously on the edge of the bed. "Yesterday afternoon, Jean-Marie left me alone in a dangerous part of the cave."

Moise looked down at her rough, beautifully made hands. "I know."

Susan spoke sharply, "He came here and told you about it?"

"No, no, Mademoiselle! He never came at all. I waited and waited."

"Then how did you know?"

"Monsieur Marc told me."

Susan sat up straight and said in a tight voice, "He told you that last evening? When he was at the Catine? Hours before he came to find me in the Violet Hole?"

Moise looked up shyly, "No, Mademoiselle. It was this morning. I met him in the lane."

Susan bent her head to adjust the lace strap slipping over her white shoulder. Then, frank and smiling, she met Moise's eyes. "What time did you see Monsieur Marc?"

"About six-thirty. I came early today. I ..."

Susan lifted her spoon. "And how late is it now?"

"Not late." Moise glanced toward the sunlit window. "Eight o'clock, perhaps." She turned back to Susan, "Mademoiselle," her hands twisted tightly, "Jean-Marie ... he's good. He wouldn't have left you all that time in the cave. Something has happened to him. Something bad."

"Yes, Moise?"

"He didn't come last night. He's always come when he's given his word. And last night was the most important of all. Everything was going to be decided."

"Everything about your marriage?"

The girl's blue eyes were dark with anxiety. Her swollen breasts rose and fell painfully. "Yes, Mademoiselle. He said that if his mother wouldn't agree to what my father can give, we'd leave here. We can go to Paris. There'll be work for both of us. Jean-Marie," she said proudly, "is strong."

Susan set her breakfast tray beside the bed, "When are you expecting the child, Moise?"

"In four months, Mademoiselle. But I don't want Jean-Marie to have to leave Volvestre. He has worked hard. He has a right to the property, but his mother controls it. When he was in the war, his father died and Jean-Marie signed a paper. That gave his rights to 'Ri. He thought he would be killed, you know. Then after he came home, he was going with a girl. She was tuberculous and after a long time she died. Then just last year Jean-Marie began speaking with me ..."

"And your dowry isn't large enough to satisfy Madame 'Ri?"

"Not now. And she never really gave her consent."

Susan slipped from the covers, "Listen, Moise, everything will be all right. I'll talk to Madame 'Ri and to your father. I have a lot of money, money of my own that I can use as I like. I'll add the sum necessary to settle the affair." She put her arm around Moise, "I promise."

Tears filled the blue eyes. "I couldn't take it."

"Of course you could. For yourself and for the child."

"Mademoiselle," Moise's voice was shy, "are you going to get married with Monsieur Marc de l'Arize?"

Color flooded Susan's face. "No, I don't believe so. No."

There was a moment's silence, then Moise spoke anxiously, "But if— something happened?"

Two girls from far worlds looked at each other in complete understanding. Last night Susan had faced death; now she had met another basic reality. "Yes," she said, "if—anything—happened, I'd marry ..."

She got up abruptly and walked over to the *armoire*. Moise stooping, picked up the dishes on which Seppel was just finishing a light rinse.

"Mademoiselle Suzanne," Moise's question was hoarse, "did Monsieur Marc tell you anything about—the dead man in the cave?"

Green linen dress on her arm Susan shut the cupboard doors. "No, Moise." She went on slowly, as if to herself, "He didn't tell me very much about anything."

"Monsieur Marc is good, too."

For a moment they were two girls trying to believe in their lovers. Then Moise said, "I'll bring you some hot water right away," and went heavily down the stairs.

A quarter of an hour later a child came up the lane. She was a tough little girl in a black pinafore, and she carried a white paper in a hand that did not match. Susan met her at the doorway and took the grubby slip on which the clerk at the St. Fiacre post office had written,

> Mademoiselle Kent, they have telephoned from Volvestre.
> Monsieur de l'Arize is waiting for you in the cave called the
> Violet Hole.

Susan read the message aloud to Moise.

"Mademoiselle, that's strange."

"Not very. Last night," her voice was soft, "I told him that whatever happened, I was going back to the cave today. He told *me* that I wasn't to go without him." She turned to the staring child, "There are some bonbons in here."

Dogged by dachshund and child, she entered the living room and lifted a candy box from her desk. Beneath it a book had been half-concealed, a small pamphlet with a green cover.

"Well, I'm off. Moise, I leave this in your hands," Susan smiled and waved her hands toward the battle waging over the chocolates. "For once I'm betting against Seppel."

Moise followed her out to the spot where the bicycle lay. "Mademoiselle, you will find out what happened to Jean-Marie?"

Susan looked at her closely, "What do you think happened?"

"I don't know," sighed Moise, "I don't know."

Against pure blue the rock of Volvestre stood out bright and gay. Green bushes and trees, purple roofs, cream walls, white limestone ridge, and below, other bright houses, the post office, the schoolhouse, the inn beside the clean ribbon of the road. There was a dark knot in front of the inn, a little huddle of people, men in the sashes and corduroys of farmers or the dark blouses of cattlemen, children in black pinafores, women with striped aprons over drab jersey. Near the schoolhouse two cars were parked, a Citroën and a powerful black machine. No individual in the crowd seemed to be talking, but a low insect hum hung over the road.

Suddenly everything was so still that one could hear the quiet steps of men in the grass. Three of them were coming out of the alders which bordered the river close against the inn. Slightly in advance walked a man in a raincoat and a black felt hat. Behind him the brigadier of gendarmes and the postmaster carried between them a rough stretcher sagging under a blanket-wrapped burden. Two other figures followed them into the sunlight, the fat *maréchal des logis* and Madame 'Ri.

The stretcher-bearers came to a stumbling halt before the door of the inn, and the brigadier turned his head toward his superior as if for orders. The *maréchal des logis* spoke a low word to the old woman. Madame 'Ri did not answer. Her wild old eyes were raking the little crowd of neighbors, searching for—what? Suddenly a terrible animal cry broke from her great body. Across the road she ploughed into the frozen group.

"Ay-yi!" she roared, and charged. Her huge hands fell upon two slender shoulders clad in green linen. Shoving Susan Kent before her to the stretcher, she held her in the cruel grip of one fist, and with the other pulled back the top of the blanket, "Take another look at what you did to my son. Murderess! *Catin!*"

A formless mass. Splinters of bone, strips of flesh, dark hairs, and over all, dried and blackened blood.

Someone in the crowd muttered, *"Nom de Dieu!* He was shot in the face."

Through a sick mist Susan heard the words, a torrent of patois curses; she felt the searing hands wrenched from her shoulders, as the chief of the gendarmes and the man in the raincoat forced old 'Ri away. Cries and struggles, and the tread of the stretcher-bearers died behind the door of the inn. Susan swayed slightly. The crowd in the road stared, hostile, but for the moment quite still. Then a figure left the group and came close to her.

"Mademoiselle, you need help." Little Father Bigorre did not look comic to her now. Kind, and, as he faced his muttering parishioners, heroic.

Susan's white lips moved. "Thank you. I'll be all right in a minute. I didn't know. It was Jean-Marie?"

"Yes, Mademoiselle."

Two cattlemen with the short goads of their calling were starting toward her.

"Where," she gasped, "is Monsieur de l'Arize?"

"I saw him go up to your cave about an hour ago," Father Bigorre watched her anxiously, watched also the two angry men.

"I'll—go up there," said Susan.

"Mademoiselle. I—don't ... know ... Ah," a great relieved sigh issued from the little priest, "*you* are here, Monsieur."

Susan looked up at a calm, impersonal face beneath a black hat brim.

"Police," the man said briefly. "I'll want to talk to you later, Mademoiselle."

A little color had returned to Susan's cheeks. "Could I wait up there, Monsieur? In a cave where I am doing archaeological work? Monsieur de l'Arize ..."

"Yes, quite all right," he interrupted. "If you can make it up the mountain after this experience. I'll join you there within an hour."

"Thank you," Susan turned away from the crowd. "No, thank you," she told Father Bigorre. "You are very kind. But at the moment, I'd rather be alone."

The familiar climb seemed long and hot, and she was terribly tired. But at the end there would be the only comfort in the world—Marc. She reached the limestone ridge. Above her the village clock struck nine cool tones. Under the violet-stained arches she entered the gray sanctuary of the cave. A man was standing there. Straight, smiling, elegant with gloved hands and cane.

"Good morning, my dear little friend," said the old Comte de l'Arize.

CHAPTER XVIII

THE STONE

"My child," he said gently, "you are very pale. It was that regrettable affair in the valley? Old 'Ri's voice rose painfully. She was always a violent woman."

Distaste tempered Susan's grief. "Jean-Marie is dead."

"I said it was regrettable, didn't I?" He spoke in a testy old voice. "So are all unnecessary things. This whole affair ... Ah, well, Mademoiselle Suzanne, I have something here that may divert you for a few moments from your sorrow." From his breast pocket he slowly drew folded papers and held them out with a graceful sweep of the arm.

Susan did not move. Command entered his tone. "Come here!"

She gave an impatient little sigh, walked to the spot where he stood by the rock wall and extended her hand. There was a small thin bundle and a single sheet of cheap ruled paper. She unfolded this sheet and saw a crude drawing; through the middle a straight line; at the top a series of scallops of varying depths punctuated by two objects, a cross and, to the right, a candle; below the line another series of scallops and a single flower, perhaps a violet. Diagonally across the page ran a smear of red.

The paper quivered in Susan's hand and fluttered to the floor of the cave. The packet of folded blue paper was an intricate pattern of figures and symbols; only a little was clear. Francs, pesetas, numbers of arms and men. She flung it from her and drew back. Her eyes stared sick and wide into the cold eyes of the Comte for a full second before she realized what else she was facing.

"A pretty little map our schoolteacher made, isn't it? Too bad to throw it in the dirt. Never mind. I shall poke it under your body with my stick after I have used *this*."

The stick lay at his feet. The gun held very steadily in his hands pointed directly at Susan's heart.

She said only one word, "Why?"

"Why the map? Or why am I about to kill you?"

"I think I am entitled to both answers." She flung back her shining head.

He smiled not without admiration. "Do you remember, Mademoiselle, the man in the cave? Why wince? That is a little thing now. The map was for him. The highway, the hills and paths, the three caves near the chateau where one might meet—a friend. That silly old knight drove us from the Cave of the Cross. You moved into the Violet Hole. Well, there was still the more difficult cave with the stalagmites that looked like candles. You noticed them, Mademoiselle? Beautiful, are they not? —No, Mademoiselle, it is not wise to move like that."

He shifted the gun ever so slightly, and went on in a dry old voice, "Thanks to the arrival of interfering fools in this quiet countryside, the day had come when it was not safe to meet anywhere. Then my friend arrived from over the mountains. We talked things over in the Cave of the Candles. He would not admit that our—friendship should end. He had this gun. But before he could use it, I used a stone. I left him there. Unfortunately, I forgot to leave the stone."

He advanced a step toward her. "You interfering little fool! Why must you find that stone covered with blood and wave it in everyone's face? So little intelligence and so much money! Well, Mademoiselle," an edge of hate warmed the coldness of his tone, "I could have used a great deal of that money. I had a right to it. You had cut off my supply from Spain. I gave you your chance and you did not take it. I am not offering you a second chance."

She said steadily, "If you did, Monsieur, I would not take it."

"No?" The thin lips curled, "Think what you have lost. The chance to be the Comtesse de l'Arize, to be the mother of the nobility of France. Perhaps the boy would not have been my son," the corners of the mouth rose in bitter mirth, "but I have every reason to believe he would have been in every sense a de l'Arize."

She caught her breath then, and he laughed. "*Touché*, Mademoiselle?" His face grew stern. "There is only one thing you will be now. I need a scapegoat. After—that affair at the inn, it is well that a guilty person be discovered. You are going to be found. Very soon, Mademoiselle. With the blood-stained documents of the Spanish agent beneath your body and with a bullet in your heart. The bullet you have put there yourself. With this gun. The gun that also killed Jean-Marie."

She answered him desperately, "But that is impossible! You can't make me commit suicide."

"Of course not. But I can make everyone believe that you shot yourself in my presence. When I accused you of espionage against my fatherland."

"But they wouldn't believe you. There is plenty of evidence that you sent for me. The priest saw you come here long before I did. You will have no witness to my—to my—"

"To your death? But I shall have, one with a most reliable character. My good friend M. Dumas has arranged to be here. In fact a moment ago, there was a step behind you and a shadow across the path. And of course he does not have to be here at the exact instant ..."

He had come very close to the girl. The steel barrel was only a foot from the spot where green linen outlined the deep point between her breasts. "Mademoiselle," he said, "I truly regret this, as I regret Jean-Marie. I was always suspicious of him and after you told me that he had found the Spaniard's pseudo-archaeological kit, he had to die. Yes, Mademoiselle, I regret that I must be your executioner. If only the forester at the Cerf..."

He broke off, his delicate deprecatory smile asking for pardon.

Again, as the night before when she waited for a slower death in the black gallery, Susan's lips formed the words, "I shall know." She held her head high and looked straight into the mean old eyes.

From the shadows to the right a voice spoke. "The forester is in prison."

The Comte de l'Arize turned his startled head and stepped backward toward the trench, but the gun did not waver in his hand. A tall figure walked into the cave.

"The schoolteacher will not be joining the party. He also is in custody. He has confessed." Steel was shining in Marc de l'Arize's hand. "I should advise you to drop your gun. It is a good many years since we have hunted together, but even when I was a kid, I was the better shot."

The old man said scornfully, "You would not shoot your father!"

"That would be an unnatural crime, wouldn't it?" Marc came a step nearer, "Father and son! How did you feel when you killed Jean-Marie?"

Susan gave a little gasp.

"Hold it, Suzanne," Mark ordered. "It won't be long now."

"No, it will not. One step forward, Marc, and she will be dead. You wouldn't kill me to save a girl like that."

"Gladly," Marc told him. "But a larger issue is at stake. What about France?"

"Really, my son! I had no idea you were such a patriot. You wouldn't put your fatherland before your father?"

"I would do anything to clean a filthy mess out of the one place I care about. Yes, Aston."

The gun was no longer so close to Susan's breast, but the aim had never faltered. The elegant old man looked up at his tall, dark son.

"That affair is closed. I give you my word, there will be no further trouble here. As for the girl, something could be arranged. After all, I remind you once again, you are my son."

Marc's shadow fell over them both, the old man at the edge of the trench, the girl by the rock. He said quietly, "Dead or alive, I shall have to take you. I am a special agent of the Sûreté."

A gun exploded, a cry rang out, and a gasping sob. Susan, fallen flat on the ground, saw through smoke the figure of the Comte wavering for a second on the edge of the trench. His hat had fallen off, and his white fluff of hair was visible through drifting fumes. She had one glimpse of the sharp agony of his face. Then he pitched backward and fell like a stone into the grave of the skeleton of Volvestre—the grave dug by his son, Jean-Marie.

CHAPTER XIX

AFTEREFFECT

In the hot sunshine outside the Violet Hole, Marc de l'Arize sat motionless, hands clasped over his knees and eyes staring straight ahead. Occasional shudders passed over his body. Susan knelt beside him, pressing her slim warmth against him, offering him her tenderness and her strength.

"Darling, you didn't kill your father," she said.

"I know. Whether his gun went off by mistake or whether he turned it on himself ..."

"... has no importance."

He said tensely, "Nothing had importance for him. Except money. Money and what it would give him. Luxury, Society, life in the Paris he knew. He was as cold and amoral as a stone. Well, he had a chance to get some money. Those old cronies of his offered it to him. He didn't want power, but they did, those fashionable little fascists driven under cover, but still flirting with the monarchists of Spain, the *Renovación Española*. They had to get and send information across the border, and so many ways were watched. So there was that famous correspondence of a lifetime, with its Eighteenth Century charm. Who would suspect letters, even in a little post office like Volvestre, that arrived in the identical handwriting or departed to identical addresses as those of the last twenty years? So," his tone was lowered, shamed, "my father agreed for a price. Payment was made at least once for services rendered. And Gaston, Comte de l'Arize, on the profits made a nice little trip to Paris, and was so dumb as to tell you about it within range of my ears."

"He wouldn't have had enough money from any legitimate source?"

"God, no, Suzanne! Long ago he sold everything salable on the estate. I know how much income he had; I sent it to him. You must have a fairly good idea of the situation. You've dined at the chateau. On *écrivisses* from the brook, I wager, and chickens from the poultry yard, chestnuts from the trees, or maybe a tasty rabbit from the traps. I tell you, to raise a penny on the property would be like drawing blood from a stone. So that reported visit to Paris led me to him for the first time."

Her arm was light now around his shoulders, her cheek near his, but not touching it. "So when you joined the Sûreté, you didn't suspect the Comte?"

He shook his head. After a pause he turned to her, feeling in his pockets for cigarettes. "Look here, Suzanne, in a few minutes they'll be through in the valley, the gendarmes and Laroque, the Sûreté man who's been working under cover at Foix. Before they come up here, you'd better know all about this vile business." He looked compassionately at her face, tired and so much older than when it had lain on the pillow. "Do you think you can stand a little more, Suzanne?"

"I? Of course," she said, "but what about you, my dear?"

For the moment the brown hand holding out the cigarettes closed over hers. Then he moved slightly away from her.

"About two months ago the Sûreté in Paris got an anonymous letter, the illiterate kind of thing that could come out of any peasant's house. It said something about dirty work going on in Aston and it was postmarked in St. Fiacre. The department knew some communications between Rightist groups in France and Spain were getting through, and they were following almost any lead. I have a friend in the Sûreté. He knew I came from Aston. I was sent for and asked how a stranger could appear in little communities like this without attracting too much attention. I said: by posing as an archaeologist. That led to inquiries at the Museum of Natural History."

"And to me." Through the smoke of her cigarette Susan studied Marc's profile, weary, unshaven, still keen and charming. "I understand that part now. Professor Boulanger, without being aware of it, was begging me to say I was enemy agent."

Marc smiled faintly. "We soon knew you probably were not—you and Sir Cyril and Neva—but before the reports on you all came in, I, as a person who could appear in the region of St. Fiacre without exciting suspicion, had been deputized by the secret service and had come down here. On the first night I met you."

"Which," Susan suggested, "added a complication?"

"Of the worst kind. When I followed my curiosity to the spot those boys had fled from, I wasn't planning to run into ... Well, we'll leave that for the moment, shall we?"

"As long as you like, Marc."

"I was on my way to see Jean-Marie and his mother, then on to Foix to make arrangements with Laroque. You see, when the police wanted everything made easy for you to come down here and start your spying, I wrote to the one person I knew I could trust to help me without asking questions and without talking to anyone about it. My half brother, Jean-Marie. So through 'Ri he got your house, and Moise agreed to work for you. And that first evening when you told me you were looking for a workman, I drove to the inn at Volvestre and he agreed to take on the job. Yes, Jean-Marie did everything I asked of him. Except trust me. And why should he?"

"Did you go on suspecting me for a long time?"

"A little, off and on. When the reports came through, you were in the clear on every point but one: I didn't know where you stood politically. As you afterwards told me, that female university you attended had turned out some fancy communists and a few fascists on the side. The F.B.I. knows more about your alma mater than you do, I'm afraid.

"The reports on your fellow spies were amusing to read. Sir Cyril, having tried a different excuse for every summer of a long married life, had invented the archaeology stunt to escape from his wife and hunt him a siren before the sun set for good. And your friend Neva was afraid of just one thing: the loss of her allowance. She's the daughter of a highly respectable attorney in Riga who is willing to pay a fair sum to maintain his problem child at a comfortable distance from home, on condition that she gets into no legal complications. That happened once, and the young lady's been told that the next time, she'll be without a stipend for keeps."

"Good-bye, Romance!" Susan smiled at herself. "But, Marc, did your father think we three were dangerous? What about the accident at the Cerf? The Seven Red Spots?"

"Oh, God, that day! As you can imagine, the forester had the job of helping the Spanish agent over the border. It's a lonely spot, and nothing has ever gone on there except a little smalltime smuggling. When my father got the message—that I was off with the three of you to the Cerf—he telephoned the forester to be on guard. That you and Sir Cyril were probably spy and counterspy. So the poor fool, quite on his own, arranged that horrible hocus-pocus. And you"—the hand lighting a fresh cigarette shook slightly, "and you were nearly killed."

"But not completely. No one can do it. I know that. Practically everyone has tried."

He did not smile. "The forester confessed all this with the greatest pride. As for the other accomplice, Dumas, it wasn't hard to get him to talk. He had gone into the thing for pure hate of France and the rest of the world. To learn that my father had actually made money out of it was to open the floodgates. He was needed as an accessory because he had knowledge of the caves and my father hadn't the faintest idea where to find a good one for meetings with the agent. Also, Dumas was the first person who would have been suspicious of a false archaeologist—you were the second."

"I'd like to make one guess," said Susan. "That the anonymous letter sent to the gendarmes on the night of the party was written by Madame

Dumas and delivered by her lovely little son."

"Right, and that message must have given the murderer a very nasty jolt. Of course the old woman didn't know the agent was dead, and she was terrified the next day when you actually found a body in a cave."

"I suppose the stone was taken from Seppel's cairn while the gendarmes had all the lights turned on me and the skeleton, and all the rest were in darkness. The next morning at the *gendarmerie*, was it you who came and made them lock me up? And then sent in those awful questions on a piece of paper that the gendarme wasn't deft enough to hide?"

He nodded. "I was always planning to spare you and always managing to put you in worse jams."

She said quietly, "You saved my life a few times, too."

"I didn't save Jean-Marie's," his voice choked. After a moment he added, "I was suspicious of him. He didn't trust me. We should have stood together like brothers." He turned back to her, his eyes grief-stricken, "Suzanne, I know I don't have to ask you to stand by Moise."

Tears filled her eyes. "We'll do it always, Marc."

He stood up. His face was stern now and determined. "I couldn't spare you very much, Suzanne. And there will still be some hard moments ahead. I think you won't be called as a witness at the trial of Dumas and the forester, but depositions will have to be taken and there'll be a few other formalities before you are free of the entire mess. Your summer has been ruined, but no more of your life need be."

For the first time in all the crises she had gone through, complete terror showed in Susan's face. "Marc," her voice shook, "are you saying 'good-bye?'"

He said, "The men have started up the hill. If you leave at once, you can climb to the village and down the other side of the rock of Volvestre. At least I can spare you the—activities of the next hour."

He glanced involuntarily into the cave behind them, where in the dark trench the body of the Comte waited for the police. He did not offer her his hand. He put both of them in his pockets and turning away from her, stood looking at the mountains.

Susan closed her eyes and leaned against the rock. When the world was no longer turning in black circles, she rose to her feet. Red-crowned head held erect and proud, she walked to Marc's side. She did not look at him or touch him. Her voice was steady and sure.

"I am staying," said Susan.

After a moment his arm came around her and held her hard against his side. Together they watched the gendarmes climbing up to the Violet Hole.

THE END

TOO MANY BONES

When Kay Ellis is offered the job of assistant anthropologist at the Henry Proutman Museum, she is at first excited to have a fulltime, well-paying job in a new town. But things turn sour when she meets the museum's owner, Zaydee Proutman, the aging and self-centered widow of the museum's founder. Zaydee has her sights set on Kay's supervisor, Dr. Gordon, as husband number two, and sees Kay as nothing more than competition. Even the director, Alpheus Harvey, seems to look at her askance—he had expected a K. Ellis, not a Kay Ellis. In fact, the only encouragement Kay receives is from Alice Barton, the museum's librarian. So when Zaydee disappears one dark night, why does the sheriff think Kay has something to do with it….?

BLOOD FROM A STONE

Susan Kent has come to France to explore caves. She has no more ulterior motive than to search for ancient archeological treasures. So why does it seem that the locals are so suspicious? First there is Marc, mysterious son of the elderly Comte de l'Arize. Her digging assistant, Jean-Marie, is certainly no open book either. Nor is the Englishman, Sir Cyril, who claims to be just as interested in archeology as Susan, but refuses to get involved in any actual discussions. The school teachers, M. Dumas and his wife, seem outright hostile. Even her companion, Neva, is acting like someone with a secret. When she almost plummets into a cave well, she wonders if it is just an accident. Or could it be that someone is actually trying to kill her?

**Ruth Sawtell Wallis Bibliography
(1895-1978)**

Fiction/Mysteries:

Too Many Bones (1943; Dodd Mead; reprinted by Dell, 1946)
No Bones About It (1944; Dodd Mead; reprinted by Bantam, 1946;
   Eric Lund series)
Blood from a Stone (1945; Dodd Mead; reprinted by Bantam, 1947)
Cold Bed in the Clay (1947; Dodd Mead; Eric Lund series)
Forget My Fate (1950; Dodd Mead; Eric Lund series)

Non-Fiction:

Primitive Hearths in the Pyrenees (1927; with Ida Treat)
"Ossification and Growth of Children from One to Eight Years of
   Age" (1929, American Journal of Diseases of Children 37:61-87)
Azilian Skeletal Remains from Montardit (Ariege) France (1931)